D1237045

Ship of the Hunted

Ship of the Hunted

· · · · ·

Yehuda Elberg

Translated from the Yiddish

Syracuse University Press

First Edition 1997
97 98 99 00 01 02   6 5 4 3 2 1

The paper used in this publication meets the minimum requirements of
American National Standard for Information Sciences—Permanence of Paper
for Printed Library Materials, ANSI Z39.48-1984. ⊗

Library of Congress Cataloging-in-Publication Data

Elberg, Yehudah.
[Oyfn shpits fun a mast. English]
Ship of the hunted / Yehuda Elberg. — 1st ed.
p.   cm. — (Library of modern Jewish literature)
ISBN 0-8156-0449-1 (cloth : alk. paper)
1. Holocaust, Jewish (1939–1945)—Fiction.   I. Title.
II. Series.
PJ5129.E5340913   1997
839'.134—dc21   96-47894

Manufactured in the United States of America

The author expresses his sincere thanks to Barbara E. Galli
for her editorial assistance on this volume.
The contributions of Max Rosenfeld, Shaindle Elberg, Nathan Elberg,
Eve Elberg and Kathy Roth are also gratefully acknowledged.

Yehuda Elberg was born in Zgierz, Poland in 1912 to a rabbinical family and is himself an ordained rabbi. He was active in the Jewish Underground throughout World War II. He established the Writers' Union and *Dos Naye Lebn,* the first Jewish newspaper in his homeland, and is the author of numerous novels, short stories, Hasidic stories, and dramas in Yiddish and Hebrew, including *The Empire of Kalman the Cripple, Under Copper Skies,* and *Jeftah and His Daughter.* Elberg now resides in Montreal.

Barbara Ellen Galli is assistant professor in the Department of Religion at Concordia University and associate faculty of Religious Studies at McGill University. She is author of *Franz Rosenzweig and Jehuda Halevi: Translating, Translations, and Translators,* as well as numerous articles on Rosenzweig's thought.

Ship of the Hunted

Book One

1

Golda Heshl sat at her sewing machine in Schultz's factory, her icy fingers guiding the heavy cloth. Her husband, Shiya (short for Yehoshua), was protected because he worked at the post office; and as of today, her teenage daughter Nenna was working with him. Wearing high heels and with her hair up, Nenna looked older and could easily pass.

Scraping the money together to pay for her own work card had been nothing short of miraculous. One hundred American dollars and a gold ring for good measure—a fortune! Little Hannele was safe now, hidden in the pile of German uniforms down the hall. They'd never dream of searching Schultz's factory—after all, he was one of their own men. God was still watching over them. But what about Yossel? Too big to hide and too young for a work card. They'd have to find something for him, with God's help. They'd—

"R-A-I-D!"

The word ripped through the factory like a gunshot. Hearts pounded, machines raced, needles clacked up and down, catching fingers on the gray fabric. A vein throbbed in Golda's temple to the rhythm of the single thought: *They won't search here, they won't search, they won't search . . .*

•   •   •   •   •

A brusque German voice below; heavy jackboots on the stairs. The door flew open. A band of Yunaks, black-uniformed Ukrainians who worked for the SS, burst in and positioned themselves around the shop, guns at the ready. Through the open door strode an SS officer.

"*Achtung!* Attention!"

They all jumped to their feet.

"Line up!"

The officer planted himself between the hastily formed lines.

Dead silence. He was so young . . . such a gentle face . . . he'd never hurt anybody. The officer sauntered back toward the door. See? It was only a scare. Thank God!

The officer turned, started back. "*Du! Du!*" The words cracked in the still air as the gloved finger pointed. "You! You! You!" The Yunaks pulled the doomed from the ranks.

A woman tore herself away. "Sir, please . . . please . . ."

Carefully the officer removed his right glove and fingered the snaps on his holster, frowning at the interruption. The woman was dragged away. He slipped the glove on again and smoothed it over his hand. "YOU! YOU! YOU!"

He reached the end of that row and turned to face the opposite one. "YOU!"

Golda stood up straight, trying to compose herself. Her face must be as white as chalk. What if he thought she was ill . . . surely he'd point to her . . .

He was coming closer, closer. "*Du!*" For the dark woman beside her. The rush of blood to Golda's head almost deafened her.

"*Du!*" For the man on her other side. Her knees trembled. Her scalp prickled beneath her hair.

The German bellowed for the foreman. The man came running and halted stiffly in front of the officer.

"Anybody hiding here?"

"No, sir!"

Off went the glove. He removed the gun from his holster and nodded at the Yunaks: "Let's see . . ." They rushed out to make their search.

"MAMA!" The Yunaks were dragging a girl by her hair. A woman staggered out of the line and ran toward her little girl.

A wild-eyed boy dodged a guard at the door, darted in and out of the two rows, and leaped into his father's arms. The man stepped out of line, his son clinging to his chest, and joined the others.

"Seven little Zhids, Jews," a Yunak reported.

The foreman swallowed. "I didn't know about this, I swear."

"*Du Schwein! Du lause Hund!*—You pig! You lousy dog!" the German raved, his face contorted with rage. He reached into a pocket for a cigarette. A Yunak was before him instantly with a light. The officer inhaled one puff, another, studying the perfect, gray smoke rings he blew into the air. His arm whipped into abrupt motion, brought his gun down on the foreman's head, again and again. The man sank to the floor. Blood gushed through his hair and down his face.

"Take him away!" the German barked. A Yunak dragged the Jew across the floor and left him in a heap among the condemned. The officer wiped the gun clean and replaced it in his holster.

"Another seven for the seven hidden!" he snapped.

A woman cried out: "Sir, let me go with my child!"

He inclined his head and gestured graciously. "*Bitte,* please, by all means. Anyone else?"

They couldn't have found Hannele, Golda tried to reassure herself. She would have been crying louder than anyone . . .

"Another seven!" the German repeated, eyeing the row.

A scream started to rise in Golda's throat. "ME! ME! TAKE ME! They must have found them all . . . let me be with my baby!"

". . . five, six, seven." The officer ticked off his quota. The scream died in her throat.

A group of men, wearing the blue caps and arm bands of the Jewish police, marched into the room and rounded up the condemned. The SS officer nodded and strode out, the Yunaks close on his heels. Their boots thundered on the steps leading to the floor above.

That policeman—wasn't he—yes, the son of Melach Blass! Golda ran up to him. *Panie* Blass, Mr. Blass! They took my Hannele! Let me go with her. Please. She's the little dark one—"

The policeman turned his back to her. Golda clutched his arm. "I will go with Hannele and you tell Mr. Renba—"

"Get away from me!"

"I'm Golda Heshl, don't you remember me? Yehoshua Heshl's wife. Tell Mr. Renba that the daughter of the rabbi of Prinsk—"

The man pried her hand away. "Nobody's special these days!" he snorted, and turned to help the other policeman herd the group toward the door.

"*Back to work!*" came the order.

The cloth bunched, the thread snapped, the needle broke. Golda sat back, her eyes glazed. What was she doing here? As soon as the Germans left, she would run to Mr. Renba. He'd have to do something. . . .

●　　●　　●　　●　　●

Midafternoon. Most people were still at work or in hiding. Golda's footsteps echoed eerily on the deserted sidewalks. German shouts carried through the streets like a pack of dogs barking. Rifle shots reverberated through abandoned streets. She stopped, listened . . . a raid somewhere . . . it was sheer madness to be out now . . .

Her heels clicked on.

She arrived safely at the Judenrat, the Jewish Community Council appointed by the Germans, but Mr. Renba was not in and they had no idea when he would be back . . .

• • • • •

Dusk. The streets began to fill with people. Crowds, commotion, bargaining. One way or another, people had to get food. The *platzuvkas,* the groups working for the Germans outside the ghetto, would return with food they smuggled in. On a corner a woman implored a *platzuvkazh:*

"Give me the whole loaf at least, mister, this is a new winter coat. Have God in your heart—"

"Lady, God's in my heart all right, but not in my pocket. Yesterday, I lost out twice. You hear me—twice! On my way to work, one guard helped himself to my goods. I had to borrow money to bring back some food. And what d'ya think happened? They took that away from me, too, the bastards."

"But look at this coat!"

"Nice, but I'll be risking my neck again to exchange it for bread. That's the way it is."

• • • • •

People milled around, looking for missing relatives, searching for new hiding places. Golda ran along the gutter toward Mila Street.

Hannele must have cried out when they found her, but all Golda had heard was the German officer's *"Du!" "Du!" "Du!"* My sweet little dove, what have they done to you, where have they taken you?

Her home on Mila Street was to the right, but she strode straight ahead. Shiya would be home by now. How would she face him? The street seemed quiet, empty. Suddenly, from nowhere, two Jewish policemen appeared, blocking her way.

"Hey! Who's chasing you?"

Who was chasing her? Hannele's cry was chasing her. She twisted around them and hurried on.

Up ahead, sentries with guns patrolled the ghetto gate, but she would not stop now.

* * * * *

At the Umschlagsplatz, the depot where they loaded the Jews into cattle trains for deportation, the massive iron gate swung open and clanged shut behind her. A Yunak, standing guard, sent her sprawling into the yard with a shove of his rifle butt. She sprang up, raced into the building before her.

From floor to floor she ran, up one hall, down another—all empty. Only a few small remnants of life lay about—a baby's shoe on a step, a woman's handkerchief crumpled on the floor, a drying pool of blood—but not a living soul, not a sound. The air still quivered with disembodied cries. The trains had left, the transport had gone! My little dove, where are you now?

Golda sank to the floor, her arms squeezing her chest. Tears streamed forth as if floodgates had opened in every pore of her body. She wept until the pain was like a mere echo of vanishing footsteps. Her thoughts were in shreds, but deep within her something still stirred faintly, like the sails of a windmill when the breeze has waned . . .

* * * * *

Suddenly feet were pounding up and down the stairs, windows rattling, doors banging, people dashing about; the clamor roused her.

A Jewish policeman appeared in the doorway; people crowded around him. "Where are we? Is this where they brought the children? Are we going to work here?"

The policeman backed off a few stops. "Don't unpack, it's not the end of your journey. There will be another train in the morning."

Golda leapt to her feet and pushed through the crowd.

"Trains?" a man shouted above the noise. "Where to?"

The policeman shrugged.

Golda dashed to the stairs. Another policeman loomed before her. "Hey, where do you think you're going?"

"I've got a valid work card."

"Nothing is valid here. The only way out of here is the train."

"I've got to get out."

"You want to get shot?"

"Please, I'm the daughter of a famous rabbi. The author, Yeho-shua Heshl, he's my husband."

"Listen—writers, rabbis, they don't count for anything here! You know what counts? Heads! Ten thousand a day, twelve thousand—today we hit thirteen thousand!"

"Let me go. Please."

"You think it depends on me? The Yunaks are crazy today—"

"I have a diamond ring."

The policeman shook his head.

"I have a gold piece. A watch, too."

"I don't even know the night guard. I can't help you."

"Please . . . can't you try?"

"They will take your things and still send you away."

"Try. I beg you!"

He studied her for a moment. "Go to the top floor. You'll find the attic door locked. Wait there for me."

•   •   •   •   •

On the first landing, a guard stopped her.

"A policeman told me to come up here."

"Is that so? What's his name, this policeman?"

"He didn't say."

"Get back down! Move!"

"I was ordered to come up here, I swear."

"Get down those stairs, dammit, before I—"

"She's with me," the first policeman called, running up the stairs.

The climb seemed endless. Finally they reached the top landing. The man unlocked a door and steered Golda into a dark room.

"Give me the stuff." His voice was close to her ear.

"Is everything arranged?"

"No guarantees!"

A few feet away an iron bathtub lay overturned on the floor. The man lifted one end. "Get under there, quick!"

"But—"

"For God's sake, hand over your things and get down!"

She ripped open the hem of her dress and counted her meager hoard into his hand. He started to lower the tub.

"Wait, what's your name?"

"Stashek. You may have to stay here till the train leaves. Be very quiet."

A padlock clicked shut. Golda squirmed under the tub, then tried to raise it with her shoulders; it wouldn't budge. How would she breathe under this thing? She pushed harder, leaning on her elbows. If she didn't get some air soon she wouldn't have to worry about the trains . . .

Time dragged on. It must be morning by now. Suppose he didn't come back at all? A lot of good a little ring and a cheap watch would do her; people a lot richer than her couldn't buy their way out . . . Shh, someone was coming up the stairs.

The padlock was sprung, the tub lifted. An unfamiliar face stared down at her, a policeman. They had tricked her! She stood up, her legs cramped and unsteady.

"Where is the man who brought me here?"

"Come on, there's no time to lose."

"He said he'd be here."

"He's around, come on!"

On the window ledge, a wooden plank formed a bridge to a window in the building opposite. The man took Golda's elbow; she froze.

"Go on! Don't look down!"

"I can't! I can't even see the board!"

"Hurry up! They'll be doubling the guard soon." He touched her arm again. "Don't be scared, it's only a few steps."

She stiffened. It was so high up . . .

"It's either this way or the train!"

She put one foot out, set it on the plank, then the other; the narrow plank swayed under her weight. "Keep going!" the man urged. She moved forward, almost slipped off the board, tripped, and found herself in someone's arms at the other end.

"Stashek!" she cried out, remembering his name.

"Shut up!" he rasped, and led her quickly down the stairs and out of the building.

At the ghetto wall, he boosted her up. "This is as far as I go. On the other side of the wall is Stawki Street. If you can sneak across and get out of the deserted area to Dzika, you'll be safe."

Golda slid down the wall, winced at the sound of glass crunching under her feet. She threw herself to the ground, listened . . . only the clickety-clack of wheels on distant rails.

Crouching, half crawling, she edged forward to the other side of the street. A single shot shattered the stillness, echoing thunderously. For a moment she hesitated, then slithered onto the sidewalk and over to the wall of a building. She pulled herself up and inched along to the entrance, hugging the wall.

The door was locked! There had to be another way in. The German guard was not more than a hundred meters away. He was bound to see her.

Heavy footsteps advanced toward her. She dropped to the sidewalk, pressed herself against the pavement. Let them think she was just another corpse . . .

The footsteps halted. The marching started up again, but the sound was receding. A change of guard? She raised her head, her heart hammering against her ribs. She filled her lungs with air. That cop, Stashek, he could have told her what to expect. There had to be an open gate somewhere!

Something creaked nearby—a scraping sound. She peered into the dark—Mama! An open window!

She dropped from the windowsill and burrowed into a corner of the room. Her body shook as if palsied, her teeth chattered. She was back in the ghetto, that was the important thing.

Dawn was breaking. She would wait here. Later, when people came out in the street, she would sneak into the Verterfassung Depot on Dzika Street, where they sorted the spoils taken from the homes of the deported. Uncle Shmuel's Boruch had a job there. He would hide her.

A sudden thought splintered into her head. Shiya will go to the deportation depot! Of course, to be with her and Hannele. "We have to stay together, the main thing is to stay together." He had said it many times since the raids began. She must get to him before it was too late.

A sharp crack roused her to her feet. What was that—just a sheet of paper? She must be going crazy. Insanity would be a welcome relief if it could stop the cries of "Mama, Mama," hammering in her ears.

Would Shiya be gone? Would everyone be gone? Was she running home just to save herself?

She jammed her fists against her temples. She must hold on to her one lucid thought: don't move until enough people are out in the street. She dug her toes into the soles of her shoes as if to nail herself to the ground.

A sudden torrent of sound. Cracks of gunfire. Howling of dogs, terrified screams. It came in furious waves from the Umschlagsplatz on the other side, driving Golda deeper into her corner. The people there were being forced into cattle cars, and she lay here in an empty house on an empty street, safe . . .

The sounds faded, the rhythmic clatter of train wheels rolled off into the distance. Her back aching, her neck stretched, Golda strained to hear—a group was presenting itself to a guard at the gate, platzuvka going to work. Time to go.

She headed for Mila Street—was her home still *her* home? They could have closed the street during the night. And how had Shiya responded to her and Hannele's disappearance? He might have heard about the raid at Schultz's and rushed to the depot with Nenna and Yossel so they would all be together. My God! Shiya and their children could have been in the crowd she had left behind when she escaped from the Umschlagsplatz.

Her fears swelled and her steps slowed. Should she turn back to the depot? Should she go home to see what happened?

Somewhere a clock chimed seven. Seven? Time to go to work. After all, Shiya, Nenna, and Yossel were probably safe at work at the post office, and she should hurry to her factory.

She raced through the empty streets. The door to Schultz's factory slammed in her face. She banged on the door; a key turned in the lock and a guard's head appeared in the crack. The Yunak shouted something in Ukrainian.

"Let me in, please," Golda pleaded, holding up her work card. The guard swore but let her in.

•   •   •   •   •

When the raid at Schultz's workshop was over, the condemned were loaded into horse-drawn wagons, guarded by the Jewish police. As the transport approached the ghetto gate, a policeman scooped up a little girl, jumped off the rear of the wagon, ran to the Verterfassung, pushed her through the door, and leapt back onto the moving vehicle.

Inside, people crowded around the child. Her arms were rigid at her sides, her eyes were glazed; she shivered with fear. "What's your name? Who is your father?" But her lips were a thin, pinched ribbon.

The foreman grew anxious. "What do we do with her? We can't just leave her here."

"That policeman—he risked his life to save her. He'll be back," someone reasoned.

"What if a German comes in? We'd better hide her in the wardrobe."

It was almost noon when the policeman returned. He held out a small yellow pill. "For the child. It's to keep her quiet if she cries." He turned to leave. "The rabbi of Prinsk is her grandfather," he added, and ran out the door.

"The rabbi of Prinsk? Then she has a cousin working here."

Someone went to fetch Boruch Ginsberg. "Yes," he confirmed, "it's Hannele, Shiya's youngest." He leaned down. "Where's Mama? Where's Papa?" Her lips did not part. Best to put her back in the wardrobe; he would try again later.

•   •   •   •   •

At the end of the day, Boruch slipped Hannele into a rucksack and carried her to her home. The family watched, astonished as he lifted her out of the bag.

"What is this?" Shiya cried.

"A policeman brought her to the Verterfassung. That's all I know."

"Where's Mama?" they all wanted to know.

Hannele stood stone-still, dry-eyed.

"They've taken Mama!" Nenna screamed. A pall of silence fell on the room.

•   •   •   •   •

The next morning they took Hannele with them to the post office, where Shiya and Nenna worked and where Yossel kept busy even though he had no work card. Shiya hid Hannele inside a wooden crate and covered the boards with stacks of mail.

At noon Shiya lifted the board just enough to reach his hand in with a piece of bread and marmalade. He waited for Hannele to take it but finally put it down beside her. Later he reached in once more with a bottle of water, and even managed to stroke her hair, now wet with perspiration. When he returned in the evening, the bread and water were still untouched.

•   •   •   •   •

Shiya trudged up the stairs, carrying Hannele in a rucksack, and barely made it through the door. Yossel ran to his father, took the rucksack off his shoulders. "Be careful," Shiya cautioned, as he collapsed into a chair. Yossel and Nenna struggled to free Hannele, a deadweight in the canvas bag.

"Come on, Hannele, get up," Yossel prodded.

Still winded, Shiya rose. "I'll get her something. She must be starved."

Yossel carried Hannele to the bed and set her down. "Don't be afraid. You're home now."

"Here, baby, eat this." Shiya offered her the soggy bread and marmalade. "Nenna, bring her some water." He smoothed back her matted hair. "Eat, Hannele, just a little bite . . ."

Yossel sat down beside her. "It's your favorite, it's marmalade . . ."

Nenna took the bread from Shiya's hand. "If you don't want it, I'll eat it myself, then you'll be sorry," she teased. She held the bread against her sister's mouth, but Hannele drew back. Shiya's bony fingers dug into his pale, sweating face, his body swaying in despair.

"Bad girl, look at what you've done to Papa!"

"Stop, Papa," Yossel begged. "You'll only frighten her worse."

"MAMA!"

Golda froze in the doorway as if Hannele's shriek had pinned her to the threshold. Then she tore across the room and threw her arms around the trembling little frame. Hannele only screamed. Golda rocked her gently back and forth, back and forth. Hannele's voice grew hoarse and faint, but her blue lips did not close even after sleep finally engulfed her . . .

2

Air-raid sirens startled them out of a restless sleep. The drone of bombers, the barrage of antiaircraft fire sent everyone scurrying out into the yards, too excited to seek shelter. Bombs dived through the air and split the earth.

"The Russians!" Shiya rejoiced. "Let them keep the Germans busy."

They craned their necks at the crisscross of beams that lit up the night like fireworks at a carnival. Bombs plummeted, igniting into giant red flowers, while the ack-ack of the guns punctuated the explosions.

The next night it was the insistent ringing of the bell at the entrance gate that disturbed their sleep. Then they heard the hoarse shouts bringing the bad news: Everyone must vacate this section of the ghetto and move to designated blocks around the post office. Anybody found here after eight the next morning would be shot.

"You see," Golda whispered to Shiya, "Russian bombers penetrated this far and the damned hunters haven't forgotten us."

Permission to form breadlines was granted, and the night curfew was lifted. In the final hurried hours, bakers used up every last gram of flour, whether smuggled or stolen from allotted rations. Everyone, even the sick and infirm, queued up at the bakeries. Many forgot that the bread would have to be paid for and, reluctant to give up their places, begged for money. But in the end, no money was needed. Half-baked loaves burned their outstretched hands as they looked at the sky—where were the planes? An air raid now would be a godsend, postponing the hour of doom . . .

• • • • •

The huge courtyard of the post office complex was jammed with people squatting beside their possessions. The area was barely large enough to hold the various sections of the Judenrat, yet outsiders forced their way in, hoping to find shelter. In the streets, the shooting continued unabated.

Steam rose from the pavement. Hannele was fretful and fidgety on Golda's lap.

"It's like a caldron," Yossel complained, wiping his brow. "No place to move. I'll see if I can find something better."

Golda seized his wrist. "Don't you move a centimeter!" she hissed.

"No use looking for anything better," Shiya sighed. "A caldron is all that's left of the ghetto, and even that shrinks with every raid."

As the sun sank lower in the cloudless sky, a cool breeze from the

Vistula River brought some relief. The shooting diminished to an occasional blast, then finally stopped altogether. The last day of the Jewish year was drawing to a close.

"Grant, O Lord, that our anguish end with the outgoing year."

"Amen, may it be so!"

• • • • •

It was not the *shofar,* the blowing of the ram's horn, that ushered in the new year 5703. This one exploded in a hail of bullets and wailing sirens. The "Days of Awe," the first ten days of the Jewish New Year, turned into days of terror, but still some prayed, some hoped . . .

Block after block fell to the raids, systematically reducing the "caldron" to a few streets. At last a piece of good news: Schultz's factory had been spared; the Tebbens factory and the brush makers would be allowed to operate again. Like many others at the post office, Shiya was almost certain the Judenrat would not fall.

• • • • •

In the courtyard of the post office complex, all the divisions of the Judenrat were lined up in separate groups. Shiya stood between Golda and Nenna among the employees of the post office section. His eyes kept drifting anxiously to the building at the left. Golda's eyes also turned stealthily in that direction. Yossel and Hannele were hidden there.

Lichtenboim, the head of the Judenrat, stood motionless. Even the jittery Furst stayed still, trying desperately to catch the eye of any German who might know him. He'd be in dire trouble if anyone were caught hiding there . . . Should have checked out the buildings while there was still time . . .

A whistle shrilled. A platoon of Yunaks scattered and ran into the buildings to search for hidden Jews and execute them. Near the gate of the main building, a truck waited to cart off the dead.

Gunshots in the nearest building; a pane of glass shattered. They had found someone! Lichtenboim's frightened eyes fastened on Furst. Furst's shoulders rose in an imperceptible shrug. He had warned them; what more could he have done?

Pinkiert's men carried stretchers into the buildings and soon brought them out laden, trailing blood in their wake.

With a wild shriek, a woman broke from the line and ran toward the gate. A man slumped to the ground; his group closed ranks around him and concealed him from view.

A gun fired again. Golda dug her fingers into Shiya's arm. The shot had come from the building to the left. Her eyes, riveted on the dark entrance, could discern nothing. Only the patter of slow, ponderous footsteps against her eardrums.

Heads lowered, bowed by their load, the men slowly emerged with a blood-spattered stretcher. It was a giant of a man! Golda's knees stopped shaking.

Near the gate the selection had begun. Lichtenboim, Furst, and all the high officials of the Judenrat were motioned to the right, their families with them. A good sign.

Obersturmführer Brandt approached the administrative officials. The line on the left lengthened and more Yunaks were brought in to guard them.

The rabbinate was next. "Left! Left!" Golda panicked. All to the left! "Shiya, they're going to deport us all! How can we get the children?"

A warning shh! from the people nearby. Shiya squeezed Golda's arm. "Just stay close to me."

"Post Office Division!" the section head called out as Brandt halted before the group.

Shiya stood rigidly on his thin legs, his narrow shoulders taut, his unblinking eyes as glassy as his spectacles. He filled his lungs with air, pushing out his hollow chest; his fingers tightened around Nenna's hand.

"Right! Left! Left!" Life or death meted out with but a single word.

Golda's turn. "Left!" the officer commanded. She ran to the right. His eyes on Nenna, the officer did not notice.

"Right!" he barked at Shiya. Shiya held on to Nenna's hand.

"Get moving, stupid!" a Jewish policeman hissed, pushing him to the right. Golda reached out and pulled him toward her.

Nenna showed her work card. The German ignored it. "Left!" he snapped. A Yunak dragged her to the left.

The guards began herding the condemned out of the courtyard. "Take care of the children," Shiya whispered to Golda and charged across the yard. A bullet narrowly missed him. Head lowered, he ran on and caught up with Nenna. He had heard about the selections where only pretty young girls were taken. He held Nenna's trembling hand in his; he would not ever leave her.

3

Outlawed streets, outlawed houses, outlawed people. The streets were a shambles. Shattered glass crunched underfoot, solitary footsteps resounded on forsaken sidewalks. On one corner, a broken street lamp hung limply from its pole like the head of a gallows victim. An open window moaned in the wind. A door swung rhythmically on its hinges. Inside, darkened corridors led from empty room to empty room, abandoned belongings strewn about like spilled entrails. A bowl of soup left standing on a table had formed a skin; the spoon jutted out like a beseeching hand from a sealed grave.

From their hideouts, miraculously undiscovered, survivors headed back to the "legal" ghetto. For two months, day after day, hour after hour, there had been only the rattle of machine guns, the barking of Nazi thugs, the screams of the hunted. Now it was quiet, but the silence only intensified the terror.

Those allowed to stay in the ghetto went to work carrying permits newly rubber-stamped with swastikas. But they knew by now these various cards were only a new deceit. They worked side by side, hardly exchanging a word all day long. Only an accident of fate had spared them thus far.

The selections were over for the moment, but those who had eluded them still moved through the streets on tiptoe. Danger lurked around every corner for the outlaws. Most threatened of all were the children, who were betrayed by their size even from a distance; living contraband, they viewed the world through a veil of terror.

• • • • •

Golda rounded a corner and hurried down the street. One thought preoccupied her; how long could she go on? How much longer could she keep the children hidden in that airless attic? If only the Judenrat would allow her to take Shiya's job. She had to belong somewhere, she had to get a new work card, real or forged.

"Aunt Golda, Aunt Golda!"

Though little more than a whisper, she recognized Pintshe's voice. They faced each other on the deserted street, avoiding each other's eyes. Golda's heart thumped, questions she couldn't bring herself to ask crammed her mouth.

"Uncle Shiya?" Pintshe finally blurted out.

Golda could only shake her head.

"The children?"

"Only Yossel and Hannele," she murmured. "Mindele?"

"In the health service."

"Amush?"

Pintshe's "no" was barely audible. He raised his voice to warn her. "You shouldn't be out in the street during working hours. You don't have a card, do you?"

"What about you—do you have one?"

"No, but Mindele does. They opened some sort of hospital on Gensia Street. She's the nurse there. Have you found somewhere to stay?"

"We're still in the hideout."

"We're billeted with the health section at Number 4 Kuzha. When it gets dark, we'll try to get your children over to our place."

•　•　•　•　•

They found an empty room on the top floor of the building. "The rabbi of Prinsk's only surviving daughter," Mindele had pleaded with the doctor responsible for assigning living quarters.

"A Jewish daughter—that's good enough for me," was his reply.

•　•　•　•　•

LOOTING AND SCAVENGING STRICTLY FORBIDDEN!
Anyone found entering a building outside the
new ghetto borders will be shot on sight.

So now there was another death penalty. The bold, red letters of the new decree did not frighten Golda.

Staying alone without a card was no less a crime, hiding a child carried the same punishment—and she was hiding two. Could they kill her three times? She would take valuables from the empty houses and exchange them for food.

• • • • •

Golda crawled into a store on Nalevski Street through a broken window. She stumbled, fell headlong, and cut her hand on a piece of glass. Groping in the dark, she felt along the edge of a shelf that protruded from the wall. Her hand recoiled. The soft, delicate touch of the tulle on the shelf was more painful to her than the lacerated fingers. This must be Number 17! Her sister Nachele had run her shop here.

Now it belonged to the Germans. She ought to take every shred she could carry and set fire to the rest. Why leave all that finery for some overfed German woman?

Golda returned home before daybreak. Only Hannele was there asleep. Where was Yossel? My God, where was he? She dashed into the hall to awaken Pintshe. The outside gate creaked.

"Yossel?"

He climbed the stairs carrying a bulging sack.

"Where have you been? What are you—"

"Shh! You'll wake the neighbors."

"Where were you so late?"

"Not so loud, Mama. We're uninvited guests here."

"Where have you been? Answer me!"

Yossel followed Golda into the room. He swung the sack from his shoulder and sat down on his cot. "They'll be moving the ghetto gate in as far as Novolipki Street any day now. We've got to take the stuff while we can."

"How do you know?"

"Everybody knows it. We won't be able to get into those streets much longer."

"So we won't!"

"This stuff buys food. We have to eat, Mama."

"Yossel, you're still a child. You know they shoot children for scavenging!"

"They shoot mothers for scavenging, too."

Golda wrung her hands in exasperation. "When there's no father, the children walk all over you."

"But Mama, I've been at this longer than you. I used to smuggle over the ghetto wall, remember?"

"Listen to me, Yossel, sit down and listen. It was different then. A grown-up had no chance on the other side; only children could get away with it. Now it's the other way 'round. There aren't supposed to be any children left. You can't go out, not even in the legal streets. You're not to leave this room, you hear me, Yossel?"

He didn't answer. Golda gazed down at his bowed head. She knew he would not obey her. Desperate, she sank to her knees in front of him.

"Have pity on me, Yossel! You and Hannele are all I have left. Swear you won't sneak out when I'm not here. Promise me—" Yossel lifted her to her feet. He buried his head in her breast and smothered his sobs, so as not to wake his little sister.

4

A blanket of snow covered the Umschlagsplatz. The gray, desolate buildings no longer brought terror to the *platzuvkaman* passing by. Now and then a child appeared in the street, a strange and unfamiliar sight.

Now the alarm of raids was heard on the other side of the wall. Poles were being seized in the streets and shipped off to labor camps in Germany. Jews who had managed to slip over to the Aryan side, hiding their identity, now came scurrying back with frightened Poles seeking a haven in the ghetto.

Smuggling thrived. A wagon hauling garbage would be pulled out of the ghetto by a half-dead nag and return with two well-fed mares. For a few days afterward, there was meat. Whatever the *platzuvkaman* could not exchange for food kept the fires going in improvised iron stoves. Furniture, delicately carved and highly polished, was chopped up for firewood. The crackling flames brought bitter satisfaction: better in the fire than for the German Verterfassung!

The rations allotted to those holding jobs inside the ghetto were not enough to sustain life; at least one smuggler was needed in each household. Golda's failure to get legitimate work at the Judenrat turned out to be a blessing. She attached herself to the day shift in the Ostban *platzuvka* at the eastern railroad depot, where Pintshe was on the night shift. Yossel, who now went by the Polish name Yurek, carried on the ghetto trade for both of them, buying goods to smuggle out of the ghetto and selling the food they smuggled back.

•　•　•　•　•

Pintshe's group was all lined up to return to the ghetto when the day shift arrived. But Aunt Golda was not among them. His eyes ranged over their ranks. That stubborn woman—she had done it again. Even if the gate was "burning," with the guards confiscating everything, she shouldn't have taken the risk and slipped away under the noses of the Germans just to save a few rags. As soon as the group entered the ghetto gate, he ran to look for Aunt Golda and found her in her room.

"Why didn't you come to work? The guards were all bribed today. What happened?"

"Nothing happened, that's the trouble. We talk and talk about building a hideout, and nothing ever happens. Any day now they'll come for us, and there won't be a place to hide."

"It's been quiet so far, hasn't it? They're finally beginning to reckon with the world."

"Are they?"

"Stalingrad is teaching them a lesson. Did you hear about the kindergarten the Judenrat is opening? The Germans sanctioned it; it was their idea."

"What are you saying—the Germans care about our children? That's the worst news of all. We've got to do something, Pintshe!"

Golda ran from neighbor to neighbor, her hair in disarray, her eyes wild, pleading: "They're planning one of their actions. I can smell it! Do something!" She came into Pintshe's room as he was putting up a length of rope to dry some clothes.

"What in the world are you doing? Who knows if we'll have time to take it down? Don't go to work tonight, Pintshe, please. We must finish that cellar, we must!"

"What's gotten into you? Calm down, Aunt Golda. Here, sit down."

She threw herself into a chair, her chest heaving, her eyes darting. "We're not doing anything, Pintshe! We're not doing anything!"

"I have to go," Mindele said, taking her coat off the rack. "Shall I make a hot drink for you before I go? It'll make you feel better."

"Don't go out, Mindele, please!"

"I work in a hospital, Aunt Golda. Somebody has to be on duty. It's my turn."

"They say there will be a raid tonight."

"They're always saying that."

"Today is different."

"How do you know?"

"Everybody says so."

"Everybody said so last week too."

"So I'm crazy, Mindele. You think I don't know what the neighbors are saying about me? All right, I'm a nuisance, but I'm still your flesh and blood, your mother's only living sister. I'm sick. Stay with me tonight."

"I can't, Aunt Golda, truly. There are serious cases waiting for me. Pintshe, you stay home with Aunt Golda." She poured a glass of chicory, placed it on the table, and left.

Leaving the steaming glass untouched, Golda also rose to go.

"I was going to bring the children down, why are you leaving?" Pintshe asked.

Golda left the room without a word. Pintsche stood in the doorway and watched her disappear down the dark corridor.

● ● ● ● ●

A frantic knocking on the door awakened Pintshe. "Who is it?"

"Get up, Pintshe, quick! Don't you hear the noise outside?"

"Aunt Golda? What noise? It's daybreak, people are going to work."

"You're wrong, Pintshe. Come out here. What's your neighbor's name, the one whose window faces the street?"

"You mean Weissman? I can't wake him in the middle of the night."

"Pintshe, get out of that bed!"

"Please, let me get some sleep!"

"Get up, quick, get—"

Pintshe heard her feet padding down the hall, her fists banging on a door. He leapt out of bed and stuck his head out into the hall. "Aunt Golda, you're not even dressed!" He grabbed Mindele's housecoat.

Weissman's head appeared in the crack of the door. Golda pushed past him and ran to the window.

"Germans!" she cried out.

"Aunt Golda, please. It's only the convoy taking the *platzuvkamen* to work. Here, put this on."

"It's a raid, I tell you—a deportation! I've got to get the children!"

• • • • •

The work of preparing the shelter had gone slowly. "Plenty of time," some had insisted. "The Russian winter will keep the Germans busy enough."

"There's nothing to worry about till spring," others agreed.

Among the labyrinths of cellars beneath the buildings, they had chosen an inconspicuous, windowless room. They had yet to cut into the water pipe for a faucet; the arrangement for a toilet was still unfinished. However, the door had already been walled up, a pit dug below floor level, and a hole cut into the foundation wall. The only entry into the shelter was through the floor, and plenty of rubble lay about to camouflage the hole, enough even to scatter around the other cellars so they all looked alike.

Golda and the children were the first ones into the cellar. Pintshe followed, still questioning the need to hide. She wedged herself into a corner, cradling the sleeping Hannele in one arm and some hastily gathered provisions in the other. At the entrance a woman struggled to pull her wares through the hole. Behind her a man insisted on dragging in his sewing machine. Idiots!

And what about her? She had run from door to door alarming everyone, while she herself had come unprepared. A few chunks of bread and a single bottle of water—that was all she had.

• • • • •

Drops of water started to leak from the ceiling. The heat from their bodies had thawed out a frozen sewer pipe over their heads, and the dripping soon became a foul-smelling flow. The asthmatic Blaustein choked and struggled to stifle a cough.

Golda's arm grew numb. She shifted Hannele to her other arm. The child woke with a cry, and Golda clamped a hand over her mouth. Yossel was furious. For so many weeks he had drilled it into Hannele's head not to make a sound. He took a piece of bread out of the bag and tried to distract her, but she pushed it away. She did the same with the water that Pintshe held out to her. She tried to say something, but Golda stifled it at once. The rumbling in the child's belly could not be suppressed, however. Golda's eyes darted left and right. So what? It was no worse than the stench from the toilet thawing overhead . . .

·   ·   ·   ·   ·

The luminous dial of a wristwatch confirmed the lateness of the hour; it was past midnight. The board was removed from the hole, and a welcome breath of air wafted in through the rubble. Weissman crawled out of the shelter. His footsteps echoed through the cellar until they faded away. The silence became as oppressive as the air around them. The water dripped with an incessant beat; time ticked away; pulses raced, slowed, raced again, as running footsteps announced Weissman's return. They saw a flash of light, heard someone stumble, a horrified outcry.

"Quick, cover the hole!" someone ordered.

"Shh! Nobody move," cautioned an anxious voice.

The light drew closer; the footsteps halted at the entrance.

"Come on out, it's all over!" It was Weissman's voice but they waited, motionless.

"What's wrong with you in there?" Weissman's head appeared in the hole. "Why are you all sitting there like dummies? Come on out!"

"You shouted. We heard you shout."

"The Greenstein sisters. I stumbled over them. They always said they wouldn't let themselves be taken alive."

"What are you talking about?"

"They must have swallowed poison. Down here, we couldn't hear the shooting . . ."

"No more deportation? They're shooting on the spot?"

"Let him finish!"

"They are shooting, but so are we. They were taking a group of Jews to the Umschlagsplatz. When they reached Zamenhof and Mila, our fighters opened fire. The Germans ran away, leaving their dead on the street . . ."

"At last! At last! It was worth staying alive just to hear this!"

"Don't get too ecstatic. Have you forgotten the revenge they took on Nalevki 9? They'll be back tomorrow and slaughter half the ghetto."

"There won't be any more Nalevki 9s! Only the Germans had guns then. Now we can shoot back!"

"We've got to find some weapons for ourselves, too."

"I think it's safe to go out for a few hours now; maybe get some sleep. But we'd better get back here before daylight."

"Who can sleep now?" someone exulted.

"Do as you please. Just don't come running in at the last minute."

Pintshe took the stairs two at a time. His room was empty. Of course, Mindele couldn't possibly come home in the middle of a raid. He returned to the shelter to help Golda with the children. "Why go all the way to the top floor? Let's go to my room."

Golda put the children to sleep in Mindele's bed and soon dozed off beside them.

· · · · ·

Thirty-six hours since Mindele had left for work. The night shift at the hospital would have changed for the second time. "It's clever of her to stay there," Pintshe rationalized. "All those streets to cross—it would have been crazy."

Golda said nothing. She could not take her eyes from Mindele's wash still hanging on the line.

"I think our fighters stopped the raids," someone speculated on the way back to the hiding place.

"At least for a while," another echoed hopefully.

They were still congratulating themselves when the news came about the raid on the hospital. Liquidated, floor by floor. On foot and by stretcher, they had been sent off—a man with an incision still open; an infant, newly born. The doctors and nurses had gone with them . . .

5

A railway security guard led the Ostban *platzuvka* to its work location. The usual traders waited for them on Targova Street in Praga. Polish urchins ran into their lines, hawking their wares.

"*Papierosi!* Cigarettes!" Golda heard a familiar voice. In a moment Yurek was beside her with a large tray of cigarettes. She began "choosing" a brand.

"Did you find something?" she whispered.

"I think so. The Wilchinskis want ten dollars a month for each of us."

"Ten dollars! Can they be trusted?"

"I've dealt with them before. Hey, are you buying or just looking? *Papierosi! Papierosi!*"

"I've got to think about it. Meet me here tomorrow."

"What if they take in someone else?"

Golda removed a sweater from her sack. "Give them this as a gift from me."

The security guard was coming toward them.

"Two lousy cigarettes for such a fine sweater?" Golda complained loudly. Yurek yanked it out of her hand and took to his heels.

The guards grinned. "A real devil, eh?"

•   •   •   •   •

Hannele's frightened face emerged as Yurek unwound the long, woolen shawl. Mrs. Wilchinski wrung her hands in horror. "Jesus Maria! Look at this, Heniek. Did anyone see you come in, boy? Was the janitor at the gate?"

"Nobody saw us," Yurek said. "I waited till there was nobody around."

"Such a face, if anyone happened to look out of a window . . ."

"The windows are all frosted up, and anyway, her face was covered," Yurek tried to calm them.

"A child all bundled up like that . . . bound to look suspicious," Heniek Wilchinski grumbled.

Hannele's eyes grew larger and darker with fright.

"But everybody is bundled up today," Yurek argued. "Listen to that wind, you can hardly breathe."

Wilchinski insisted: "You've got to get her out of here."

"We'll pay you more. I'll see my mother tomorrow, I'll tell her she has to pay you more."

"No amount of money is worth it," Mrs. Wilchinski said grimly.

"Fifty American dollars a month, not one grosz less," her husband interjected.

• • • • •

The children were safely in Praga, on the other side of the Vistula. Golda fingered the four thousand zlotys she had managed to save for their refuge. How far would it go when she converted it to American dollars on the black market? She'd have to go on smuggling.

An old acquaintance of Shiya's introduced her to Guzik of the prewar American Jewish Distribution Committee. He came to her aid, but cautioned: "Watch out. How well do you know these people? We've had reports of cases where Jews were tricked out of their money and then turned out into the street."

Go to the Wilchinskis with all that money? What did she know about them except that long ago they had bought a few things from Yossel? She would have to stay in the ghetto as long as possible and pay the fifty dollars month by month.

6

The night shift of the Ostban *platzuvka* marched in formation along the gutter approaching Targovna Street. Golda peered into the dusk, trying to catch sight of Yossel. Every day for a week he had waited for her, but could not get past the roving gangs of the Naro, the Polish anti-Semitic youth organization, which was determined to stop the trading between Poles and Jews. Yesterday, her last time on the day shift, Yossel had managed to get close to her, but a Naro member had grabbed his collar: "Jew lover, selling to the Zhids!" She had leaned her head on her hands, simulating sleep. Had Yossel noticed? Had he understood her signal that from now on she'd be on the night shift?

The work was easier at night. The men unloaded coal from freight cars while the women scrubbed floors in the offices of the transport administration.

• • • • •

She had learned a lot as a *platzuvkazh,* but not enough. She shouldn't have put on a well-fitting dress when she went out at night, and especially not here. The peculiar glances of Shimek, the Jewish group leader . . . and the Ukrainian rail guard captain, he was too attentive to her tonight. What would happen when they finished work and stretched out on the straw waiting for the escort back to the ghetto? How would she escape their clutching hands in those dark hours before dawn?

"Would you like to trade dresses with me?" Golda suddenly asked a woman scrubbing the floor beside her.

The woman's eyes widened. "Sure, but where would we change?"

"Never mind," Golda said, her eyes falling on the black coal in the scuttle near the stove.

The captain came by again. His eyes traveled from one woman to the other, rested briefly on Golda, and moved on.

It had worked. The same dress—soiled, fastened with buttons awry, coal dust smeared across her face, and hair rumpled—had achieved the purpose. Even Shimek would be discouraged. Anyway, she could handle him, her fingernails were long enough.

•　•　•　•　•

Yurek hadn't shown up. Maybe she should break away and go to the Wilchinskis herself. Yes, but with those Naro hooligans dogging her footsteps, how would she join up with her work group again? She wasn't ready yet to leave for good.

If only Pintshe were here. He had gone on a mission to Otwock; she should have asked him to contact Yossel on the way.

No, the Wilchinskis would be furious—another person knowing about the children. But they'd be even more furious if they didn't get their money on time. What on earth should she do?

Bring the children back into the ghetto? The hideout at Kuzha was better equipped now, but how long could Hannele's weak lungs last there? And how would she make it back? It wasn't cold enough now to bundle her up to hide her face.

In her own Warsaw, and not a soul to turn to. Not long ago, she would have found a relative at any street corner. Now the city had become one huge graveyard.

Yossel showed up at the next night shift. He managed to grab the fifty dollars from her before that bully got to him. One day they had ground his cigarettes into the dirt and wrestled him to the sidewalk. If he lost the money for the Wilchinskis . . .

The next evening Yurek was marching along with the Naro gang following the *platzuvka*. He grabbed a placard from the hands of a youngster and joined the demonstrators. Golda winced. This was carrying it too far.

"Poles, don't help the Christ-killers!" a youth shouted. "The Zhids are Poland's worst enemies!" screamed another. Yurek jumped in among the Jewish workers, lunged at Golda, bringing the placard down on her head, and ran off.

"That hoodlum!" a woman muttered. "May they all drop dead!"

God forbid, Golda whispered, as she pulled the placard off her neck. JEWISH RAGS SPREAD TYPHUS, it read. There had to be more to it than that. She folded it quickly and carried it away with her.

The moment she found an opportunity to leave her work, she examined the paper under the light. In the lower left-hand corner was Yurek's penciled note:

"*W porzadku*—all went well."

She would have to talk to him about that; he should never take such risks. But what a clever boy he was. With his quick wits they might still have a chance. But who knew what trick he'd have to invent for the next payment?

Why not give Yossel all the money? The Wilchinskis wouldn't have to know about it.

Good idea, but first she needed to talk to him. They would need a plan. He would pretend he had to go out somewhere to get each payment. Yes, that would be safer. If only she could ask someone, if only Pintshe would return.

7

"Ya don't know me, y'never seen me, y'hear? Tell that to the kid, Yurek. If they catch ya, just run away from the ghetto, remember that. Almost three months I risked my neck for ya. I can't do it no more."

Wilchinski went out to check if the way was clear, and crooked a finger; Yossel and Hannele followed him on tiptoe. The sky was starting to get light. An alarm clock clamored nearby. Yossel pulled Hannele closer to the wall.

"Come on, faster!" Wilchinski hissed. He unlocked the gate,

pushed it open a crack, and looked out. "Like I told ya, y'never been here." He locked the gate behind them.

They shuffled along, close to the wall. Hannele shivered in the early morning chill. The air was thick and acrid from the smoke and soot of the burning ghetto. Her eyes questioning, Hannele pointed to the red sky. "It's the sun coming up," Yossel said gently. She was frightened enough as it was . . .

"They've finished off the Jews, now they're burning down their houses," Wilchinski had told Yossel the night before. "Your old lady is gone—who'll pay for ya now?"

All through the sleepless night, plans had catapulted through his head but he couldn't sort them out. He'd better stop and think clearly. They were heading toward Yagelonska Street, was that where he wanted to go? How could he bring Hannele across the Vistula when the bridges were swarming with cops?

They'd have to go farther east. On the Otwock line there was a forest—maybe they could hide there for a while. The Wilchinskis might even take them back again when the search for Jewish escapees was over.

An empty streetcar screeched to a halt at the corner. Hannele stopped, Yurek tugged at her hand. The tram started forward again and disappeared from sight. They continued down the street. A volley of rifle shots punctured the quiet. He pulled Hannele into an entranceway. She buried her face in his coat.

"A thunderstorm somewhere, it's only a thunderstorm," Yossel explained, patting her arm.

"It's not, it's not. It's shooting."

He'd better get as far away from Warsaw as he could. The woods around Shwider, that's where he would take her. Before the war, they used to rent a summer cottage there every year. He knew each pathway, every tree . . . They'd never recognize him now—fourteen and all grown up. He might even find work with the peasants.

The streets were slowly coming to life. Out of the corner of his eye, Yurek saw people staring at them. At night there was the curfew; in the early morning two children attracted attention; during the day the streets crawled with informers. What could he do?

He turned around. That tall, skinny man had been behind them for quite a while. He'd slow down and see if the man passed them.

Better not—what if he grabbed them. Run? No, that would be worse; everybody on the street would chase them. Just walk faster.

They'd jump on the first streetcar that came along. He looked at his sister and bit his lip. Not so easy. Jumping on a moving streetcar was no problem for him, but Hannele could hardly keep up with him even now. He stole a quick glance behind him; the man was still there, a *shmaltzovnik,* a blackmailer, for sure.

"A streetcar is coming," Yurek whispered. "When it stops at the corner, we'll run across the street, but we won't get on it."

"Why?"

"I'll tell you later, just run as fast as you can."

They arrived at the corner as the tram came to a stop. Yurek glanced behind him; the tall man was no longer there. Still, he couldn't be sure. He dragged Hannele to the other side of the street and into a courtyard. He heard the tram pull away and peeked out into the street. The man was nowhere to be seen. The kerchief on Hannele's head had slipped; he pulled it forward to cover the dark hair and returned to the street. If only he could do something about her Jewish eyes!

It was now broad daylight. In the distance, a factory siren announced the start of another workday. An approaching streetcar rattled along, drowning out the clomp-clomp of a military patrol coming in their direction. Yurek grabbed Hannele's hand. When the streetcar came to a stop, he leapt aboard, dragging her after him.

The car was packed. Yurek pushed Hannele into a corner of the open platform and stationed himself in front of her. This tram went as far as Grokhow. From there they could make their way to Shwider through the fields.

At each stop people got off, one or two got on. Fewer and fewer passengers remained as the tram came closer to the end of the line. The conductor opened the door to the platform. "Why don't you come inside, kids? There's plenty of seats."

"Thank you, sir, but we're getting off soon," Yurek said. The conductor closed the door. I must have a great face if he doesn't suspect us by now, Yurek thought, a real gem of a face . . .

A crowd of boisterous schoolchildren was waiting for the tram when it pulled into the Grokhow terminal. With the brakes still grinding, some of the youngsters piled onto the platform. Yurek cleared a path through them with his elbows and pulled Hannele after him, off the streetcar.

"Zhidzi! Jews!" a child's squeal rose above the noisy chatter.

The children howled excitedly. Some of them leapt off the tram in pursuit. The conductor shouted, the streetcar bell clanged as if in alarm. As Yurek fought his way through the crowd, an outstretched leg tripped him, and several boys piled on his back. Hannele stood to one side, petrified.

The uproar resounded through the street. "They've caught some Jews," the news spread. A man ran up. "*Was ist los?* What's wrong?"

"Jews!" the children shouted in a chorus.

The man lifted Yurek from the tangle of arms and legs and shook him violently. The crowd grew larger. He pulled a revolver out of his pocket and gripped Yurek's arm. "Let's go! You too!" he barked at Hannele.

With a final clang of the bell, the streetcar pulled out. Yurek and Hannele moved slowly forward, the man following them with drawn revolver.

"I saw them, it was me," one youngster boasted. "No, I was first!" a little girl yelled louder. The crowd began to follow.

The man turned around. "Scram!" He pointed the weapon threateningly. "Beat it, all of you!" The crowd refused to budge. Another streetcar screeched into the terminal. The German shoved his prisoners across the track. Grumbling, the children reluctantly boarded the waiting tram.

Yurek took Hannele's hand and jerked her forward. She was moving too slowly; the German might get mad and start shooting. His eyes searched frantically. Somewhere they'd have to make a break for it. The houses stood farther and farther apart; the German was leading them outside the city. He would shoot them in an open field somewhere. God, Hannele was such a baby! If she saw him being shot . . . let him kill her first . . .

The man stopped at the highway. "Go," he said.

Yurek waited, his mouth agape.

"Go on!"

Yurek didn't move. Did he mean to shoot them in the back?

"Run, you're free! *Loyft, Kinder, loyft!* Run, children, run!"

Yurek stared at him in disbelief. Was he talking in Yiddish?

"I have to go," the man continued in Yiddish. "Beware of children, they're often more dangerous than their parents."

Yurek was still in a daze when Hannele suddenly turned and bolted into the field. His trembling legs could hardly catch up with her.

• • • • •

They made their way along narrow paths through the fields. Yurek had no idea where they would lead him. The sun was high in the sky. It must have been five or six hours since they had left the Wilchinskis.

Hannele began to limp. Where was he dragging her and how long would she be able to carry on? No food, not even a drop of water. The warm clothes they had put on before dawn now made them sweat in the full heat of day. But it would be cold again at night. He had to find a place before dusk.

The path skirted a huge boulder. "Let's rest a minute," he proposed.

As they sat down on the rock, Yurek came up with a surprise. There was a piece of bread in his outstretched hand. Hannele did not take it.

"Here, eat," he urged her.

She turned her head away.

"Aren't you hungry?"

She didn't answer.

"Don't be afraid, Hannele, we are far from Warsaw. The worst is behind us."

Actually, with Hannele's snail-like pace, they hadn't gotten very far at all. He put away the piece of bread. "All right, you'll have it later. Now we have to go on."

He got up and readied himself, but she stayed sitting.

"Come on, silly. If we wait here till dark, how will we find a place to sleep?"

Hannele shivered. She did not stir.

"You're not at home. I can't pamper you here. Do you want me to go on alone?"

She got up. Tears gushed from her eyes and she sank slowly back on the boulder.

"What's wrong, Hannele? Does something hurt?"

She nodded.

"What hurts you? Where?"

She pointed to her right foot.

Yurek bent over, untied the shoelace, and pulled off her shoe and sock.

"Don't cry, Hannele. I know it hurts." The sock had bunched up under her foot and chafed the skin. "Don't worry. I'll make it stop hurting."

But he didn't know what to do. Some ointment might help. Where could he find a pharmacy and how could he leave her here while he looked for one? He untied his bundle and took out a pair of clean socks. He found a white shirt, tore off a strip with his teeth, and bandaged her blistered toe. From her grimaces, he could guess how much it hurt, but what could he do? He put her shoe back on her foot and urged her to get up.

She stayed where she was.

"Hannele, I know it hurts, but we have to go, we just have to!"

She clenched her fists and remained sitting.

"I'm leaving," he said and turned as if to walk away. She still didn't move. He walked a few steps and turned back. He grabbed her hand and pulled her up, but she slipped out of his grasp and fell to the ground. He sank down beside her. He curled up with his head between his knees and broke into distraught sobs.

"*Sha* . . ."

Hannele's whisper came from above him. He opened his eyes. She was standing near him, ready to go.

A locomotive whistle made it clear that they were still on the train line to Otwock. He would have to take a chance and travel a few stops by train. There was no other way.

•   •   •   •   •

When the train pulled into Shwider, they jumped off the platform and hurried toward the woods. Dense shadows invaded the forest, lengthening and entangling each other, covering the bush like a spiderweb. Light still hovered over the treetops, but below, tentacles of night crept up the pine trunks. The day was doomed.

8

Shwider lay on a hillside overlooking the forest. Yurek stopped at the edge of the woods; from behind a tree his searching glance moved from hut to hut. Only the roofs were distinguishable, some thatched with straw, others covered with tin; one flat, another sloped. But under those roofs—were there people he could trust?

It didn't matter. All he needed was a place to hide: an attic, a cellar, a bin, anything safe from prying eyes.

The outskirts of the village. Here the houses were far apart, each one surrounded by its own field and clump of trees. He paused at a weather-beaten fence. This house stood well back from the street. A dog bounded out of the tall grass, barking ferociously. Yurek stopped dead.

A woman poked her head out of a window. "Quiet, Wilk, down!" she shouted. "You out there, who're you lookin' for?"

"May I come in?" Yurek asked, and waited for the dog to retreat. The dog bared his teeth, growled deep in his throat, and stayed put. The woman withdrew her head from the window.

Farmhands are not afraid of dogs, Yurek reminded himself. He vaulted the fence as the woman came out of the house and advanced toward her, the dog snarling at his feet.

"What do you want?" the woman asked.

"I'm looking for work."

"A kid like you, out on your own? G'wan home to your mama."

"The Shwabes—the Krauts—sent her to Prussia, to work. My father's a prisoner of war . . ."

"Go to a relative, to someone you know."

"I don't have anyone around here. I'm from Posman, they chased us all out."

Yurek felt tears come to his eyes. A peasant boy doesn't cry, he chided himself. The tears rolled down his face.

"Poor kid! A curse on them, those Shwabes, those cockroaches! Drove everybody off our holy Polish earth. May lightning strike them all! Bandits, cutthroats! Are ya hungry, boy? I can give ya something to eat. Wacek! Wacek!"

Her husband came in from the field.

She pointed to Yurek. "He wants to work here."

"Him? He still needs someone to wipe his nose!"

"I'll pasture your cows, I can do all your chores."

"Ha! Wacek the lout, with a farmhand like a fancy squire! Come on in and put down your things, boy. I'll get you some soup."

Yurek lifted the steaming bowl to his lips and set it down again. Could he carry this off? Tell them . . .? The woman seemed a decent sort. But once she knew, she wouldn't be the same. Better to keep quiet. And those kids out in the yard must belong here. Kids are snoopy, they're bound to find Hannele sooner or later. Anyway, how would he get her past the dog?

"Ain't ya gonna eat the soup?" Krysia asked.

"Maybe it ain't good enough for 'im," Wacek snickered. "We don't waste food around here, boy!"

Yurek gulped down the thin gruel. He hadn't even had a chance to look the place over, see if there were a corner to hide Hannele in. He had to get her out of the bushes, if only for a few days.

• • • • •

The master led Yurek through the barn, which was a sort of annex to the house, their feet sinking into slimy dung. At the far end they climbed a rickety ladder to a trapdoor, which opened into the attic. It was a large space, and the chimney from the kitchen stove made a pillar in the middle. There were a few bundles of straw, a pile of hay, nothing else. Yurek felt a flicker of hope, as though God himself had prepared the perfect hiding place for Hannele. As long as he was looking after the cow, there would be no reason for anyone else to climb up to the loft. It must be God's doing, as the man in Grok-how had been God's doing—a German with a revolver who spoke Yiddish.

"This is where you sleep," the peasant said. "Pile some straw around the chimney, you'll be warmer there." He went back to the trap and lowered himself down the ladder.

"Couldn't be better," Yurek whispered to himself jubilantly. Now, if only that dog would go away so he could sneak Hannele in . . .

• • • • •

The trapdoor opened silently, but the ladder groaned under his weight. No matter! When the weather was warm, wood creaked even when no one touched it. Outside, it was pitch dark. Good! If the farmer woke up and looked out, he wouldn't see a thing.

Stepping from the last rung of the ladder, Yurek slipped in the manure. He grabbed the ladder to right himself. Luckily the stuff was soft; his fall had made no sound. They would have laughed to see him all covered with filth. If he could just get Hannele safely into the loft, he would laugh too.

He groped his way toward what he thought was the door but instead found himself sprawling on top of the sow. She lurched and he lost his balance again. But she hadn't uttered a squeal. Good pig, good little pig . . . just stay quiet, that's a good girl.

If the sty were here, the barn door must be to the right. He turned and blundered into the cow's stall. If he turned left now he'd—there it was!

The door groaned. He squeezed through a narrow wedge. If he woke up the family, he was done for. He raced across the yard, tumbled over the fence. The dog growled and went back to sleep.

He had cautioned Hannele again and again; he had even frightened her into absolute silence. Now he wished she would make a sound. How else would he find her in this black confusion? Call her name? Too dangerous. He whistled softly once, again. Echoes came from all sides.

A rustling sound, a muffled sob. At last!

He lifted Hannele out from under the bush. She pounded his chest with both little fists. "I'm sorry it took so long," he soothed. "It's all right, everything will be fine now, you'll see." Her body shook convulsively as he led her up the hill.

Had he shut the barn door? He panicked. The animals would escape!

On his way to get her he hadn't made a sound, but now pebbles rolled, twigs snapped, leaves and sticks crackled under every step she took. Damn!

They stopped near the fence. "Shh!" he warned her. He climbed up first, reached down, and pulled her up beside him. Thank goodness, the boards hadn't creaked. It was so still, as though even the wind were holding its breath.

All of a sudden, the fence shook, and the yard was filled with the dog's barking. Yurek quickly covered Hannele's mouth.

He hesitated only a moment, took his hand from her mouth, and held one finger on her lips. When he sensed that she understood, he lowered himself into the yard.

The dog's fangs sank into his flesh. He clenched his teeth and stretched his arms out to Hannele. But she clung to the fence for dear life. Anger engulfed him, and he almost began yelling at her.

"Who's there?" The mistress's voice pierced the blackness. Yurek felt himself go numb. This was the end. It had all been for nothing.

"Who the devil's out there?"

"It's me. I had to use the outhouse. The dog doesn't know me yet."

"Go ahead and crap and let people sleep!" the mistress yelled. "Shut up, Wilk, you damned mutt! Into your kennel!"

The dog refused to retreat, but his bark turned into a low growl.

They finally reached the barn. He latched the door from the inside and waited until everyone was asleep before he helped Hannele up the ladder.

•   •   •   •   •

Wilk was true to his name; he looked like a wolf and was just as ravenous. A true hunter, he treated everything within reach as his prey: cats, rodents, even birds on the wing. He had to be chained to his kennel before the hens were let out in the morning. They had learned how far his chain extended and kept well clear of him. If a neighbor's hen strayed into the yard, he made short work of it.

"I'll take Wilk's food out to him," Yurek offered one day.

"Like fun you will!" Hella, the little tomboy, jumped to her feet. "Papa gave him to me, and he's *my* dog!"

"I want him to get used to me," Yurek explained. "You can feed the cat." He took the tin of soup from the mistress, and Hella followed him out.

"I'm not going to let you gobble it up! He's my dog!"

So that was why she was so eager to feed him. All that fuss about Wilk being her dog! He would gladly give Wilk some of his own food if he didn't have to share it with Hannele. The dog would be a valuable ally, keeping strangers away . . .

Although Wilk was the terror of the neighborhood, within range of his master's boots he turned into a cringing puppy. A well-placed kick and he cowered in a corner, whining abjectly. The young Wojtek, imitating his father, would pull the dog's ears, and Wilk would run away, tail between his legs. The dog didn't have it so easy either, Yurek decided. He stroked the animal's back and Wilk stretched out at his feet. He began to feel a kinship with the hound.

• • • • •

The lingering half-light of dusk faded. Night slipped gently over the village; only the western sky still glowed red. Yurek leaned on the fence. Was Mama still there in the burning ghetto? Was she in one of the trains that rolled past the village every night on the way to Treblinka?

And how would it end here? Only this morning a Jew, jumping from a boxcar, had been shot. The Germans would never have caught him without the help of the villagers, one of whom could very well have been the master.

Soft lights blinked at him from behind the curtained windows, beguiling lights that seemed warm and friendly. A gentle breeze ruffled his hair, but it made him shiver. Danger lurked behind those curtains. If anyone recognized him, they would run him down the same way they had run down the Jew this morning.

Yurek felt the warmth of Wilk's body at his feet and leaned down to stroke his neck. The dog nuzzled his cheek. He put his arm around him. Wilk had become the one friend he had here.

The next morning, Yurek broke loose several rungs from the ladder leading to the loft. The master was too lazy to climb it; the mistress wouldn't venture up a broken ladder. Hella—he would have to watch out for her.

9

Yurek's day began early. He worked long and hard, but the master always found fault. "You're bedding down the cow like she's a damn princess! What'll you do when there's no more leaves—spread out your shitty drawers?"

The mistress came to Yurek's defense. "The cow needs a dry bed. Every farm boy knows that, even if you don't."

"There's hardly a leaf left in the barn now! What'll we use— straw? There ain't even enough of that left for your mattress."

"In the fall there were enough leaves on the ground for ten cows, but where the devil were you then? When the farmer's a good-for-nothing, the whole damn farm goes to hell, may a black plague take

. . ." But Wacek turned on his heel and slammed the door behind him.

They're fighting over me again, Yurek fretted. Once she started cursing, there was no stopping her. Then they'd find the master in a drunken stupor somewhere, and the whole thing would start all over again. They'd throw him out on his ear—that's how it would end.

· · · · ·

The fields were coming into bloom—velvety green carpets sprinkled with multicolored wildflowers. The air was fragrant, the woods alive with birdcalls. The cow, grazing hungrily on the lush meadow grass, shed her winter fur along with the clumps of dung that stuck to it like scales. Her hide became smooth and silky and glistened in the warm sunshine.

Krysia sold the first of the spring radishes and the new scallions. That boy was a real treasure; the vegetable garden had never been so well tended. There was enough milk now to churn a little butter, and by the next frost she'd have enough money saved to buy another cow. With two milk cows, she wouldn't have to skimp on feeding the children. If only that husband of hers didn't find her nest egg and squander it.

Yurek came into the kitchen balancing two pails of water. He emptied them into a barrel.

"Sit down and eat with us," Krysia suggested.

"Thank you, mistress, but the barrel is empty, I have to fill it. I'll eat . . ."

"Leave him be," Wacek interrupted. "He can't eat away from the stink of the barn."

"And what about you—do you smell better than the cow?"

Yurek slipped out of the kitchen. They'd catch on one day if he kept insisting on eating in the attic. They were still at each other when he came back with more water.

"Ya hear that? There it is again," the master said, pointing to the ceiling.

The mistress turned to Yurek. "Mice have gotten into the attic."

"What'll ya do if they chew up your pet from Posnan?"

"What'll I do, you lazy lout? It's your work my pet from Posnan is doing. Hey Yurek, don't you ever see any mice when you're up there?"

"I sleep like a log, I've never seen any."

"It's rats for sure. Fix the ladder, Yurek, and I'll spread some poison around. I'll have to do it before we put in the fresh hay."

How could he ask Hannele to keep totally still? She had to turn, she had to stretch her legs sometimes. If only the house and the stalls weren't under one attic, one roof—every little sound carried.

"What else can you expect when your little helper carries bread up there? We ain't had any rats in this house since we got Wilk."

"Wilk's gotten to be as lazy as your rotten cat. Some hunter that hound turned out to be!"

Yurek jumped in with a suggestion. "If the master would let me take the dog up there, you wouldn't need to spend any money on rat poison."

"If your fleas and the dog's fleas get together, the whole damn house will be crawling with vermin!" the farmer exploded.

"Look who's talking about vermin. If you'd wash once in a while I wouldn't have to delouse your clothes."

"For all I care the dog can sleep in the attic and the damn kid in the doghouse. It's all the same to me!" Yurek carried Wilk up the ladder and pushed open the trapdoor. The dog sniffed and with a menacing growl tried to break loose from Yurek's grip.

"Easy boy, it's all right." He knelt down on the other side of the chimney, still struggling with the dog. His hand reached into the straw to find Hannele. "It's all right," he repeated, his lips almost touching the straw. "Down, down," he pleaded, until Wilk lowered his tail and stretched out near his feet.

Yurek picked the straw off Hannele's face. "Don't be afraid, he won't hurt you." He pulled her up, brought her close to him, and encouraged her to stroke the dog's back. Wilk sniffed and huddled close to them, content.

With the first rays of the sun, Wilk began to scamper playfully around the huge loft. Yurek tried to quiet him. The crazy dog would wake everybody. As he bounded across the attic, a loose floorboard flew up. Yurek rose to put it back and his mouth dropped open—a rifle lay there under the board!

A rifle? Terror seized him. The Germans would burn down the house if they ever found it. Terror soon gave way to a sudden gleam of hope. If they weren't afraid to hide a weapon, why should they be afraid to hide Jews? If the master didn't hate him so, he would tell them . . . What if he only told the mistress?

Below, Hella was awakened by the cavorting dog. How many mice had Wilk caught during the night, she wondered. The dog was the first to hear her footsteps on the ladder. He pricked up his ears and barked at the trapdoor. Hella tried to push it up. Yurek motioned to Hannele to hide and bounded to the trap.

Yurek was struggling with Hella at the foot of the ladder when the rest of the family came scurrying into the barn.

"What's going on here?" the mistress wanted to know.

"You've really taken over around here, eh?" the master shouted. "What's this about not letting Hella into the attic? You have treasures hidden up there, or what?"

"No, but the master has," Yurek whispered.

"Vodka?" the mistress asked, her voice tightening.

"Worse," Yurek said, and indicated that he couldn't talk in front of Hella and Wojtek.

Krysia chased the children out of the barn.

"What kind of stories are you cooking up, you runt? I'll push your rotten teeth in for you," Wacek blustered.

Yurek extended one arm like a rifle and pretended to pull the trigger with the index finger of his other hand.

"You nosy little sneak. Why were you tearing up the floorboards?"

"Wilk did it by accident. If the master will give me a couple of nails, I'll fasten the board down."

The mistress was dismayed. She had known nothing about a rifle.

"You'll bring trouble down on all our heads, you drunkard you!" she shrieked.

"I'll say it belongs to me," Yurek volunteered. "I'm the one who sleeps up there."

"You keep out of this, snotnose!"

Yurek threw back his shoulders. "Everybody has a weapon hidden now. The day will come when we'll run the Schwabes off our Polish earth! We'll need all the guns we can find."

"Yes, everybody has one . . . there'll come a day . . ." the farmer parroted uncertainly.

The mistress crossed herself. "May the Lord Jesus protect our sainted Polish earth from the Antichrist, may the Holy Mother of God protect us from the enemy and guard this house against misfortune."

. . . . .

The dog suddenly dashed from the barn with a yelp and chased around the corner. The mistress followed him to the front door. Someone was approaching.

Almost fondly the master clapped Yurek on the back. "There'll come a day, eh? Women don't have to know everything, right?"

Yurek moved the ladder out of the stall and hid it in the grain shed. Now the mistress would be just as anxious as he to keep Hella away from the loft.

Wacek's praise was grudging. "Brainy little bastard . . ."

. . . . .

The sun lay like a lazy cat atop the red clay tiles over the hayloft. All day long the attic was a glowing furnace.

Yurek's promise to Hannele that he would bring her more water had to be put off again and again. Whenever he came in from the meadow, someone was too near the barn.

The day the mistress had discovered the vinegar bottle missing, she had ranted and cursed for hours, accusing everyone in the household. All he needed now was to be caught with it at the pump.

Yurek finally got up to the loft in the late afternoon. Hannele had already thrown off the last of her grimy clothes; the straw clung to her like a second skin. He took one look at her and knew he would have to steal the two empty flasks the master had hidden in the shed. The master would run him through with a pitchfork if he caught him with his vodka bottles. That cursed war—even a dirty old bottle had become a treasure . . .

Yurek watched Hannele drain one bottle after another. Incredible! How could such a tiny body hold it all? He'd better get back to the pump while it was still safe. Scooping up the empty bottles, he started for the trapdoor, and stopped short. Wait a minute! Why show himself in the yard with stolen bottles when he could fetch water in the bucket and fill them in the barn?

"Your brother is a big fool," he said.

"I know," Hannele agreed.

Yurek's harried face broke into a smile.

• • • • •

A tall green bottle leaned against the neighbor's pump and shone like a jewel in the pale rays of the setting sun. Yurek let the cow go on ahead. He took a drink at the pump. Nobody seemed to be around, not even a dog. He grabbed the bottle and ran after the cow. Now Hannele would have four bottles, and this potbellied wine bottle held twice as much as the others.

• • • • •

The cow rested in the shade of a tree, chewing her cud. Yurek was helping the mistress in the vegetable garden.

"Pity we can't grow salt," she complained. "They just raised the price again, damn their souls! As if we can cook without it. Even cows need more salt in this heat."

Yurek almost jumped. So that's why Hannele had grown so weak! He should have remembered. Mama used to say the body needed extra salt when you sweated. With all that drinking and sweating, what would he do if she got sick?

He was taking too many risks. If Hannele had gotten along without salt so far, she could survive one more day. It would have been foolhardy to steal the salt while the mistress was out in the yard; she had seen him leave the house. God help him if he had left any traces. The master stole, Hella and Wojtek stole—she had to put up with them. But him? She would split his head open—and she'd be right.

Yurek left a bucket of water in the stall and started up the ladder. As he pushed up the trapdoor, he recoiled. The stench in the attic was so overpowering he could hardly breathe. He had grown accustomed to the smells in the barn, but this was nauseating. The puddles around the overflowing improvised chamber pot quickly evaporated in the heat, but the odor of the putrefying straw was so pervasive it might give them away.

Before he did anything else, he'd better run down and fill the bottles. Only three? "There was a big green bottle here—where is it?" Hannele said nothing. He searched for it in the straw but could not find it.

He hurried down the ladder, filled the bottles with water, and rushed up to the loft again. It was time to get back to the field. Wait, he'd almost forgotten to give Hannele the salt.

Hannele thought it was sugar, and gulped it down. She choked and coughed and tore at her gullet.

"Don't, Hannele, it's good for you. You have to swallow it all or you'll get sick."

She pushed his hand away, scattering the salt into the straw. He pulled a piece of bread out of his pocket and rubbed it in the straw, hoping to save a few grains. When he tried to push the bread into her mouth, she resisted desperately.

"You spoiled brat, you think you're still Papa's pet?"

A lump formed in Yurek's throat and his lips began to quiver. "You remember Papa?" he asked softly.

Hannele was still intently spitting out the salt.

"You don't remember Papa? A strip of beard around his face, brown eyes like yours, thick glasses—remember?"

Hannele gave no sign she had even heard him.

•   •   •   •   •

The chamber pot was full to the brim. Hannele tried to hold back, crossing her legs so tightly together that tears came to her eyes. Where was he? Why didn't he come? He was always telling her to hold it in. Easy for him to say—he could drink when he wanted to and pee when he wanted to. "Hold it in, hold it in!" Anyway, some of it came out and she might as well let it all go. But it burned her thighs so bad. She wouldn't tell him. All he ever did was yell at her.

•   •   •   •   •

Yurek started for the shed. He still had to shred the straw for the cow. Overhead there was a scraping on the bricks—Hannele's signal. He scurried up the ladder. Tears and sweat and straw and raw flesh met his startled eyes. He had put salt into Hannele's drinking water, and she had used it to cool the chafed and reddened skin on her thighs. In agonizing pain, she had stuffed her mouth with straw, but her tears ran down her cheeks in rivers.

He scrambled down the ladder. In the kitchen that morning he had seen the mistress hide a crock of lard. He felt a twinge in the pit of his stomach. He was the only one she trusted, but what else could he do now? He had to find something to soothe that red, oozing skin.

His last chore done, Yurek wearily made his way to the attic. He went limp at the sight of Hannele lying there motionless, her teeth clamped over her parched lips. Her silent agony tore at his insides. Why hadn't he tasted the fat? He should have known that it would have salt in it.

He would have to find some way of emptying the chamber pot into the barn. It couldn't be done through the trapdoor—Hannele would never be able to lift it. It would be too dangerous, anyhow. More pots? Where would he get them? Every rusty old container on the farm was patched a thousand times before it was thrown away.

But the solution turned out to be easier than he had imagined. The floorboard had been eaten away by termites and crumbled under his knife. Between the floor of the attic and the ceiling of the barn was a layer of clay; it was easy enough to scrape away. But the board under the clay was thick and solid. He chiseled away at it half the night.

When the tip of his knife finally went through the board, he sighed with relief, then suddenly sat back. Why was he so happy? Down in the barn, a fresh cut in the ceiling would strike the eye in a minute. Why hadn't he realized it before?

At the earliest light he went to the barn and looked at the hole. Even if he could enlarge it a bit, it would still be too small. If only he could get a funnel. There was one in the house, but it was for pouring milk into customers' bottles. When the mistress discovered some of her lard missing, she had slapped Hella and called her a glutton. Whom would she suspect if the funnel disappeared?

•   •   •   •   •

It was still too early in the day to begin his chores. Yurek went back to the attic and lay down beside his sleeping sister. Something in the straw pressed up against his ribs. He reached for it. The missing wine bottle! The size of it—it would almost double the reserve of water. Hold on—there was a better use for this bottle! If he could knock out the bottom without breaking the neck, it would make a perfect funnel. He was so pleased with the idea that he awakened Hannele to tell her about it. She pounced on the bottle and grabbed it out of his hands with a cry:

"Libbe!"

Below, a bed creaked. Yurek felt the blood rush to his head. Now she had brought the house down on them. He wanted to slap her. She was getting worse every day.

He bent his head to listen. No more sound down there. But what if she yelled again? She was rocking back and forth, cuddling that silly wine bottle. Libbe, of all things! What in the world had made her think of Libbe now?

•   •   •   •   •

It had been during the move from their spacious apartment in Praga to the one-room flat in the ghetto. Their possessions were thrown onto a wagon that they had to pull by themselves. The streets were full of such vehicles, Jews converging from all corners of Warsaw and moving into the ghetto. Papa harnessed himself between the traces like a horse while Mama pushed from behind. He and Nenna had lent support at the sides, and Hannele sat on top of the load.

Their father was soon wheezing and breathing heavily but refused to let their mother take his place. By the time he finally gave in, he could barely drag his feet. There was nothing to do but lighten the load. Half the household goods were jettisoned before they even got to the bridge. Libbe, Hannele's doll, was lost somewhere along the way.

"May I never have worse troubles," Mama had said. "People are losing their lives and I should worry about a rag doll?"

They had arrived at their new home exhausted, but the beds had to be set up. It had taken hours, and all that time Hannele lay on the floor, banging her feet and screaming for her Libbe. Mama had tried to calm her, and ended up threatening her, but her tears continued to flow in a steady stream. Papa had found a way to pacify her. Libbe had gone to a faraway land. She was eating and sleeping there; and after the war she would come back looking for Hannele. Would a grown-up Libbe want to play with a teeny-weeny little girl? Of course not. So Hannele must behave herself and eat, and grow up, just like Libbe. Hannele's tantrums came to an end at last. "Children forget quickly," Mama had philosophized.

Ever since then, the doll had never been mentioned, but now, from out of nowhere, it had come back to life as an empty wine bottle. As if he hadn't enough to worry about . . . He used to resent the way his father treated Hannele. Papa never came home without something in his pocket for her; he even made a game of it. "Here's a stone for you," he would laugh, and throw her a candy or a nut.

So this is what Papa had accomplished by spoiling his pet. She'd forgotten him but she remembered her rag doll.

Yurek's voice was brittle. "Give me that, you little brat! It took me hours to find it, so you wouldn't rot here." He yanked the bottle out of her hands and ran to the trapdoor.

• • • • •

With one eye on the grazing cow, Yurek examined the result of his work. There was a long crack in the glass; if he put it very carefully into the hole, it would work. The jagged edges might be a problem for his clumsy sister.

He managed to get to the attic during the noon milking. He pulled a crust of bread out of his pocket, laid it on the straw in front of Hannele, and rushed to fit the glass funnel into the hole in the floor.

"There, it's perfect!" he cried happily. His excitement struck no chord in Hannele; she had not even touched the bread.

"You think Libbe hasn't grown bigger than a bottle?" Yurek asked, using his father's approach. "If you don't eat, you'll be a pip-squeak forever and Libbe will never play with you."

He might as well have said nothing. Hannele only turned away in silence. Below, Wilk started barking. Someone must be coming for milk. He looked at the bread nestled in the straw, and his mouth watered. He could devour ten pieces like it, but she turned up her nose. She must be hungry. How could she starve herself just to spite him? He started down the ladder. He would make her eat it if he had to stuff it down her throat.

Poor Hannele, she was only a kid and he was making her the target of all his misery. If a green bottle was what she wanted, he'd get one for her!

• • • • •

He was halfway into the loft when a commotion started in the yard. "Don't tell me you don't know!" the mistress was yelling. "Another bottle for your stinkin' vodka?"

"Shut your filthy mouth, woman, or I'll throw this hammer at you! I never even saw Sherinska's lousy bottle!"

Yurek's chest tightened. He shouldn't have done it. But how could he turn back now, with Hannele's eyes glued to the bottle in his hand? "Here, take it!" he whispered. She didn't move. He held out the bottle.

"Here's your Libbe."

Hannele's eyes grew moist, but her hands were two clenched fists.

Still holding the bottle, he slid down the ladder and sneaked out to the pump.

"What have you got there, you little thief?"

"I'm washing Mrs. Sherinska's bottle."

"Why in blazes didn't you tell somebody you were taking it, you damn fool?"

Sherinska came to Yurek's side and patted his shoulder. "Thank you."

The master pointed a mocking finger at his wife. "If the house disappeared she'd look for it in my pocket!"

"If you could, you'd carry it away. I know you—you'd sell your own mother for a drink."

10

Hella's first communion was approaching. The priest would have to be paid, the family clothed, and a party arranged. Her mother's little nest egg had grown but it was "blood" money. Every grosz had already been wrenched from their meager food allowance for buying a second cow. If this money was squandered, they would eat watery soup again next winter.

All the hens were laying. There was enough milk to supply the customers and still churn butter for sale. If that husband of hers didn't drink so much, she could put away enough for a cow and still prepare a communion party for Hella that she would be proud of. If only that good-for-nothing were a good smuggler. The rest of the village was raking in money. However, even if Wacek tried smuggling, she'd never see the money. This was something she'd have to try herself.

• • • • •

Hella sat hunched over the table. She licked the point of a pencil and thought about what to add to the list in front of her. The cat warmed itself languidly in the sun. Hella wasn't around to step on its tail. Wilk was left in peace to enjoy the bone he'd dug up somewhere— nobody chased him into the shed. The hens strutted undisturbed, pecked the ground for a stray kernel or bread crumb—no one interfered with their wanderings. The brown hen had laid an egg; it still rested in the straw in a corner of the shed. Wojtek had not learned the art of snatching the eggs before his mother collected them; Hella knew the laying schedule, but she hadn't stirred all morning.

Wojtek chased the pig around the yard. The farmer heard the grunts and came running all the way from the vegetable garden. The little dunce, couldn't he see the sow's belly was practically scraping the ground? She could lose her litter. "Leave her alone, you good-for-nothing, or I'll make you a head shorter!"

Her father's shouts brought Hella to the window. She put one leg over the sill, thought better of it, and returned to the table.

This coming Sunday she would go to her first confession. She had just drawn up a list of all her sins, so she wouldn't forget to confess them. She went over it again. Was it worth going all the way to Otwock for this? A feast was being planned, a new white dress for her, new clothes for Mama and Papa, even for Wojtek. All this for the sake of a few measly sins? Forgot to count her rosary one morning, maybe one time in the evening—her mother always made sure she said her prayers in a good loud voice. What real sins could she bring to the priest? Her mother's confessions lasted at least half an hour, but she'd be through before she even got started.

Should she write down about the neighbor's chicken that Wojtek had strangled? It had been her idea, but he had done it. Anyway, she'd better leave something for him to confess.

Oh, she remembered something. "Mama," she called, "is stealing a rabbit a sin?"

"Of course," her mother replied, "stealing *anything* is a sin."

"And obeying Papa?"

"Obeying Papa is right."

"What if Papa told me to steal a rabbit and I obeyed him?"

"A black plague on you and your father both."

She recalled the business with the rabbit well enough. Guests had arrived, and there was nothing in the larder, not even a bone of the hog they had slaughtered for Easter. The hens were all laying. After pampering them all winter, it was senseless to kill them just when they had begun to pay off. Wacek had wanted to "borrow" a hen from their neighbor Jozef. "I'll pay him back someday, Krysia, and anyway he steals plenty from me." She wouldn't hear of it.

"It's criminal to kill a layer, even the neighbor's," she had insisted. Then they remembered that the Przybulskis were raising rabbits. Hella disappeared and came back with one. Krysia turned it into a real feast—black soup from the blood, the belly stuffed with oats and stewed—they had dined like kings.

With a houseful of guests, what else could she have done? Krysia would never permit stealing for themselves. If only Wacek, that sponge, didn't soak everything up, they'd have enough to eat. But there had been guests and his cousin Wykcia, that babbler, would have wagged her tongue to the whole family if they hadn't produced a good meal. After that incident, Krysia had started raising her own rabbits.

Now it all had to be confessed to the priest. This backwoods village! The whole lot of them were nothing but wicked thieves, and the children were turning into savages. May this whole rotten place sink deep into the earth and disappear without a trace! May a fire burn it down from end to end, and it wouldn't hurt if Wacek's thieving family, including the witch Wykcia, went up in smoke along with it—but may the Lord God not punish her for such sinful thoughts.

Ah, what's the use weeping over the rabbit? Wacek didn't confine himself to stealing from strangers. He even snitched things from her linen chest. If only he'd work and earn enough for a bottle; but all he did was lie around like a pile of cowshit. If she didn't keep on his tail every step of the way, he'd never plow a furrow or plant a seed; he'd just soak himself blind and chase every whore in the village. He set the children a fine example. That daughter of his—she's looking for sins! In a few years there won't be enough priests in the whole province to hear her confession.

Still, they had to have a party, and a nice one at that. She was not going to fall into her gossiping neighbors' mouths, not if she could help it. But dip into her bundle? She'd rather starve. Again and again she had tried to save for a second cow, but one way or another it had all gone down the drain. Not this time!

Carefully, day by day, Krysia had hidden the eggs, and already she could stack them in mounds of fifteen. She had whipped the butter into round pats and wrapped them in moist white muslin, ready for market. Their heft had felt good in her hands. It would bring twice as much in Warsaw as in Otwock.

It was still dark when Krysia rose to pack up her goods. Sixty-eight eggs—a windfall!

She placed the eggs in the basket, one snug against the other, so they wouldn't be jostled. But the Germans were starved for butter. She'd better put that at the bottom of the basket, on top of it the eggs, then the radishes and onions to hide the smell of fresh country butter. Into a second basket went the cheeses, and over them a large loaf of homemade yeast bread. The Warsaw housewives would pay handsomely for that.

Why not take the young cocks too? She would raise the little hens as layers, but what use were the roosters? She would take all the half-grown ones to Warsaw, and everything added up would bring in so much money there would be no need to touch her savings.

But how was she going to carry it all? She shook her husband. "Wacek, wake up!"

"Let me sleep, woman," he snarled, and turned his face to the wall.

"Wacek, get up! You've got to come with me to Warsaw. We need the money for the communion."

"You think I'm crazy? You're not getting me on any train—not with all the raids going on."

"I can't handle all this stuff alone."

"Well, I ain't goin'! Take your farmhand."

For once he was right. She'd be much better off with the boy.

Krysia gave Yurek two carrots for the rabbits. Once in the barn, he managed to get to the loft to leave Hannele a piece of bread. He took the ladder out of the barn and hid it so well even the master wouldn't be able to find it. He milked the cow and led her out to pasture.

The mistress dragged her husband out of bed. "Make sure the cow doesn't get into the garden. Water the vegetables, d'ya hear? It's going to be a scorcher today. The tomatoes need lots o' water, don't forget. And see that Hella gets to school on time. C'mon, get moving. I'll miss the train."

11

Wacek sat under a tree, sprinkled a few grains of tobacco onto a square of tissue paper, and deftly rolled a cigarette. The blast of the train whistle told him that Krysia was on her way. Clever wench, that wife of his, but he was no fool either. He chuckled; little did she know. The white hen had found herself a new place to lay, and no matter where Krysia searched, she couldn't find its eggs.

She might have, all the same, if he hadn't been so quick to clean them out. The moment the hen started clucking he stalked her until she squatted and laid her egg. He had found six eggs there and daily he enlarged his hoard. Three more days and he'd have enough for half a liter of vodka.

Three days? By then Krysia might find the eggs. Now was the time to act. But that Marysia, the bitch in the tavern, wouldn't trust him a grosz. If her father, old Stakh, were serving, he'd probably give him credit. It was nicer, though, when Marysia was at the bar. That body of hers, the heat she gave off, devil take her. If you bit into her cheeks, the blood would spurt to the ceiling. She had already slapped his face once, the bitch. Ah, they're all alike. You say yes and she says no; you say yes and she says no; you say yes, she says no again until you say yes and she says nothing; then at the crucial moment old Stakh shows up and ruins the whole thing.

So, only three eggs to go for half a liter of vodka. Why did she have to take everything to Warsaw? There was still some flour she had been saving for Hella's communion. One kilo of flour was worth every bit as much as three eggs.

The cigarette burned down and scorched his lips. Wacek spat out the butt and ran home to get the flour before the children woke up. When he had packed the flour down and smoothed it over and swept away the telltale traces, he woke Hella. "Get up, you little bitch! Half the morning's gone, and she lies there snoring. Get out there and make sure the cow doesn't get into the vegetables."

On his way to the tavern, Wacek met old Stakh. "Where to so early?"

"To Karczew for sausage," the old man replied, hurrying off.

To Karczew? He couldn't possibly get back before afternoon. So Marysia was alone in the tavern.

At the door of the tavern Wacek turned on his heels and ran home. He wouldn't get very far with Marysia if he came in smelling like a stable. He dashed into the house and grabbed his new pants.

"Hella, are you watching the cow?"

"Yes, Papa, I am," came the answer, not from the pasture, but from the barn next door. In his rush to get out of the house, Wacek didn't notice, and even forgot to shut the door behind him.

Hella indeed went to tend the cow, even tweaked her ears and pulled her tail, but in a few minutes she ran back to the yard for a drink. She pumped the handle until the cool spring water flowed into her cupped hands. Some swallows flew by overhead, and Hella watched them in wonder. Where were so many birds coming from? She forgot her thirst and took off after the swallows, who were heading straight for the eaves of the barn. Maybe they had built a nest— she would get a ladder and have a look. Oh, the cow! She leapt through the open window and shook her sleeping brother.

"Get up, lazybones!"

The boy looked at her, his eyes heavy with sleep, and turned to the wall. Hella shook him again.

"Get up, dammit! It's your turn to watch the cow!"

"You watch," he grunted sleepily.

Hella pulled him off the bed. "I've got to study for my communion."

Wojtek scrambled back under the covers. She gave up and went into the barn to look for the ladder. Her eyes fell on two fresh carrots in the rabbit's cage. She snatched them out and wolfed one down as the rabbits watched timidly. About to start on the second, she stopped, and ran back to her brother's bed.

"Wojtek, Wojtek, want a carrot?"

Her plan worked. Chewing on the carrot, he stumbled out to the meadow. Hella ran back to the swallows. The ladder leading to the loft had disappeared and the big barn ladder was too heavy.

"Wojtek, come back, I need you!"

The dog would watch the cow, she decided. He'd done it many times before. She let Wilk off his chain. He promptly lunged at a hen; the chicken squawked and flew to the top of the fence. Hella burst out laughing. That Wilk was a real terror. She caught hold of the dog's collar and dragged him out to the cow in the field.

"Now, Wilk, don't let her out of here! That's a good dog!"

Even with Wojtek's help she couldn't move the heavy ladder. She sent him to fetch Bobek, the neighbor's boy. Together the three barely managed to drag the long ladder outside, but it was well worth their effort. Up in the eaves they found the nest full of tiny eggs.

Hella organized a game; they would play store. To start with, they had the eggs. Wojtek brought out some flour and Bobek contributed a slab of bacon. But a few things were missing. The store in the village stocked a variety of household items. They persuaded Wojtek to cut the buttons off one of his mother's dresses. Bobek came back with a cracked glass and a battered old pot. Hella forgot all about the sins she had wanted to add to her list. She even forgot to go to school.

Meanwhile Wilk was busy with his own game. Birds rose in the air, grasshoppers took flight, anything that moved was a potential victim. He leapt to snare a fly and noticed the cow stray to the edge of the meadow. In a flash he blocked her way and chased her back.

The sun climbed steadily, drinking up the early morning dew. A band of humid air settled heavily over the field. The cow, sated, lay down to chew her cud. Wilk trotted back to the house.

The barnyard was empty; the children had gone to the river.

The barn door stood ajar. With a nudge of his muzzle, Wilk widened the gap and sauntered in. Inside a crate sat three small rabbits. Wilk stood stock still, tail pointed, nose quivering. A rumbling growl started far back in his throat until it erupted in a savage howl. He lunged. The rabbits fled to the farthest corner of the cage and cowered, trying to hide behind each other. He flashed his fangs and tore at the cage. It shook violently but the makeshift door was securely latched. He leapt to the top of the crate, ripped at the slats with his paws; everything shook, but the boards held.

The rabbits shrank into a ball, their fur standing up stiffly like porcupine quills. Their terrified eyes clouded over, their small pink noses sniffed and trembled.

Wilk shoved his paw between the slats and stretched his leg into the cage, but he couldn't reach the rabbits' corner. He tried another slat, and another; each time his paw fell short of its goal. A bloodthirsty yowl tore from his throat, foam frothed around his jaw. Suddenly, one rabbit broke away and raced across the crate. Wilk stopped barking, his eyes fastened on the rabbit. He tensed and waited to pounce. His paw, a streak of lightning, swooped down and a faint squeal came from the bottom of the cage. He rolled his victim back and forth until a little blue tongue emerged from the rabbit's rigid mouth.

He bared his teeth at the other cringing little creatures. His paw came down, blood spurted from the small, pink nose. Another rabbit lay dead.

The smell of blood aroused Wilk to even greater fury. His paw aimed at the head of the last rabbit. It twisted away and fled to the other end of the cage. Wilk jumped back and forth on top of the crate, his fangs bared, snarling and yelping. He jabbed his paw through one opening, through another, as the rabbit darted from corner to corner. His paw caught on a splinter. Half crazed, he jumped off the crate and bolted from the barn.

Curled up in his kennel, Wilk nipped at his leg until the splinter came out. He licked the wound clean and charged out of the kennel again.

A hen clucking in the shed now caught his attention. He promptly chased after her as she fluttered out to the yard and up the ladder, feathers. flying. A freshly laid egg gleamed in the straw. He trampled it, and with a final growl at the hen, headed for the garbage bin to rummage for food.

A chirp came from the front of the house. Wilk's ears stood straight up.

Though the shed served as the chicken house, a heap of straw had been piled in a corner of the kitchen for the brood hen and her eggs. It was only three days since the chicks had hatched and the door was kept locked to prevent them from wandering out and the dog from coming in.

Now the door was not quite shut. Wilk peered through the crack—the chicks were all over the kitchen floor. The mother hen sensed danger lurking. She sprang from her roost squawking and clucking, hopped around the kitchen, tried to collect her young. Wilk shoved his snout into the crack and swung the door open. With measured treads he marched into the room.

The hen spread her wings, stiffened her neck, and swooped down on the dog. With wings spread, feathers ruffled, she appeared large and menacing. Wilk saw her pointed beak aimed directly at his eyes and his hide shriveled. He fled from the house, his tail between his legs.

12

"I have to go away, Hannele. Don't be scared. I'll hide the ladder and nobody will be able to get up here. I'm going to Warsaw, I'll bring you something."

"Will you see Mama?"

"I don't know. I'm going with the mistress."

"Will you see Mama?"

"Maybe."

Yossel can do anything, Hannele reassured herself when the trap-door shut behind him. If he promised to do something, he did it. A long time ago, when Yossel went away, Mama would cry and cry. But it wasn't really so bad when he went out; he always came back with something good for her. Once he'd brought her a piece of chocolate. Nenna said that before the war there was chocolate in the house all the time, and Mama said that after the war there would be lots and lots of chocolate again. They kept saying "before the war . . . after the war" all the time. Does "war" mean when you run and run, looking for a place to hide? Back then she remembered, they weren't hiding yet, but there wasn't any chocolate. Still, Yossel had found some anyway; Yossel could do anything.

Somebody was moving around below, first in the house, then in the barn. The sounds finally stopped. Very carefully she crept to the open window. It was so pretty out there. Hella and Wojtek were chasing each other around a big tree. Would she ever be able to go out and play?

It was like that in the ghetto when Mama used to take her out. They would walk and walk and walk until they came to a place with a wall in the middle of the street. She could see branches full of pretty leaves, but between her and the leaves was the high brick wall. And now, right down there, the children were rolling in the grass with the little yellow flowers, but she had to stay here in the attic.

She took a deep breath, filling her lungs with fresh air. When Mama used to take her on those long walks, she would say, "Take deep breaths, Hannele, so you'll grow up to be a big healthy girl." She was a bad girl though; she hadn't done what her mama told her. Mama would be proud to see the deep breaths she was taking now. She would say, "Good, Hannele, you're a good little girl." And she would hug and kiss her. She used to hug her and kiss her all the time.

She must remember to tell Yossel that she wouldn't cry or stamp her feet anymore. She should have made him promise to tell that to Mama. Yossel wasn't a tattletale, he wouldn't tell Mama that she had been a bad girl.

Why had she said that she didn't remember Papa? As soon as Yossel came back, she'd tell him that she *did* remember him, she really did, his big eyeglasses, his little beard, everything. But Papa shouldn't have gone away with Nenna . . .

Hella and Wojtek were back with a stranger. She had never seen the boy before. Why was he hollering about a ladder? Had Yossel forgotten to hide the ladder? Now they would find her. "Zhidova, Zhidova," they'd scream, like that time on the streetcar, and Yossel wasn't even here.

Hannele dashed back to the hay pile. The boards never creaked so loud . . . Who put that pot there?

Deeper, deeper into the hay she wriggled. Oh no, she mustn't sneeze. She clamped the palm of her hand over her nose. Even her breathing was too loud, but they wouldn't hear anything, they were making so much noise themselves. Maybe they hadn't even heard the clang of the pot when she kicked it.

The children's laughing voices drifted farther and farther away. See, scaredy-cat, they didn't hear you!

It had been nice at the window—all those trees, and the flowers were so pretty. Back in the ghetto, she could see only a few branches that grew over the wall. Still, it was nicer there, Mama was with her to hold her hand.

•   •   •   •   •

The train pulled into the Grokhov terminal. Buyers milled around them the moment they stepped down.

"We could sell everything right here and get back home earlier," Yurek suggested.

The mistress held the basket close to her body. "No, we'll do better in the city."

"All right, then let's take a tram straight to the center of town. These buyers would take quite a slice of your profit."

The red Warsaw tram rolled over familiar streets toward the Poniatowski bridge. His mother had stayed there, on the western shore of the Vistula. What was happening behind those ghetto walls? Had anything been left after the fires had burned themselves out? Not far from here, there had been a *meto,* a contact point for smugglers. A hole was dug under the ghetto wall or you went over it on a ladder. Right here, where the tram came to a stop, Bolek had been caught.

They had been walking close, with Bolek just ahead. Jews never walked together on the Aryan side. Somebody had recognized Bolek and started shouting "Zhid! Zhid!"

People had come running from everywhere. He had walked right past Bolek without looking back, not even when he heard the shot. The sound of that shot had stayed with him the whole time it had taken to walk to Bolek's house in the ghetto. He had waited and waited, and Bolek had not come home. But the next morning he closed his ears to his mother's cries. She had thrown herself in front of the door. "You'll go out only over my dead body, God forbid . . ." He had climbed out of a window and run to the *meto.*

Hadn't he been frightened then, even a little? He couldn't remember. It was good to come back with bundles of food. How they had fussed over him, especially Mama. Even Papa had not been allowed to scold him when his mind wandered from his studies. There had been no lack of food in their house, while in the ghetto, people were starving in the streets. He had been the provider, and not once had he forgotten to bring something for Hannele. "You're spoiling the child," Mama had complained, just as she used to say to Papa in the old days.

It was true that Papa had given in to every whim of Hannele's, but when it came to studies, he wouldn't back down, not one bit. "More than four years old, and she can barely read a word!"

"Can't you see the child has no strength?" his mother had protested.

·   ·   ·   ·   ·

The day his mother had taken Hannele to the doctor came vividly to his mind. He had wanted to go with them; not that he was so eager to go to the doctor, but how long could he sit in one place and study? School went on all day. First, the Talmud. Other children were still asleep while his father was filling his head with talmudic deliberations. Later in the morning, when the neighbors' children were sent off to the improvised ghetto school, he had to go too. After school the children played in the yard, but his father would call him in to study Bible. That day the book was open at Isaiah.

"O sinful nation, a people laden with iniquities: a seed of evil-doers, children who deal corruptly . . ."

What did Papa find so fascinating about this? The prophet blamed the Jews themselves for all their troubles.

"Yossel, pay attention!" his father demanded. "You're almost a bar mitzvah boy. When I was your age . . ."

Nenna was past fifteen already, and she didn't have to study as much as he did. Papa wanted him to learn the Talmud and Scriptures and Polish and arithmetic and Hebrew and Yiddish and grammar and history—as many subjects as he had pockmarks on his face. The girls didn't have to learn all those things, just he. "His face isn't much to look at, at least let him have a good brain . . ."

"*Ehkho hoyso l'zoyno kirya nemonah*—how has the faithful city become a harlot . . ."

"That means that Jerusalem, which was a faithful city, has turned away from the right path."

"How can a city turn away from a path?"

"The prophet means the people who live in the city."

"The right path is the *derekh hayosher,* the path of righteousness?"

"Yes."

"And what is a harlot?"

"Read further. It becomes clear from the other half of the verse: *m'leyasi michpot, tsedek yolin bo*—she that was full of justice, righteousness lodged within her—"

"What does the first half mean? What does harlot mean?"

His father blushed. "That means—it means . . ."

He had waited stubbornly for an answer. If a pockmarked kid had to study so much, his father would have to explain more.

"It means a woman who has turned away from the right path," his father blurted out.

"What is the right path? How does a woman turn away from it?"

Beads of sweat broke out on his father's forehead.

Yossel tried to give his father an easy way out. "I know, Papa, it means she steals things."

"No, no, that's not what it means. It means . . . it means she doesn't live a decent life, she sells herself for money."

"Sells? Like a slave is sold?" He was tempted to ask another question, but a vein was protruding on his father's forehead. "I know, Papa, I know what it means now."

"You know? How do you know? What kind of friends are you hanging around with?"

Yossel had wanted to get even with his father, but it had turned against him. Now he had to study the next chapter as well, where the prophet spoke of the good days that were to come. Even after he finished that and his father had gone to his desk to do his writing, he had to go over the weekly portion of the Scriptures on his own. He thought he'd wait until Papa was engrossed in his work and then slip out of the house. But before he could make a move, his mother had come back.

"You're writing again?"

His father didn't notice the resentment in her tone. He merely nodded, not looking up.

"Aren't you interested in what the doctor said?"

"What did the doctor say?"

"What did the doctor say, what did the doctor say? Do you really care?"

"Goldele," he said reprovingly, with a faint motion of his head toward the children.

"What do you care, go ahead and write your books!"

His father shrugged, dipped his pen into the inkwell, and bent over his papers again. His mother lunged forward, swept her hand across the table, and papers flew all over the room. The inkwell lay on its side, spilling its dark fluid over the manuscripts, the books, over his father's gray sleeves and white hands, like blood from an open wound. He did not move from his chair.

"The child has bronchitis, it could turn into tuberculosis," his mother said as if she were talking to herself. "She needs eggs, she needs milk, and butter . . . Other people do everything for their children . . ."

Usually when Papa was writing, Mama would tiptoe around the house, not letting anyone breathe too loud. Bronchitis must be a terrible thing if she acted like this, but now she appeared to be sorry.

He decided then and there that tomorrow he'd go over the wall.

The next day, when Yossel returned home late, his mother met him at the door with a stream of tears.

"God in heaven, what we have to endure because of this boy!"

"Where were you all day?" His father's voice was loud and angry.

"We didn't know what to think," Mama tried to soften the confrontation.

"You weren't in school, you weren't home for your lesson . . ."

"You didn't even come home to eat, Yossel. You could get sick. Did they catch you for a labor squad—you're so young . . ." Mama had found an excuse and was ready to accept it.

"Out from morning till night, like a common hoodlum . . ." Papa couldn't forgive him.

Yossel started pulling packages out of his pockets, from under his shirt: a linen sack full of white flour, a small bottle of milk, a flask of oil, two apples, an egg . . .

"What is this?" His mother could not believe her eyes.

"The friends he picks out!" His father wrung his hands. "You— you—"

"I didn't steal it, Papa."

"Then where did you get it?"

"I was over at Grandfather's. I told him that Hannele was sick, and he gave me ten zlotys."

His mother lowered her eyes. "Your grandfather gave you ten zlotys? These things cost at least thirty, forty—"

"And Mrs. Wilchinski said I should bring her some used clothes— a dress, a jacket. I could put them on under my shirt—"

"Are you delirious or what? Who is this Mrs. Wilchinski?"

"I was in her house in Praga, on the other side of the Vistula River. She'll sell the used clothes and buy food for me. They get food very cheap there. All this stuff cost ten zlotys."

"Have you lost your mind? Don't you know what they do to a Jew if they catch him on the Aryan side? Never do this again!"

"Don't worry, I know how to take care of myself. Just look at all this," he pointed to the packages. "You think I go by myself? There were at least ten kids from our street."

"You see what this war has led to? Once and for all, you're to stop running around with smugglers. Children are supposed to stay home and . . . and study. A bar mitzvah boy already and he'd rather climb over walls than open a book."

His father's anger did not move Yossel at all.

"I'm still young enough to sit at home, but I'm old enough to study like crazy for my bar mitzvah, seven months away. Mama knows better. Hannele is sick and needs an egg."

"I'd rather go hungry, Yossel, I'd rather go out and steal." His mother wept, wringing her hands. "They shoot people at the wall . . ."

"Goldele, is that a way to talk to a child? Yossel, your mother won't steal and you won't smuggle." His father's tone now had the ring of finality.

Yossel's eyes shifted from his father to his mother and back again. They must have made up while he was on the other side. Papa shouldn't really worry about what Mama had said. She would never go out and steal. But how would they get any food into the house? There were raids for the labor camps every day. God help them if his father should ever be caught. How would he survive with just one good lung? And Hannele—yesterday when Mama was yelling and Papa was so mad, she just sat there and played with her stupid doll. He could have killed her. Let her have bronchitis, let her get tuberculosis, let her . . .

No, he didn't mean it. He would go over the wall like the other kids and bring back the food she needed. She would get better just like Papa had. And once he took off his arm band with the star, there would be no reason to worry at all, nobody could tell he was a Jew . . .

•　•　•　•　•

She had such plump rosy cheeks and dimpled little hands. Now she was all giggles and smiles. If he went ahead and did it, she'd cry and stamp her feet like Hannele had when she'd lost Libbe. It didn't hurt a growing child to cry once in a while; it was good for the lungs. Anyway, she wouldn't cry too long, look at all the good things her mother was buying from the mistress. She could give her a piece of sausage, maybe a crust of that delicious white bread smeared thick with butter, maybe even chocolate.

Whether she was a fat little girl or a skinny one, if he took something that didn't belong to him, it was stealing. He'd better stop staring at that little girl's doll.

The woman was examining the eggs, weighing them in her hands, comparing one egg with another and messing up the whole basket. She beat down the price of a small pat of butter, then reached for a larger one. The mistress was losing patience. Yurek shifted his weight from one leg to the other. If that woman didn't stop bothering the mistress, he would grab the baskets and everything in sight, even the fat girl's doll, and whoosh!

The woman began to pay for her purchases as if she had read his mind. The mistress counted the money as Yurek rewrapped the butter and put the remaining eggs back in the basket. He was still looking at the doll from the corner of his eye when the woman pushed a chunk of white bread into his hand. He looked at her amazed. Now she was breaking off a piece of sausage from a long link. "Here boy, eat; you must be starved."

He bent to kiss the woman's hand, caught himself, and drew back. Only a city boy would do such a thing; certainly not a farmhand. Ah, what did it matter, so long as he had something to bring back to Hannele. He wrapped the bread and sausage in a cloth and pushed it deep into the basket though his stomach was contracting with hunger.

What had the mistress thought when he'd almost kissed that woman's hand back there? She must have noticed. The mistress fed him every day. Was the Warsaw woman more worthy of respect because she was a city lady, while the mistress was only a peasant? He would have liked to rip those amber beads off that woman's fat neck and give them to his mistress. The necklace must have come from the ghetto—and wasn't the mistress feeding Jewish children? Not that she knew, but she would soon know. With all the money she was making here, she would be in a good mood, and he would confess everything. How nice it would be to find something to give her right now—a brooch, a ring, anything. He walked behind the mistress, his eyes scouting the sidewalk. In a big city like Warsaw it shouldn't be impossible to find something.

When he told her, he must remember to ask her not to confide in her husband yet. The master was so nasty . . . if he could find a present for him—a pocketknife, a nice leather belt. People are always dropping things in the street. A bottle of vodka would be even better. How silly; even if somebody had lost a package with liquor in it, the bottle would be broken. But if he found some money, he could buy anything, even vodka. He would give it all to the mistress for another cow—but he would put away a few zlotys for the master. He wouldn't give him all of it at once, only a bit at a time, enough for a half-liter. You're our savior, Yurek, our good luck, the mistress would say. And he would answer: The mistress and the master are my saviors. My little sister Hannele is up in your attic.

"Idiot, are you blind or asleep? Walks right into a telephone pole with his eyes open! Are you hurt?"

"No, mistress."

"If you had broken those eggs . . ."

"No, I only bumped it with my left arm."

They knocked on many doors and climbed countless steps but the effort was well worth it. At dusk when they came back to the station in Grokhov, the mistress's big bosom was bulging with money. It had been a good day's trade. They sat down on a bench and waited for the train. They hadn't had anything to eat since the ride to Warsaw.

"The lady gave you a piece of bread, what are you saving it for?" the mistress asked Yurek.

He took the bread and sausage out of the basket and handed it to her. She broke each in two and gave him his share.

She devoured her portion before he had even bitten into his. "You're hungry, so eat!"

This was the perfect time to tell her. He started to put the food back into the basket, but the mistress caught his hand. "Who are you hiding this for? They steal enough as it is. You think I don't know about the eggs and butter that keep disappearing? Eat!"

She thought he was saving it for her children! How could he possibly tell his story now?

But he had to! A woman appeared from nowhere and sat down beside them. Dammit, now he would have to keep quiet. Well, they had a long ride home, there would be plenty of time to talk.

The woman opened a paper bag, took out a cherry, and popped it into her mouth. Yurek fixed his eyes on her. The lady in Warsaw had given him bread, maybe this one would give him a couple of cherries. There wasn't a thing left for Hannele. All alone there the whole day—he had promised to bring her something. He watched the woman toss the plum-red cherries into her mouth and spit out the pits, without so much as a glance in his direction.

She threw away the paper bag, and he sprang to retrieve it. A lonely pit rattled around in it. One by one he gathered up the pits that lay at her feet. It wasn't much, but he would have something to give his sister. He could split them open with a rock. No, not a rock—he would do it with a hammer on the kitchen table. He sat down again and wondered if the mistress was thinking he had lost his mind. She would soon know who the pits were for, he would tell her all about it on the ride home.

The mistress fell asleep the moment they boarded the train, and slept so soundly that he had to wake her when they arrived at their station. She raced on ahead of him for the short walk home. How could he tell her now? There would be no time to explain.

There had to be something he could do for Hannele. He reached into the basket, pulled out a damp rag, and stuffed it into the back pocket of his pants. The cloth must have soaked up a good bit of the butter that was wrapped in it during the long, hot day. He would give it to Hannele to suck. Or maybe it would be even better to put the greasy cloth on her poor inflamed thighs. Anyway, it was something.

13

At noontime the cow trotted in from the meadow on her own and made straight for the pump. The mistress always kept a bucket of fresh water ready, but today the bucket was rolling around on the ground empty and dry. The cow sniffed at the puddle at the foot of the pump and jerked her muzzle away—a dead chick was floating in the shallow pool. Closer to the house she sniffed at a watering can. It had been standing there since early morning ready for Wacek to water the tomato plants. The water was hot from the broiling sun and brown with rust. The cow turned and lumbered off in search of fresh water. She found nothing and came back to the can. Desperate, she tried to lap at the water but the opening was too narrow for more than the few drops that splashed tantalizingly against her mouth. A second attempt turned the can over and the water ran into the sand.

Her mouth too dry to chew her cud, her udder painfully full and heavy, the cow plodded into the barn and took her accustomed place near the milking stool. A plaintive moo issued from her throat.

In the late afternoon, Wacek staggered home, grabbed the milk pail, and shuffled to the stall. His fingers tugged at the teats but no milk came. "She's holding back, the bitch!" All right, all right, I'll bring you water!"

"Here, choke on it!" Wacek snarled. Before he could settle himself on the stool again, the water bucket was empty. He filled it once more, stood it in front of the cow, and after kicking her viciously, set to milking her. He watched the milk stream into the pail and could almost taste the vodka it would buy. He took it without bothering to strain it.

At nightfall, Wacek finally floundered into the house on splayed, shaky legs and collapsed on his bed, rumpled clothes, muddy boots, and all.

A suspicious crackling beneath the window make him sit up with a groan. "Hella! Wojtek! That whoring cow must have gotten into the vegetables! Where the devil are you, you little bastard?"

He rolled off the bed, dragged himself to the garden. Grunting and waving his arms, he chased the cow while she trotted from one end of the garden to the other, stomping on the plants she hadn't already chewed. At the far end of the enclosure she leapt over a wooden bar and galloped across the fields. Wacek started after her, but his feet slid out from under him and he landed squarely in a mud hole. He flailed his arms in an attempt to stand upright again. Grimacing, he finally managed to crawl out of the hole on his hands and knees. The cow was gone.

•　　•　　•　　•　　•

Wacek heard Hella's voice and quickly hid behind a pine. She drew nearer, skipping and humming, but stopped abruptly as she caught sight of the havoc in the garden. She turned and fled. Finding Wojtek loitering at the gate, she sent him on ahead. Let him be the one to get it. He walked right into the trap.

"Bastard, no-good-lazy runt! That's how you watched the cow, eh? I'll flatten you right here!" As Wacek undid his belt, Wojtek ducked and ran for the road, his spindly legs churning. His father raced after him, brandishing the heavy leather belt and screaming: "I'll murder you, you worthless son of a bitch!" His trousers slid below his knees, tripped him, and he sank into the mud. His furious swearing brought out the neighbors. They slapped their thighs with mocking laughter. Wacek's anger compounded his confusion. He struggled to his feet and pulled his pants over his muddy drawers. Holding them up with one hand, he swung the belt over his head with the other and resumed his pursuit of Wojtek.

The distance widened between them. Wacek could scarcely drag one leg after the other. He stopped and swallowed great gulps of air. "Come on, Wojtek," he called to the shadow down the road. "Help me find the cow and I won't beat you."

"It wasn't my fault, Papa. Hella started the whole thing," Wojtek shouted from a safe distance.

"I'll kill her, that tart, I'll kill her!"

Satisfied that his father's rage had been diverted, Wojtek started homeward, taking the long way around. It was well past milking time when he entered the yard. He looked into the stall but the cow wasn't there, nor was the pig in the barn, and the rabbit cage was upside down.

"Papa, come quick, look what's happened!"

Wacek burst into the barn, took one look, and advanced on his son, shaking his fist. The boy tried to sidestep the oncoming blow and slipped in the dung. Wacek laid into him with the belt savagely and repeatedly.

The hoot of a passing train cut into Wojtek's screams of pain and terror. Wacek's arm stopped in midair—Krysia might be on that very train. He left the boy lying in the muck and rushed out to round up the missing animals.

From behind the shed Hella saw her father leave the barn. "*Malyushka, malyushka!* Little sweetheart, come home!" he was calling to the pig.

"I'll kill that pig of his," Hella swore through her teeth. "Me he calls bitch, and that old shit of a filthy pig he calls *malyushka!* I ought to run away from home. Then he'd chase around looking for me. Helenka, he would call, Helenka sweetheart, come home! Well, he'd just have to keep on calling, because I wouldn't be there to answer. I'd never come back to this awful place . . ."

"Blackie! Blackie! Where's that damn cow? *Malyushka! Malyushka!*" His voice receded into the distance, and Hella came out of her hiding place. She helped Wojtek out of the barn and put a wet towel to his head.

Wacek soon found the pig, all battered and bloody. She had strayed into a neighbor's field and trampled the grain. The farmer had driven her off with a stick.

Wacek patted the sow's rump and gently urged her on. "Get along, *malyushka*, old girl!" His misgivings were growing worse by the minute. Who knows, the little pigs might be stillborn after such a beating.

"Blackie's back in her stall!" Hella greeted him with the good news. His eyes fell on Wojtek and the towel pressed to his swollen face. Jesus, wait till Krysia saw him, there'd be hell to pay. He drove the pig into the barn and saw the cow standing there contentedly chewing her cud. Blood rushed to his head. It was all her fault, that bitch of a cow! He picked up a pole and hit her with such force that the pole snapped and the cow sank to her knees. He looked for something else with which to punish her, but nothing came to his hand.

Just then a customer stuck his head through the barn door, and Wacek went hunting for the milk pail. It wasn't anywhere to be found in the barn. He looked in the yard, searched through the house, turned the shed upside down, rousing the sleeping hens. How could that goddamn pail have disappeared? The customer had left before he finally recalled that he had taken it to the tavern in the afternoon. The cow's water bucket would have to do. He emptied and rinsed it at the pump.

"Up, Blackie, up!" The cow pushed herself to her feet. Wacek sat down on the milking stool and started pumping.

"Damn her to hell, not even a quarter of a bucket!"

"You almost killed her when you hit her with that pole," Hella volunteered. "Her milk must have dried up."

"You go to hell! Who asked you?" He kept tugging at the teats. The cow stamped at the ground, a turd flew into the bucket, and the milk turned green. Wacek tossed the contents of the bucket into the cow's muzzle, threw the bucket across the barn, and stormed out.

He sat down on a tree stump and scratched his mud-caked head. He was really in for it. Once Krysia opened her crummy mouth nothing would help him—not swearing, not beating, not Satan, not God himself. If only he could pick up a few zlotys somewhere and hand them to her before she reckoned up all the damage. . . . "Here," he would say, "take this! While you were running all over Warsaw I earned a few zlotys right here . . ."

Hella, still afraid to approach her father, watched him from a distance. She could tell what he was thinking just from the way he spat, the way he sighed and scratched behind his ear. "Papa," she called, her voice dripping honey, "I saw cherries in the squire's garden, they're big and ripe!"

It took a moment for the idea to sink into his befuddled brain. "Will you go with me?" His question was a plea.

"Sure, Papa!"

He ran into the house for a basket. The first cherries of the season always fetched a good price and a basketful would bring a pretty penny in the Otwock market. If he could show Krysia a bushel of new cherries . . .

They worked quickly; the basket was almost full. Suddenly a dog howled. Hella tugged at her father's sleeve and a light went on in the watchman's shack. The door banged open, throwing a beam of light into the orchard, and a dog streaked down the path. The two slid down the tree, abandoned the basket, and scrambled for the fence. Hella landed on the other side with a single leap, but Wacek, his foot catching in the barbed wire, barely managed to get to the top. The massive hound threw himself against the fence. Wacek dropped to the other side but half his trousers remained on top of the fence.

"D'ya think he saw me? Nah, he couldn't have." Wacek studied his mutilated trousers. "Two hundred and fifty zlotys," he moaned.

"Fifty-two," Hella corrected him.

His head hung low. The old nag would walk in on them any minute now and in one glance she would know the whole stinking story. The cow, the pig, the boy—all battered and bruised. Milk all over the barn, eggs trampled into the ground, two rabbits gone and three chicks drowned, the garden in ruins, and his new suit in tatters—things couldn't be worse. His bloodshot eyes traveled desperately around the room. There had to be something he could trade for a shot of vodka. What did he have to lose now? And where had his old pants gone?

"What will you wear to Hella's communion, Papa?" Wotjek asked stupidly.

"Suppose somebody recognizes your pants on the fence?" Hella worried.

Panic spread through Wacek's chest and he sank onto a bench. A new thought raised him to his feet again. "Nothing to worry about," he beamed, "those are my new pants. Everybody in the village knows my old pants. These—how will anybody know whose they are? Nobody's seen 'em yet."

Hella's voice was sweet innocence: "Papa thinks of everything. It was real smart to put on the new pants that nobody would recognize."

"Right, so in case anything happened, nobody could tell." Wacek was delighted with the excuse he now had for Krysia. How could he tell her he got all dressed up for the wench in the tavern?

"Don't worry," he boasted. "Your father still has a head on his shoulders." He was so pleased with himself he took the last bit of change out of his pocket and gave it to the children.

• • • • •

Krysia was glad to be getting home. The long, hot day tramping around Warsaw had been exhausting, though it had paid off handsomely. No doubt about it, her luck was changing for the better. The cow was giving milk, all the hens were laying, and Wacek had even planted a bigger garden this year. True, she could never get him out of bed to water the vegetables and he was never around for the evening chores, but the good Lord Jesus had sent her this lad Yurek. Everything was growing fine now. In another few weeks the summer vacationers would be arriving, and they would pay well for every tomato, every carrot. She would save all the money and guard it with her life. This year they would finally have that second cow. With two cows in the barn, they wouldn't have to scrimp for every slice of bread. Yes, her luck had changed for the better at last.

14

Shouts and screams and curses rang through the house and hammered against the floorboards of the attic like claps of thunder. The mistress wouldn't stop yelling, Hella and Wojtek cried and cried, and Yossel—he hadn't come, she hadn't even heard his voice. Something must be happening to him. Maybe somebody had recognized him in Warsaw and taken him away. How would she get down? They would soon find her, and Hella and Wojtek would jump around and holler "Zhidova" just like the children on the streetcar, and Yossel wasn't even there.

That day they had hit him, they had knocked him to the ground and hollered "Zhidy! Zhidy!" Their accusing eyes flashed at her now from the darkened corners of the attic. "Zhidova! Zhidova!" The sound attacked her from every direction—from the guttural grunts of the pig below, from the shrill chirps of the crickets in the rafters.

It must have been Yossel the master was beating in the barn before. He would never have beat his own boy so hard. She had felt the attic shake every time he hit him. Yossel must still be lying down there all banged up, the cow stomping on him, the pig biting him. She ought to scream for help.

Her lips parted, her teeth chattered as if they too would scream at her, Zhidova! Zhidova! She stuck her fist into her mouth and sank to the floor. Everybody had deserted her, everybody. First Papa went off with Nenna, then Mama sent her away with Yossel, and now Yossel had left her all alone in the barn with a wild pig and a mad cow and angry voices calling her Zhidova.

Footsteps . . . she could hear them, just like that time when Mama had hidden her and Yossel in a closet. Yossel had crept outside to where they were shooting and hadn't come back. Footsteps, footsteps, she had seen the soldiers through the crack in the door coming closer and closer and . . . and her pants had gotten wet just like now.

That other time the Germans had gone away and Yossel had come back, and Mama had come back, but Papa and Nenna—they had never come back . . .

Were those really footsteps? Maybe it was only the shredding machine; Yossel was always saying he had to go to the shed and cut straw for the cow. It always made that sound. Maybe it was really Yossel down there shredding straw.

The thudding noise stopped, the door of the barn creaked.

"Back, lady, back!"

Yossel! A sob tore from her throat. The trapdoor burst open, Yossel leapt across the attic and put his hand over her mouth. Her body shook with stifled sobs. He knelt in the straw and held her close, and all he could utter was a tremulous "shh!"

•　•　•　•　•

Only a few kernels remained of the cherry pits that Yossel had gathered that day in Warsaw. They were too hard to crack open with his teeth; a blow with a rock crushed a kernel; a light tap and the pit flew away. All his fingers were bruised, and just a few measly kernels were left to show for it. Hannele stared at them with dark, sorrowful eyes and refused to touch any. "Take it, silly girl," he said, forcing one into her mouth, "it's good." It slid down her throat and choked her. Tears flowed from her eyes, and she couldn't stop coughing. Yossel slapped her on the back and prayed that nobody would hear them.

"You know what, Hannele? I'll take these pits and plant them in the ground, right out there in the yard, and soon a cherry tree will grow. We'll have our own cherry tree with heaps and heaps of cherries to eat and . . .

"Can you eat the cherry too?"

"Silly, that's the best part. You eat the *cherry* and spit out the *pit!* Cherries are sweet as sugar. Remember sugar, Hannele? Sure you do. It looks like tiny crumbs of glass and it tastes so sweet. Cherries are just like that but full of juice—like a bubble full of sweet red juice. It's true, Hannele, I'm not making it up, honest to God."

Her eyes grew dreamy. If only he would stay here and talk to her. Yossel's words were like . . . like . . . better than cherries, better than . . .

Yossel's heart ached. Imagine having forgotten the taste of sugar or cherries. Soon she would forget her own name. How could she help it, lying here cut off from the world? He must find a way to make her think, he must try to teach her something. His father was right, a child had to learn or he turned into a moron.

He slept fitfully and wakened with a start. It couldn't be more than four o'clock. Hannele was sitting up, moving her index finger in and out of a faint beam of light coming through a crack in the roof. He could hear the animals stirring below. The master's grunting snores were a counterpoint to the twitter of the birds outside. Yossel got to his feet and motioned to Hannele to follow him to the window. He pulled a crumpled piece of newspaper from his back pocket and flattened it out in front of her. Rubbing the sleep out of his eyes and stifling a yawn, he pointed to a letter: "This is an *A,* it reads *AH.* Now you say it, Hannele: *AH.*"

No response.

"Come on, open your mouth: *AH.*"

He couldn't understand it. Papa had begun to teach her, and whenever Nenna had read her a story, she had always tried to follow the lines in the book; now she couldn't even say *AH.* Beads of sweat dotted his forehead, but Yossel persisted. It took less effort to turn the heavy wheel of the shredding machine than to grind one letter into Hannele's stubborn head. But he could be stubborn too; she had to learn.

It took several mornings before Hannele could repeat what he told her to say, but when he asked her to identify a letter on the paper, she sealed her lips. Maybe he was being too hard on her.

Maybe it would be easier for her if he used Yiddish letters instead of Polish. His father had taught her to recite a blessing even before she could talk properly, and he must have taught her the Hebrew *aleph-beis*. Yes, that would be better—the Yiddish alphabet was the same.

Hannele watched the movement of Yossel's fingers as he laid out bits of straw to form Yiddish letters; she did not respond. Yossel stood up, bent over, and formed the shape of an aleph with his arms and legs.

"What is this?" he asked.

"You."

"What am I when I twist like this?"

"A crooked you."

The child was lazy, too lazy to learn anything. "Listen, Hannele," he said, "I'll teach you a beautiful song:

> *Aleph* is for *adler*—an eagle flies high
> *Beis* is for *boym*—a tree grows to the sky
> *Gimmel* is for *galakh*—a priest who kneels
> *Daled* is for *doctor*—a man who heals
> *Hey* is for *hoon*—a hen that crows
> *Vov* is for *vasser*—water that flows

Nothing, no sound at all. Had she even heard him? He would get through to her if he had to pound it into her brain.

Later in the day, when Hannele reached for the bowl of gruel Yossel had brought her, he held it back and raised a finger. "This is ONE, Hannele." He fed her a spoonful. "One spoon of soup." He held up two fingers and fed her another spoonful. "TWO, Hannele, two fingers, two spoons of soup."

Her eyes filled with tears. Yurek ignored them. THREE, three fingers, three spoons of soup." He counted off each spoonful until the bowl was empty, but when he asked how many, she had only one answer:

"You're mean, you're mean, and I don't like you!"

15

Everybody was up early. The house buzzed with activity. Yurek was on his hands and knees scrubbing the kitchen floor. Wojtek hobbled around on one foot looking for his missing shoe. Hella preened in front of the cracked mirror, while her mother struggled to fasten the snaps on her white communion dress. "You can't even get a decent snap nowadays. Will you stand still for a minute? We'll never get to church on time."

The master stomped around in his underwear. "Get the hell out of my way," he snarled at Yurek. "*Pshakrev!* Goddamn it! Where are those lousy pants?"

The mistress had hidden his pants and now went to get them. "That thieving, drunken slob! Had to rush all the way to Otwock to get a second pair. It would serve him right if he had to go to church in his drawers. Here," she threw the trousers at him.

"Bitch," the master hissed under his breath, "we're late and she's still playing games."

"Look at Yurek," Wojtek pointed, "he hasn't even started to get dressed."

"Never mind about him. If you're ready, go outside and wait. And don't let me see one speck of dirt on your clothes," the mistress warned.

Hella turned away from the mirror. "Isn't Yurek going too?"

"No, somebody has to keep an eye on things."

Yurek guessed that he would not be asked to go with them, but what a relief it was to hear the mistress say it. He hadn't the faintest notion how to behave in a church.

The mistress made a final inspection of her family. "You look like a real squire," she complimented her husband. "If you'd wash now and then, the girls would still be chasing you." The master looked into the mirror, threw back his shoulders, and smiled at himself with pride.

The usual tension had given way to a mood of festivity, and in a most unwonted gesture everyone bade Yurek good-bye. Everyone but the master, that is. He was still in a rage about the eggs. When Yurek had found four eggs behind a log in the yard, he had taken them straight to the mistress. How was he to know the master had hidden them there? He hadn't known a moment's peace since. No matter how hard he tried, everything always fell wrong side up.

He watched them disappear down the road and walked back to the house. He would take some food to Hannele and get on with his chores.

That morning's milk had been sold out and yesterday's had been used all up in the baking. The cakes and loaves of bread lay spread out on a white cloth on the bed, each loaf almost the size of a tabletop. One of the loaves had been started. Yurek had the knife in his hand ready to cut off a slice, but quickly drew back. A series of fine lines had been scored on top of the bread. The mistress wouldn't have done this. It must have been the master, to trap him, to be rid of him for once and for all.

Yurek went up to the loft carrying only a bottle of fresh water. "Later there'll be bread, cake too," he promised Hannele. He left her and ran to the meadow.

•   •   •   •   •

The boisterous voices of the guests in the house carried as far as the pasture and made Yurek uneasy. The day was hot. Someone was bound to come out and nose around. He'd better stay close to the house. Anyway, it was time to water the cow. He led her to the pump and filled the bucket. He stole a moment to check the trapdoor to the attic and raced back. The cow had slurped up all the water and was waiting for more.

"Who's that out there with your cow?" one of the guests inquired.

"My farmhand," Wacek beamed with pride.

"A farmhand? You must have struck it rich. Bootleg whisky or bootleg Jews?"

How d'ya know this farmhand of yours is not a Zhid himself?" a woman teased, her voice high, raspy.

"Leave it to Wacek," he assured her. "I can smell one of *them* with my eyes shut. This kid's family was chased out of Prussia, or Mazowsze, or wherever the hell it was. His father's a war prisoner, the mother's in a labor camp somewhere. Hey, Yurek, c'm'ere."

Yurek's heart leapt to his throat. He stopped just inside the door while curious eyes looked him up and down.

"Those gangsters, look what the rotten Schwabes have done to our children," a guest spat out, her voice loud with indignation.

A hand reached out. "Here, have a piece of cake." Yurek recognized the grating voice that had wondered if he was a Zhid.

"Thank you, ma'am," he muttered and took the cake.

"You can tell right off he's from around Mazowasze, even the lowliest of them always give you their 'thank you's' and 'excuse me's.'"

"That face of his—must be a real gem, if it makes up for all his blunders. . . ."

Each guest now tried to outdo the other in a show of patriotism, with everyone handing him a delicacy from the table. Even the master presented him with a generous piece of sausage. Nothing was too good for the son of a Polish prisoner of war.

· · · · ·

The sun had moved toward the western horizon, but the festivities showed no signs of slackening. Now and then a squeal of laughter rose above the din. Yurek recognized that kind of giggle; some peasant would soon be dragging a wench up to the hayloft. Not that they'd be able to get up there; all the ladders were well hidden.

"Yurek! Yurek!" The master's summons came all the way across the meadow. "Where's the ladder? Where've they all disappeared to?"

"The ladder? Why does the master need a ladder?"

"None of your stinkin' business! What the hell did you do with all the damn ladders?"

"I hid them from the kids. If the master needs something from the attic, I'll be glad to fetch it."

"Stay out of my way, I said! Where's the goddamn ladder?"

Yurek dragged the ladder back to the barn. "Why should the master climb all the way up to the attic in his new suit?" he asked, raising his voice as a warning to Hannele. Maybe the mistress would hear him too and think the master wanted to drag some woman up there for a roll in the hay.

"Don't stick your snotty nose where it doesn't belong, you pit-faced bastard. Get the hell back to the cow!"

The master grabbed the ladder, his unsteady legs wobbling under its weight, and Yurek rushed to take it from him. "Let me," Yurek pleaded.

"Out of my way, runt! Who d'you think you're bossing around, you nosy bastard!"

Yurek watched the drunken master struggling up the broken ladder and prayed he wouldn't make it. He almost tumbled when he threw the door open.

"Beat it!" the master yelled down and disappeared into the loft.

Inside the house, pandemonium broke loose. Chairs crashed to the floor, peals of laughter exploded and shattered like a stack of broken plates, and in the attic, too, something cracked and creaked. Yurek leapt onto the ladder. The master appeared in the opening of the trap with the rifle in his hand.

So it was the rifle he was after! Tears of relief filled Yurek's eyes but froze quickly on his lashes. "Mr. Boss, somebody might tell."

"Get back to the cow, you miserable meddler." He raised the rifle. Out of my sight or I'll shoot!"

Yurek took cover behind a tree. The master tried to steady his wobbly legs, then hoisted the rifle to his shoulder and marched into the house. Yurek kept his eyes on the door. If they drink anymore they'll be at each other's throats and before you know it one of them will end up informing about the rifle . . .

The door swung open; one of the guests was dragging a woman out to the yard. The ladder was in the barn, the trapdoor was open. God! Let them go to the straw in the shed, not to the hay in the attic. The kids are down at the river. If they come home . . . if Hella finds the ladder and an open attic . . .

He must sneak Hannele out this minute.

The master lurched out of the house still carrying the rifle. If he puts it back, maybe he'll close the trap and take away the ladder. That Hella, if she comes home . . .

A shot ripped the air, and Yurek plunged through the tall grass. It's the end, it's all over. God, it's all over . . .

In the yard, the master had struck a pose with the rifle shouldered, as if his picture were being taken. The mistress tried to tear it away. "You drunken fool, you'll get us all killed!"

"What're you scared of, woman?" His tongue tripped over itself. "I ain't scared of nothing. Let 'em send a whole damn regiment—I'll lay 'em all out with my good old rifle, and they'll never find it anyhow . . ."

"Stupid fool! So they won't find the gun. But what about the cow? Are you giving the Germans their quota of milk? Y'know the cow's not registered. D'ya have to go looking for trouble? Krysia reached for the rifle and Wacek sprawled on the ground. She wrestled it away from him and handed it to Yurek. "Here, hide it where he'll never find it. I oughta break it into pieces and burn it!"

Yurek held the rifle in one hand and with the other helped the master to his feet. "No, mistress," he said, winking at the master. "There will come a day when we'll need it, remember? My father will come back, and he and the master will march on Berlin, side by side. We'll need guns then."

"Tha's right, side by side," Wacek repeated and reached for the rifle.

"But not yet, master. Dead Poles can't take Berlin."

"Right, dead Poles can't take Berlin . . ." Wacek had no idea what Yurek meant, but it sounded patriotic.

The master was still in the yard when Yurek climbed to the loft to put the rifle away. He stuck his hand into the haypile and patted Hannele's head to reassure. Her hair was dripping wet. He pulled a chunk of cake out of his pocket, found Hannele's hand, and closed her fingers around it. They were limp and ice-cold.

16

A bright, intense light stabbed at Yurek's closed eyelids and tore into his sleep in the middle of tangled dream. The dream snapped like a taut thread. He wanted to bring the ends together again but couldn't catch hold of them. The dream still fluttered within him, warm and pleasant; he could hear its faint rustle, but it eluded his grasp. His eyes were closed but his sleep oozed out, giving way to an awareness of the sound and movement all around him. He sat up abruptly and forced his eyes open.

It was only the familiar attic. What had seemed loud and grating in his half-sleep was now a soft hum—the whirring of thousands of tiny creatures. Flies buzzed against razor-sharp beams of light knifing through slits in the roof. Crickets chirped their monotonous, clicking chorus. Minuscule ants hauled massive lengths of straw. A multitude of insects wove nests around their eggs. Termites drilled into roof beams with machinelike precision, sweeping yellow sawdust out of fresh holes. The whole attic seemed to be in motion, teeming with life. Amazing! And all the time he had believed that he and Hannele were alone in the hayloft. But the hot sun brought all these creatures back to life. Tiny crawlers, black and trim and shining, moving in a ruler-straight line like a regiment on dress parade. Tinier ones massed in a solid phalanx on a beam, completely covering the wood. Seemingly ordinary lice revealed wings and soared into the air.

There, a little spider was nimbly and rapidly spinning a web across a hole in the roof. Watching, enchanted by the artistic delicacy of the web, it struck him all of a sudden: this beautiful web was a perfectly designed death trap!

Death! He had seen a lot of it. But this, an angel of death with a silken trap . . . Yurek picked up a twig and rose to his feet but a giant horsefly got there first. Flying out through the hole, it had pulled most of the web with it, leaving but a few ragged strands. The spider went back to work. It spun new threads, patched the old, and soon the web was whole again. The spider moved slowly to the edge, to wait for prey. A breeze rippled over the rooftop, the tile shifted and demolished half the web.

Now she'll look for a safer place, Yurek thought. Out of its corner came the spider and once again began its work.

Hannele stirred. Yurek leaned over and gently shook her shoulder. She got to her knees and snuggled against her brother. "Yesterday somebody came up here, I hid. I heard a shot. I was so scared."

Yurek brushed her hair back from her forehead. "Nothing to be scared of, Hannele. They like me here. I'm almost like a member of the family. Soon I'll tell them, and you won't have to be afraid anymore."

"They'll chase us away, just like the Wilchinskis."

"No, they won't. The mistress is kind. Only yesterday she found a sick little bird and took it right into the house."

"A bird, yes; but not me."

"Don't be silly. Maybe I'll even talk to her tonight. Did I tell you there is still some cake left from the party? The cake was good, eh? Later I'll bring you some more. Shh! They're waking up . . ."

•   •   •   •   •

The hay was ready for harvest. Krysia brought the scythe from the barn and dropped it at Wacek's feet. "Get to work and sharpen the blade," she ordered. A retort came to his lips, but he thought better of it. There was no way to recoup the losses they had already suffered; he would have to make the most of what was left on the farm.

The cow munched on the sweet-smelling clover, twitching her muzzle at the flies that clustered around her nostrils. A flurry of birds swooped down, soared up, banked, dipped, and finally landed among the rustling branches of the tree over Yurek's head. Their high-pitched chatter filled the air and suddenly, as if in answer to some unheard command, they took off again. Yurek followed their flight until they dissolved into the blue of the sky.

Another perfect day. If the weather held, the hay would dry quickly, and they'd bring it up to the attic. They'd all come up, the master, the mistress, even Hella. He couldn't put it off any longer, not one more minute. He would have to talk to the mistress.

In the kitchen Hella was puttering at the stove and didn't look up when Yurek stuck his head in the door.

"Where's your mother?"

"She isn't here."

"I can see that. Where is she?"

"Out smuggling."

"When is she coming back?"

"How should I know? In the evening, I guess, like always."

·   ·   ·   ·   ·

The household was fast asleep. Yurek kept throwing wood into the stove to keep the fire going under the pot of soup he had prepared.

It was close to midnight when Krysia returned, exhausted and troubled. The raids had gone on all day, she had barely made it home. Half her merchandise was gone.

Before she even put a spoon into the bowl, her face flushed with anger. "Look how that idiot wastes the potatoes. The cellar's almost empty and he uses up a whole basket of potatoes for one pot of soup. What, groats too?" Did Grandmother die and leave him a fortune or something?"

"It wasn't the master," Yurek confessed. "I cooked the soup especially for the mistress."

"So now you're a cook too? This ain't your Posnan, you know. We're poor people here. Every potato has to be counted; we have to be careful with the groats. And another thing, when you put everything you own into the same pot, at least stir it so it won't scorch."

Yurek was crestfallen.

"And why are you hanging around here half the night?" the mistress went on. "Go to sleep. Tomorrow you won't be able to keep your eyes open and that whore of a cow will get into the vegetables again."

• • • • •

Someone was in the kitchen buying all the butter. The mistress unwrapped the moist strips of muslin and dumped each pat into the buyer's huge earthen crock. Yurek waited his chance and took some of the butter-soaked cloths for Hannele to suck on.

Later that day he returned to the kitchen to put the cloths back, but found the other pieces had already been washed and ironed. He'd have to wait until she sold more butter. Then again, the cloth would make a fine patch for Hannele's dress. What he ought to do was get a needle and thread.

Yurek walked into the empty barn. A trickle of fluid splashed down from above, a smile came to his lips. The funnel was working just fine.

Hannele was back at the chimney when he got to the loft. "See, you were so mad at me when I made a funnel out of the green bottle. Look at your legs now, they're all healed." Hannele's eyes grew misty at the mention of the bottle. Yossel's face lit up. "You know something, Hannele, if you're a good girl and pay attention to what I teach you, Libbe will come back to you. Come on, let's see if we can count your fingers."

Hannele turned away from him.

"I promise you, Hannele, Libbe will come back. I swear."

The next morning when Hannele awoke, Yossel was not beside her, but she could hear him whistling under his breath. He was sitting near the window, his hands busy with something. She would pretend to be asleep or else he'd be at her again with his alphabet. Through the slit of one eye she saw him coming toward her, one hand behind his back.

Yurek noticed her eyes move under her closed lids. "It's too bad you're still asleep, Hannele. If you were awake, I'd show you something nice."

She didn't stir.

"I always keep my promises," he whispered. She sat up at once, her eyes two big questioning circles.

Yurek brought his arm forward. In his hand was a rag doll, fashioned from the strips of muslin. Hannele lunged at him, snatched the doll away, and threw herself face down into the straw. Yurek's eyes filled with tears. He hitched up his pants and walked to the trapdoor. He had chores to do.

• • • • •

"You lazy little girl," Hannele prodded the doll. "Say after me— *aleph* is an *adler, beis* is a *boym* . . ." She could hear Yossel's tread on the ladder. Hastily she scrambled the pieces of straw that she had laid out in the Yiddish letters for Libbe.

17

The hay had been cut and left to dry. Time was racing, and Yurek felt every passing moment hammering in his skull. He had done everything he could think of to please the mistress. When she'd been after her husband to mend the leaning fence, Yurek had run to do it. He had gathered stones at the river's edge, carted them back in a wheelbarrow, and laid them out around the pump.

After lunch, the mistress was finally alone. As Yurek approached the house, she charged through the doorway, her face mottled with rage. "Have you seen him?" she cried. "Vanished without a trace, that sneaky bastard. Who knows what he's stolen this time! Now he'll come home stewed to the gills." She hurried to the gate.

Yurek was surprised to see the master return on steady legs. When he was drunk, Yurek lived in terror of him, because no one could predict what he would do. This one time he wouldn't have minded at all if he were drunk and out of the way, but as if to spite him, Wacek puttered around the house all afternoon.

The sun went down and with it his last chance to talk to the mistress alone. He would have to tell her with the master present.

"What're you hanging around for?" the mistress demanded testily. "Get to sleep! Tomorrow we start bringing in the hay."

Yurek climbed the ladder to the attic and felt the weight of doom pressing down on him inexorably.

• • • • •

Hannele shifted onto her side but did not awaken when he lay down beside her. What should he do? He couldn't just leave her in the hay; she might suffocate there with big bundles of new hay piled over her. Even worse, she could be run through with a pitchfork.

The last precious minutes of the night were running out. Better lie on the trapdoor, at least he'd be awakened when they came up.

He was drifting off to sleep when he felt someone pushing against the opening. "Who the devil is holding that door?"

"Why were you holding down the door?"

"I was lying on it."

"What the hell for?"

"That's where I sleep."

"Are you crazy?"

"It's because of the gun, ever since the master fired that shot."

"Where is it?"

"Under a board. I nailed it down."

"Pull the nails out and give me the gun."

"What's happened?"

"Don't just stand there! Get me the gun! What happened, he wants to know. Plenty happened. I dreamt I lost a tooth, and when a dream like that wakes me up in the middle of the night, I know bad luck is just around the corner. I'm going to bury that gun in the woods."

Whether the mistress's dream was a bad omen for her or not, Yurek couldn't say, but for him it was indeed a misfortune. She would be bound to recognize Hannele as the bad luck promised by her dream. He held the ladder for the mistress as she descended into the fetid blackness of the barn. He remained silent at the open trap, enveloped by a numbing terror.

·   ·   ·   ·   ·

Yurek piled the bundles of hay into neat stacks. Still in a daze, he tried to sort out the events of the morning. He couldn't remember taking the cow to pasture, he hadn't heard the children leave for school. All he knew was that there they were, the three of them, with pitchforks—the mistress out in the yard tossing bundles to the master in the barn, the master throwing them up to him. The bundles were bigger than he was, but his feet stayed anchored to the top rung of the ladder. Then, without a word, the master had disappeared. God bless his thirsty gullet. If only it would keep him away until the hay was stored.

"Wacek! Wacek!" the mistress's cries rang through the yard.

Yurek looked through the open trapdoor and saw her tear into the barn.

"Is he up there?"

"No, mistress, he didn't come back."

"May the black cholera take him! I kill myself to earn a zloty and that thief guzzles it up! The new sheet, my best bedsheet, seventy-five zloty I paid for it. When I dreamed about that tooth, I knew it meant bad luck!"

The mistress was really upset. Yurek was half-ashamed of his feeling of relief that the predicted misfortune should turn out to be merely the loss of a bedsheet.

18

The first light of dawn had hardly begun to streak the morning sky when Yurek was awakened by a noise in the barn. If the sow was about to drop her litter, better now, before the family took off for the market in Karchev. He opened the trap, looked down into the barn. The cow lay quietly in her usual place, but the sow was running back and forth as if performing some kind of ritual dance. He lay back in the straw wide awake. He heard the family getting up, heard them leave for Karchev. Down below, the persistent, pounding hoofbeats continued. Yurek glanced at Hannele. She was still sleeping soundly. He climbed quietly down the ladder. The sow made no attempt to get out when he opened the barn door. Too early in the day even for a pig, he thought.

He filled the cow's trough and went back to the kitchen to get slops for the pig. "What's the matter, lady? You're waddling around like an old woman." He sat down to milk the cow, but the pig kept brushing against his legs. She sniffed at the stall, burrowed into the spot where the cow had been lying, picking up a bit of straw and carried it off to a corner, came back, repeated the procedure. What was she looking for? Outside, there was a feast of cooked potato peelings waiting for her, what did she—? Of course! She was preparing a bed!

He hurried through the milking and led the cow out to graze. He set Wilk to watch over her while he rushed back to the barn. The sow was lying on the mound she had made out of straw and leaves, her breath coming in snorts.

Yurek stared in wonder: she lay in the corner, her forefeet braced against one wall, her hind legs propped against the other, pushing. Her body made a natural barrier, fencing off the rest of the barn.

The sow's skin was drenched, her veins stood out like straining lengths of rope. Her belly heaved, an explosion of air, and a small piglet slid out. It stood up, its legs awkward and shaky, but it ran forward immediately, and the umbilical cord snapped. In the next instant it was at its mother's belly, sucking.

The cord hanging from the piglet's belly was covered with barn dung. Yurek wondered if he ought to tie a knot in it. Another burst of air, another shiny piglet. It ran to break the cord and stumbled back to its mother's belly, tried to push the first piglet aside. They competed awkwardly until one of them found a second teat. As each new piglet was born, it battled with the others for a place to suck and pushed the weaker ones away.

· · · · ·

"Eleven? Eleven pigs!" The mistress's mouth dropped open when Yurek told her the news. She ran to the barn and scooped up the piglets one by one, showering them with kisses. Such pretty little creatures with their round, rosy bodies and nimble little legs; such beautiful hair, like golden, shimmering silk.

She would raise two or three of the litter and sell the others. In a few months they should bring thirty to fifty zlotys apiece. She sighed over the smallest ones: "These two won't survive. Fifty zloty apiece— a decent farmer would see them all through, all eleven of them."

"Nine ain't good enough for you, you greedy bitch? Show me another farm in all the village with a litter of nine!"

"And you're the one who did it, hah?"

"Who else—you? You have to know how to handle a hog. Son of a bitch, nine ain't good enough for her!"

"If the Lord Jesus sent me eleven then nine ain't enough. These two have to be helped—make sure they suck."

"How? My tits don't give milk. For Chrissake, woman, stop nagging. Piotr's sow dropped only five, and nobody's bitching. Nine is a blessing from the Lord, it deserves to be celebrated."

"Not so fast with the celebrating. When we collect the money for the pigs, then we'll see."

Yurek watched the master's face turn purple, and quietly slipped away before he could take out his disappointment on his farmhand.

At noon, when Yurek brought the cow in, he found the mistress holding a bottle of milk with a rubber nipple, trying to shove it into the mouth of one of the undersized pigs. "Suck, dammit, four zloty I spent on this." The piglet turned its head aside, and the mistress pushed it off her lap. "Go ahead and croak—" The sow sprawled on the ground, the litter clustered at her teats. Yurek took the bottle and pushed it under the sow's belly with only the nipple visible. The larger pigs took possession of the full teats as before, and the smallest two were again left hungry. The protruding rubber nipple was untouched. He picked up one of the piglets and tried to feed it with a spoon, but only a few drops slid into the animal's mouth.

Among eleven piglets, there had to be two with some sense. Again Yurek put the bottle under the sow's belly, and again it was ignored. The sow suddenly lurched to her feet and waddled away, leaving her litter pawing the air. One of the larger piglets sniffed at the rubber nipple, shoved the bottle away. Before it could wander off, Yurek snatched it up and rubbed the nipple across its snout; the piglet licked the few drops of milk around its mouth and eagerly looked for more.

The trick, it appeared, was to smear some milk on the outside of the nipple. Before long, Yurek had the animal eagerly sucking at the bottle. He chose two of the larger pigs and trained them to feed from the bottle. He had only to keep them locked in the house while the sow suckled the others. Now the two smallest had full teats of their own at their mother's belly. The mistress was full of praise for him. Even when one of the little pigs died, she comforted him: "It was too far gone, nothing could have saved it." For the first time, she patted his head.

With a ration of milk for the bottle-fed pig, Yurek managed to put aside a few mouthfuls for Hannele, and it was doing her good, renewing her strength.

The sow isn't really such a beast after all, Yurek observed. Look how placidly she suckles her young as they rummage and scramble for her milk. On the sly, he put extra peels in her feed.

One morning the mistress met him in the yard and handed him a bowl. "Give this to the piglets, they need something more than milk now." He sniffed at it. "I mixed some grated potato with flour, that'll put the fat on 'em," she explained. Yurek took the bowl into the barn and set it down. The sow made a dive for it and downed the whole thing before he could chase her away.

"You numbskull!" the master fumed. "Where do you keep your brains? Couldn't you lock the hog in her pen? You think I wouldn't like a bowl of that stuff myself?"

"I didn't know—" Yurek tried to explain.

"What the hell *do* you know—how to make honey cake out of horse turds? You couldn't tie a knot in a cat's tail. Who needs you here, anyway? You know as much about farming as a . . ."

"What about the half-pail of milk Papa spilled yesterday?" Hella jumped to Yurek's defense.

"You keep your trap shut or I'll shut it for you! You know what we could have bought for what that lousy hog just ate up? At least two pounds of bread, or half a kilo of sausage, or . . ."

"Or a quart of vodka," Hella broke in.

"You too? I need you to bitch about my vodka too? And how come you're standing up for this smart ass all of a sudden?" He stuck his fist under Yurek's nose. "Listen here, you little bastard, if I ever ketch ya even lookin' at her I'll chop you up and feed you to the pigs myself!"

Yurek was as puzzled by Hella's sudden support as the master had been. The one time she decided to defy her father, why was it over him? And why should the master scold him about looking at her? It was all he could do just to stay out of her reach. She trailed around after him every day.

Not that she was stupid. He had learned many things from her: she knew how to make a whistle out of fresh green reeds, how to whittle designs out of bark. There was nothing she couldn't do, that girl: she could run as fast as any boy, and knew a million hiding places . . . so why did she always let him find her when they played hide-and-seek? From now on he'd better be more careful.

• • • • •

"Stop following me like a puppy, Wojtek, go play somewhere else," Yurek heard Hella's voice coming from the barn. He hurried the cow into her stall and found Hella on the ladder, blocking her brother's way up.

"Hey, what are you doing there? Get down!" Yurek shouted.

"And if I don't?"

"Get down this minute or I'll—"

"You'll what?"

"I'll drag you down by the hair!"

"Lemme see you try it."

Yurek pushed Wojtek aside and flew up the ladder. Hella leaned forward and threw her arms around him.

"I bet ya can't carry me down."

With her hands clasped around his neck and her breath hot in his face, Yurek had no choice. He started down the ladder, Hella clinging to him. The ladder tilted dangerously and righted itself. He put a tighter grip around her. She was only twelve years old, but lately she had sprung up like a weed and was almost as tall as he.

Somehow they got to the bottom without toppling. He put her down. She circled behind him and hung on his back. "Carry me piggyback!"

"Let go or I'll call your father."

"Ha-ha, call him all you like, nobody's home." She laughed into his face and pinched him.

"What do you want of me? What have I ever done to you?"

"Then pinch me back if you don't like it."

Wojtek wanted to play too. Yurek turned on him. "Beat it before I break every bone in your body!"

Hella moved closer and punched him. "There, I hit you. Now hit me back, I dare you!"

Yurek couldn't shake them off. He watered the vegetables and they followed him, he got ready to milk the cow and there they were. Muffled sounds came from the attic. Yurek turned quickly, asked Hella to fetch water from the pump. Hella sent her brother. Overhead the dull sound continued. Yurek rattled the milk pail, tipped over the stool. Hella grabbed his hand. "Wait a minute! Did you hear something?"

"Let go, I have to milk the cow."

"Listen, don't you hear anything?"

"I don't hear a thing."

"The cat's in the hayloft again."

"Go away, let me do my chores."

Hella stuck out her tongue, made a flapping noise with her lips, and flounced out of the barn. Yurek raced up to the attic. Hannele had both hands over her mouth, her tears running over them.

"What's the matter, what happened?"

"You know. I heard them, I heard them!" she gasped between sobs.

"Shh! They can hear you downstairs."

She bit her lips. Yurek held her and stroked her hair until her sobbing eased. "I heard them, they were torturing you," she blurted out, and again tears coursed down her cheeks.

"What are you talking about?"

"They were pinching you, they hit you. Let's run away from here."

"You don't understand. You see . . ." He groped for words. Hella had pinched him all right, but it wasn't torture. How could he explain that to Hannele? "Anyway, don't worry, it won't be much longer," he said distractedly.

•   •   •   •   •

Yurek stuck his head around the door of the house. The master was rolling a cigarette and had his back to him. The mistress looked up, and he motioned for her to come outside. "The rifle, does the master know it's not up there anymore?" he whispered.

"What do you care?"

"When you and the master were away today, a kid down the road told me that in Jozefow the Schwabes found a rifle in a house. They set fire to the house and killed the whole family."

"Holy Mother of God! And that damn fool fired it in broad daylight. I'll see him dead before he ever finds out where that gun is."

"The best thing is to keep the trapdoor closed and the ladder hidden, like before. That way the master will think the rifle is still up there."

The mistress rumpled his hair. "You are a shrewd one," she chuckled.

19

It had been a warm and peaceful Sunday. The soup had been delicious, with even a few bones in it. The master had stayed sober all day, and best of all, in the afternoon he had come back from the village with an underground newspaper carrying good tidings: the

Allied armies had landed on Pantelleria, an Italian island somewhere. Soon they would open a real second front in the West, and the terrible war would be over.

It had truly been a fine day, and it wasn't spoiled even by the incident of Yurek's wet pants. He had begged Hannele to use some of the water to wash herself, but there never seemed to be even enough for her to drink. He had tucked a wet cloth into his pants to bring to the attic, and in moments it had spread a dark stain down the front of his trousers. Hella and Wojtek had roared with glee, and he had joined in their laughter. It didn't matter what they thought as long as he could get Hannele cleaned up a bit.

"It can't last much longer," he comforted her as he sponged her with the cloth. "Soon I'll get you out of this oven. You know what, I may be able to sneak you out to the woods for a while, maybe even a dip into the river. You'll feel brand-new after you've bathed."

He should have thought of a wet cloth long ago. The attic was swarming with insects. Hannele's dress was a breeding ground for lice, and they multiplied faster than he could pick them out. Her poor little body was all chewed up. His own clothes were a problem too. The mistress had noticed him scratching. She had urged him to wash in the kitchen and use plenty of water. It would certainly be a wonderful thing to do. But what about the master and Wojtek? What if they saw him naked? He usually bathed in the river early in the morning, when the village was still asleep. Last Sunday someone had come along; there had barely been enough time to grab his clothes and hide behind a tree.

Hannele's dress was falling apart. He filched a needle and thread to sew it up as best he could. While he was threading the needle, Hannele accidentally bumped his arm. The needle slipped through his fingers.

"Don't move! Sit still!" he exclaimed.

"Shh! They'll hear you!"

"Don't move, the needle fell into the hay!"

"You can get another one."

"Be quiet, clumsy! I've got to find that needle!"

Hannele pouted. Yossel had never sounded so cross with her.

"Something terrible could happen if the cow should swallow that needle with her hay," Yurek explained, and instantly regretted his words. What good was it to alarm her too?

He felt around in the hay where he had been sitting. No needle.

He motioned Hannele to stay where she was. The family had begun to stir and it was time for him to tend to the cow.

Before he led the cow out he ran up to the attic to search again. If the cow swallowed that needle, it would kill her. What then? Even if they suspected nothing, they would no longer have any need for him. And if they slaughtered the cow and discovered he was to blame, the master would beat him to death.

The days passed. Yurek had painstakingly sifted through every inch of the haystack but found no needle. He kept his eyes on the cow every minute, examined everything she ate. "Blackie," he pleaded, "eat slowly, please. If you feel something hard, spit it out. If the needle must stick you, let it be your lip, your tongue, but for God's sake, don't swallow it . . ."

20

Summer vacationers started arriving in the village. The small room at the far end of the house had been rented to a Mrs. Jankowska of Warsaw, and late in June she settled in with her ten-year-old son, Janushek. Yurek had overheard her say that her husband was a Polish army officer, a prisoner of the Russians. That worried him, for the Polish officers had always been Jew haters. Now the Germans were spreading rumors that the "Jewish Communists" were torturing and murdering Polish officers. With that kind of talk, Mrs. Jankowska must be ready to kill every Jew on sight. God help him if she were to hear movements in the attic and suspect something.

As it turned out, she was good to him. When he ran an errand for her, or chopped some wood for her stove, she rewarded him with a slice of white bread and butter, at times a handful of cherries, once even a piece of sausage. If Mrs. Jankowska, with her snooty nose, ever found out who he was, her pink face would turn green.

•   •   •   •   •

Yurek forced his eyes open. The dog was barking wildly. Who would be coming here in the middle of the night? Mrs. Jankowska, she must have found him out somehow, and she hadn't lost any time informing . . .

"What's the matter?" Hannele asked, rousing from sleep.

"Shhh!" was all he could get through his chattering teeth.

Jump out the window? The whole house must be surrounded.

But why were they breaking down the barn door? It wasn't even locked. Silently, he raised the trapdoor a crack and looked down. It was the cow beating her horns against the door.

The knots in his stomach slowly unwound and left him limp. "It's nothing, only the cow," he told Hannele. Nothing? Could it be the needle? Maybe she had swallowed the needle and the pain was driving her wild.

• • • • •

He must tell the mistress. Maybe they could still do something. But first, he had to get Hannele out of the attic and hide her in the woods. He should have spoken up as soon as he lost the needle. They might have had to throw out all the hay but the cow would have been saved. Big, brave Yurek . . . finally ruined everything.

Hannele fell asleep again. He sat up and waited for daybreak, although he didn't know what he would do when it came. The cow was so wild now it was dangerous to go down there. Where was everybody? Didn't they hear the racket?

Inside the house all was quiet, but from the little room where the summer guests lived he could hear light footsteps. A hinge creaked, a door opened.

"*Gospodarzu,* what's the matter?"

"Nothing to worry about," the master laughed. "The cow's in heat. Tomorrow I'll take her to the bull."

• • • • •

Yurek had never seen anything like it. Overnight, it seemed, a strange force had been unleashed in the world. At dawn the master took the cow to the bull; in the meadows, cows tried to mount each other; the rooster was chasing the hens; flies mated; children threw pebbles at coupling dogs. He thought back on all the summers he had spent in the countryside, but he couldn't remember anything like this. People too were behaving peculiarly, and so was he. Just this morning he had stood and peeked through a crack while the mistress, half naked, washed herself at the pump. Hannele was scraping the chimney brick with her fingernail, but he couldn't tear himself away to answer her signal until the mistress went back into the house.

An aroma like freshly drawn milk rose from the steaming fields. Hella came back from the village with a gang of peasant girls. They whispered together and giggled until he was sure they were up to no good. Soon they were throwing burrs at him, pulling his hair and taunting him until he chased them, and they fled into the tall corn.

"What're you standing there like a scarecrow for?" Hella teased. "C'mon, catch me!"

"If I do, I'll crack your ribs!" He turned back to the cow.

"Come over here, I'll show you . . ."

He glanced over his shoulder. They were all there, almost hidden by the tall stalks, but he could swear they all had their skirts over their heads. His face burned, and their giggles followed him out of the field.

There was no end to Hella's pestering. It was at her instigation that Wojtek spat in his soup. When he went to open the barn door one night, he found the handle smeared with dung; another time it was wrapped in barbed wire.

"I know you did it," he warned her. "Don't push me too far!"

"And what if I do?"

He seized her by the shoulders, started to shake her, and his fingers sank into soft, warm flesh. How long was it since he'd arrived here? She had been a bony, skinny-looking kid then. Now—she would soon have a bosom as big as her mother's. She didn't struggle to get away from him; she only laughed, the same squealing laughter he heard when girls disappeared into the tall corn with young fellows. Later that day she tracked him down near the shredder and handed him a chunk of white bread. She'd stolen it somewhere, no doubt.

It could be worth his while to play up to her. If he got closer to her, she would be on his side. He might need her help.

No, no, no! What was happening to him in this damn village that such thoughts could even enter his head?

21

The rains came day after day, hour after hour. Up to their ankles in mud, they dug up the last of the potatoes. When they had to pick some during the summer, they'd done so sparingly. Leave them in the ground until autumn, the mistress had insisted, and they would grow to their fullest and most profitable size. Profitable? What did it matter that they were big when they were stolen? "May this whole wretched village sink into the earth!" the mistress ranted. "We eat water for soup, and those thieves dig up the fields! That old Stakh, may his fingers fall off one by one! But what good would it do? The pot calling the kettle black! Who knows how much my own spouse has torn out of the earth to fill his gullet?"

•   •   •   •   •

It had become obvious that the winter was going to be a hard one. There were too few potatoes in the cellar; hardly enough of the pickled cabbage; the cow was giving less and less milk each day. Yurek was worried. Why should they keep him now—he was an extra mouth to feed. There were still a few chores for him to do, but they could manage well enough without him.

The two little pigs the mistress was rearing would bring a nice profit in a year or so, but right now, they only added to the burden. They had made a deposit to buy a second cow, but the way things stood, there wasn't a chance in the world they could pay the balance by the deadline on New Year's Day; they might even lose the deposit.

•   •   •   •   •

Everyone was pinning his hopes on a second front. In the house, in the village store, in the fields, it was the only topic of conversation. But as yet there was no sign of it. They talked about a city called Zhitomir— one day the Russians liberated it, the next day the Germans recaptured it. They talked about American victories in countries he had never even heard of, at the other end of the world. But here, things weren't moving at all. Some day the Schwabes would get what was coming to them, but would there be one Jew left alive to see it? In Otwock, a Jewish family had been found hiding. They were all shot.

What would he do if something should happen to Hannele? It was true that he was the one exposed to all the risks. But what would happen to Hannele if he . . .

He shouldn't torment himself with such thoughts. The Germans were being beaten everywhere; it couldn't last much longer.

• • • • •

If only he could get rid of his cold. They were all drenched with rain in the fields, but only he was coughing his lungs out. "Why don't you sleep here in the kitchen?" the mistress had suggested. "It must be bitter cold up there in the attic."

What did she know about cold, about freezing winds, unstopped by shattered tiles, Hannele clinging to him and shivering as if the wind were blowing right through her bones. He brought logs from the woods and stuffed the oven to bursting. The wood burned furiously and for a little while it heated up the bricks of the chimney that passed through the attic. Hannele curled up beside it, but the fire soon sputtered and died, and the wind kept howling as if it would never stop.

• • • • •

A breeze came into the yard like an advance scout—rattled a tile in the roof, rocked a fence to test the strength of the posts, knocked over a barrel, and then withdrew. The fence slumbered, leaning on the rotting timbers; the trees, their heads covered with white snow-caps, swayed gently, as if in silent prayer.

Then an onrush of wind tore loose like a pack of wolves and swooped down with savage howls. The fence shook and toppled over. A windowpane blew out and hit the ground with a crash; a shutter flew open and banged against the wall. Somewhere a roof was lifted into the air, laying an attic bare. Pieces of washing were ripped off the line into the twisting gale; sleeves ballooned out like embracing arms and wrapped themselves around naked branches. The wind lashed them unmercifully, tearing them to shreds. In the barn the cow lowed woefully, stamped on the ground, and rammed its flanks against the stall. The pigs snorted and tore at the board that fenced off their corner. The hog leapt over it and nestled against the cow, leaving her young squealing helplessly.

• • • • •

Yurek plugged up the new holes torn out by the wind and tried to calm Hannele. "Don't worry, our roof is the strongest in the village." He took off his jacket and covered her. Her forehead felt hot, her eyes were glassy, her feet ice-cold. His heart sank; she must be running a fever!

"Let's go home," Hannele begged, her teeth chattering, "I want to go home to Mama."

"I told you, Mama wants us to hide here."

"I don't want to anymore. I want to go home."

"As soon as you feel better."

"I want to go now."

"Who can go out in this weather, silly? As soon as it gets warm, we'll go. Mama must be worrying about us. Just imagine, I'll knock on the door, and Mama will say, 'Who's there?'"

"I want to go home!"

"That's just what I was telling you. But first you must get well. Hey, do you remember the fluffy quilt on Mama's bed? That's where you'll sleep, in the big, soft bed, and you'll cover yourself with Mama's quilt. Nenna will put plenty of coal in the stove—"

"Nenna?"

"Nenna must have come back already, and Papa too. They were sent away to work, remember? Now the work is finished, so they must be back in the ghetto."

"But the big bed . . . we left it . . ."

"Yes, I remember. You think I don't remember? In our last place in the ghetto I slept in the same bed as Uncle Pintshe, and you and Mama slept in another bed, a little iron cot. Uncle Pintshe must have brought the big bed from the old house by now. He and . . ."

"I want to go home."

The wind tore a few more tiles off the roof. Yurek had nothing left to stuff up the holes with. He tried to hold down the hay covering Hannele. The wind cut his back like a lash, but he kept talking.

"The first thing Mama will do is give you a bath. She'll throw these dirty clothes right into the trash. She'll scrub you all over, rub you dry with a soft towel, then she'll brush your hair and . . ."

A coughing spell choked off his words. The cold knifed into his mouth, but he caught his breath and continued. "You'll have clean hair, clean clothes, you'll smell so nice. Oh, from habit you'll still scratch yourself, then you'll remember you don't itch any more . . ." He tried to laugh, but the wind snatched up the sound and carried it off. It came back from the other end of the loft, brittle, sardonic . . .

"You're almost naked, Yossel. All your clothes are on me."

"I'm not cold. I was just thinking of how it will be when we come home, that's why I'm shivering. I'm not a bit cold."

"I'm afraid, Yossel. I want to go home . . . take me home now . . ."

•   •   •   •   •

This time nothing would stop him, Yurek resolved. He would tell the mistress everything. Hannele was sick and needed help. He couldn't put it off, not a minute longer.

"What kind of shit head are you?" the master greeted him when he charged into the kitchen. "You keep complaining you're cold, you're sick, you drag every rag you can find up to the attic; and then you come down here half naked. All night long you hack and cough, and now you run around without your clothes on."

"I'm not cold," Yurek said, and ran out of the house.

"To hell with you!" the master shouted after him. "We ought to kick you out anyway!"

Yurek returned with an armful of firewood and stuffed it into the stove. He blew into the fire; it flickered feebly and went out.

The door flew open. In strode a neighbor, red with cold, smiling broadly.

"What the hell are you so pleased about, Antek?" the master asked.

"Just nabbed myself a Zhid!"

"Where are there Jews these days?"

"Right out in the street. Over by the green fence, I see this beggar coughing his guts out, his face swollen, his eyes all puffed up. I look and look—somethin' about his mug is familiar. Who d'ya think it was? Moshek the shoemaker!"

"The shoemaker? From Otwock?"

"The same son of a bitch! I'll be damned, I says to him, you're still among the living? He could barely breathe, but he starts to run, would you believe it, Wacek? Three steps and I ketch up with him. I let 'im have one on his big snout, and the blood pours out like somebody's pumpin' it. We think we're rid of them, but every time you turn around, another Zhid crawls out of a rat hole."

Yurek's hands tightened around a log, his body coiled like an animal about to spring. He shoved the log into the stove with all his might and kicked at the cat brushing against his legs.

"You little hoodlum!" Antek turned on him. "What did that

poor animal ever do to you? How'd you like to be kicked in the guts like that?"

Yurek stumbled into the barn, tears streaming down his cheeks, his guts twisted into a knot of suppressed and frustrated rage.

22

Things were looking up again. Hannele's fever had subsided and for the first time in days she felt hungry. The mistress had a fine feast prepared for Christmas and there would be plenty of food for all. She already had the money for the cow, and the master wanted to lose no time in getting her. But the mistress objected.

"We're not going to register the cow and give all the milk to the Germans. If you run into a German patrol and they take one look at a cow without a registration earring—you know what that means? It means you pay out all our good money for a cow and come home with nothing."

"So how will waiting help you?"

"I figured it all out. We'll wait until New Year's eve. With all the celebrating and drinking, there won't be many German patrols, and it'll be easier to get the cow home without any trouble."

That would be his chance, Yurek hoped. With the master away, it would be easier to talk; and, in getting her second cow at last, the mistress would be in good spirits. God would surely reward her for the good deed of saving a sick little girl. He would tell her so.

•　　•　　•　　•　　•

The mistress had cooked a batch of dumplings filled with sauerkraut and stored them in the cellar, but when they were brought up to be readied for the holiday meal, there were telltale signs that the mice had been nibbling at them. "The house takes after its master, full of mice and crawling with lice, a plague—" She interrupted herself, remembering it was Christmas Eve, and directed her curses at the rodents. "A plague on the filthy mice!"

The mistress was about to throw the dumplings into the garbage—let the pigs have a merry Christmas too. Yurek quickly put out his hand. "Might as well let Wilk eat them," he mumbled, and took them out to the kennel. He gave one to the dog and took the rest up to the attic.

Sitting around the festive table that evening, Yurek suddenly burst into tears. The master squirmed in his chair, but the mistress was overcome with sympathy. "A horrible end to those Schwabes, dear Jesus! On this holy night, a child has to sit at a stranger's table."

"We're not strangers," Hella protested.

"He has his own Mama and Papa; he would be with them now if not for the Germans."

Faint sounds coming from the loft reached Yurek's keen ears and he instantly dried the tears he had been unable to contain. He jumped to his feet and groped for an excuse. "I . . . I . . . I have to go," he stammered, grabbing his stomach, and ran out of the house.

Up in the loft he found his sister doubled over, vomiting and retching. The sauerkraut dumplings had been too much for her.

* * * * *

Through the little attic window, Yurek's eyes glided over the virginal white snow to the gold-threaded clouds that dotted the darkening sky. The setting sun grasped the horizon and held on as if the day refused to withdraw, as if the year 1943 would not release him from its clutches. May all the evil cease with the old year, may deliverance come with the new, Yurek chanted and swayed as if at prayer on Rosh Hashanah.

The delicate aroma of fresh chicken soup reached his nostrils. Hannele was running a fever again, and he couldn't get her to swallow a crumb. Chicken soup was just what she needed. Maybe the new year would really bring him relief. After supper, when the master went for the new cow, he would tell the mistress everything. Hannele would sip hot raspberry juice and sweat out her fever in a nice warm bed.

* * * * *

His hair plastered down and his trousers brushed, Yurek walked into the house to join the family. Everything was ready for the new-year dinner, but the master wasn't there. The mistress moved the pots on the stove, she changed her apron, she ran to look through the peephole she made with her warm breath in the frosted window—there was no sign of him.

"I'll go out and look for him," Hella volunteered, grabbing her coat. Yurek went back to Hannele.

Krysia stirred the soup impatiently, shifting her weight from one leg to the other. Now both of them had disappeared. With a clatter of the wooden spoon, she bolted out the door.

It was late when Krysia and Hella returned, dragging Wacek between them. They dumped him on the bed.

"I should have left you to rot in the gutter where you belong, damn your soul to hell!"

"Christ," he moaned. "They must have given me poison, not vodka—"

"Sober up, you slob. Get on your feet and go for the cow!" She pulled him up, he fell back on the bed.

"Jesus Maria! What do you do with a souse like that? The last train will leave soon and everything will be lost."

She tried to pull him up again but he tumbled to the floor in a heap.

"YUREK! YUREK! Where the devil are you?"

Yurek flew down the ladder and dashed into the kitchen.

"You're going to get the new cow," the mistress said, hanging a little moneybag around his neck.

"Me? I can't—I never—I don't even know where—"

"Stop stammering! Here, I've written everything down on this paper. Have some soup and bundle up. Hurry, or you'll miss the train."

"I've got to get my mittens," Yurek muttered, and ran up to the attic. "Here, Hannele, chicken soup . . ."

She didn't move. He tried feeding her a spoonful. It ran down her face. How could he leave her now?

"Yurek! Yurek! Stop wasting time!"

He ran down and pleaded tearfully, "I can't—I—"

"I'll take an ax and split your empty head open! Comes mealtime, everybody's here. When there's work to be done, they've all got excuses. Now get a move on!"

"I have a sister—"

"A pox on you and your sister both! If you're not out of here—"

Yurek ran all the way to the station. With any luck, he'd be back

before dawn. He'd be the one bringing home the new cow . . . maybe
it was really for the best.

23

"Ho! Ho!" Yurek urged the cow, and she ambled placidly along before
him. The farmer had warned him that she was wild, had even given
him a stick to beat her with and a hobble for her front legs so she
couldn't run away. But she was no trouble at all. Yurek tucked the stick
under his arm. "Ho! Ho!" It was a cheery sound on a lonely road.

The shadowy huts with their darkened windows melted into the
blackness of the night. A village deep in refreshing sleep; a child
close to its mother's side; a cat drowsing by a warm oven. "Ho! Ho!"
If he kept up this speed, he'd be home in two or three hours. It must
have been the hand of God, the master getting drunk, leaving his
farmhand to bring the cow home.

"Ho! Ho!" Past the third village, more than halfway. Soon they
would come to the forest and the road to the left—home. Maybe
Hannele's getting sick had a purpose too; now he would be forced to
tell the mistress. No, he wouldn't say anything. He would simply
carry Hannele into the house. He should have brought her down long
ago, when the mistress took in that sick little sparrow. She had tried
so hard to save it; wouldn't she do the same for a sick little girl? Of
course, they would still have to keep Hannele out of sight during the
day, but in the evening she could be in the house with the rest of the
family. She'd be clean, she'd eat at the table, sleep in a proper bed—
how many times had they daydreamed about it? Now he would make
it all come true.

A road sign. This must be the fork in the road; this was where he
should turn left. A little farther on, just before the next village, he
would turn onto a narrow path, go through a field, and then the road
would lead straight home.

"Ho! Ho! Good, Metcha, go left!"

If his mother could see him now with this cow, she'd be scared.
Hannele was scared of cows, and of the dark too. What was there to
be afraid of? He wasn't afraid of the dark at all—especially when it
protected him from searching German eyes . . . Soon the war would
be over, and the first thing Mama would do was go to the Wil-

chinskis. She'd think the worst when she found them gone, but when he brought Hannele back . . . It was me, he would say, me, Yurek, Yossel frog-face, Yossel pock-nose, it was me who saved her . . .

"Whoa! Stop, Metcha, stop!"

How had he gotten into the forest? The peasant had told him the forest was to the right. Had the man made a mistake? Had he taken a wrong turn? He could swear he had turned left. There should be a village here, not a forest. "Stop, Metcha, turn around! Go back!"

The cow kept going, and Yurek ran in front of her, waving the stick at her muzzle. The cow bent her head aside and continued forward. He grabbed hold of one of her horns, tried to turn her around. The cow tossed her head once, and he was tossed from her horns like wood chips from an ax.

His right leg was bruised, blood dripped from his nose, but he picked himself up. He had to catch that animal. Her strides were cramped by the short rope attached to her forelegs, and he caught up with her quickly. Once more he ran in front of her, trying to bar her way. "Back, Metcha, back! Turn around!" He waved the stick, hit her a few cracks on the muzzle—the cow turned and stopped dead.

"Good girl! Now go! Ho! Ho!"

The cow didn't move.

"Move, Metcha! Go, I tell you!" He prodded her lightly on the flanks.

The cow didn't budge.

"Move, dammit, or I'll make you move!" He hit her with all his might.

Nothing. Not a step. Maybe it was the rope—it might have irritated her legs. He'd been on a farm long enough to know that. He barely got one leg untied—the cow shot forward and tore off into the woods.

"Stop, Metcha, stop!"

The cow galloped ahead wildly, Yurek after her. He fell over a stump, got up and ran on. The rags the mistress had tied around his shoes loosened, and he tripped over them at every step. He bent down to tighten them again, and when he looked up he could no longer see the cow. The beat of her hooves on the frozen ground sent echoes through the woods that came back to him from all sides. He kept running. His knees were giving way. He tried to drag his feet forward but pitched to the ground like a felled tree.

The snow against his brow cleared his head, and he pushed himself up. He couldn't see or hear any movement. The cow was gone—gone forever!

It was all over. He would have to sneak Hannele out before daybreak. Where would he take her?

Standing there wouldn't solve anything either. He had to go on.

Snow got under the rags, the frost pierced his mittens, penetrated his shoes; red-hot needles were stabbing at his toes. His eyelids grew heavy, his head dragged him down. He had hardly slept a wink since Hannele had taken sick. Bushes and thorns tore at his skin through his trousers. Just as well—if it weren't for the pain, he might fall asleep on his feet.

An upended stump projected from the snow as if someone had thoughtfully provided a stool. If he rested a moment, closed his eyes to squeeze out the cold, he would see better. It would help him find the cow. He wouldn't even sit down, just close his eyes . . .

His eyelids came together. Oh, that felt good. That's how he and Mama would fall into each other's arms and no one could part them ever again. He wavered and fell. Mama! I'm falling asleep . . . I mustn't . . .

He forced his eyes open and crawled over to a tree, pulling himself up, What . . .? Tracks! The cow's footprints in the snow, right at his feet! His drowsiness disappeared.

Night extinguished its lights one by one; day had not yet kindled its own. Suddenly the tracks were gone. Twigs crackled nearby. It must be the cow, it had to be! He took one step, listened, another step and listened again; he could hear the cow's heavy breathing.

There! The rope dragging from the cow's leg had caught in the underbrush. She strained and pulled at it but could not free herself. Yurek bent down to untangle the rope. The cow yanked mightily and galloped away.

The trees were close together here, and Yurek could maneuvre more easily than the cow. He caught up with her, blocked her way, and smacked her hard between the eyes with the stick. She reared and landed on her knees. The stick came down savagely again and again until the cow sprawled in the snow.

God, have I lost my mind? His breath came in gasps. He tucked the stick under his jacket. "Up, girl, up!" he urged, gently nudging her flanks. "Your leg, Metcha," he commanded, lifting her foot off the rope on the ground. The cow waited obediently as he tied the end of the rope around the other leg. Now I won't get her to move, he worried.

"Go, Metcha!"

To his great surprise, the cow started forward. But where was he to lead her? The route that brought her here would take her out, he reasoned, and lead her back over her tracks.

The rope kept catching in the underbrush; he stopped and untied it from the cow's legs. This time the animal followed his commands. He patted her flanks happily.

"You're a smart cow, Metcha. You found out I was stronger, huh? Now be a good little cow and make up for lost time, it's getting late."

The cow allowed herself to be led, not the same Metcha at all. When Yurek came out of the woods, the rising sun had begun to light up the sky.

• • • • •

"It's about time!" Wacek scolded when he caught sight of Yurek. "He brings the cow home in broad daylight. You want the Germans to get her? What the hell were you doin' all night—sleepin'?" Only then did he notice Yurek's bruised and bloody face. The cow too was covered with welts. "What have you been up to, you little bastard?"

"She's a wild one, worse than a bull," Yurek explained.

"You're a lazy blockhead, that's what!"

"She got stubborn wouldn't budge—"

"Some farmhand, can't even handle a dumb cow!" He wrenched the stick from Yurek's hand. "Go to your mama and let her wash the blood off your mug." He gave Yurek a shove and took over. "Ho! Ho!" The cow obeyed him like a docile kitten.

Yurek's eyes followed the cow down the path. What are you doing to me, Metcha? Stop, run, kick—do something!

The cow trotted submissively, the master behind her smacking her rump with the stick. She didn't veer a centimeter from the path.

"A cow like a lamb!" the master shouted over his shoulder.

24

Yurek raced up the ladder. "Hannele, I'm back! I've got fresh milk for you, straight from the milking pail. Hannele, Hannele, where are you?"

He set the milk down, dropped to his knees beside her and shook her gently. She did not awaken. He shook her more vigorously and pulled her up; her arms hung down like two broken sticks. He shook her until his teeth rattled, but her head rolled to one side, like a chicken with its neck wrung. Slowly, carefully, he laid her back in the straw and rose to his feet.

In the barn the pigs were grubbing in the dirt; the black cow contentedly chewed her cud; the new cow licked at the empty trough. All at once, Yurek leapt from the ladder and ran. The pigs scattered out of his way, a startled hen flew high on the ladder. Wilk raised a howl. Yurek kept running, out of the yard, into the field.

Wacek had already gone to buy vodka for the celebration to "wet down" the new cow. Krysia was busy in the kitchen cooking up fodder. The children were still in bed. The village was sleeping off its new-year hangover. Only Wilk was witness to Yurek's wild chase and started after him.

Yurek flew across the meadow, across the frozen river, like an arrow shot from a bow. Then suddenly he sank into the snow. Wilk whined, ran in circles around him, dug his forepaws into the snow, and let out a mighty yowl. Somewhere in the distance a lone dog responded. Yurek lay motionless. The dog laid its paws on the boy's chest and licked his face. Yurek's eyes flickered behind his closed lids, his hands moved as if to brush the dog away. He tried to get up, but the dog's frantic leaps knocked him down again.

He pushed his head up as if to lift it out of a fog and forced his eyes open. His ears listened for the rustle of life that used to fill the air here—a rush of sound as cheerful as his hopes had been. Now only silence, a vast desolation like the emptiness within him. All that was left was the lifeless little body lying in the attic. He pushed Wilk away, staggered to his feet, and started back.

• • • • •

All was quiet when Yurek came into the yard. He paused at the barn door, turned away, and went into the toolshed instead. There he picked up an ax and a shovel, and took off again. He could do this one last thing for Hannele . . .

He stopped at a clearing in the woods and set to work. The

ground was frozen hard beneath the snow, and the ax chopped out chunks of ice. The strokes echoed and reechoed through the woods. He cut deeper, down to tangled, unyielding roots; the ax grew so heavy he could barely hold it.

"YUREK! YUREK!"

They were calling him. Let them. "Yurek! Yurek!" The echo bounced from tree to tree. He drove the blade into the earth, and it seemed to him that the ax was chopping their calls apart along with the roots.

It was evening when he finally dragged himself into the barn. His father's face swam before his eyes. "God's will," Papa said.

Why? Why did God will it this way? I led her through the streets of Warsaw, I carried her across open fields, I gave her my own crusts of bread, I . . . I'm the one who did it all! Why does God . . . why didn't He let me?

His father's eyes were hard, accusing.

Am I to blame for everything? Didn't I try a thousand times to talk to the mistress? I couldn't help it, I had to wait for the right moment.

I waited and waited, and Hannele froze to death while I waited. How could I have known?

The question gouged Yurek's head like jagged teeth, but no answers came. He shut himself off from his father's image; to his father, God was always right and Yossel always to blame.

Wilk came bounding over. "*You* know what happened, Wilk. You're the only one who knows."

He groped up the ladder and made his way to the chimney. Hannele was not there! He crept along the floor, feverishly combing through the hay. A fearsome wail tore his mouth open and hurtled through the attic.

They all came running "Yurek! Yurek!" What had they done to poor, dead Hannele?

The master dragged him down the ladder. "What kind of animal are you?" the master shouted. "Chases around and leaves a sick child in the attic!"

"The dog has more feeling than you!" the mistress cried. "She almost froze to death!"

Almost froze to death? *Almost?* He lunged forward. The mistress caught his arm. "Shh! No noise! She's barely alive."

• • • • •

A fire blazed in the stove, but Yurek kept piling on more wood. The
master poured vodka into the mistress's palms, and she rubbed it
into Hannele's emaciated body. The master ran his tongue over his
lips. One more minute and he would be tipping the bottle into his
mouth, Yurek thought. But no, the mistress put out her hands again,
and again the master poured the vodka into them. Yurek felt his
heart spill over; a silent blessing trembled on his lips.

The alcohol burned into Hannele's open sores, and her eyes rolled
in pain.

"Maybe it's enough," Yurek pleaded.

"No time to lose," the mistress said, her face flushed, "it's either—or."

The master kept pouring until the bottle was empty. The mistress wrapped Hannele in a wet sheet and covered her with a huge
down comforter. She brought a glassful of steaming liquid; the smell
of raspberry juice trailed in the air. The red fluid ran over the child's
mouth. "Drink! Please, drink!" The mistress's voice was stern. Yurek
wanted to help, but she pushed him away and went on with her
coaxing. A few spoonfuls slid down Hannele's throat.

• • • • •

Long after the others had gone to sleep, Yurek sat beside the mistress
at Hannele's bedside. Again and again he forced his eyelids open as
they drooped of their own weight. He awoke with a start. The mistress was shaking him.

"You can go to sleep now. She'll pull through."

The next morning Hannele opened her eyes; it seemed to Yurek
that she smiled at him. She breathed more easily, her fever was down,
but she could swallow no more than a spoonful or two of sweetened
water.

25

The master steadied the bucket under the new cow; already it was
half-full and the stream of milk still whooshed and rang into the

pail. The master looked up at Yurek with exultant pride. "A pig in a poke, eh? When I buy a cow, I know what I buy, and she knows that by now."

"That's what I call a milker," Yurek agreed, smiling broadly. Thank God something good had come to these kind people at last.

The master was still chuckling over his triumph when Yurek ran to the house. "Mistress, you should see Metcha." The mistress stuck her head out of the room where Hannele lay sleeping. "Stop that yelling! What're ya carrying on about?"

"Metcha is even better than Blackie. Just wait till she gets out on the grass this spring, the pail will run over!"

The news about Wacek's second cow spread through the village, bringing flocks of well-wishers, and Saturday's new-year celebration spilled over into Sunday. The children were sent away, and the drinking started all over again.

After everybody had gone, Antek's wife came bustling in, and Krysia stared at her in surprise. Earlier, Antek had come alone; his wife was ill, he said. Now here she was large as life, throwing herself on Krysia's neck with kisses and blessings. Her inquisitive eyes scanned the room. She settled herself on a bench opposite the closed door separating the kitchen from the rest of the house. Aye, that Wacek, she mused, he's making home brew in there, the whole house reeks of whiskey.

Antkova folded her plump arms across her ample bosom and slyly glanced at Wacek. "You certainly put out a spread. My Antek hasn't sobered up yet. With the price old Stakh is charging for vodka these days, I can imagine what it cost you. Raised it just before the holidays, the old skinflint. The price keeps going up and the quality keeps going down. It's high time someone got smart and put up a still. It would teach that old leech a lesson."

"Yeah, it's high time," Wacek nodded eagerly.

"Maybe you know somebody," Antkova persisted. He might not be making vodka in there, but something was going on behind that door. If they thought they could get rid of her before she found out . . . She almost jumped as a sound came from the other room.

"Who's that coughing in there?"

"The farmhand," Krysia was quick to answer. "City kids! The first frost, and he's sick as a dog."

Antkova knew better. Sick or not, a farmhand's place was in the barn, not the bedroom. She stayed on.

Krysia stood at the stove and nervously stirred the mash for the animals. "Holiday or no holiday, the animals have to eat," she said and added pointedly, "When do you feed your animals, Antkova?"

"I cook for them all week. Sundays, I don't care what Antek gives them."

Wacek lifted the caldron off the stove and stamped out of the house without a word. It was growing dark, and Antkova still sat there. That fat cow, Krysia thought, her eyes glaring. She hated to leave her alone in the kitchen, but the fire in the stove was petering out. She ran to the shed to get more wood. No sooner had the door banged shut than Antkova sprang to her feet. Her catlike steps moving toward the bedroom did not escape Yurek's ears. The knob turned, the door opened a crack, but he barred her way in. "The mistress is outside."

"The way your mistress talked, I thought you were ready for the priest. You look as healthy as a horse to me," she said, and tried to force the door. He held on to it, and called out, "Mistress, your guest is looking for you!"

Krysia came running. She put a firm grip on Antkova's arm. "If you've made up your mind to go in there, Antkova, let's go."

"Not if you have something to hide."

"The best way to find out is to go in and see. I've got a lover hidden in the bed, maybe two. I know you won't tell Wacek."

"Don't be so touchy."

"Who's touchy? I just thought you wanted to go in. No? Then come sit down. You want a piece of bread? You must be hungry, sitting here for so long."

•　•　•　•　•

"She didn't see a thing," Yurek assured the mistress after the woman had left.

"May the Holy Mother of God protect us from the trouble that old slut can stir up!" Krysia cried, and ran into the bedroom to kneel before her porcelain Madonna. On top of the chest of drawers, behind the figurine, stood a tub of freshly churned butter. The cat had been licking at it, and startled by the mistress, it leapt down. The icon fell to the ground and shattered. Yurek's lips turned chalk-white; the mistress would surely see a bad omen in this.

Throughout the night at Hannele's bedside, the thought of the smashed figure gnawed at him. The mistress must be thinking the Madonna was angry because a good Christian was sheltering Jews. Finding Hannele alive in the mistress's bed was a real miracle; now he needed another miracle to make the icon whole again.

The next morning Yurek ran into the kitchen, words tumbling around in his head, but the mistress was calmly stirring farina into some hot milk. When it cooled, she took it into the bedroom and forced some of it into Hannele's mouth. In seconds, it came frothing up. The fever was gone, but she was too weak to open her eyes. Getting the doctor from Otwock was out of the question. Even if he agreed to come, there would be no way to get him to the house without the whole village knowing about it.

The mistress kept the children away all day, and the house was strangely still. Dusk rolled into the room like a gray fog, erasing the window, swallowing up the walls. Yurek could barely distinguish Hannele's wan face from the white linen; only her dark, matted hair outlined the shape of her head. He felt as if he were floating, as if they had been cast adrift, he and the bed and Hannele, floating in a gray fog . . . no, he mustn't sleep . . . he must bend down and listen to her breathe . . . Where had she found the strength to gasp like that?

He jumped to his feet. Hannele's breathing had grown loud and labored. Her hands were icy and the bottles the mistress had put at her feet weren't enough. More hot bottles, that's what she needed. He ran to get the mistress. Where could he find more bottles?

Krysia ran into the room ahead of him and bent over Hannele. A moment later she straightened up and crossed herself. "We won't need bottles anymore . . ."

·   ·   ·   ·   ·

The village awoke after a restful night. Little clouds of smoke curled out of chimneys, rose into the crisp, cold air, and floated away to reveal a clear blue sky. The snow sparkled like frosty jewels on the treetops and covered the fields with a downy white blanket. Only in one spot in the woods had the snow been disturbed, and in the hay above a peasant's hut there remained the gaping imprint of a child's small frame.

• • • • •

The local train from Shwider to Warsaw cut a path through the gray, snow-covered landscape and rocked a weary young body to sleep. His head jerked up with every jilt of the car and fell back again. A thatch of dirty blond hair and a pitted forehead, with a bead of sweat in each hollow, drooped over a shabby gray coat.

"Yossel?"

"My name is Yurek. Yurek Kovalski."

"Yossel!"

"Oh, it's you, Grandpa. Shh! Here I'm Yurek."

"Where is Hannele?"

"How—what are you doing here, Grandfather?"

"Where is Hannele?"

"It started with Papa . . ."

"Where *is* Papa?"

"In Treblinka, gassed."

"Golda?"

"Mama? In the ghetto. You know they burned it down."

"Nenna?"

"With Papa . . . they were . . ."

"And Hannele, with Mama? With Papa?"

"Oh no, I got her out of the ghetto. I smuggled Hannele out and . . ."

"You did? So where is she?"

"It's a long story, Grandpa. . . ."

The locomotive shrieked and Yurek started. He tried to sit up, but his heavy lids soon drooped again and sealed his clouded eyes. Grandpa was back in an instant, questioning, "Where is Hannele?"

"It happened . . . but what about you?"

"Gassed, in Treblinka. Uncle Mayer?"

"Shot in the street."

"Mindele?"

"Taken from her job in the Children's Hospital."

"And Hannele?"

Yurek shook his head.

"Gassed, shot, burned?"

"No, no, no. She only caught cold. She was in the mistress's bed getting better, suddenly . . ."

"In bed? She died a natural death? Thank God."

"Grandpa! Grandpa!"

Grandfather was fading away, and Yurek wanted to ask him to make the icon whole again. But what did he need a good omen for now, when . . . Oh, there was Grandfather on the other side of the window. He pointed his thumb at his pockmarked face and winked. "Don't worry about me, Grandpa, I've got a gem of a face . . ."

Book Two

1

Once, Jews used to wish each other a "kosher Passover." They trembled lest a crumb of *hometz,* leavened bread, somehow be missed in the general cleansing. Now Passover was approaching and the rabbis were saying one could eat anything—the greatest sin was dying of starvation; the greatest virtue, survival.

Maybe a piece of *matzo,* an unleavened wafer, would turn up, maybe even a drop of the traditional wine—the traditional Haggadah would be recited, but with a new pharaoh, and the fat for the holiday rendered from the once-forbidden flesh of horses. What sort of blessing is made over a delicacy cooked in unkosher horse fat? Should those who remain after the great slaughter recite the Hallel prayer, the odes in praise of a just and merciful God?

She must not allow herself such sinful thoughts. Out of the whole group working at the Ostban, both day shift and night shift, she was the only one with two children who were alive and safe on the other side. She didn't have enough money to join them yet, but people were saying the war would end soon.

Meanwhile she could go on smuggling. Perhaps she would be able to find Guzhik again and get some American dollars. Yossel took all kinds of risks, why not she? God seemed to watch over Yossel—He would help her too.

The rucksack on her back would have been heavy even for a peasant. Never mind—she had succeeded in smuggling out a silver-fox fur, although possession of furs was now almost as dangerous as possession of weapons. More than two years ago, Jews had been forced to surrender their furs; if caught, she could have gotten a bullet through her head. But to stay in the ghetto too long was no less dangerous. She needed more dollars fast. She also smuggled risky stuff back into the ghetto— dried salami and preserves—rather than potatoes, which even the most vicious cop would overlook. Food that didn't spoil was worth its weight in gold these days, because people were buying it to stock in the shelters. And she desperately needed gold and dollars!

She arrived at the checkpoint where the night shift left for work.

"A few officers at the watchtower on Nizka Street," people were whispering, "but everything's going through. They're not even searching the rucksacks."

Officers on duty usually meant bad news. They didn't bribe so easily, and the Polish police fell all over themselves trying to impress their superiors by confiscating every last scrap of smuggled goods.

"I'll be right back," Golda told Shimek, the group leader. "I have stomach cramps."

She ran all the way back to her house. Cramps! She had eaten nothing since breakfast. By the time she got back to the checkpoint, Shimek and the group were gone. Unobtrusively, she attached herself to another group.

"Is the watch still good?"

"Everything's going out with no inspection."

"And in?"

"If it goes out, it'll come in."

"And those who have already come in?"

"The day shift hasn't returned yet."

"Do they always come back so late?"

"You're full of questions. The metal workers are supposed to return at five, but sometimes . . ."

The man turned away, leaving her with unanswered questions. Not that she didn't know the answers herself. But she didn't trust German officers, especially when they were kind. She broke away from the queue and ran back home.

•   •   •   •   •

Her group never returned to the ghetto. Neither did the others. They had all been interned that night near their place of work.

Had they detained the *platzuvkas* outside the ghetto to frighten smugglers? Would they be satisfied with detention alone? She'd better wait to see what would happen with the other work details. Monday was the eve of Passover. She would wait until after the first two days of the holiday.

• • • • •

Pintshe always said of her that she could smell danger the way a wild animal did. Where was that sixth sense now? Was the detention of the Ostban *platsuvka* a bad sign?

The air was thick with rumors. One day, too many Germans around the ghetto gates, and everyone ran to the shelters to hide; another day, no Germans at all near the Gensia gate, and again, fear and confusion. Each hour brought contradictory pieces of news.

Good news. The Tebbens and Schultz factories needed more workers. That vicious Jew baiter Brandt had promised the Judenrat flour for matzos. Germans bearing gifts—this had to be a bad omen. And here she was, so mixed up and uncertain. If only Pintshe were here . . .

• • • • •

"No, it can't be, it's not possible!" Golda shouted as she ran to the hideout. The neighbors eyed her with amazement. Wasn't she the one who had raised the alarm about the raid back in January, when no one had suspected anything? Now, when everyone knew that a whole German army was surrounding the ghetto, she was insisting it wasn't possible!

"It must be a raid against the illegals," she tried to convince herself. Her work card from Schultz's factory had expired long ago. Her Ostban card was useless if she wasn't with her group. Again she was an "outlaw." Did it matter anymore? Unless this was a total liquidation, someone would be able to get out afterward, that's what mattered. If not she, then someone else, someone who could get the money to the children.

Each crashing bomb and exploding grenade, each round of bullets, drove home the truth: this was the end, really the end. Yet her whole being protested. No, no, no! It can't be! It mustn't be! There, listen—it has quieted down. Her eyes searched desperately in the blackness for an answering nod.

• • • • •

The first night of Passover. Outside all was quiet. The holiday candles were lit. Someone intended to conduct a seder, a traditional service for the eve of Passover. The electricity in the cellar was turned on for the first time, and everyone was delighted at the way they had outsmarted the Germans in preparing the "bunker." The news was heartening: the resistance was well organized and was holding key positions; there were German corpses on Nalevki Street, on Shvienta-Yerska. People embraced and congratulated each other. They plotted revenge.

Was she the only sane one or the only lunatic here? Saving Jewish lives was more important than killing Germans. If only someone would talk to her, convince her there was still hope. If the little uprising in January had forced the Germans to delay—maybe this time too. Dr. Stillman danced for joy when he heard a German tank had been blown up. If the Germans were really surprised, if they hadn't known what was in store for them . . . If they delayed for a month, a week, she would manage somehow to get the money out to Yossel. Then she would dance too.

The lights went out. The current had been cut. In the dark someone muttered, "After all, smuggling in a generator was impossible."

Another groaned, "Who knows when they'll cut off the water?" And just when they had filled every conceivable container, the taps went dry. Now rationing would be necessary.

•   •   •   •   •

Nalevki Street was burning. Maybe they should brick up the holes in the attic. When it had become dangerous to be seen on the streets, they had broken open passageways in the attics so they could go from building to building throughout the ghetto without being seen by the Germans. Now the fire would spread through the open attic walls.

Resistance fighters, escapees from Nalevki, set up a base in the cellar. Seventy-four people now crowded the space instead of the original twenty-two. So far there was enough food, but water would soon be a problem. People came in clutching their worldly possessions. Ridiculous! Yet hadn't she done the same? Hadn't she carried a rucksack packed with smuggling goods? All she had now that mattered were the two bottles of water and a small pouch of food—some dried prunes, a few lumps of sugar, a few husks of bread. If only it were possible to hoard a breath of air . . .

The quickest way out of Nalevki was through the lofts to Kurza

Street. The numbers in the shelter swelled to suffocation; the air thickened with sweat and dust and smoke. If the fumes had come this far, how long before the Germans would follow?

Night descended like a redeemer. When the Germans withdrew beyond the ghetto walls, they crawled out of the cellar as if released from bondage. The smoke stung their eyes, but the air was cool, a gust of fresh life. The idea of returning to the cramped cellar was hard to bear. But the few shelters left must be as jammed as this one.

The fire was so close. What if it reached her during the day? The attic passageways could no longer be relied on. To run through the streets in broad daylight was to become a target for German sharp-shooters. Why not now, while it was dark and there was still a chance?

Golda went to the street. Some people were running *away* from Kurza, others were running *to* Kurza. One said he was going *to* Gensia, another was coming *from* Gensia. They ran like poisoned mice and burrowed into the cellars. If they didn't know what to do, how could she know? Her survival instinct, which Pintshe had always admired so much, was failing her—there was no longer any way to survive. Let the others gasp for air like trapped animals, let them bury themselves in their airless tombs. She would find some open space with air and sky around her and wait for whatever was destined.

High above, a full Passover moon. Tongues of fire threw a dawn-like haze over the night. The *rat-tat-tat* of distant machine guns reached Golda's ears and shook her out of her paralysis. She lurched forward, ran through streets, leaped down a flight of stairs to another bunker, pounded with both fists on the heavy door.

•   •   •   •   •

The cellar was dense with smoke. Although the roof had barely caught fire, the ventilation shafts drove the thick, gray-black smoke quickly down into the room. Choking, gasping, they were forced up into the courtyard while the German patrols were still making their rounds in the ghetto. Not until night fell did they dare go into the street.

Walls of fire on all sides. This could hardly be a result of haphaz-ard bombings. No, this was systematic, deliberate extermination of the ghetto. Soon the flames would reach into every corner, consume every street, burn everything. Everything! Golda ran with one group, tore away, ran with another group in the opposite direction. A hail of bullets. She ducked into a blackened ruin, pressed against the wall.

"'*Raus, 'raus,* everybody out!"

A dark figure moved out of the shadows, arms raised high. A burst of gunfire, and it slumped to the ground. The crackle of bullets echoed in all directions.

• • • • •

The Germans were leaving. Had they not seen her? Had they not heard her breathe? From the opposite wall, a shadow detached itself, ran out into the street. Golda remained riveted to her place. At least she still had her food and water.

• • • • •

An overpowering stench assailed her as she neared the cellar. She steeled herself and crawled in. The sound of scampering paws made her flesh crawl. Rats in a burning ghetto? Weren't they supposed to be the first to flee? With each step she took, puffs of feathers from torn featherbeds billowed around her, attacked her like locusts, settled on her brows, her eyelids, tickled her nose.

She grew somewhat accustomed to the stench, but the continuous swish and patter of the rats unnerved her. She clutched her scraps of food to her breast; she beat on the earthen floor with her hand but could not frighten them away. All through the night, she could hear their persistent gnawing. As the first light of dawn penetrated the cellar, she gasped, nearly screamed at what she saw. She shoved a trembling fist into her mouth. Mustn't scream. The Germans were all around. One sound, and she herself would become the rats' next midnight feast. Her body shook uncontrollably, her teeth bit into her fist, but no sound, not even a gasp.

Footsteps approached, paused, moved on. If there were Germans out there, the stink of the corpses must have driven them away. Perhaps she was safer here than in a well-camouflaged hideout. But those rats—when they finished with the dead, they'd start on her. They were huge, fat, and so many of them!

Golda clambered out of the ruin and ran blindly. Just as abruptly, she stopped, almost losing her balance. Where was she running to? The street was an inferno. Black smoke, sheets of flame, falling debris all around. Was she the only one left alive? She would scream. If Jews heard, good. If only Germans heard, what did it matter, anyway?

She picked her way along the blackened skeletons of gutted buildings, the sound of gunfire in the distance, the dull crash of fire-ravaged hulks collapsing on all sides. She trudged on, not recognizing any of the streets. She came upon some dead Jews—women, children, men—and barely avoided stepping on them. Dear God, was there no one left?

Footsteps. She turned. One man, alone in the night. He had to be a Jew. A living Jew! She ran to him, fell on his neck and burst into tears. He drew back with a groan of pain. She looked at him more closely. His hair was singed, his clothing charred, he smelled of—scorched flesh? She drew her bottle of water. She watched him drain it dry but could not bring herself to stop him.

Leaning on her, moaning with every step, he dragged himself along as they climbed over the rubble blocking the streets. No, they were not the last Jews in the ghetto. Some came running toward them. "Where to?" they asked, and kept running. The real question was: What for?

Was it the brilliance of the flames or the blackness of the smoke that had wiped out the division between night and day? Morning fell upon them as if it had been waiting in ambush. The man leaned heavily upon her, slowing her down. Suddenly a burst of gunfire, German commands, and on both sides of the street, houses aflame or starting to burn.

She ran into a house. The roof was already in flames. The cry of a child led her to a cellar doorway, where a gust of ovenlike air struck her in the face. Inside it was black as pitch.

The injured man still clung to her. A whole bottle of water gone. He should have known better. She had dragged it around, denying herself one drop, and now she was dying for a sip to wet her tongue. Falling beams collapsed with a roar on the upper floors. The fire was moving closer. Could they hold out here until dark?

"The second floor is on fire," a lookout reported.

"Where will we hide?"

"The fire's only at the second floor. It'll take time for it to get all the way down here."

Another lookout came running in from the street, bursting with good news. "The Polish underground have attacked the Germans at the ghetto walls. Our resistance sparked a Polish uprising, and it's spreading throughout the country. The Allies are parachuting weapons in."

"This time the Nazis have gone too far. Now they'll pay dearly, just wait and see."

"Sure, we knew it would happen. The world won't just stand by and let this barbarism go on."

Golda listened as their excited cries mingled with the crackling of the flames above them. They were doomed here, all of them. Still, it was good to know the world was not simply watching in silence.

The fire had not yet burned down to the cellar, but the smoke rolled in thickening layers. With each passing minute, more timbers gave way. Part of the ceiling caved in with a thunderous crash. Flailing arms, shuffling feet, cries, groans. Wasn't there an opening anywhere? A clearing to crawl through? A cloud of fiery parching dust hung in midair as the flames licked at the gaping boards.

The ghetto was ablaze, and out of each flaming hulk came the horrifying smell of scorched human flesh. Some survivors were being led away with their hands over their heads. Where to? The cemetery, to be shot? The Umschlagsplatz, to be deported?

•　•　•　•　•

The Umschlagsplatz had not changed; only the surrounding area was different. There was no longer a ghetto to escape to.

One German let slip a secret: they were to be sent to Skazisk. Could it be true?

Why not? Schultz's shop had been transferred to Skazisk. The Germans of course would need all the workers they could get now. Golda's mania for holding on to all her work cards might turn out to be—yes, Schultz's expired card was still in her pocket. Was it fate? She had never really believed it was all over for her, not even here, right next to the trains. No, she did not see death before her, she felt life pulsing in her veins. She would—she must—"Even with the sword at your throat you must continue to hope," she remembered, a phrase from some holy book.

2

The doors of the cattle cars slid open to a blast of fresh air and the sounds of shouted orders:

"*Heraus!* Out!"

Germans, Ukrainians, guns, clubs, leather whips. "*Schnell!* Fast! Move!"

Skazisk? A whip slashed Golda's back, a club smashed against her head. She staggered, clawed the air, regained her balance. Mustn't fall . . . she would be trampled under thousands of stampeding feet. The shouts of the floggers and the flogged, the barking of enraged dogs, the whining scream of well-aimed whips, the pounding of hearts and shuffling of feet all blended into one sharp, mad, staccato rhythm, which halted abruptly as they were brought up short before a barbed-wire fence.

"*Frauen, rechts austretten*—women, step to the right!"

Scrambling, colliding in a tangle of arms and legs, the women were herded to the right. In the confusion, several men were carried along but were quickly weeded out.

To the right? In the ghetto the condemned were always sent to the left. But why were they separating the women from the men?

"Forward, march!" The command was to the men, who were prodded along in ragged formation. All of a sudden, an explosion—flying metal, clumps of earth, bits of human flesh, patches of gray and black from German uniforms, screams.

The watchtower opened fire. A grenade? Yes, a ghetto fighter had managed to sneak it in with him. No good would come of this.

"*Strip!*"

Silence—dreadful, palpable. No one stirred.

A hundred mouths bellowed at once:

"*Undress! Strip!*"

Whips arched, bullets whistled past Golda's ears, blood ran over her arm. Her own? Was she standing on her own two feet, or was she suspended in air by the pressing mass herded together like sheep in a pen?

"MAMA!" The word cut through the air like the wail of a siren, and the quiet shattered into wild screams. Dogs charged with bared, ravenous teeth; flashing whips tore away ribbons of cloth and bits of flesh. Red—everything was red! Spurting blood, dripping canine jaws, leather gleaming red, cavernous red mouths blaring:

"Strip! Strip!"

An eerie silence descended as the last of the garments fell to the ground. Hands fluttered desperately here, there, not knowing what to cover first. A gate was flung open, bare feet ran through, as if to escape from nakedness. The clear light of day cut at their naked bodies. The very air, hushed and still, seemed naked without the screams.

• • • • •

The sun was low in the western sky when they drove another transport of women into the compound. Golda pushed herself against the rush of bodies to keep herself from being jammed against the fence. The barbed wire must be charged with electricity, and she was almost on top of it.

Electrocution, instant death. So what? Better than the gas chamber. But she kept pushing against the crowd. Strange, the newly arrived women were naked too, but all day long, men were marched by, still fully clothed. Had the grenade frightened the Germans? They must be delivering the men straight from the cars to the gas. Weren't the men putting up any resistance? If so, only briefly. As soon as they were herded into the buildings, the screams and the shots ceased; even the dogs stopped barking until the next transport arrived.

Night fell with a chill wind. Why were they being kept there so long? There were no guards down here, only up there in the distant watchtowers. They knew that naked women would not try to escape. Please God, let them put us into the gas chambers before daylight comes . . .

What sort of mad thought was that? As long as she was not in the gas chamber, there was still hope—the trees on the other side of the fence there looked like a small wood. Where did it lead?

A beam from a tower searchlight sliced the night and moved off in its probing circuit, the blackness closing quickly behind it. Here was the path leading to death. There—what could there be but more barbed wire on the other side? Probably another camp. Could it be worse than this one, on the very threshold of the gas chambers? But there were guards with machine guns up there. What if they saw?

So what? Let them shoot!

Golda started her way toward the fence. No one seemed annoyed or angry: a mass of motionless, mute, shivering bodies. She bumped accidentally against someone. The woman stumbled, fell against the barbed wire, picked herself up without a sound. No electric current!

She had seen the wires before nightfall, but now could not remember how apart the strands were. She could easily get caught in the barbs and not be able to move one way or the other. Unless— what if she dug underneath the wire?

If she had something to dig with . . .

Golda dropped to her knees and dug her nails into the grass under the fence. She stood up and turned to the woman beside her. "Are you the one I pushed? I didn't mean to hurt you. I was trying to get to the fence. We could dig under there and get out. It will go much faster if we both do it."

The woman did not answer.

"Come on! There isn't much time."

No response. Golda grabbed the woman's arm and shook her. "It's dark now. We're not being watched. We've got to try—"

"They'll shoot," the woman finally muttered.

"So you won't live to go into the gas? Get down and dig!" Golda hissed, and crouched to the ground. The woman remained standing. Golda grabbed her leg and pulled her down. The woman moved close against her, trembling. Golda tore out a clump of grass by the roots, dug deeper and scooped out handfuls of soil. Underneath the sod, the earth was soft and easier to loosen. After a while Golda felt another pair of hands near her own.

"It won't stay dark for long. We've got to hurry, but stay absolutely still when the searchlight passes over us."

Only this morning she'd been rushing headlong toward the gas chamber to escape from her nakedness, and now, naked as the day she was born, she was trying to escape.

Dig! Don't think! Just dig!

The woman uttered a stifled scream and sat up. Golda continued to scratch at the earth. "What's wrong?"

"My whole nail broke off," the woman whimpered.

"Dig!"

"It hurts so bad I could die . . ."

"If you don't dig, you'll die for sure. What's your name?"

"Leah."

"Dig, Leah, a tiny bit more, and we'll be able to crawl through."

"It still won't help."

"It's worth a try. Is a bullet worse than the gas chamber? Dig, Leah."

Golda reached out and tugged at someone standing near her. "Help us dig—we're trying to get out!" The woman did not respond. Leah gasped each time she dug her fingers into the earth.

"Don't be afraid to cry, Leah. It's a sign you're still alive."

"My fingers are bleeding. The pain—"

"Look at them, Leah, all those people standing around. They're not crying. They've lost their spirit along with their clothes. Dig, Leah!"

•   •   •   •   •

Golda flattened her back against the ground and pushed herself under the fence. Her hair caught in the wire. She dug her heels into the earth and pushed; a tuft of hair stayed on the wire. Don't get stuck; keep moving! A barb gashed her breast. Her lips parted in agony, but the scream died in her throat. A bow of light arched near her as if to impale her on its beam. She shut her eyes and lay still. She sensed the beam pause above her, relentless, cruel, invading. God, let them not see the tunnel!

An eternity? A moment? The red haze receded from her closed eyelids. She opened them. The light was a moving finger in the distance.

Not a sound, not a shot—they hadn't seen her!

Why hadn't she kept her eyes open in that accursed light—she would have seen where to move and not cut herself to ribbons.

•   •   •   •   •

They lay on the other side of the fence, motionless, listening. Only the leaves rustled in the wind. On hands and knees, they began to crawl. A streak of light from the mobile reflector—they threw themselves flat on the ground. The beam moved slowly over them, touched every pore of their naked bodies and glided away. On their stomachs, they slithered through the coarse grass. The dense blackness began to fade. On the horizon, to the right, a vermilion sliver appeared in the sky. Daylight was advancing upon them slowly, silently, like a murderer stalking his victim.

"On your feet, quick! Hurry!"

Damn! How had that Leah got ahead of her? And why was she screaming like that? Now they were finished!

Golda freed Leah's bleeding hand from the barbed wire. Behind them, the watchtowers. Ahead, a new fence. To the right, the ever-brightening sky.

"Trap! A death trap!" Leah cried, and sank to her knees.

"Get up!" Golda urged, tugging at her arm.

"O God, what do you want of me?"

"It's getting light! We'll have to hide here somewhere until dark."

* * * * *

A trenchful of bodies and stacks of lumber. A mere touch of the finger set all the boards quivering. Golda moved toward the trench.

"What if they come to fill it in? What if they take them out to be burned?" Leah refused to move.

"Leah, for the love of God, we can't just stay here!"

The silence was riddled by a deafening burst of gunfire, an eruption of shouts. Golda dived into the ditch, Leah close behind. The uproar subsided as quickly as it had begun; again everything was still, as if nothing had happened. Silence, the silence of the dead—except for their own trembling bodies. For those women back there in the field—she'd have been better off to die with them. In the ghetto she had been alone among the dead, but apart from them. Here—broad daylight and the silence of death. Corpses, cold, remote, alien as stones, and—God forgive her—so repulsive . . .

How could she even think it? They were Jews, her sisters and brothers! She had to stay calm. She mustn't shake so! Just let the night come. Obstacles, no matter how many, could also be overcome.

Clatter of boards. Without seeing them, Golda knew that the workmen had come; they were dragging away the planks from the pile. All she heard was the rasp of metal against wood; not a sound from the mouths of the laborers. The sun was already warm and red on her eyelids when Golda heard footsteps near the trench.

"Pretty soon we'll be lying here ourselves," she heard someone say.

"Shut your dirty mouth!" came the hissed reply. "Do you think I could forget that for one minute?"

Close by, someone was busily moving about. She peeked through the slit of one eye. The workmen were putting straps around the corpses, piling them up and hauling them away. She would be burned alive! Her eyes shot open as if the lids had been burned off; a searing heat flashed through her body as if she were already engulfed in flames. She started to sit up—a uniformed guard stood over the trench. Her eyes pressed shut. One minute passed, another. No movement in her direction. She took a deep breath. Thank God, he hadn't seen her.

A tug at her leg. A leather strap swung over her face. Two terror-stricken eyes stared down into her own for a paralyzing second and instantly turned as if scalded by her gaze. Another moment and the strap was thrown around the body beside her.

The workmen moved cautiously toward the other end of the long trench. Someone swore in a mixture of German and Ukrainian. "Get moving, you lazy Jew bastards! You call this work?"

Were they deliberately delaying, trying to give her a chance? But the guard must have frightened them; they moved closer. Wait! A body was placed beside her. It was warm . . . Leah! In a few minutes the men returned and piled several dead bodies on top of them.

"Who's going to carry the heavy ones?" the guard demanded angrily. A whip cracked and found its mark but the scream was far away.

A break in the work. Midday? Something was moving up there. Golda cautiously opened one eye and peered through the tangle of limbs. She shuddered. Directly above her, naked buttocks squatted over the edge of the ditch. Who would do such a vile thing? But from beyond the bare rump, almost inaudible, came a whisper: "On the other side of the fence lies freedom . . . run to the woods, tell them what's happening here . . ."

She longed to see his face, but his voice vanished as suddenly as it had come. Hope stirred once more but quickly dissolved in doubt. If escape from this place were really possible, why didn't he too hide among the dead?

Evening. The men were lined up and the count began. Of course! If anyone was missing, there would be a search. Another count, a search again; it would go on and on. How good it was to lie among the dead and not be counted. . . .

• • • • •

Night. Crawling, sprinting, lying prone when the beam of light threatened, slowly gaining ground. Golda and Leah finally reached the fence—and almost stumbled over a board. They had not seen it yesterday. The workmen must have forgotten it. Golda dug her nails into the grass. The earth was packed hard and enmeshed by thickly gnarled roots. Impossible to dig here.

"Wait, that board!" Golda whispered. "The men must have left it for us! Help me lean it up against the fence." Golda held it while Leah tried to climb up. She wobbled and fell back. "You can't do it if you crawl. Run, run!" Leah didn't budge. Impatiently, Golda moved back a few steps, ran swiftly up the plank and jumped, landing on the other side of the fence.

"Don't just stand there," Golda commanded through her teeth. "Come on, or I'll go on without you!"

With no one to steady the board, Leah found it even more difficult. She burst into tears. Golda turned and walked away. The barbed wire clanged, the board crashed, and Leah tumbled over the fence with a thud. Golda hurried back and pulled at her arm.

"Get up! Hurry!"

Leah gasped. "I can't. My knee!"

Golda spun around and started running. A few moments later she heard Leah hobbling behind her.

Guns fired, and the outline of the trees appeared against the night sky. Running as fast as they could, the two women entered the woods.

• • • • •

The pebbles on the road cut their mangled feet worse than the underbrush in the woods, but it was easier not having to watch out for trailing branches and hidden stumps. There was still no moon, no stars, only the thick, impenetrable blackness. Did this road lead away from the camp, or back to it?

Noise in the distance. Golda pulled Leah off the road and hunched down behind some bushes fringing the woods. The night air cooled the perspiration on Golda's skin. After days without water, how could her body still produce moisture? From the drops of dew she had licked off the leaves in the woods?

A metallic clang; iron wheels on gravel. A peasant's cart? Golda bent her head to the ground and listened. A steady crunch of wheels, the rhythmic sound of hoofbeats. The darkness was fading to a murky gray. She ran behind a tree and peered cautiously around it. Yes, there it was, a horse and wagon. The animal moved sluggishly, and the distance seemed to lengthen as she watched. It was getting relentlessly brighter, and here she stood, stark naked. A swaybacked horse came into view, pulling a weather-beaten old wagon. An aged man sat nodding on his perch. Leah's head bobbed up from behind a shrub, and Golda put a cautioning finger to her lips. Suddenly, the sound of her own voice frightened her:

"*Gospodarzu*—master, sir!"

The peasant reined in the horse and looked around. Not a soul in sight. He snapped the reins and the horse started slowly forward again.

"Sir! Please!"

The old man looked to the right, to the left, and quickly crossed himself.

"I ran away from Treblinka—I'm naked—"

The peasant scratched his head under his cap and crossed himself again. Golda poked her head out from behind the tree. The old man could not see her. The measured clip-clop of the horse's hooves was out of beat with her racing heart. She ran onto the road.

The peasant tugged at the reins and brought the horse to an abrupt halt. He slipped out of his jacket and threw it to Golda. She grabbed it and covered herself.

"There are two of us, sir—" She pointed to Leah looking out at them from behind the bush.

The old man took hold of a sack, emptied its contents into the wagon, and threw it to the side of the road.

"Help us, sir."

"Get away—they're all over the place."

"Without clothes? How far could we get?"

The peasant frowned and scratched his head again. "People say there are Jews in the woods near Parchew. Hide here till dark. I'll bring you something to wear."

"And something to eat," Leah begged.

"And a little water," Golda pleaded.

•   •   •   •   •

They read the signposts as they passed: KOSOV, SOKOLOV. There had been other towns and villages. They had lost track of time, walking by the side of winding roads and crossing tangled fields. If only they could meet another friendly person like that kind peasant. Most of the time, doors were slammed in their faces. Sometimes they were chased by eager bounty hunters. The Germans were offering ten kilos of sugar and two liters of whiskey for every Jew handed over to them, dead or alive.

•   •   •   •   •

Night again. Stomachs growling with hunger, feet lacerated and sore, they were on still another road. Every step sent agonizing pain through their empty intestines and up into their heads. Leah limped to the edge of the road and sat down.

"We don't have a chance."

"Come on," Golda pleaded. "As long as it's dark, we can walk on the road."

"We don't have a chance," Leah insisted and didn't budge.

"What do you want of me?" Golda cried in despair. No, it was the other way around: What did *she* want of that poor soul? She just had to keep going, and who else did she have but Leah?

Her skin tingled. Something, somebody—close by—a whispering sound—she dug her fingers into Leah's hair, dragged her into a field and sank down among the tall stalks. Running feet! Rifle fire! It was over in an instant. She lay rigid, trying not to breathe. The dying stars faded one by one. Nothing stirred but the swaying stalks of grain and her own quivering body. She stretched out her arms and felt the ground around her. Where had Leah disappeared to?

In a ditch at the edge of the road, she found her. Golda flung herself down. Leah! Leah! The body was cold, clammy, repugnant, like the ones back there in the trench.

"Leyishe!" Golda wept. "When I begged you to run, you wouldn't move. When you should have stayed down, you ran."

• • • • •

Gray dawn. Golda lifted her head and looked at Leah—still not a drop of blood. She turned her over and ran her fingers over the skin—no sign of a wound. Nothing but the icy stare saying for the last time, "Leave me alone. . . ."

Golda sprang out of the ditch. Enough of dead bodies! Enough! Enough!

Wheels on the dirt. The first of the peasants out on the road. She leaned against a signpost. If Leah had died without a bullet, maybe she would too. Let them come. Wearily, she opened her eyes and the words leapt at her:

PARCHEW

48 KILOMETERS

Parchew? Oh God! Parchew!

A military truck sped by, covering the road with a cloud of dust. The particles drifted down, the top of the post came out of the cloud, and slowly the sign spread itself before her eyes—"Parchew: 48 Kilometers." The Jewish partisans—only forty-eight kilometers!

3

What the devil were they staring at? They had come to work in the fields; let them work. Why were they following her with scoffing eyes as if she had sprouted horns? She remembered a Russian plane the Germans had caught in the cross beam of their searchlights one summer night. That's how these peasants had her now, pinned in the hostile beam of their eyes. In a moment someone would run toward her, point an accusing finger and scream Zhidova! Jew! Or come at her with an upraised pitchfork. She would be better off on the open road.

As she approached the road, she heard the sound of distant engines—an advancing motorcade. Golda hesitated a moment, retreated into the field, and dropped to her knees amid the stalks.

But Parchew was so close! She could not afford to lose a whole day hiding in the grain. She crawled along in the furrows, tearing her skin on the stubble and broken glass. After a while she stopped, listened, but heard only the buzzing of insects. Nobody was after her. Peering through the stalks, she could see the edge of the field, but the dark outline of the woods was still far away on the horizon. It seemed no closer than when she had first discerned it yesterday across the expanse of grain, and her heart leapt with hope. She had walked and crawled, but the wooded horizon only seemed to recede.

•   •   •   •   •

The darkness in the distance must be the Parchew woods. But why take a chance now that her goal was in sight? The roads were alive with Germans and the fields with hostile peasants. She would rest here for a while. She broke off the heads of a few husks and squeezed the kernels out with her teeth. The grain was not yet ripe, but it was better than the bitter grass.

Again she studied the dark outline on the horizon: it began to melt into the darkening sky. She trudged on. The hunched contours of village huts began to emerge out of the dense blackness one by one. A dog barked, and soon all the dogs in the village were yelping in a cacophonous choir. She stumbled over something and fell. A trough? She plunged her hands into it. It was empty, but she managed to scrape off some of the swill left by the pig.

After all the roots and bitter grass she had consumed, the bits of chaff and cooked potato peelings made a delicious feast. She scraped and ate until a light came on in the hut.

•   •   •   •   •

The twitter of waking birds announced the start of another day. How many mornings and nights had passed since she had entered these woods? She stumbled through the thick summer undergrowth, trying to memorize landmarks. Was this the same fallen tree she had seen before? The same clearing she had already passed? No trace of a human footprint anywhere, much less a sign of any partisans. Surely they would camp in a dense area like this one. She would find them deeper in the forest. She mustn't tire, mustn't give up.

The woods were thinning. Was she imagining it? Voices! Human voices! She ran forward. Among the trees, meandering toward her, was a gray, winding ribbon—a road.

• • • • •

The rain stopped. The wind whipped her muddy dress against her body until it seemed glued to her wet skin; the nipples of her shrunken breasts jutted through the fabric. She felt naked, exposed. How could she show herself like this in a village?

Night after night she had foraged for food, but lately she hadn't even scared up the scrapings in a pig's trough. She would have to leave the woods in the middle of the day, come what may, or else her churning belly would consume itself.

A shred of sunlight thrust its way through a rip in the clouds. She stuck her tongue out at the ragged ray and just as quickly drew it back. Wisps of vapor rose from her sodden dress. Yes, that's what she would do, walk into the village in broad daylight. What was there to lose? Parchew, her great hope, had turned into a wild-goose chase. She had been in the woods around Parchew and found nothing. To stay alive all alone was worse, a lot worse, than to die along with the others. Yes, she would go to the village as soon as the sun had dried her dress, if her legs would carry her that far. No strength to go on, no strength to put an end to the whole ghastly business. Leah had more sense.

• • • • •

A dog leapt at her before she reached the door. She held him off with her stick, pleading from a distance. "A crust of bread, a potato! Something to eat!"

"Go away, old hag! Beat it!" the woman shouted from the doorway.

What had happened to the peasants? What had this abominable war done to them? In the old days, when she used to spend summers in the countryside, the peasants had never turned a beggar away. She remembered—when an old beggar, a *dziad,* came to a door, he would chant some sort of incantation. Where was she to learn a Christian prayer? All she knew was that it ended with "amen."

A troop of noisy children from a nearby house poured into the street, stopped short, stared at her, their mouths dropping open, their eyes wide. She stiffened. How could she get away from so many children at once?

"Look, Crazy Mary!" a small boy screeched.

"Cuck-oo!" another trilled.

"Cuck-oo!" came the cry all around her.

A snubnosed, pigtailed girl tossed a pebble through the air. It grazed Golda's shoulder. Immediately, a hail of pebbles rained down on her to the rhythmic chant of "Crazy! Crazy! Cuck-oo!"

Crazy! Cuck-oo! The delighted lilt of the childish singsong surged in through her nerve ends to rouse an answering lilt in her spirit. She felt the knots in her limbs relax. "Ba-a-a!" She stuck her tongue out at them. The children squealed with laughter. She stamped her feet, she grunted and crowed and bleated. The children howled in glee. She flopped down in a puddle near the pump, splashing and kicking.

"Bread, a little piece of bread, something to eat," she cackled.

Bits of bread, hardened crusts struck her face, her arms, landed at her feet. Golda chewed and grinned broadly at her benefactors. Let them taunt her, chase her, scream insults at her. Let them laugh their heads off. If she was crazy, she didn't have to say any prayers, she didn't have to utter one single sensible word. If she was crazy she could come and go at any time.

·   ·   ·   ·   ·

Near her shelter in the woods, Golda discovered a pool of stagnant rainwater. She pulled the lice-infested dress over her head and knelt to wash, but the foul muck encrusting her pores would not dissolve. Maybe it was better, more suited to her role. A shopkeeper had chased her. "Get out, you mangy hag, before you contaminate my place!" People turned away from her in revulsion, gave her a wide berth when she appeared in the village street, but they didn't harm her. What matter if some of the food they threw at her landed in the mud? Bread crusts, potato scraps, sometimes even pork rinds—she wasn't going hungry any more.

Today she overheard one of them ask another: "Why does a creature like that even want to exist?" She knew why. Every filthy lice-ridden fiber of her body knew why—to survive.

The leaves began to turn, the days grew shorter. Golda found a small rise in the woods surrounded by dense shrubbery, a tiny glade amid a thicket. She stuffed all the crevices in the wall of bushes with bits of tin, rags, twigs—anything she could lay her hands on. She wove a kind of mat from pine boughs, plastered it with mud, and fashioned a roof. Heaps of dry leaves and pine needles stuffed into an old sack stolen in the village formed a comfortable enough bed.

Weary from long hours of work, Golda stretched out in her new dwelling, proud of her accomplishment. Here she would be snug and safe when the winter storms blew up. Her eyelids grew heavy. She was floating up, up on tinted clouds, higher, higher, above the rows of houses lining both sides of the street. Novolipki Street? A ripple of laughter like a fountain in a summer garden . . . voices, gentle, familiar voices . . .

With a start, she swept an enormous red ant from her face and tore the delicate web of her dream to shreds. Her eyes opened to behold the darkness of the shelter.

Only a speck, a black patch in the dark woods, a tiny ripple in an endless sea of trees, fields, villages, stretching as far as—as far as Warsaw. She had only to shut her eyes and she was home—Warsaw.

4

An early fall. Although it was still quite mild in the autumn wind, the ground had turned into a sea of slime. Golda eyed the bundle of rags she had collected. Pity to use them now. She would need them to bind her feet when the snows fell. No sense wasting them on mud. She left for the village, barefoot as usual. She had trudged only a short distance, her feet sinking into the mud, when something sharp stabbed through the callused sole of her left foot. Just her stupid luck! With all that space to walk on, she would pick the one spot with broken glass. She examined the foot. Not too deep. The blood was flowing freely, so no glass had remained inside.

A shiny fragment glinted up at her through the slime. A broken piece of mirror she realized with horror when she picked it up. She flung it as far away from her as she could and fled. It would do her no good to see herself in a mirror, not if she wished to survive.

As if pulled by some unseen hand, she turned, walked back, carefully estimated the distance of her throw, and knelt down in the grass. She searched and found the jagged bit of glass. She stuck it back into her pocket and walked quickly back to her shelter, where she thrust it deep among the leaves of her bed.

What had gotten into her? She had been on her way to the village to beg for food. What had possessed her to pick up the mirror? To succumb to such nonsense after all she'd been through—she must have really lost her mind. If she didn't hurry she wouldn't get back from the village before nightfall. But her feet were rooted to the ground. Her hand—as if it had a will of its own—began to rummage among the leaves, found the glass, and held it to her bosom.

•   •   •   •   •

A mirror, the large, full-length mirror in her bedroom, a room bathed in sunlight. She was brushing her hair, admiring the reflection of her milk-white face. In the mirror she saw the bedroom door open slowly as Shiya tiptoed in. He moved stealthily behind her, playfully covered her eyes with his hands.

"Guess who?"

"Who?"

"Guess!"

"I can't!"

"The door's unlatched, a thief could sneak in."

"Let him."

His arms encircled her tightly. What strength he had in those slender arms. She could hardly breathe. Their eyes met in the glass, and he blushed at his boldness. His arms relaxed, but his large adoring eyes couldn't disguise their wonder, as if he were seeing her for the first time.

•   •   •   •   •

The whole thing had begun when they were still children, when Shiya's grandfather, the rabbi of Klerotsk, had visited Golda's family in Prinsk. He and Golda's father were distant relatives and close friends. Before long, the two rabbis were deeply immersed in learned argument. Golda's mother served them tea. Behind her trailed Golda, shyly offering a plate of cookies.

"This is my Goldele," her father beamed.

"How old are you, Goldele?" the rabbi of Klerotsk asked kindly, stroking her hair with gentle fingers.

"I turned six on Hanukkah."

"My grandson Shiya turned six on L'ag b'Omer."

Golda grew up to be as tall as her father, with a thick golden braid that hung almost to her waist, enormous blue eyes, and a radiantly fresh complexion, as if she had grown up in the countryside among fields of golden grain instead of on the Shulgass, in Prinsk, and the crowded Panska Street, after her father accepted the rabbinic position in Warsaw.

One day, her father introduced her to a guest. "This is Berish Heshl—he is the son of the rabbi of Klerotsk. You remember the rabbi? Berish and his son, Shiya, will be spending the summer vacation in Shwider, near Warsaw, and so will we.

In Shwider, where Golda met Shiya for the first time, he was suntanned and handsome. They strolled through the woods, and Shiya spoke of nature, of golden flowers nodding in the breeze. As his words flowed, the countryside became even lovelier. She tried to match his elegant phrases and was delighted that almost every observation she ventured led him to some biblical quotation. After he left, he wrote her such beautiful, poetic letters that she was frequently moved to tears of happiness.

She did not see Shiya again until Hanukkah. He came to visit on her birthday and presented her with a string of exquisite pearls. But this was a different Shiya. The summer tan had worn off; he was pale, drawn, whiter than the pearls. If his eyes had not been so dark, they would hardly have been visible behind the thick lenses.

Golda's mother took her into the bedroom and locked the door. "Goldele, your father and I have talked it over. Shiya is obviously not a very strong young man. If that worries you, we can reconsider the whole thing. You are as robust as a peasant."

"If Shiya is weak, he needs a strong wife to look after him," she had replied.

Her mother's face had positively glowed. "Your father thinks the world of him."

Summer arrived early that year. At their wedding in June, Shiya again had the same tanned and healthy look as when they had first met.

After their marriage, Shiya set up a small printing shop for letterheads, wedding invitations, and the like. But the competition was brutal. The other printers worked long hours, set their own type, operated their own presses. Shiya, weak and frail, could not tolerate the paper dust. When he fed the press, he would drip with perspiration and his legs would grow weary on the pedals. By autumn he began running a light fever almost every night, and the doctor advised him to go to Otwock for a complete rest.

Golda, five months pregnant, took over responsibility for the business. Evening after evening, she came home exhausted to an empty house, with only the daily letter from Shiya to cheer her. Sometimes there was a clipping of an article he had written in the *Togblatt;* once, a poem he had written for her. Shiya wrote a great deal during his stay in Otwock, which made her happy. She knew what the writing meant to him, how content he was when he could work all day at his desk, pen in hand.

Shiya's illness and her pregnancy depleted what was left of her dowry. Her father found Shiya a position in the Jewish Community Organization. They would never get rich on his salary, but they never went hungry.

On Sabbath afternoons, all the children and grandchildren gathered at her parents' home. Her mother noticed Golda's sidelong envious glances at her sister Sarah's diamond brooch. "Shiya's Torah and his wisdom are your jewels," she whispered. Golda held little Yossel closer to her breast. "And Shiya's children."

Nenna was the first-born, then came Yossel and Hannele. Nenna was a beauty from the moment she was born, with her mother's blonde hair and blue eyes and her father's finely chiseled features. The grandchildren of the rabbi of Klerotsk and the rabbi of Warsaw would not grow up to be nonentities.

But with the children, the housework became more arduous and the zloty scarce, for, although Shiya was no longer ill, he was not strong enough to work a full day. Golda started a little business of her own. In the evening, when Shiya was home to keep an eye on the children, she went out with a stock of fine linen, silverware, and jewelry supplied by her well-to-do brothers-in-law. Selling was easy for her; collecting the weekly payments was another matter.

After climbing stairs all evening she could barely drag herself home. She would kick the shoes off her aching feet, hoping Shiya would serve her a hot drink, but he was always bent over his desk, buried in his writing. Finally she would get up and boil water, pour herself a glass of tea, and serve him as well.

Yossel was a mischievous youngster, not at all what one would expect from the grandson of that noble scholar in Israel whose name he bore, the rabbi of Klerotsk. From the moment he began to crawl he was a menace: overturning flowerpots, pulling off the tablecloth with all the dishes on it, spilling hot soup all over himself and cold milk on the rug. A little devil. How could the son of delicate, gentle Shiya turn out to be such a roughneck? Nenna would catch cold if you so much as breathed on her. Yossel could run barefoot onto the snow-covered balcony and stay the picture of health.

However, on the rare occasions when he did get sick, he was always in mortal danger. When Nenna came down with scarlet fever she recovered in a few days. But Yossel's temperature rose to forty-two degrees Celsius and he barely survived. The same thing happened with the smallpox. Nenna took sick first and had only a little scar to show for it. Yossel caught it from her and his entire body was covered with sores. It broke her heart. She had to tie his hands to the bed to keep him from scratching himself to shreds.

He was sick, but she had to leave him alone with Shiya nonetheless. In the installment business one could not afford to skip a collection. So Shiya told Yossel stories about Jewish heroes, about brave Jewish children, about King Solomon, who could talk with birds and animals—and eventually Yossel fell asleep. Shiya sighed with relief and went back to his paper-laden desk.

This one night Golda came home late. From the bottom of the stairs she could hear the commotion in the house: Nenna on the floor sobbing, Shiya wringing his hands, and Yossel—in bed, his face raw and bloody. No one had to explain to her what had happened. Shiya had become deeply involved in his writing; the boy had managed to free one hand . . .

Even after that terrible night, she kept the house quiet whenever Shiya was writing. Often, as she lay in bed listening to the scraping of his pen and the shuffling of papers, her mother's words would come back to her: "Shiya's Torah is your crown." Sometimes she felt the crown grow heavy on her head.

Yet, for whom was he writing if not for her? Through his writings, he said things to her that he was too shy to say out loud. He wooed her with his pen, his words embraced her from the page. Moreover, his eyes had a darkly eloquent language all their own. True, his manner was naïve, modest, reserved, like that of a Yeshiva boy, but he knew how to love.

The blouse she had made from an old dress; how he had loved her in it! She had tried it on before the mirror. The blue of the collar around her slender neck reflected the blue of her eyes. Shiya watched from the other side of the room. In the mirror she could see his eyes grow soft, his hands move as if to reach out to her. But no, not in the middle of the day. Nenna might come running into the room. She clenched her fingers to keep herself from caressing him.

• • • • •

Golda had just come home from work. She undressed the children, put them to bed. Shiya was still bent over his desk. She removed the pins from her hair, let the golden mass fall around her shoulders. She would step softly into the study, then he'd—anger built up within her like steam. He shouldn't have said "Leave me alone." Her eyes filled with tears, a sob escaped her throat. He jumped up quickly from his chair, came to her, stroked her hair. Her anger subsided. He'd had a hard day; she knew he did not mean to hurt her. Yet the tears continued to trickle down her face.

"Why can't you understand?" Shiya asked, his voice gentle, consoling.

Through the tears, her eyes glistened. A smile around her lips said, I understand, I have understood for a long time. Shiya was annoyed. Then why did you torment me for nothing? If only he would stroke her hair once more with his long fingers. If only—

Yossel, the little imp, had climbed out of his crib and marched into the study, trailing his blanket. He scrambled into her lap. She hugged him close, kissed his forehead, his sleep-heavy eyes, and crooned, "Yossele, Yossele, my sweet little boy . . . Your papa is a little boy like you, Mama has two sweet little boys . . ."

• • • • •

A sudden pain jolted her. The jagged glass clenched in her fist had cut the skin. Had all of that really happened? Had those two innocents ever existed: gentle, aristocratic Shiya Heshl and his loving and beloved Goldele? Were they any more than a madwoman's delusion?

The wounded hand that had instinctively thrown away the mirror retrieved it hastily. She wiped it on her dress and crawled out of the shelter into the daylight. The image of a madwoman sprang at her, mocking, vengeful. The glass fell to the ground. She stamped on it until her feet bled, but it stayed intact. She searched the ground frantically, found a rock, and smashed it with insane fury until it was nothing but glinting, silvery bits.

What did she want with a mirror? Whom did she hope to find in it? The Golda with the golden hair and the creamy skin? That one had remained in Treblinka. That one had been stripped from her, torn away, hurled to the ground along with her clothes. The other one, the madwoman of the mirror, eaten by lice and covered with scabs, she was alive.

Was it for this she had run naked from Treblinka? For this she had turned herself into a buffoon for the peasants to revile and the children to spit at? This was an ugly, murderous world. She too would become a killer . . . Treblinka had murdered Golda Heshl; she would destroy this festering madwoman in the mirror. Never again would she go to the village. Never!

The dirt on her face moistened and ran in sluggish rivulets down her cheeks. Did she still have tears left? Nenna and Shiya—ashes, long since, ashes. With a face like Hannele's, she and Yossel must surely have been caught, shot. And she had tears for herself?

The mirror had shown her the truth. The mirror would be her salvation. She frantically scooped up the bits of smashed glass, now mixed with earth. She stuffed them into her mouth, ran into the shelter, lay down on her dry leaves. This was where it would end. She tried to swallow. Her tongue thickened, her throat locked. She spat out the mouthful of filth-encrusted glass. No! the mirror image commanded her. What makes you think you've earned such an easy way out? Go on! You must at least find out what really happened at the Wilchinskis.

Grains of glass and sand grated her teeth, but it was not the glass that churned in her belly. Hunger ate at her vitals.

No! She would not go! Nothing could make her take a single step toward the village.

The children . . . maybe, somehow . . . maybe the Wilchinskis had spared them even after the money was gone. Maybe they had found another place. Even the Poles who informed on adults could not easily bring themselves to send children to certain death. Maybe . . .

On his own, Yossel might have got away. But his mother had hung Hannele like a millstone around his neck so that she herself would be free to run. How could she have escaped Treblinka if Hannele had been with her? Clever Golda! She wasn't crazy at all.

She was an accomplished actress. She could play any role! A devoted mother in Warsaw, a madwoman in Przybilovka. Anything, anywhere, so long as it saved her own wretched hide.

5

Winds whipped through the forest with a fearsome roar, tearing great chunks out of Golda's shelter. Snow whirled aloft as if afraid to settle on the shuddering earth. The trees shivered in a violent dance, throwing their white crowns into the air and hurling them down in an eerie cascade as if to bury this interloper in their primeval retreat. Frantically she dug her way out of the lean-to and ran from it as swiftly as her feet could move in the drifting snow. Maybe she would find an open barn, an unlocked grain shed. Let the peasants beat her, chase her, turn her over to the Germans. She could no longer stay here. The howling wind would drive her out of her mind.

The rags on her feet caught in straggling bushes and dragged her to her knees. She struggled to her feet, ran forward clumsily, the raging wind pursuing her, the forest heaving and groaning like a sinking ship. Blindly, she plowed ahead through the rising drifting mounds of snow.

"MAMA!" Her desperate shriek of terror echoed through the deserted forest and sank down together with her into the soft, cold whiteness.

Had the earth split open? Was everything sinking into a white abyss?

A bottomless pit in a snow-covered world . . . and she was sinking into it deeper and deeper. The harder she tried to pull herself out, the deeper she sank. Now she was up to her waist. Her legs were being clamped in white, relentless shackles.

"Help me! Help me! Somebody help me!" Her screams flew into the darkness and were lost in the roar of the cruel wind.

•   •   •   •   •

Not until the first gray light dawned above the treetops did the wind subside. The snowflakes now fell silently, gracefully. Innocent white blossoms covered the ravages of the storm's destructive fury—cruelly severed branches, mangled, uprooted trees—and Golda, held upright in a vise of snow.

"Heh—hev-hevp—" She tried to cry for help, but only unintelligible sounds rose from her throat. Something was towering over her, covering her mouth, stifling her cries. She felt both hot and cold, and in the dark she began to discern the contours of a huge figure. Was she in her grave? Was this the Dark Angel come to summon her soul?

"*Amkho*—one of us?" the man asked.

Her straining eyes could make out only the humps and ridges of an enormous featherbed. This heavy weight on the pillow must be her head. The lump lower down must be the groan that had stuck in her throat. Was there anything beyond that?

Maybe she would be able to see better if she wiped her eyes. Yes, she had eyes too, and they were drenched with tears or sweat—how could she wipe them? Where were her arms, her—

"*Amkho?*" the man asked again and removed his hand from her mouth.

She could see the outlines of the featherbed as it undulated in the darkness. Was there anything underneath it or was she only a dismembered head attached to—

"*Ah yeed*—Jewish?" he insisted.

Her reply was a deep sigh.

"I found you in the snow."

"Where am I?"

"This is my hideout. My name is Hertzke. Don't be afraid. I was covering your mouth only because you were screaming."

"I was?"

"Yes. Before you woke. If anyone hears, we'll all go up in smoke—Bronek, his wife, all of us."

"Bronek?"

"We're in a basement under Bronek's hut. I carried you here. Bronek is a farmer. I'm paying him well for hiding me, but if a passerby hears a scream—"

His voice rose almost to a shout—or did it? Just a moment ago his voice had come to her as if from far away and she could barely make out a word; now it painfully pierced her ears. His words fell heavily upon her, pressing on her eyes. No, she mustn't close her eyes, the world might disappear again . . .

The man had stopped talking but the heaviness still lingered.

Was silence heavy too? This quivering featherbed—it seemed to be breathing. A pinpoint of pain struggled through it and reached her head, piercing and stabbing, but it was a relief—the pain had charted a line below her head.

Oy, Mama! Now she felt it—shoulders, kneecaps, knuckles—they came back and rejoined her body, each one with a new wave of agony.

The man appeared again, bent over her, and held a bottle to her lips. She clamped her teeth shut as the sting of alcohol burned her nostrils.

"Drink. It's good for you."

She sipped slowly. A warm glow began to spread within her, mingled with the merciless stabbing of icy needles and burning skin. Only now were the man's words reaching her mind. *Amkho!* This strange man, this hulking figure whose face she couldn't see was a Jew? She wasn't completely alone?

"The war—what's happening with the war?" she finally asked.

"Practically over. They're getting it from all sides."

If she had been able to escape from the very mouth of the gas chamber, then why not the others? Maybe Nenna? Shiya? And even if Yossel and Hannele had been driven out by the Wilchinskis, couldn't they have been found by such a man as this one? Miracles still happened in this world—one had happened to her.

A prayerful murmur rose to her lips but died in her throat. If the Almighty had any miracles left, He should have revealed them in the ghetto, where German machine guns sowed bullets and reaped death, where His Jews were cut down like wheat under a summer sky, a blue sky smeared with the smoke of blazing houses and the stench of blackened flesh.

And what about Treblinka? Of his own free will, Shiya had joined the condemned there so that he could watch over Nenna. When Nenna had stripped off her clothes and exposed her young breasts to the ogling of arrogant German eyes—what had happened to Shiya then? Did his eyeglasses shatter? Was he struck blind? Did the sky turn red from the wanton outrage? No. The sky stayed blue, while below the victims writhed in mortal anguish.

But she had been spared, so why was she torturing herself? Wasn't it enough that her body was being lashed with thongs of fire and ice? Where was the madwoman of Przybilovka with her gift of oblivion? Or was this the madwoman cunningly turning her thoughts to Treblinka and away from her own pain? That would be real madness!

* * * * *

Her body was a burning mass of agony. Flames seared her legs, swelled, flashed through her bowel, and wrapped her in a sheet of fire. Could there still be living flesh on her frame, a living cell left in her head? The pain throbbed with life, clamped down on her scalp, yanked each strand of hair amid the nits, hummed like beads strung on her exposed nerves. Nothing was left of her breasts but the burning nipples, drawing the shrunken tissue up into red-hot pain. Three precious babies had suckled at those nipples and raised so they could end up—no, God forbid! Three precious babies she had fondled and nestled and raised, and they were found by a Jew like Hertzke and brought to a shelter like this . . .

"Oh God, how it burns . . ."

The man bent over her. "Good. Anything that hurts is alive. How are your feet?"

"They're on fire."

"Good. Very good. I was worried about your feet. In the morning I'll light a candle and have a look. I can't do it now; the light would show through the cracks."

Golda became aware of a scraping sound overhead. A trapdoor opened in the low ceiling, and a shaft of light fell on the man below. He was tall, broad, with a wide stern face and drooping whiskers. Did he have to hide in a cellar, even with a face like a Polish peasant?

Someone lowered a steaming pot, and the trapdoor snapped shut. Again, the scraping sound, as if furniture were being moved.

"Y'think y'can sit up?" the man asked, then thought better of it. "Nah, you'd better stay where you are."

He sat by her side and ladled the soup into her mouth, spoonful by spoonful. She felt the moisture but tasted nothing. She tried to swallow, but the soup gurgled at the back of her mouth and made her gag. The brandy he had forced into her earlier rose in her gullet, and a sudden torrent of foul-smelling vomit splattered them both.

Calmly, gently, he cleaned her up and then attended to himself. Who was this man—a saint? Or only someone conjured up by her feverish brain?

Stifled moans broke through her clenched teeth. Unremitting

pain racked every nerve and fiber of her body. Hertzke sent Bronek for aspirin, but when it was fed to her she could not keep it down. After a time, her moaning gradually ceased and the room became very still. Alarmed, the man bent low over the bed and listened intently. Her breathing was deep, regular. He sat at her bedside in the darkened room, keeping his lonely, patient vigil.

•   •   •   •   •

She was nursing Yossele. The child must be cutting teeth. He was biting both nipples at the same time. How was that possible? Don't, baby, stop it, you're hurting Mama.

•   •   •   •   •

Hertzke pulled back the layers of quilts and blankets he had piled on Golda, took her right hand in his huge one, and asked, "Can y'move your fingers? All of them? Good. Your elbow bends just fine." He took hold of her left hand—the fingers moved easily. He uncovered her feet and ran his hand over them. Yes, she could feel his touch on the soul of the right foot. The left foot? No, not everywhere, parts still felt numb. He squeezed the toes. No, no feeling there, maybe one or two on the left foot, she wasn't sure. Yes, oh yes, they hurt, but she couldn't tell where the numbness ended and the pain began.

•   •   •   •   •

He cut her hair off to the roots. Nothing much he could do about her running nose, her watering eyes, her wheezing chest. If he could only get her to eat properly, the welts and sores on her body would gradually heal. But what about the toes? Some of the toes on the right foot were turning black. They would have to come off. And Bronek would not allow a doctor; they couldn't be trusted, he said.

"Same thing happened to my wife, Kayla, God rest her soul. She was sick, and Bronek wouldn't let me get a doctor. 'What,' he said, 'take Kayla to a doctor? Are you out of your mind, with her black hair and black eyes like a Gypsy?'" Hertzke paused. "She's lying out there near the barn."

"Is there still room near the barn?" Golda asked.

"God forbid. Listen to me. My face is good. No problem with my looks. It's when I open my mouth . . . I used to be kosher butcher, y'know, all my customers were Jews. You speak good Polish? You do? So there you are. I'll carry you, and you do the talking. The only thing is, they know me in this district . . ."

"I'll go alone. Just tell me how to get there."

"Don't be silly. We can't wait till y'can walk. It's a long way from here. Don't worry. Leave it to me."

"Are you crazy? You want to burn my place down? You want to get me arrested?" Bronek shouted more in terror than in anger. He usually hired a horse for plowing and planting; but what farmer in his right mind would need a horse in the middle of winter?

Hertzke stopped arguing. It was useless, and besides, he saw Bronek's point. "It's only eleven kilometers. If we start walking at midnight, we'll get there before dawn."

"How can I walk eleven kilometers?" Golda protested. "I can't even take one step without fainting from the pain."

Hertzke laughed. "Who said anything about you walking? I'll carry you. I've got broad enough shoulders."

* * * * *

Hertzke pounded on the doctor's door. At last a sleep-eyed old woman appeared.

"The doctor isn't here."

"Where is he? When will he be back?"

"Where? Ask the Schwabes. They took him away."

"How far to the nearest doctor?"

"Liptzin. Thirty-three kilometers to the east."

The miracles that happen to me, thought Golda bitterly. I could have just gone to sleep in the white snow like a little bird. But he had to find me, so that now I can rot from the feet up with gangrene.

Hertzke put her down—almost threw her down. He pushed past the old woman and charged into the doctor's house.

* * * * *

Can't she see what I'm going to do? Why doesn't she say something? Hertzke wondered. He laid out the things he had removed from the doctor's cabinet—iodine, alcohol, peroxide. Beside them, he placed a roll of cotton and some sterile gauze. Bronek stood near the table on which Golda was sitting. Each time she emptied the glass of vodka beside her, he refilled it.

"I'll have to strap you to the table," Hertzke apologized.

Golda said nothing.

"Don't be afraid. I know exactly where to cut—I'm an expert butcher."

She watched him take a long sharp knife out of a pan of boiling water. Silently, she gulped down another mouthful of vodka.

"It hasn't spread yet," Hertzke assured her. "You'll eat well and heal fast, and in no time at all you'll be as good as new."

He poured iodine on the open wounds. Golda bit down on her lip with such force that he could see her teeth redden, but not a sound come from her lips. What had happened to her blue eyes? Her eyeballs were red knots of criss-crossed veins. He pulled the bandages tighter. Still the blood oozed through them. "It won't stop bleeding," he groaned.

"It's all right," she wanted to tell him, but the words faded, sank beyond her reach. She felt herself sinking after them . . .

•   •   •   •   •

Again she became aware of the hard table under her back. The leather straps were gone, but her teeth were still embedded in her lower lip as if they had grown there. She raised her head. The bandaged foot was packed all around with snow, pink-marbled snow. Where was he? She looked around. He was stretched out on the bench, holding snow to his face. Had he fainted too?

When Hertzke realized she was awake, he threw down the melting snow and came quickly to her side.

"Feeling any better, Golda?" he asked with a feeble smile.

She barely nodded her head.

"Now we'll have to do the left foot. One toe, the big one. Nothing to it."

Nothing! She began to resent his hearty tone and his forced smile. Did he think he was carving up a cow? Mama, pray for me, and pray that God steady his hand.

• • • • •

The wounds were still draining, but she was feeling better. Her appetite had returned. She ate every last drop of the hot soups and stews lowered through the trapdoor. When the cold weather eased, Hertzke wrapped her in blankets and carried her to the attic where he arranged a spot for her near the window. She needed fresh air and sunshine, he said, if she was to recover completely. She stayed there from early morning to nightfall. Her hair, growing back, now framed her face. Her skin was smooth and clear and showed hardly a trace of the old sores and scabs.

"You're a pretty woman," Hertzke blurted out one morning. Golda blushed to the roots of her new hair. It was not so much his words as her sudden recollection of something he had said soon after he had found her and brought her to his hideout. He had described how he had carried her here and—and rubbed her frozen body all over with snow. She caught her breath as she remembered how she had looked then: her hair a nest of lice, her skin eaten by vermin, her breasts like two empty sacks, her feet swollen and blistered. She felt the shame overwhelming her again. She looked up at Hertzke, caught his admiring eyes studying her, and lowered her lashes.

A simple man, this Hertzke, but certainly no fool. He addressed her with the familiar "you," but somehow she couldn't bring herself to do the same with him. Why? Because he was just a common butcher?

6

"Children? I never had any. We tried everything—doctors, rabbis, quacks, all kinds, but nothing came of it. All her insides, overgrown with fat. That's what the doctors said."

"Never mind," Golda consoled him, "a few children less in Treblinka."

"She liked to eat, my Kayla."

Golda smiled. "I'll grow fat too, with all the food you're pushing at me."

"Yeah," Hertzke nodded. "When we first came here, Kayla, may she rest in peace, got even fatter. She could hardly move. Then she started to lose weight, got so thin her ribs stuck out. That's when her belly began to grow. I thought, that's it; the fat's gone and it's finally happened. We counted the months and prayed for the war to end."

"So she died in childbirth?"

"There was no childbirth. The war didn't end and neither did the pregnancy. It was a sickness, not a baby. Nine months, ten, eleven, her belly got bigger and bigger and she herself got smaller and smaller. She was only skin and bones. Then the pains started. She wasn't even allowed to cry, and no doctor, no nothin'."

"I can imagine how you suffered," Golda said softly.

"I'd have given half my life just to ease her pain," Hertzke sighed. "But enough about myself. Tell me about your husband."

"What can I tell you? A good man—learned, pious, a good father. A writer, he was. Wrote poems, some of them just for me. A gentle man, cultured . . ." Her eyes shone, remembering.

She became aware of Hertzke's darkening face, his uneasiness. What had she said to offend him? Perhaps she shouldn't have mentioned Shiya's knowledge, his refinement. She hadn't said it to belittle Hertzke, God, no. She knew some rabbis who could have used a little of the sensitivity that lay beneath his rough exterior. Not many people would have had the strength, let alone the courage, to do what he had done for her. Was it really the fresh air and good food that was restoring her? Or was it only the passage of time? Perhaps it was Hertzke's ever-present, devoted care. The wounds stopped draining and began to heal. He patiently taught her to walk again, how to balance herself on her heels, and encouraged her whenever she faltered.

"I'll be crippled for life," she groaned.

He looked down at her, started to say something, and merely shrugged his shoulders, as if to say that such foolish talk didn't even warrant an answer.

"But you know these intellectuals," Golda continued in a changed tone. "He was good at writing poems, but when it came to everyday matters—he squandered my dowry in no time. In the end, I had to find a way to support the family and I had to leave him to look after the children. It was awful—he couldn't even boil an egg. Once I left him with Yossel, our son—Yossel had the smallpox at the time—and when I came back, don't ask what I found. Yossel bears the scars to this day."

• • • • •

To this day? Here she sat telling stories about her children. Why wasn't she on her way to Warsaw to find out what had happened to them?

Hertzke wouldn't hear of it. She couldn't even take a proper step yet! He would be glad to go himself, but when it came to speaking Polish, he might as well be mute. "I'll send Bronek."

"Will he go?"

"If you grease the wheel . . ."

"I don't think it will work. The Wilchinskis will resent a total stranger coming to them. They'll deny everything."

"You think I'd send Bronek empty-handed? The color of American dollars will open their mouths."

"They'll keep asking for more."

"So we'll give them more."

"I already owe them a fortune."

"Two children are a *real* fortune."

If she weren't so embarrassed, she would have kissed him. A man who earned his living by slaughtering cows—and yet so gentle. As if what he had done to save her were not enough, he was now looking for ways to save her children. Would Shiya . . . Hush! It was sinful to make such comparisons.

Bronek left for the railway station. Golda curled up near the attic window and followed his footsteps with a prayer. She stayed there long after he had disappeared from view. She stood up, faced the east, and swayed. Shiya used to pray at home that way, wrapped in prayer shawl and phylacteries. When she finally sank down on the straw, Hertzke offered her a slice of bread. She shook her head.

Hertzke, also silent, stretched out at the other end of the attic. He chewed on a straw and bit the ends of his moustache. Was she angry with him? He had sent twenty American dollars with Bronek. Maybe she thought it wasn't enough. That was all Bronek needed to see, that he was loaded with dollars. Then his whole hidden treasure wouldn't be enough to satisfy that peasant's appetite. He should have explained that to Golda before. Now it was impossible to talk to her. If only Bronek would come back with good news.

Bronek did not return until late at night with his story. The Wilchinskis had first denied everything. But when he took the money out of his pocket, Wilchinski had volunteered a few words. Yes, there were these two kids—but he had never known they were

Jews, though come to think of it, the little girl was black as the devil. When the Jews in the ghetto had made their revolt, the boy—Yurek—decided to run away from Warsaw. He didn't have a penny to his name, but he was a cunning lad, knew his way around. He might show up again any day.

"That's what you said yourself," Hertzke tried to comfort Golda. "You told me that Yossel knew his way around."

"He was always very resourceful," Golda readily agreed, eager to pin her hopes on it, but her hopes quickly dissolved. If Yossel would—if Yossel was still . . . would he give up hope that she, that somebody, had survived? He would have kept in touch with the Wilchinskis.

Maybe Bronek had put the twenty dollars in his pocket and never seen the Wilchinskis. He had brought nothing back with him, no proof. But he must have been there. How else would he have known about Yossel being so quick-witted and all the rest of it? Quick-witted, but what could Yossel do with Hannele? She had such a distinct Jewish face.

•   •   •   •   •

Hertzke did have a treasure hidden away somewhere. From time to time he left the hideout and returned with money for food and board.

"Keep the money here? Don't be a child! It would be too easy for Bronek to make himself my heir. And if I hadn't gone out that day, who'd have found you?"

•   •   •   •   •

Where had Hertzke gotten so much money? Before the war butchers had to form partnerships just to buy one cow. The Jews had been so poor that they ate meat only on the Sabbath. How had he gotten so rich on that?

So if he hadn't made his money before the war, maybe he had made it smuggling meat into the ghetto—so what? Wasn't Yossel a smuggler? And hadn't she done it herself? If anything, smuggling food into the starving ghetto was an act of charity. And suppose it wasn't from smuggling at all. Suppose he knew about treasures hidden by deported Jews—who had a better right to inherit them? Certainly not the Germans.

• • • • •

Some weeks later, Hertzke went off in the dead of night, leaving Golda in the attic. He had to get more money, he told her, but he would be back before daybreak. But morning arrived, and he was not back. She could hear Bronek's wife ranting; her voice seemed to come from all directions at once. She cursed the animals, banged the stall gate, swore at the rusty pump handle. The woman seemed to be trying to do all the chores herself. Where was Bronek? Golda dragged herself over to the attic window and looked down into the yard. At this time of day he should be watering the vegetables. Considering Hertzke's fear of Bronek's finding the money, they could not have gone out together. Something was wrong. She peered anxiously down the empty road.

Late in the afternoon, the peasant returned. His wife let loose a long tirade, and soon they were both shouting and quarreling. What were they arguing about?

The day gave way to a moonless night. Golda's legs were numb, her wounds throbbed. She buried her face in the straw and wept.

"God in heaven, have I really sinned so terribly that you must still tease me? If only I had those rotting toes back . . . Have pity on me, fill me with the poison again, every part of me, from my toes to my hair, and let there be an end to it."

Morning seeped through the circular attic window, as forbidding as the endless, sleepless night. Golda sat up and looked out into the gray mist.

"Mama dearest, Mama, I know how you loved Shiya, and Papa too. I know nothing is hidden from those in heaven, not even our innermost secrets. Forgive me, and plead with Shiya to forgive me. Hertzke saved my life and tried to save the children. I am afraid that Hertzke is gone too, and I am left here to die slowly, limb by limb. Plead for me, dear Mama, that I may soon be with you. Pray to the Almighty for your daughter who has been so harshly punished."

Golda heard the creak of the barn door and a clatter of metal. Probably the milk pail. Suddenly there was a commotion: footsteps running in the yard, noises in the barn. Was that the farm wife yelling? Wasn't that Hertzke's voice she just heard? That was crazy—if Hertzke had returned, wouldn't he have come to her first? The farm wife was sobbing, her husband cursing, and Hertzke—it was his voice, she was sure. What was going on? Had the Germans caught him and made him talk?

•   •   •   •   •

When he had got as far as the road, Hertzke looked back at the attic. A light suddenly went on in the house, the door opened, and Bronek came out. Hertzke smiled to himself. The glutton must have stuffed himself with sauerkraut; if he didn't hurry, he wouldn't make it to the toilet.

Hertzke continued on his way. Something rustled behind him— a cat? No, it was footsteps all right, stalking him. He stopped, listened. The footsteps stopped. He started walking. There they were again. He left the road and turned onto a path. Whoever it was, he mustn't let on in which direction he was headed.

He jumped into a ditch and squatted there for a long while. A cricket chirped, a frog croaked, and the only breathing he could hear was his own. He climbed out of the ditch, but as soon as he started walking, the footsteps were behind him again. He walked on until he got into the thick of the woods, then darted behind a clump of trees and waited until he was certain he had finally shaken off his "shadow." But by now it was daylight—impossible to go on. He would have to wait until nightfall again before he could start moving. To save time, he took a side road home—and lost his way in the dark. Another morning was beginning when he saw the outline of Bronek's house at last.

He hurried into the barn, started for the attic, and stopped in his tracks. The cow—bloated like a blimp—was lying on the ground near the trough, which was still full. He ran to get Bronek. There was only one thing they could do to save the cow—lance the stomach to let the gas out.

The farm wife ran up to the attic and knelt beside Golda. "Is it true your father was a holy rabbi? Please, Hertzke says to pray to your father so the cow won't die. Please, the cow is our whole life . . ."

•   •   •   •   •

The cow was well on her way to recovery. The farm wife prepared a sumptuous meal, and Hertzke carried it up to the attic. Famished, he wolfed down the food. Golda ate only the bread. Just this morning she had felt so close to her mother, and here—globs of pork fat floating on the soup. She turned her head away.

"Did they really believe my prayers helped them? It was clever of you to think it up."

"I didn't think anything up. It's the truth. I figured it out: if a lanced cow can never be kosher, it means that it's a serious situation. It was a good cow, it would have been a pity. Your father brought the punishment on them, so I thought it might help if you pleaded with him."

"My father brought punishment . . . Hertzke, what are you talking about?"

"Bronek followed me. If he hadn't, the cow wouldn't have wandered into a meadow and gorged herself on drying hay."

"What's wrong with hay? Isn't it good for cows?"

"When the grass is growing it's good. Then, when the grass is cut and dried into hay, that's good too. But when the grass is cut and left in the fields to dry, it begins to ferment, and that's poison for a cow."

•   •   •   •   •

He shouldn't look at her like that. Only this morning she had begged her mother and father to intercede for her. She could still feel their presence, her prayers still vibrated all around her, and Hertzke looked at her so strangely. She was a married woman!

A wave of heat washed over her. She raised her hands to loosen the collar of her dress. Hertzke's eyes followed her fingers. Quickly she drew them back. She still felt his eyes on her. She would cover herself all the way to the tip of her nose if she could. Why was the attic so hot? Was it the sun beating down or Hertzke's breath, so close . . .? She should ask him to move away from her, but she felt so guilty. Even if it was a momentary thought she had wronged him today. He was no informer. He wouldn't have talked even if he were caught and tortured. If he were a scholar like Shiya, such a thought would never have occurred to her. No, if there was one fine, decent person in the attic, it was Hertzke.

•   •   •   •   •

Hertzke helped her down the ladder to the cellar as usual. He went first and held the ladder steady as Golda descended rung by rung, lowering the trapdoor as she stepped down. He guided her just as he had the evening before, and the one before that, but never before had the touch of her body stirred him to such trembling. The ladder slid, the trapdoor slammed, and so did her heart as they fell together onto his bed.

A warm haze enveloped her and everything seemed to float away. Reality lurked somewhere, but the clasp of his strong arms barricaded her against it. Now there were only his hands moving gently over her skin; his lips, like fluttering butterflies' wings against her face.

She said nothing and he was silent too, as if he knew that it wasn't enough for her to hide in darkness . . .

The next morning, Golda asked to be left alone in the cellar, and he went to the attic without her. She sat on the bed and stared into the dark. What had happened last night was inevitable. She knew how it had happened, why it had happened. The excuses were sound, the reasons valid; still . . .

She recalled an anecdote Shiya had told her once, about a Jew who was desperately ill with consumption. His doctor advised him to eat fatty foods—with the rabbi's permission, even pork. One day the rabbi happened to see him eating it and sternly reprimanded him. "What kind of Jew are you, gorging yourself on pork?" The man was puzzled. "But you sanctioned it, Rabbi." "I permitted it, yes, for the sake of your health. But to smack your lips over it . . ."

· · · · ·

It was a hot day. Golda lay in the attic bathed in perspiration. The old-time remedies with which the farm wife had plied her had no effect; she stayed pregnant. What would happen if the Germans were still here when the time came? Who would deliver the child— Hertzke?

From giant Hertzke, she could well be carrying triplets, and who knew what harm those potions might have done to her system? What would they do when her time came? Would Hertzke boil his butcher's knife, fill her full of whiskey, and do a Caesarean section?

Hertzke could do anything if he had to, she thought, as she watched his brawny figure enter the attic. He sat down beside her, smiled, stroked her face tenderly and gently wiped the sweat from her brow. In the next instant he had eased her down on the straw, pressing her close, his hot breath urgent on her cheek. She had told him before that the dark cellar was one thing, but it was another to act like dogs in the street . . .

Yet here, now, in the attic's brilliant sunlight, he was pulling off her clothes and she was uttering no word of protest. Her eyes clamped shut at the sight of her body. Shiya had never seen her like this. Even the walls of her bedroom had never seen her naked in the revealing daylight. The sun's rays cut through the cracks in the roof. Behind her closed eyelids, red wheels spun inside each other as her body quivered under Hertzke's rough hands and coarse hair.

In the cellar it started all over again. She could have managed to climb down herself by now, but Hertzke, tender, insistent, carried her to his bed. And she did sleep more soundly, nestled in his arms.

By day it was "like dogs" in the attic; in the evening, in the dark of the cellar, it was as Hertzke wished. But at night, in her sleep, she was back with Shiya, modest, shy as he had always been. Shiya's long fingers on the pages of a book, but his words and boyish glances stroking her, caressing her. When he turned out the light and came to bed, his slender arms and delicate mouth were as tender as his words, as thrilling as his glance. She could still feel his lips on one cheek even as Hertzke's hairy chest tickled the other. She sprang from the cot in a cold sweat. Shiya was alive, she knew it now. Shiya was alive!

Hertzke awoke, tried to soothe her.

"Let me alone!" she cried and moved away.

Hertzke withdrew without a word. With one hand she felt in the dark for her clothes, with the other she tried to cover her breasts, though the room was dark. She would have killed herself rather than let Shiya find her pregnant with a bastard . . .

7

"Last stop!"

The conductor's shout startled Yurek out of a deep sleep. His eyes snapped open in fear. It took him a second to realize that the train was pulling into Grokhov. The other passengers were already pushing to get off.

"Is that yours?" A man pointed to a bundle under the seat.

Yurek picked it up. All he had were a few pieces of torn underwear, but the mistress had given him a chunk of bread and two kilos of butter. He would sell the butter and have a few zloty in his pocket.

"Last stop! Everybody out!"

He moved toward the exit. An icy wind struck his perspiring body. Across from the train was a tram stop. Which line should he take? He hadn't given a thought to where he would go. The Wilchinskis? They had turned him out because of Hannele, but now . . .

"Where is Hannele?" How real the image of his grandfather had been in his dream, the piercing blue eyes demanding, "Where is Hannele!"

He had walked to the number eight tram, but now, as it started to move, he jumped down off the step. He couldn't go to the Wilchinskis. When that man had locked the door behind them, he had sentenced Hannele to death. "Don't worry, Mama," he had said when she had entrusted Hannele to him, "I'll take good care of her." But he had only watched her life drain away day by day.

He shook his head. If he had come here only to torture himself with these thoughts, he needn't have accepted the butter from the mistress—God knew she was poor enough.

The butter! It would melt under his arm. He took a running leap onto a tram that went across the bridge to the main streets of Warsaw. He would get off at Bratzka. That day when he had gone with the mistress, the lady had paid a good price for butter and had given him some food in the bargain.

Then the blossoms from the chestnut trees had carpeted the sidewalks; now the streets were covered with snow and all the windows coated with frost. He would never recognize the house, even if she came to the door. How long could he wander in the cold? His shoes were filling with snow. Where would he sleep? He would have to—was this the house? It looked the same. He pushed open the gate and walked in. No, this couldn't be it. The house he wanted didn't have marble steps.

A door opened. "Who ya lookin' for?" the janitor asked.

"Nobody in particular. I have fresh butter to sell. Can you tell me who'll give me a decent price for it?"

"Let's see."

"My mother made it just yesterday."

The janitor bought it all and paid him well. He surely wouldn't use it all himself; he'd probably sell it and make a nice profit. Apparently the price of butter was even higher now. Perhaps he could go partners with the mistress and stay on in Shwider. Why had he left anyway?

· · · · ·

Hannele's grave was ready. No sooner had he cleared the snow from the grave and climbed out of the pit than the master had grabbed her little body and thrown it in. The cry he had heard must have been his own, but at that moment it had seemed to him that Hannele had cried out for her nose. It had snapped off like an icicle! Suddenly, he was in the grave, lying beside her as he had done in the attic. He'd just wanted to comfort her. The smell of whiskey filled the grave even before the master's hand reached him. Back on his feet, he had run to the house to pack his rags.

Was it true you could ask a dead person's forgiveness for a wrong you had done him, or was he consoling himself with fairy tales? In his dream, when he told Grandpa what had happened to Hannele, he had said, "Thank God!" Maybe he really meant it? Hannele was the only one in the family who had a grave. He would go to her grave and beg forgiveness for her broken-off nose . . .

One thing he mustn't do: think. Thinking was deadlier than a German bullet.

· · · · ·

He went back to the janitor. "Could you please give me a little hot water? It's so cold outside."

"You've sold your butter, haven't you? Why don't you go on home?"

"I still have a few things to buy."

"Go over to Jerusalimska Street, to the public kitchen. They'll give you a bowl of hot soup."

The kitchen was closed. It was only noon, and it didn't open till half past two. He walked up one street and down another, his feet freezing; his ears felt as if they were being squeezed with hot pliers. The trams were heated; he'd ride one for a while.

Two ragged boys got on after him. The bigger one started singing; the smaller one, cap in hand, walked up and down the car begging for coins. Was it a coincidence? A song about Polish refugees from Pomern, but the melody—it was the ghetto song, "I Want to See My Home Once More." If these boys knew where it came from, they wouldn't be singing it. They looked like real Polish kids. Yurek couldn't take his eyes off the bigger one. That potato nose and the straw-colored hair falling over his eyes. Yes, he had seen him somewhere. If they *were* Jews and had a place to sleep, they shouldn't risk riding around in streetcars.

They were heading for the door. He sprang up and followed them as they jumped from the tram and boarded another one. He kept following them. Real Polish kids wouldn't run away like that. He must find a way to meet them. They could help each other.

He took a seat near a window. One of the boys started singing again. Good. When the smaller one held out his cap to him he would . . .

The youngster walked right past him. He got up, handed the kid a coin, and winked. The damn fool didn't notice, or pretended not to. Here they were—back on Jerusalimska. He would get off at the soup kitchen and stop squandering his little bit of money on trams and charity. He'd better use the few remaining daylight hours to find a place to sleep.

This time the boys followed him off the tram and all the way to the soup kitchen. He would sit near them and find an excuse to start up a conversation. He could get along with them even if they weren't Jews; with his face, they would never suspect.

The soup kitchen was crowded with children—newspaper hawkers, cigarette dealers. The Poles must be poor these days. He was gulping down the hot soup when he remembered the chunk of country bread in his bundle. It would have been a good way to introduce himself: he could have offered them some bread to go with the soup. Maybe he could still do it. No, they were already headed for the door. He'd have to talk to them outside.

They walked so fast that he would have lost them if they hadn't stopped. As he got closer, they started walking again. Was there another place to get free soup? A bunch of the kids he had seen in the soup kitchen were walking in the same direction. The two from the tram in front of him, the others behind him. What was going on?

The two tram singers stopped again, turned, and went through a gate. If they were running away from him, it was no use chasing them. Suddenly, he was shoved from behind. Inside the gate he tripped over somebody's foot and fell headlong to the ground. His cry was stifled by a big kid who sat on him and covered his mouth.

"His pants!" someone ordered, and the boys started undoing the buttons.

A gem of a face, he taunted himself. But there were other giveaways.

His eyes almost popped out of his head when someone lit a match and brought it close to—those bastards were going to burn his—"I've got a little money," he started to say, but the hand pressed down harder on his mouth. This was his punishment for letting Hannele's nose be broken off. He shut his eyes. When he opened them again, the kid who had been sitting on him held his hand out.

"Shake, pal. You're among friends. We had to make sure."

Wicek, the leader of the gang, took Yurek to his hiding place, although Yurek got a little nervous when he saw it was the room of the building's janitor. He knew from his smuggling days that most janitors were informers.

Wicek nodded. "Sometimes I think this janitor suspects something. But he cooperates, and anyway, with a face like yours, you don't have to worry."

8

It was all so unbelievable. Yurek awoke each morning ready to run down and tend the cow, then he opened his eyes and found Wicek beside him on the cot. Strange: in Shwider it was almost a superhuman effort for him to tear his eyes open; here, while Wicek slept like a log and the janitor and his wife snored away, he lay in the dark with his eyes wide open.

It was a little bewildering. He had worked hard on the farm, but black-market street trading was no picnic either. Raids by German and Polish police, attacks by competing gangs. You had to be able to maneuvre; you had to know what to buy, where to buy it. Wicek knew it all. He was a good teacher, and Yurek watched, listened, and followed him everywhere.

Every day the gang met in the soup kitchen. Yurek kept an eye out for the two tram singers, but they didn't show up for several days running. He mentioned it to Wicek, who was also worried. "I took a kid, Stefcha, to their hideout. I hope she didn't cause any trouble. I think we should find out."

They found Stefcha in tears. She didn't know what had happened, but something was wrong. Bolek and Milush had left Sunday morning, as usual. Milush hadn't come back till Monday night. He had left some food for her and some money for the mistress, but then he had gone out again and that was the last she had seen of him.

"His eyes were swollen," the mistress told them. "He said that Bolek was in the hospital."

"The hospital isn't so bad," Wicek remarked as they left the building. "At least he wasn't caught by the Germans."

"But what'll happen when they take his pants off?" Yurek asked.

"We'd better find out where they're keeping him, so we can keep an eye on him."

They found Milush standing in a corner of the hospital corridor. "What happened?"

"His foot—his whole foot came off!"

"What?" they both cried out in horror. "What the hell are you talking about?"

"He jumped off a moving tram . . . the street was icy . . . he slipped and his foot . . . they found it on the other side of the street with the shoe still on it."

Yurek's fingers clenched around Wicek's arm. Wicek leaned against the wall, his legs suddenly unable to support him. He composed himself quickly, however, and tried to clear the tightness from his throat.

"So what are you hanging around here for?" he asked Milush reproachfully. "There are plenty of people to look after him. Let's get out of here."

"They know he's a Jew."

"Why do you say that?"

"She asked me if I was a Jew too."

"She?"

"The gray nurse. I told her no. She believed me. So help me, she even gave me a bowl of soup."

"If they're still keeping him here, they won't inform. Come on Milush, you can't help him by standing around here."

•   •   •   •   •

Wicek spread the word—the gang would have to lie low for a while. With Bolek in the hospital, and all those nurses and orderlies and doctors all over the place—there were too many who knew about him already. Somebody was sure to talk. Somebody might even go to the Germans, and heaven help them if the Germans got their hands on Bolek. They must stay away from the soup kitchen or any of the places where they usually met. They were to avoid Bolek's hideout at all costs.

•   •   •   •   •

Wicek gave Yurek a wintry smile. "It's all right to tell everybody what to do, but what about Stefcha? We can take Milush with us, he's got a pretty good face, but you saw Stefcha—nobody wants her."

"What about the underground? Don't they help you find places?"

"Well, yes, when my contact shows up, he may be of help. It's tonight I'm worried about. I have to find a place for her tonight."

Yurek's face brightened. "I can ask my farmers. They're decent people—they'll take her. I'll ride out to Shwider and speak to them, but I can't make it back before tomorrow."

"Don't ask them. Just go and take her with you. If nothing comes of it, at least we'll have gained a night or two."

•   •   •   •   •

Wilk was all over Yurek the moment he caught sight of him. His excited barking brought the mistress to the door, and she broke into a grin at the sight of him. As she ran to embrace him, her eyes fell on Stefcha and widened in alarm.

"Yurek! Hey, Yurek!" Hella shouted from the doorway. "You've come back!" She came running, Wojtek right behind her. "Who's she?" Hella pointed to little Stefcha.

"Go get your father, both of you. Tell him Yurek is here."

When the children were out of earshot, the mistress lowered her voice to a whisper. "Where are you taking her?" she asked, nodding toward the child. "If you cart her around in the open, she'll get you in a peck of trouble."

"She's all right. Nobody even looked at her on the train. What trouble can there be with a little blonde kid?"

"Anyone could tell it's not real. And what would you do with her eyes, bleach them too? Where are you taking her?"

Yurek hesitated. He knew all too well about Stefcha's eyes— dark, frightened, so much like Hannele's. "I thought I could leave her here," he said finally.

"Here? You know how Wacek runs off at the mouth when he gets drunk. And Hella's just as bad."

The master rounded the barn. Yurek ran to greet him, his hand outstretched. *"Dzien dobry!* Good day, master!"

"So you've come back, eh?" Wacek noticed the girl standing in the yard. "Who's that?"

Before Yurek could reply, he saw the mistress beckoning to them. He and Wacek followed her into the house.

"Yurek wants to leave the kid with us."

Wacek looked out the window and turned on Yurek angrily. "Not a chance! She'll croak like the other one."

"It's only for a few days, master. A week at most," Yurek pleaded, and added quickly, "We'll pay you well."

"And what if somebody squeals on us? They burn people in their houses for that. What good's your money then, eh?"

"The underground will find a place for her in a few days."

"The underground?" Wacek's eyebrows shot up in disbelief.

"Our boys have contacts—the next time I come out, I'll bring the master an underground newspaper."

"How do you like this little runt? Ain't he something! The underground, eh?" Wacek slapped Yurek's shoulder. "The day will come—remember?" He threw out his chest and clicked his heels.

• • • • •

The trip to Shwider was successful in more ways than one. With money he had borrowed from Wicek, Yurek bought some of the farm produce, took it back to Warsaw, and turned a handsome profit. In a week, he was able to return to Shwider for more goods.

Yurek was thankful they hadn't reminded him of his promise to take the little girl back. But no sooner had he gotten through the door than Stefcha threw herself at him, almost knocking the parcels out of his arms.

"I'm going with you! I want to be with you!" she sobbed. God, another stubborn kid on his hands. He looked down at her tear-stained face and felt his anger melt away. He put his arm around her shoulder and led her back into the house. He sat her down in a corner, just as he used to do with Hannele, and whispered: "Listen to me, Stefcha. You're a big girl. You know I have to go now and you have to stay here with these nice people. I'll come to see you as often as I can. Please be a good girl." He stroked her bleached hair and she nestled closer to him. "Promise you won't cry, Stefcha."

She nodded her head.

"What does that mean? Yes, you'll cry, or yes, you promise not to cry?"

"I won't cry," she answered, with a catch in her throat, but a brave smile on her tear-smudged face.

* * * * *

He strode into his quarters and his greeting stuck in his throat. Two Polish policemen were there, checking the tenant register with the janitor. Too late to turn back.

"Salute!" he called out brazenly. Nodding politely at the policemen, he turned to the janitor. Do you have any rich ladies here who'll pay a good price for fresh delicatessen?"

The janitor looked at him stupidly, his face ashen.

"If I make a good sale in this house, I'll give you a few eggs out of my profit."

"Who are you? What do you want here?" one of the policemen demanded.

"I want to do some business, officer." He pointed to his parcels. "We can't earn enough for new seed from our little piece of land and our one registered cow. But we make the best sausage in Karchew, so I bring it here to sell."

"What the hell is this—a smuggler's nest?" The cop stared suspiciously at a large carton of cigarette tubes on the table. "You come here often?"

"I'm not sure, sir. Whenever I bring stuff to Warsaw I come straight to this neighborhood. Rich people pay a much better price."

"I asked you if you come here often!"

"I may have been here before; then again, I may not. These places all look alike. I always go to the janitors first, and they tell me who the richest tenants are. I come to Warsaw once a week. If the officer would like, I could bring him something too."

"How much for the sausage?"

"It will be cheaper for officers."

The policemen bought the smoked sausage for a song, but there was still plenty of stock left. Yurek knocked at several doors and earned a few zloty. Coming down from the upper floors, he saw Milush shoot through the gate like a bolt of lightning.

9

Milush's features and fair coloring usually stood him in good stead, but clearly at the hospital he was an object of suspicion now. Wicek therefore decided that it would be wise to keep the boy indoors and out of sight for a while. For the first day or two, Milush had lain on the cot in the alcove and slept the hours away, but after a while he grew restless.

"I ain't gonna lie around here doin' nothin'" he complained to Wicek. "I'm goin' out sellin' in the streets like you guys."

"What if somebody from the hospital sees you? What if they decide to follow you here?"

"I can take care of myself. I can earn money and help out, just like anybody else."

Wicek turned from him brusquely, his patience at an end. Then an idea struck him. "Milush, I know just what you can do!"

"What?" Milush asked dubiously, still ready to do battle.

"You know how much time we wasted every night making the cigarettes. If you do it during the day, they'd be ready for us to sell every morning."

The next morning they supplied Milush with a sack of tobacco, a large box of tubes, and a stuffer, and put him to work. When the police had knocked at the door, he barely had time to hide the to-bacco under the janitor's bed. As soon as the police left, he crawled out and made straight for the door.

"Son of a bitch!" the janitor told Yurek. "The little squirt skedaddled like a bat out of hell! I didn't even have a chance to warn him not to come back!"

• • • • •

Yurek looked up and down the street. He'd better find that kid. What had happened to Bolek was enough to break anyone, but Milush had held up well so far. Maybe those cops coming out of the blue was the last straw. He just had to find him. He soon bumped into Wicek and told him what had happened. Together they looked for Milush. They found him sitting on the curb of Marshalkovska Street, bawling like a baby. Franek had taken away his tobacco.

• • • • •

Milush had run through the Square of the Three Crosses, over to Ujazdovska Street, but there was no sign of any of the gang. Franek, a polish acquaintance from the soup kitchen, was standing on the corner.

"Hey, you seen Wicek?"

"Ain't you singing in the streetcars no more?"

"I'm looking for Wicek. You seen him?"

"Whatcha got there, kid?"

Milush realized for the first time that he was still clutching the sack of tobacco in his fist.

"Listen, if you're lookin' for a partner, you just found one."

"He wasn't around here at all?"

"Who?"

"Wicek. I'm looking for Wicek."

"Where's that other guy, the one who sang in the trams with you? D'ja break off with him? Where'd ya get such a load of tobacco, anyway?"

"Wicek, he's all over me, tellin' me what to do all the time, but when somethin' happens—" Milush was having a hard time keeping his voice from breaking.

"Whatcha blubbering about? You one of them Zhids or somethin'?"

Milush burst into a loud yammer. Franek snatched the tobacco and took off.

• • • • •

"You thieving son of a bitch! Hand over that tobacco before I knock your ugly block off!" Wicek grabbed the box with all of Franek's wards and walked away. Yurek kept up with Wicek's long strides; Milush had to run to catch up with them. At the end of the long block, Wicek looked back. "Franek's gone. You think he's given up?"

Yurek jerked his head toward the corner across the street. Franek was heading for them from a side street and soon caught up with them, a gang of boys behind them.

"That kid ya got there, he's a Zhidek. If you're protecting him, you and your whole gang must be Zhideks too!"

Wicek realized that until a few more of his own gang showed up, the best thing to do was stall for time.

"If anybody here is a Zhid, it's you, Franek! A real Pole wouldn't mug a helpless little kid."

"Milush is a Zhid! He said so himself!"

"If he did, he was only kidding you, and you're an ass for believing him!"

"He should pull down his pants," someone proposed.

"Franek first," countered Wicek. "How do we know he's not one?"

"Okay. Let's go inside the gate. Me first, then Milush, and you next, Wicek!"

"Right!" the others agreed.

"Fine with me, Franek, but you'll have to pay for insulting the son of a Polish soldier. His father gave his life for the fatherland, and you're going around spreading lies about him. You put up your cigarettes. Milush will pull his pants down. If you lied, he gets all your stuff."

"That smart alec wants to swipe my stock," Franek whined, backing off.

"All we want is justice. If you're right, then you win all of Milush's tobacco and my cigarettes too."

"Up your ass! You're all—"

"SIX!"

Franek had no time to finish his sentence. The lookout's shout had signaled danger. Marching down the street was a German patrol of the anti-black-market brigade.

· · · · ·

"My mama would have said they were angels from heaven, not cops," said Yurek. "You take too damn many chances, Wicek. You almost started a war over a lousy sack of tobacco."

"It wouldn't have ended with the tobacco. If we'd given in to him, they'd have known for sure we're Jews."

"But what happens tomorrow?"

"You haven't met Romek yet, have you? Last summer he crawled into a grain shed to get some sleep. You should see his arms, even his face is full of scars. He got all chewed up by rats."

"Don't tell me rats aren't scared of people?"

"They certainly are," Wicek explained. "But Romek invaded their territory. He was alone and they were many, so they attacked him from all sides. They didn't care how big he was. If Franek doesn't lay off, you'll see what'll happen here. How do you think we won our own territory? Rat strategy!"

• • • • •

"What kind of strategy are you planning now?" Yurek asked.

"Just watch and keep quiet!" Wicek snapped.

In front of them walked Milush, with his merchandise spread out on a box tray. A short distance behind him, Wicek, Yurek, and a few others of the *amkho* gang fanned out across the square and waited. As planned, the treasure in Milush's hands proved too strong a temptation to resist, but before Franek's boys could get too close, they were surrounded. Blows rained down on them from all sides.

Franek, however, had a "rat strategy" of his own. Reinforcements arrived, although Wicek's gang still had the upper hand.

"Zhidzhi!" the Polish boys hollered. Passersby stopped.

"Zhidzhi!" Wicek yelled back, pointing to the Polish kids.

If both sides were accusing, it must be an internal squabble. Kids! Some of the adults walked away. Others stood and watched as if it were a sporting match. All at once, two black-uniforms appeared out of nowhere.

"*Was ist los?* What's going on here?"

Too late to run—and none of Wicek's gang was trying to. The two guards were punching away, but Yurek noticed how selective they were. As one of them took a swing at him, Wicek grabbed the guy's arm. Yurek could have sworn the fellow winked as he backed off. Yurek was still marveling at how far the "greasing" had gone when Wicek introduced him.

"This is Yurek, the new one. An expert at smuggling, but still a bit green around here."

With a startled look on his face, Yurek leaned over to whisper something in Wicek's ear, but before he could ask the question, the young fellow in the uniform supplied the answer: "*Amkho!*"

"They carry out some pretty dangerous work," Wicek explained. "The uniforms are stolen, but they're real. They get them from the underground, along with forged identity cards of the German Todt Formation."

• • • • •

On his way back from a smuggling trip to Shwider, Yurek found Milush, his eyes swollen, waiting for him at the Grokhov depot. This kid would get into trouble with his constant crying.

Patiently he managed to piece together Milush's story. Franek had dug up a money-hungry informer to confront Wicek, and when Yuzek had come to Wicek's aid, the informer and Franek had overpowered them both and taken them away in a streetcar.

What could they do? The fellows in the black uniforms had a connection with the underground, but only Wicek knew where to reach them. Grzegorz of the A.L. always came around alone and no one even knew where to look for him. Wicek should never have taken such risks when the safety of the whole gang depended on him. He was always warning them not to tell anybody where they lived, because the strongest man would break under torture. But Wicek himself knew all the hideouts and territories, where all the stuff came from. Had he told Wicek the address in Shwider? Should he go back there and take Milush with him? No, he had to try to help Wicek. They must find someone who would know what to do.

"Stop blubbering! Cut it out!" His harsh tone had more effect on Milush than any kind words. "That's better. Now listen. I want you to wait for me in Praga around five o'clock. Wait for me on Targova Street, near Jaglonska, but don't go into the shelter till I come for you, understand?"

Milush nodded, still gulping down his tears.

"Where will you go now?" Yurek asked.

"I don't know."

"Before you met Wicek, who told you what to do? Who told you to go singing in the trams?"

"Nobody."

"Okay then, wait for me on Targova Street. Five o'clock, not a minute earlier."

Yurek tossed his box of cigarettes to the janitor at Wicek's old hideout and hurried to all the territories he knew of. But he found none of the gang anywhere. Were they already hiding? He waited impatiently for the soup kitchen to open. He would have to warn anyone in the gang who didn't know yet. He might also find someone there who could give him some advice . . .

He had almost reached the kitchen when he changed his mind. If he got there too early, he would attract attention. When he came back later the kitchen was open, and crowded. Near the door—it couldn't be! Wicek! He ran to him, brushing away the tears that started to fill his eyes.

"Don't make a scene!" Wicek muttered, pushing Yurek away. "People are watching . . ."

Yurek dashed to the toilet, dried his eyes, and tried to compose himself. In a few minutes he rejoined Wicek.

"Have you seen Milush anywhere?" Wicek asked.

"Yes, that's how I found out about you."

"Poor kid, he must be scared to death."

• • • • •

When Franek and his *shmaltzovnik* had taken them by surprise, Wicek started arguing with them as he looked around for an escape route. Jumping onto a tram was too risky even if he left his pursuers behind. A streetcar could turn into a trap. There weren't enough people on the street for him to get lost in a crowd, and anyway, Franek's gang must be close by—they wouldn't let him get very far. What other choices did he have? He had to make a run for it. At least it would cause some excitement and perhaps alert the rest of his gang.

Suddenly his eyes lit up. Standing just across the street were Mr. Grzegorz, the contact man from the underground, and little Yuzek. If Yuzek could be made aware of what was going on, he'd get Grzegorz to do something. Now, if there were only some way to give Yuzek the high sign without Franek and the informer seeing.

Damn! Yuzek had not caught on at all. Grzegorz was hurrying away and Yuzek was calmly strolling across the street. If Franek saw him—what the—he was coming straight toward them! Had the kid lost his mind?

"Salute, Wicek!" Yuzek greeted him cheerfully. Wicek began to wonder; Yuzek wasn't that dumb.

"He's another one!" Franek said to the informer.

"Your papers!" the informer demanded of Yuzek.

Yuzek rummaged in his pockets. "Heck! I left them at home."

"Don't give me that! You're a Zhid!"

"Honest to God, I have them at home. My mama keeps them along with the money."

What mama? What money? Wicek could not understand this strategy. It was an open admission that he was a Jew and that his mother would pay to protect him. Wicek kept silent and prayed. Yuzek must know what he was doing.

"Where does your mama keep this money and your papers?" the informer jeered.

"I've got a birth certificate at home, I swear. My mother's afraid I'll lose it, so she won't let me carry it around."

"Where do you live?"

"I could be back here in an hour with my certificate."

"Why go to all that trouble? Just give me your address."

"All the way over in Praga. Maybe I can make it back in less than an hour."

"Praga, eh? Whereabouts in Praga?"

Yuzek pointed to Franek. "I don't want him to know."

The informer grabbed him by the collar. "Okay, whisper it to me!"

Yuzek said something in his ear.

"Let's go, Zhidek! And you're coming too," he barked at Wicek, grabbing him by the arm.

Poor Yuzek, he looked as if he were shaking in his boots. What kind of game was he playing? Wicek wondered as they were taken across the bridge into Praga.

At the corner of Sheroka Street, Wicek almost hooted out loud. Grzegorz himself was lounging idly near one of the entrances.

"That's my house, over there," Yuzek pointed.

"If you're lying, Zhid, you're going straight to the Gestapo!"

They walked through the gate, turned into an entrance, and went inside.

"Freeze!" Two men emerged from the darkness of the hallway,

pointing revolvers. Grzegorz stepped in from behind, emptied the informer's pockets and quickly scanned his identification papers. He then pulled a paper out of his own pocket, stood stiffly at attention, and read aloud:

"Tcheslav Kazelski, you have been tried *in absentia* by the Military Court of the Underground People's Army for persecuting orphans of Polish soldiers, for collaboration with the enemy, for blackmailing Poles of the Mosaic faith. You have been sentenced to death. The execution is to be carried out as soon as possible."

Grzegorz folded the paper and returned it to his pocket. He faced the man once more. "Have you anything to say before you die?"

The informer seemed to shrink visibly before Wicek's eyes. He opened his mouth but no sound came out.

"Beat it, kids," one of the armed men said. "This is not for your eyes."

The informer's lips began to twitch, his legs buckled. They propped him up against the wall.

Wicek and Yuzek turned to walk away, Franek close at their heels. One of the men yanked him back.

"Not you, punk! We're not finished with you yet! You deserve it too, but we never shoot a Pole without a trial. You're under arrest!"

"Don't shoot me, sir. I didn't know, so help me God. I thought they were Zhids."

"The enemy of our country is killing Jews, and you're helping him? You'll have to answer to the judges."

The informer slumped to the ground. A kick in the ribs sat him up straight.

"I'll never do it again," Franek whined. "Don't shoot me."

"Don't shoot," the informer echoed. "Mercy! Don't shoot—"

"Did you ever show mercy to your victims?"

The informer dragged himself to his feet. "I never turned anybody in, I only took money. Don't kill me. I know plenty of guys who are doing this. I'll help you find them."

"Let's have the names, *all* of them."

One of the men wrote each name into a little book as the informer called them out. When the list of traitors was finished, the "underground committee" conferred together in whispers. At last, Grzegorz turned to the informer.

"We're granting you a stay of execution, but if you ever try it again, or if those names don't check out, we know where to find you.

And you," thrusting a finger into Franek's face, "keep your lousy trap shut! If you so much as breathe a word of 'underground' to anybody, we won't even bother with a trial."

• • • • •

One week later, the informer was found shot dead on the street. The tension among the boys eased: Wicek felt sure it would be safe now to go back to the old hideout. The janitor agreed to take Wicek and Yurek, but objected to Milush. "The police keep coming around all the time, and ya never know what that little snot will do next."

Grzegorz told them about a good possibility for Milush in Skerniewice, west of Warsaw.

"He won't stay there," said Yurek. "He'll get lonely again and run away. I'm having the same trouble with Stefcha—she gets hysterical whenever I have to leave. I'm afraid we'll have to find a place for both of them."

"Yurek, you're a genius!" Wicek exclaimed. "That's what we'll do, keep them together."

"You know a place?"

"No, but you do. Take Milush to Shwider."

"They'll never agree to it."

"Even if we build them a good hideout?" Grzegorz said. "We could send an expert."

• • • • •

The master was speechless. Standing before him was a real, live representative of the underground. The fellow had brought him an underground newspaper and even showed him his pistol, a real automatic.

"I thought Yurek was making the whole thing up," Wacek said, still shaking his head. "Y'know how kids like to brag." He was so overcome he even brushed aside the extra money for Milush's keep. The mistress quickly stepped in, took the money, and tucked it into her blouse. "We're only poor peasants, we've hardly enough to eat ourselves."

"That newspaper," Yurek whispered to her as he was leaving, "the man from the underground says you should pass it around, but sometimes . . . well, sometimes a man has one drink too many and can't keep his mouth shut."

"My Wacek is a patriot," she said, a little hurt. All the same, she tied a knot in her apron string as a reminder to burn the paper.

• • • • •

The raids in the Warsaw streets were stepped up to a feverish pace; the German factories were now desperate for slave labor. In the trains, where the raids had been sporadic, they were now carried out systematically. Despite the mounting perils, the black market flourished. The greater the risk, the higher the profit. The more dangerous the run, the more closely the smugglers banded together. An elaborate system of signals between trains traveling in opposite directions warned smugglers of danger points along the route. The engineer knew just where to slow down, so that people could unload the cargo or jump off. A perilous procedure, but it worked.

The signal had come at the last moment. Yurek threw out his rucksack, jumped from the platform between two coaches, and somersaulted into the deep snow. Hardly waiting to catch his breath, he ran along the track and gathered up the packages that had been thrown from the windows of the train. He piled them up in the snow and waited.

His breath made little puffs of vapor in the frosty air. He stamped his feet briskly and beat his arms against his chest. It seemed to him that he had been waiting forever when finally he saw them coming to pick up their stuff.

After all of them had gone, there were still some unclaimed bundles at his feet. What the hell should he do with them? The clatter of a train coming down the track broke into his thoughts. In a few minutes it came into view, a belching black monster against the white backdrop of the snow. Bundles flew from the windows. He could almost make out the features of the engineer. That guy must be nuts, he thought, as a piece of coal narrowly missed his head. Then he noticed the white piece of paper wrapped around the coal. A note, obviously scribbled in a hurry, directed him to look for a certain package. It wasn't hard to identify the engineer's coal-smudged bundle.

• • • • •

All the workers connected with the Otwock line were housed in a settlement close to the terminal yards in Grokhow. Yurek finally located the house in which the engineer lived.

"I'm glad to see you," the man said, taking the parcel. "I almost gave you up."

"I had a little trouble getting back."

"Yeah, it's almost the curfew hour. I hope you don't have too far to go."

"I had no idea it was so late. I have to get all the way back to the city."

"You're welcome to spend the night here, young fellow. After what you did for me, it's the least I can do."

Early the next morning, the engineer suggested that Yurek accompany him to the yards and get a ride on the train to the terminal. There he could pick up the tram to get back to town.

Yurek declined the offer. "The terminal is too dangerous. I'd rather walk to a streetcar. It's far, but it's a lot safer."

The engineer gripped Yurek's shoulder. "You just gave me a great idea! Why don't we work together? You won't have to get off at the terminal at all. You can take the train right into the yards and then it's only a few steps to my house."

This proposal led to a profitable three-way partnership. All the purchasing was done by the mistress in Shwider. Yurek brought the stuff to Warsaw on the train and sold it in the city. But his activities kept him out too late to get him to his quarters in Warsaw, so most of the time he had to sleep in the engineer's house. He missed Wicek and the camaraderie of the street gang.

One night he rushed to the hideout, arriving just a moment ahead of curfew.

"Hey, where've you been?" Wicek greeted him. "Good to see you!"

"What's doing?" Yurek asked, slipping out of the rucksack. "How's the gang?"

"Look at you, your jowls have filled out. You look well-off. Have you seen the kids in Shwider lately?"

"Today, yesterday, practically every day." Yurek's voice was muffled as he pulled his shirt over his head. "Milush has taken to farming as if he were born to it. Of course, that's only when he can come out of the hideout in the cellar. Stefcha's still a pain in the neck."

He squeezed into bed beside Wicek. Whispering far into the night, they almost overslept. Groggy, heavy-lidded, bumping into each other, they threw on their clothes. Yurek brought a wad of banknotes out of his pocket and offered it to Wicek. "Here, you must know someone who needs help."

Wicek whistled. "Wow, you're really loaded!"

"Yeah, my pockets are bulging."

"Hold onto it," Wicek advised. "Listen, Yurek, don't get carried away. Why don't you lay off for a while?"

"Are you crazy? Why should I stop now that I can sell things faster than I can get them?"

"Easter is only three weeks away. If you think the raids are bad now, wait and see. You don't have a scrap of identification on you, not even a forged piece of paper."

"As you can see, I've managed okay."

"I'm telling you, Yurek, lay off for a while. You trade in hams, sausages, butter, the very things the Germans want so bad to send home for the holidays. They're also short of working hands and you may end up in a factory in the Nazi fatherland."

Although he felt that Wicek was overly cautious, Yurek was inclined to take his advice. The engineer, however, was disdainful. "And here I thought you weren't scared of anything. The train takes you practically inside my house, and here you are shittin' your pants. For smuggling you need guts!"

•　•　•　•　•

The week before Easter, the Germans struck. They simply posted guards at the door of each car and let no one off until the train reached the end of the line. At Grokhov they checked everyone's papers, and if they suspected anyone of smuggling, shoved him into a waiting army truck.

The passengers left their packages behind and lined up, documents in hand. Baskets and rucksacks lay in the baggage racks, on the seats, on the floor. The cars were emptied of people. A duck quacked from one of the baskets. Boots clicked through the empty car. Yurek, under one of the seats, tried to make himself invisible.

Blockhead! He should have gone to the door, documents or no documents. Or he could have stayed in his seat and pretended to be asleep. Now he was in for it! Him and his smuggler's guts! If he really had guts he would have gotten off while there was still time. All his stuff was with the engineer; empty-handed, he could have made it.

Why did they keep hanging around this spot? There were so many bundles right out in the open, maybe they wouldn't search under the seat. The toe of a boot grazed him—and moved on. If only the train would start! He might still get into the terminal before curfew.

More footsteps. Something toppled over. A big hand grabbed his foot and pulled him out from under the seat.

"*Was machst du denn hier?* What are you doing here?"

Yurek rubbed his eyes and yawned.

"*Was machst du denn hier?*"

He shrugged. "*Nix zloty, nix bilet.* No money, no ticket."

For a Polish boy that was good enough German. The guard understood what Yurek was trying to tell him. He was hiding under the seat because he had no money for a ticket.

"*Hast du ein Packet?* Do you have a package?"

"*Nix zloty, nix bilet.*"

"*Nehm' das Gepäck und 'raus!* Take your package and get out!"

A Polish boy would not have understood all that, but everybody knew that *'raus* meant "out." Yurek bowed politely and started for the door.

"*Kein Gepäck?* No baggage?"

"*Nix zloty, nix bilet.*"

The German picked up a basket and handed it to Yurek. "*Lass den Knabe durch!* Let the boy through!" he called to the guard at the exit.

Yurek took to his heels.

•　•　•　•　•

He decided to stay in Shwider for the Easter holiday. Within hours he had settled into his old routine and was surprised to find how much he enjoyed it. Even the pungent smells in the barn seemed a welcome change from the stuffy trains. He finished his chores in record time, faster than he'd ever done them in the old days.

The mistress was busy with the holiday cooking. The master was out somewhere, probably celebrating the good news from the front. Yurek made for the entrance to the cellar and called Hella to cover the trapdoor behind him.

"I'm coming down with you."

"Who'll cover the trap?"

"Mama will."

"I'm only going down for a few minutes; I haven't seen the kids today."

"I'm coming too."

"What for? You never go down when I'm not here."

Stefcha threw her arms around Yurek's neck and covered his face with kisses. She must really be lonesome, even with Milush around.

"You never play with me like that," Hella complained.

"You're not a kid anymore."

"You'd rather play with that snot nose? Bobek doesn't mind that I'm a big girl . . ."

"Are you fooling around with Bobek again? I'll tell your mother."

"Go right ahead! Tell my father and the priest, too. See if I care! If you don't want to play, I'll go find Bobek. At least he's not a tattler."

"All right, take it easy. What do you want to play?"

"I know a good game. It's like tag, but if you catch me, you have to kiss me. Or the other way 'round."

How brazen could a girl get? But if he argued with her, she would only take it out on the kids.

As he was kissing Hella, Stefcha tugged at his arm. Hella pushed her away. Stefcha fell down and started crying. He pushed Hella away and she started bawling too. Girls! When they weren't kissing, they were crying. Ugh!"

* * * * *

Easter Sunday. They all sat around the table—Milush and Stefcha too—one big happy family. Even Hella was on her best behavior. The holiday talk whirled unheeded 'round his head; the tasty food stuck in his throat. His eyes were riveted on two gleaming candlesticks in the center of the table. The mistress had bought them in the Otwock market. And why not? There were no Jewish mothers left to bless the candles anyway. Whoever had said the blessings over these candlesticks was now in the same place as his mother. Had he, Yurek Dzobak, ever really had a mother? Whose table were his mother's silver candlesticks gracing tonight?

Papa, Mama, Nenna, Hannele, Grandpa—all of them, all of them! And he was sitting here, stuffing himself on roast pork and washing it down with vodka, as if nothing had happened.

10

The eastern front burst into life again, picked up momentum, rolled westward, and poured across the river Bug. The news reports were sprinkled with the names of familiar cities and towns. Chelm and Lublin liberated. Pulawa. Demblin. Lukow. The front was moving closer and closer to Warsaw, and now every hour brought new rumors, every day fresh tidings.

It was no secret that Warsaw would not wait for the Russians to march in and liberate it.

"In Warsaw, the war will end the same glorious way it began: the city will rise up and liberate itself by its own power."

"The world saluted Warsaw's heroism in its defeat; soon the world will have cause to admire it in its victory."

The talk was everywhere, in the factories and markets, in elegant cafés and soup kitchens. Nor was the mood of the city kept a secret from the Germans, who doubled their patrols and set up defense posts at strategic corners.

●　　●　　●　　●　　●

Yurek gave up his smuggling activities and volunteered for the work of breaking through cellar walls to create underground passages. The air-raid sirens were going constantly, but no one wanted to run to the shelters when historic events might break out at any moment. The artillery fire from the front lines was now audible.

"What are we waiting for?" people demanded impatiently.

"A Polish brigade from Berling's army is preparing to attack Warsaw."

"General Berling is in the pay of the Russians. The Poles in his army carry out orders from Moscow. No, Warsaw will be liberated by Polish patriots."

"So what are we waiting for?"

"For an order from the Polish National Government in London."

●　　●　　●　　●　　●

Friday, July 28, 1944. The front was already at Michelin, on the Otwock line, less than twenty kilometers east of Warsaw.

Monday, July 31. A Soviet communiqué reported the capture of the commander of all German operations east of Warsaw. German resistance would crumble at any moment.

"For God's sake, what are we waiting for?"

"Keep quiet and do your work. They're preparing for something big."

Food was stored in the shelters. Homemade antitank bombs were prepared.

"We're losing precious time. Every minute counts and all we do is talk."

"Don't get all worked up. It starts tomorrow."

"Tomorrow?"

"At five in the afternoon."

"How d'you know?"

"Everybody knows."

"Everybody knows? That's terrible! An offensive should be a complete surprise. Maybe the Germans themselves are spreading the rumor as a provocation. They're experts at that."

"Shut up, don't start a panic. The underground has put up posters."

"That could also be a provocation."

"If you listened to Radio London, you'd know what's going on."

"What do they say?"

"How should I know? It's all in code. But we know they're getting ready for something big."

●　　●　　●　　●　　●

Tuesday, August 1. All eyes were glued to the clocks; everyone was holding his breath as the seconds ticked away; the hours rang out somber as church bells on a feast day. The hands on the dials crept as if they were collaborating with the enemy . . .

Four. The clocks struck four. Pulses beat rapidly, but the unfeeling clock wheels ticked away with German regularity, each minute an eternity. The big hand reached twelve again. At last!

The clocks had hardly begun to strike five when church bells pealed, factory whistles blew, machine guns exploded. No, that was not the distant sound of artillery from the front; the shooting was right here, in the middle of the street.

"*Na Schwaby!* Get the Krauts! Hurrah!"

Red-and-white flags fluttered from windows; a red-and-white arm band on every sleeve. People dragged furniture from their homes, turned over tramcars, improvised barricades. German autos, trapped in the blockaded streets, raced back and forth like poisoned rats, easy targets for Polish bullets.

•   •   •   •   •

Was it possible that the enemy had been caught unprepared? Warehouses piled high with food and German weapons fell easily into the hands of the rebels. Entire sections of Warsaw were liberated. The German resistance focused on the main streets and the bridges over the Vistula. Sections of the city celebrated their liberation, but across from the barricaded streets with their Polish flags, German troops moved eastward to the Russian front and westward to the hinterland. Volya, a working-class suburb on the west side of Warsaw, posed a threat to this deployment, and the enemy concentrated its forces for an attack on the area.

The celebrating ceased. Jubilation turned to horror as the news filtered in about the slaughter at Volya. When a street was captured, the people were driven out of their homes, herded into enclosures, and riddled with machine-gun fire or blown to bits by grenades. Only a handful succeeded in escaping to the liberated portions of the city.

"If the Germans are preparing the same fate for Polish Warsaw as they did for the Jewish ghetto, then they don't know what's in store for them . . . Warsaw will not surrender a second time! Vengeance will be swift and thorough . . . We'll chase them all the way back to Berlin, and in Berlin we'll do the same to them as they did to us in Volya . . . Not a brick will remain in place, not one German son of a bitch will be left to tell the story."

•   •   •   •   •

The battles grew increasingly bitter on both sides. The Germans put up stubborn resistance even at the Pawiak prison, but the rebels finally took over. No more Polish patriots in German prisons! Along with people from the Polish underground, several hundred German and Romanian Jews were freed.

"Hurrah! We outsmarted Stalin! Poland is not Lithuania or Latvia, where the 'liberating' Red Army can impose its Red rule. When the Russians come marching into Warsaw, they'll find a functioning Polish national government."

"You think Stalin will allow himself to be outsmarted?"

"Look at the Polish leftist underground. They wanted to wait for an order from Moscow, but when the patriots took up arms, they couldn't just sit around, they were forced to join in an action ordered by the Polish National Government in London, even if it went against their own plans. Confronted with an accomplished fact, Stalin will just have to swallow it. The Red Army's victories are being won with American planes and British tanks. Roosevelt and Churchill will know how to keep a tight rein on Stalin . . ."

•   •   •   •   •

The skies were showering bullets, yet no one could sit still in the shelters. Warsaw's streets were Polish again! In one building, someone had planted a Polish flag in the hole torn out by a German grenade. Fighters and civilians alike fell in the streets, but to the *rat-tat-tat* of German machine guns, patriotic hearts beat out one defiant answer: "We are free, we are free!"

"We've retaken the courthouse on Leshno!" Someone brought cheerful news. "We're recapturing Volya!"

"The German front is crumbling like a rotten bridge! German soldiers are deserting in droves!"

"I only wish it were true! From my observation post I saw a whole Panzer division going off to the front."

"Maybe it was only half a division, Mr. Strategist? Or maybe it was a whole damn army? Are you one of them Volkdeutschen, or just a plain idiot?"

German planes dropped leaflets bearing the signature of the Polish premier in London. "Brother Poles, help the German army drive the Bolsheviks out of our Polish fatherland! The British deceived us but the Bolsheviks will destroy us."

Nobody believed the Germans, but they ran to catch the leaflets as if they were manna from heaven. "They see now, the Schwabes, that they won't accomplish anything with violence, so they're trying to appease us."

The last of the leaflets were still floating down on the breeze when the German planes returned. People ran out again to see. What are they going to tell us this time? From the planes came a deadly deluge of bullets.

"You can't trust a German even when he's dying. Goddamn their black souls!"

Bullets, grenades, firebombs. But one could not just sit in the shelters. Smoke from the burning buildings seared the eyes but could not stifle the spirit. Soldiers marched on the streets wearing Polish military caps. Over the highest building in Warsaw, an enormous red-and-white flag billowed and waved as if this were a holiday. Phonographs blared Polish military marches through open windows. Warsaw was jubilant! Five humiliating years under the boot of the "master race" and—how did that hymn go?—'Poland is not yet lost' . . ."

•   •   •   •   •

On the first day of the uprising, Yurek reported to the recruiting office on Bracka Street. One man wore a Polish army hat, another an army jacket, others only red-and-white arm bands. Machine guns rattled, grenades whistled, but the long line of volunteers hardly moved.

In front of Yurek stood a tall man with a haggard face. His hat was pulled down over his eyes, sweat poured down his long nose onto his thick moustache, but neither the moustache nor the military hat fooled anybody. People were staring at him with curiosity and contempt. Yurek wondered too. Didn't he realize there was no need to hide his identity any longer?

"How long do we have to stand here?" the man with the moustache complained. "If they'd only give us some weapons, we'd show them how Poles can fight!"

"What are you butting in for?" someone baited him. "You wouldn't know what to do with a gun if they gave you one."

"Must have crippled himself to stay out of the Polish army!" another joined in.

"Keep your big mouth shut!" Yurek broke in. "He came of his own free will, didn't he?"

"Shut up yourself, runt! Go home to your mama so she can wipe your nose!"

The argument grew louder. A man came out of the office. "What's the trouble?"

"Give us guns, we want to fight the Schwabes!"

"We don't have any guns. You want to fight? Find weapons—clubs, knives, axes—kill German soldiers, that's the way to get guns." The man's tone changed. "Are there any officers here?"

The tall man with the long nose stepped forward and followed the other into the office.

Yurek watched in astonishment. He would have sworn the man was a Jew. In the Polish army they rarely allowed a Jew to reach the rank of officer. Poor guy! He must have suffered plenty from the *shmaltzovniks,* even if he wasn't a Jew.

• • • • •

The older men were assigned to cleaning weapons, kitchen duty, helping the fighters in any way they could. Younger boys were used mainly as message runners. Yurek was assigned to a foraging detail, which searched abandoned houses for food. Doctor Jendrichowski—the one they had thought was a Jew—was made chief of a first-aid station for wounded fighters.

There was a growing shortage of medical supplies, and when Yurek, returning from one of his missions, brought the doctor bottles of iodine, packages of cotton and bandages, he received lavish praise for his initiative and good sense.

"That Zhidek is sweet on you," one of the boys said to Yurek. "Jewish officers—they get all the good jobs. Either they're put into offices or into hospitals. Jews can't fight."

"Just yesterday he crawled out there under heavy fire to help a wounded man. And what makes you so damn sure he's a Jew?"

"What's the matter—are you one of them Zhideks too?"

"And maybe you're one of them Schwabes who wants to stir up bad feeling between one Pole and another?"

Early one morning a priest appeared at staff headquarters. He was Father Jendrichowski, an uncle of the doctor's. From then on, the doctor was left in peace.

• • • • •

The German army drove wedges into the liberated sections of Warsaw. Streets still under control of the rebels became islands in a sea of destruction. Communications and movement between the various liberated sections became impossible. The seriously wounded could no longer be transferred to hospitals. Doctor Jendrichowski had to do the surgery himself.

"If only I had proper instruments," he confided to Yurek. "And drugs—I'd give a whole ham for one small bottle of iodine."

From headquarters, they could see a pharmacy in the no-man's-land on Jerusalimska Street, but the Germans had set up a gun emplacement near it, and a barrage greeted anyone who ventured in that direction.

* * * * *

A new Russian offensive on the Warsaw front. Yes, the Polish government-in-exile was right. Warsaw was drowning in blood, but it was still under the control of a Polish national army. The Warsaw rebellion was a victory no matter what the losses—a victory over Hitler and Stalin!

The Russian offensive at the Vistula was soon beaten back. Inside the city, entire neighborhoods were ablaze. The fighters were being massacred. Radio London reported that the British had offered to send help, but Stalin had refused to allow British planes to refuel behind Russian lines. Rumor had it that the Russians were parachuting blood plasma, drugs, and small quantities of arms, but most of it was falling into enemy hands.

"Why was Premier Mikolaichik doing nothing in London? If Churchill would send an ultimatum to Stalin . . . Hadn't the Polish leaders in London consulted with England and the United States before they gave the order to start the revolt? If England and the United States had given their approval, why weren't they sending aid? By the time Stalin decided to move, there wouldn't be anyone left to liberate. Or was that just what he was waiting for?

The red-and-white flags that had adorned the streets were charred with smoke and shredded by bullets. Where would it all end? Would the world once again look on indifferently while Poland was slaughtered and dismembered?

News from the western front was more heartening. Paris had been liberated. The British army had broken through the German lines and, in four days, had pushed on to Holland. American tanks had reached the Rhine near Aachen. To hell with Stalin! If he insisted on digging in his heels on the banks of the Vistula, then screw him! The war would end at the Rhine. The Germans had lost half a million men and all their weapons. Any day, any hour, they would surrender. Maybe the SS in Warsaw had lost contact with their general staff. In the west they were getting the hell knocked out of them; and here they arrogantly sowed destruction, not knowing that their own doom was at hand.

* * * * *

It must have been shortly after the middle of the month, by the Jewish calendar; a three-quarter moon hung in a spot that lit up all of Jerusalimska. Yurek could now see clearly the two German corpses that he had studied so often from his observation post. How he had longed to crawl out there and take their weapons! But the Germans were just as aware of the temptation those weapons offered to the rebels. None of the attempts to get close had succeeded.

To hell with the weapons! His goal was the pharmacy. Were the Germans asleep at their posts? Yurek almost reached the door and so far nothing had happened. Damn! So many windows were smashed, so many walls shot full of holes, and here—everything was intact. Not even a crack to stick his hand through. Maybe a back door . . .

The gate creaked. Well, at least he would be safe from stray bullets inside. How would he make his way back? No use worrying about that now; just grab the medicines. This must be the back door—damn, damn, damn! Another iron bar! Maybe there was a window—the store must have one.

* * * * *

The bright moonlight now proved helpful. Yes, here was the window, but again, unbroken panes covered with an iron grating. Why hadn't he taken along some kind of tool to break in with? The grating would be no problem at all with a crowbar. Here he was with just a pocketknife to chip away at the mortar between the bricks around the window frame. He tugged with all his might, but the bricks held as if set in steel.

No choice but to break the glass; maybe he could squeeze through a space in the grating. He wrapped his cap around his right hand and punched at the glass. His hand felt fractured, but the glass remained intact. A shoe—that should do the trick. Wham! Was that a German rocket lighting up the sky or did it only seem that way as he slid his hand through the glass splinters?

There was no time to stop. It was only a surface cut. But he'd better pull out the pieces of glass from his hand. Even if he couldn't climb into the shop, he could still reach into the nearest shelves. He turned suddenly, cutting his hand more. A dark silhouette had run into an entrance at the other end of the yard. He shouldn't have gone alone. But that shadow was running away—it couldn't be a German. Maybe someone who got trapped here when the fighting broke out? Possible.

The moon had shifted. It was almost hidden by the building, but its upper rim still peeked over the wall, as if waiting to see what brainless thing Yurek would do next. Soon it would be morning. How would he ever get out of here alive? He'd have to get into one of the apartments upstairs and wait for night again.

What a bonehead he was! Scratching at bricks with a tiny blade, and he hadn't thought of getting into one of the apartments to look for a tool to pry open the grating. The doctor must have given him up by now. But tomorrow—tomorrow the doctor would be amazed by the bagful of drugs and medicines he would bring back.

He should really look for something to eat, but he was dead tired. A little nap might help him think straight. No, first he must find some way to get that damn grating off.

He could make out four entrances leading from the courtyard to the apartments. He'd try the first. Little of the moonlight penetrated to the hall, but he soon found the stairs leading to the upper floors. If he—what was that?

The stairs below creaked.

"Who's there?" he whispered.

No reply.

He held his breath. Another long silence, unbearable, unnerving. He just had to find out. He took a deep breath.

"Who's down there, goddammit!"

"Not so loud," came a hoarse whisper from below.

Yurek scooted down the stairs. The footsteps echoed in the other direction, in flight. He grabbed the banister to steady himself. The fellow was clearly scared as hell; why make it worse?

Again a long silence, again a cautious footstep. Yurek didn't move. Another step, a whisper from below.

"Who is up there?"

"A friend."

"You sound so young—"

"I am. Who are you?"

"I got stuck here."

"I'm coming down, okay?"

No answer. Yurek waited a few moments, then started down. No footsteps running away.

Words came pouring out of the man even before he reached him. "I got stuck here when the fighting started. I can't get out now in the cross fire. How did you get in? What's the news? I can hear the artillery from the front line, but the Germans are still here. What's happening out there?"

Dawn was breaking, but even in the dim light on the staircase, Yurek could make out the unmistakable features of a Jewish face.

"*Amkho?*"

The man wobbled, held himself up on the banister. "No, I— what did you say?"

"*Ich bin amkho,*" Yurek said. The man began to shake. Yurek comforted him, as if he were a child.

The man brushed away the tears that had welled up in his eyes. "Did you really come here from the outside or is your hideout in this building?"

"I've just come from the front."

"You mean the Russians have crossed the Vistula?"

"No, I'm talking about the rebel front. We need drugs badly."

"What's the news? My radio isn't working. Are the Germans still holding on the Russian front?"

"Things will break any day now."

"What's taking them so long?"

"Not much longer. Paris, Antwerp, Bucharest—they're being driven back everywhere. They may be surrendering right now as we stand here."

"I hope so! God, I hope so! My name is Stakh—Stakh Bielinski. I've got good Aryan papers, but my face kills me. The *shmaltzovniks* have sucked the marrow out of my bones. I was afraid to go out there. At least I can hide here. Maybe I'm a coward—"

"You don't have to explain to—"

Stakh kept talking, as if it were a relief to hear his own voice.

"Are you sure the Germans are losing the war? If they come back we won't survive half a day . . . you say the Jews are coming out in the open . . . I'm afraid that—did you?"

"Nobody asked me. If they asked me—"

"Me, they don't even have to ask. Tell me—what's your name, friend?"

"Yurek."

"Tell me, Yurek, can I go out there with this face?"

"The doctor at our headquarters is a real Pole, he even has an uncle who's a priest, and his face still gets him into trouble. We all fight side by side, but they still hate us."

"There, you see!"

"The Germans are burning all the buildings in this area. You'll be smoked out anyhow. There are some decent Poles too, you know. Doctor Jendrichowski is no anti-Semite, I'm sure of that."

"I'd be a doctor myself now if the war hadn't interfered with my studies."

"You studied medicine? The doctor would be glad to use you. He's swamped."

They found some iron hooks that were used to rake fires in stoves. With these they succeeded in forcing open a padlock and loosen the iron bar holding the door. Stakh ran to his hideout, brought down the largest rucksacks he could find, and showed Yurek what to take. The pharmacy was large and fairly well stocked.

•   •   •   •   •

Night fell and again the moon lighted up an inky sky. Flat on their bellies, they started for the other side of the street, directly in the line of German fire. A flare exploded high above their heads. Gunfire shattered the silence. Too late to retreat. Stakh stirred. Yurek grabbed his leg; they lay motionless. Another flare, then quiet. The moon itself seemed to fade after the flare died away. Had the bulky sacks on their shoulders so changed their shapes that the Germans didn't recognize them as humans?

They slithered along on the other side of the street, hugging the walls of the buildings. Suddenly, another flare burst, followed by another hail of bullets. Were their own people shooting at them? They knew he was due back. He called out the password, but the shooting didn't stop. Hell! He was giving yesterday's password. They hadn't planned on the possibility that he might not return the same night.

They had almost reached the Polish position when another flare went up. Now the bullets came from both sides. Again he and Stakh flattened themselves to the ground. The firing continued. Yurek jumped in pain. Stakh pulled him into a nearby gate.

"Where?"

"In the shoulder."

Stakh slipped off Yurek's rucksack. "Where in the shoulder? Your whole back is wet."

"Blood?"

"Blood is sticky. This is kind of watery. It smells like—where does it hurt the most?"

"All over."

Stakh laughed out loud. Yurek sat bolt upright. "What the hell's so funny?"

"I can't tell for sure, it's too dark, but I think this rucksack saved your life. The bullet must've hit a bottle of peroxide."

"But it hurts."

"You felt the impact of the bullet, your shoulder got wet—auto-suggestion—"

"What does that mean?"

"You're imagining the pain."

"Hell, I know when something hurts! I'm not crazy, you stupid—"

"Take it easy! When it gets lighter, we'll make sure."

"When it gets lighter, we'll be hit by more than one lousy bullet!"

"We'll just have to wait until dark again. It'll give us time to think. If we're not careful, we'll never live to get there . . ."

Stakh's examination of Yurek's shoulder in the daylight confirmed his guess: the bullet had hit the rucksack. But how were they ever going to make it to the Polish lines in one piece?

Stakh had another idea: they would duck into a building and find some pillows. With pieces of red ticking and white pillowcases pinned to their chest, and with the Germans behind them, only the Poles would recognize them.

"That's the lousiest idea I ever heard," Yurek scoffed. "We'd be full of holes before they had time to look."

"What do we do then?"

"Keep on sliding like snakes. It's our only chance. Wait a minute—the cellars! When we were preparing for the revolt we broke through passageways between some of the buildings. Let's look down there. We may be able to get to our position without using the street."

They found the walls broken through, only in three adjacent buildings, not in the fourth. They ran their hands along the walls in the dark, but there wasn't a crack.

The whole day went by while they searched. Finally they had to make a move.

Yurek slapped his forehead. "Where the hell are my brains! No wonder they were shooting! When I left there, I was alone."

"I don't understand."

"If I had come back alone, they'd have known it was me. When they saw two—"

"You're the one who talked me into coming with you."

"I'll go first."

"And leave me here?"

"You'll follow, but not until I have a chance to tell them. If I get there okay, I'll give you a sign—two flares, one right after the other. Then you come."

•   •   •   •   •

The night before, Doctor Jendrichowski had pleaded with them to hold their fire. He was sure it was Yurek coming back. He also knew that if Yurek had survived the cross fire, he would try again. Finally, an order was issued to the sentries not to shoot until the two persons came close enough to be identified.

Yurek crouched low, listened, advanced a few steps. Was the watch asleep? No flares, no shots. He wasn't more than a hundred yards from the Polish position. Maybe they had retreated. Had the whole rebellion collapsed?

"Halt or I'll shoot! Who goes there?"

"A friend."

"The password!"

"Jan Sobieski was the password, day before yesterday, when I left."

"Advance with your hands up!"

Yurek stood up. Damn fools, if a flare went up now, he was a sitting duck!

"Halt! Identify yourself!"

"Yurek. On an official mission."

"Come in slowly—and keep you hands up!"

A few minutes later, two rocket flares soared upward, one right after the other.

• • • • •

"You've brought a treasure," the doctor praised them. "A real treasure! How did you know what to pick?"

"Stakh was a medical student—"

"Only one year," Stakh interjected.

"Stakh, you're a treasure too. You'll work with me."

• • • • •

Yurek dressed wounds, took pulse counts, learned the Latin names of drugs and when to use them. By day he was kept busy at the doctor's side; by night he helped carry the wounded through the sewers to better facilities. The doctor and Stakh were full of praise. A real medic, they said.

Yurek caught one of the other medics snitching a bottle of alcohol.

"Who the hell made you boss?" the culprit shouted belligerently. "Just because you brought back some medicine, you're a big hero, eh? You wanna know the truth? You wanna know why nobody else could get through the German fire? Because you were on a mission for *them,* that's why! They sent us a goddamn present back with you—two bags of stuff and one German spy!"

"You must be delirious!"

"Open your eyes, jerk! You came back all in one piece—right under the fuckin' German guns! How did you manage that, wise guy?"

"Flat on my belly the whole way. They never even saw me."

"In bright moonlight, with a big rucksack on your goddamn back, rocket flares on both sides, and they never saw you? They could've seen an ant crawlin' if they'd wanted to. They did it on purpose, stupid, because you were bringing back one of their own guys!"

"You mean Stakh?"

"Well, well, you're finally catchin' on!"

"But he's the best medic here!"

"What better spot for a German spy?"

"Sounds like you've already used that alcohol."

"Ask Sergeant Schupak. Ask Lieutenant Sokol. Everybody around here will tell you the same thing."

"But if Stakh is a Jew, how could he be working for the Germans?"

"You never heard of the Judenrat? And what about the ghetto police? Plenty of Jews worked for the Germans . . ."

* * * * *

Finally, the doctor counseled Stakh to find another company, much as he would regret losing him. There were just too many anti-Semites in this one.

"Come with me," Stakh begged Yurek.

"How can I leave? With you gone, I'm the best medic they have here. If I left now, it would be deserting."

"How can you desert me, Yurek? How many of us are there left?"

Yurek was still in a quandary when Lieutenant Sokol called Stakh in and gave him the transfer. "As far as I'm concerned, you proved your loyalty. But the others . . . well, you'll be safer somewhere else."

The moment he saw the transfer in Stakh's hand, Yurek went to the lieutenant and asked to be sent along. The commander hesitated.

"I'm a Jew too," Yurek announced.

"You too? You little bastard! You're a damn good kid and you've made yourself real useful around here. But if you've made your mind up, go ahead, and good luck . . ."

* * * * *

After the sixth week of the rebellion, the Russian front finally stirred and liberated the suburb of Praga. But they dug in once more on the eastern shore of the Vistula. Now Russian planes dominated the skies over Warsaw. German bombing raids on the rebels ceased, but the artillery did not stop bellowing. The weapons that the Russians parachuted down, even when they reached the rebels, could not alter the course of events. Little remained of the early victories. The most important rebel positions were now in German hands. Hungry, thirsty, exhausted, overcome with despair, the rebels had to keep fighting just to get out of German traps.

* * * * *

Stakh and Yurek arrived in the area of Grzybowski Square. They had carefully armed themselves with explanations for leaving their previous position, but so many people were milling about that no questions were asked. Only Lieutenant Wilk, the deputy commander, asked Yurek: "And you—you're a Jew too?"

"Me?" His tone implied that the question was absurd.

"I see you've attached yourself to this Stakh."

"He feeds me," Yurek explained, and expected to hear him mutter something about Jews having food while Poles were starving. But the officer said nothing.

* * * * *

It was clear to everyone now that it would be impossible for the rebels to resist the German pressure much longer. Ever since the Russians had taken Praga, the Germans were attacking the rebels with larger forces and greater persistence. Stakh had resolved that under no circumstances would he surrender to the Germans. Even if they didn't recognize him as a Jew, someone was bound to come along who would be only too happy to point out their oversight.

On Twarda Street he discovered a likely cellar and began building a hideout. Two other Jews—Zbigniew and Pawel—joined him. Though their "looks" were not as bad as his, they had made the mistake of revealing their identity and were now afraid of the possible consequences. Yurek organized the scavenging for food in abandoned houses.

* * * * *

"SURRENDER!"

The terrible word came almost as a relief. For sixty-six days they had hovered between delirious joy and hopeless grief. The leaders of the rebellion saw no sense in continuing the struggle. The Russians were now dropping more food and weapons, but the pockets of resistance in Warsaw continued to shrink. The Russian front was still stalled on the eastern banks of the Vistula; it appeared they would not launch an offensive much before winter. The Germans were promising that the rebels would be taken prisoner by the regular army, not the SS, and that they would be treated as prisoners of war. Sorrow, disappointment, yet also a certain sense of relief. Many lives had been lost, and all in vain.

11

At the transfer camp, Yurek explained that he was a country boy from Karchew, that he had come to Warsaw to sell sausage, and had gotten stuck there when the rebellion broke out. They handed him a slip of paper declaring him a refugee from Warsaw—an official document at last. He was pleased that he had talked his way out of being sent to a children's camp. Smuggling had never been as easy or as profitable as now.

The Germans, with troubles of their own, left the traders pretty much alone. The customers believed that all they needed was enough provisions to hold out until the new offensive began, and they paid good prices.

There was also no lack of sources of merchandise. The peasants were more than eager to sell their products; the retreating Germans would confiscate them anyway. The barns were emptied of grain, the cellars of potatoes; they were filled instead with linens, a variety of garments, and even furs. A bomb could hit a barn and destroy everything, but what of it? They stood to lose a lot more. When the front lines passed through this area, their lives would hang by a hair. In the meantime, life had to go on, and as long as they were alive, better to hoard all they could.

The occupation zloty no longer had any value; trading reverted to primitive barter. The refugees had no place to store things anyway, and the peasants had huge barns.

Constantly on the move, Yurek never slept twice in the same place. He carried his earnings, in the form of goods, on his back. American dollars were hard to come by. There was no limit to what people asked in exchange for that precious currency. He traded a smoked ham for a small ring set with a "diamond." He knew nothing about diamonds, but the peasants knew even less. If he could exchange it for food, it was a diamond, even if it was only a bit of old polished glass.

During the day, he was in his element—hustling, making deals, even trading with German soldiers who were clearing out the food warehouses before setting them afire. It was the nights that filled him with dread. These were lawless times, and it was no secret that refugees carried all their belongings with them. If somebody split his head open and stole his belongings, who would miss him? Or even know about it for that matter? What was the point in getting rich when he had no one with whom to share his earnings?

Why had he ever let himself be separated from his friends? How many of them had perished in the fighting? There had been fierce battles near Josefow, only a few kilometers from Shwider. And Wicek—almost his brother—would he ever see him again? Everyone he had ever loved was gone; his loneliness choked him, enveloped him, oppressed him like an icy breath. There was no warmth to be found even under the featherbed he could now afford, if he could find one.

·　·　·　·　·

The swirling snow had already blanketed the countryside when Yurek arrived in the village near Skernovice. The products he had come to buy were packed and ready, but he had stayed, hoping to wait out the storm. Now the gusting wind rattled the windows, the driving snow obscured the road, and the short winter's day had almost ended.

"It's a sin to put a dog out in this blizzard," the farm wife said. "Ya can spend the night here." She invited him to have a bowl of soup with the family.

She had a round face with a ruddy complexion, and she seemed pleasant enough, but her husband might turn out to be a proper brute. "When is your husband coming home?" he asked.

"My husband?" The woman broke into a laugh. "Why are you asking about my husband?"

"It's almost curfew time and he's not back."

"Don't worry about him." She slapped her ample thigh and threw back her head with a loud guffaw. "One night he got drunk, shoved a German soldier, and ffft, no more husband."

"I'm sorry. When did it happen?"

"Soon after the war began."

"When the war began? But your youngest child is still a baby."

"My husband, of blessed memory, was a drunk and a damn fool and a son of a bitch. He's dead, I'm alive."

"But how can the mistress have such a young child?" Yurek persisted.

"In the same old way," she replied earnestly. He blushed to the roots of his hair and began to examine his shoes as if he had never seen them before. "A blanket on the floor will be enough for me," he told her.

"You'll freeze to death down there, jump in here," she said, uncovering a bed piled up with pillows and an enormous featherbed.

How nice of her to give him her bed. She'd probably sleep with the children in the other bed, Yurek thought as he undressed.

"In you go," she sang out, playfully pushing him into bed, and turned out the lamp. Heavily she climbed in beside him. Good. If she had any notions about going through his rucksack, he would be sure to wake up. The woman turned her back to him and almost at once, began to snore.

He found it hard to fall asleep. Damn it! He was a successful smuggler and lived like one. Only restaurants and taverns; no more public kitchens for him. He even had a beer now and then, sometimes a shot of vodka. After all, if he was a smuggler, he had to do what other smugglers did: he had to show some guts and take risks; he had to use rough language, be ready to use his fists. Then he'd be respected. Other smugglers were continuously bragging about their conquests—women practically fell into their laps. Occasionally he did some bragging too, but no pretty girls really threw themselves at him. He was ashamed to admit it, but he would have given a whole chain of sausages just to look at a girl's naked body; a glimpse of a décolleté dress still held mystery for him. He had watched mothers nursing their babies, but how totally different that was from a girl's breast curving out of a blouse, rising and falling with every breath, a secret terrain, enticing, calling out to be explored!

By next Passover he would be sixteen, and he could hear the fellows laughing their heads off if they learned that he had once stood for hours behind a window waiting to watch a girl across the way undress. He could have had an eyeful when Hella used to hang around him, but he'd always chased her away. If only she hadn't been the master's daughter . . .

The woman had crawled into bed the moment she had turned the light out—had she taken all her clothes off? She was so fat, she must have—only a few months ago she was nursing an infant. This was no Hella lying next to him; this was the mother of a child!

* * * * *

Yurek awoke drenched in perspiration. He tried to throw off the featherbed and realized it wasn't what was smothering him. He was scared out of his wits but could not utter a sound; his vocal cords had dried up. A pungent warmth was enveloping him. He sank into a mass of glowing flesh, and only after it was all over did he shake himself awake. She pushed a huge breast toward his mouth. "Here, sonny, suck . . ." She was startled when he burst out crying.

* * * * *

The peasant woman cooked up a tasty soup for breakfast. Yurek barely touched it, but gulped down the glass of vodka she set before him. She must have realized he was a Jew, but she said nothing about it. He was grateful, too, that she said nothing about what had happened during the night.

* * * * *

Several days later in a tavern, Yurek listened intently to a fellow smuggler regaling his friends with details of his prowess the night before. He described it all minutely, almost drooling as he did. Yurek wondered about his own experience. Something had finally happened to him too, and he didn't even know how it had all come about. It was dark, he was sleepy, or devil knew what. Maybe he had really dreamt the whole thing. The smuggler was giving an account of a beauty mark on his girl's belly or a navel or anything. If a girl came to his bed tonight, he wouldn't even know where to begin. A lot his big experience had done for him . . .

* * * * *

Yurek went back to the village near Skernovice. This time he wouldn't let her turn out the lamp. This time his eyes would be open, his mouth and his hands would not be idle. He strode along with a determined air. As soon as he walked into the house, he would kiss her. No, that wouldn't impress her. He would pinch her, right on the behind. Even better, he'd stick his hand down the front of her dress . . .

The door was locked from the inside. He knocked. He could hear the giggling—was that a man's voice? He knocked again. The door opened a crack; the sour stench of bad whiskey burned his nostrils. The door opened a bit wider and he saw a stocky peasant woman. God, she could have been his mother—no!—how could he even think of his beautiful, gentle mother in that way?

"Whaddya want, sonny? I've got nothing to sell today!" the woman shouted, and slammed the door.

That old hag! She had nothing to sell today! Who would buy what she had to sell, anyway?

Book Three

1

Hordes of smugglers and scavengers followed the victorious Soviet troops. Yurek hitched rides westward on Russian army trucks. Once again endless columns of German soldiers marched, but this time eastward, as prisoners, not conquerors. Now they limped along, feet wrapped in dirty rags: shoes, if they had any, were slung over their shoulders. One Russian soldier was enough to guard hundreds of wretched, ragged Germans. The Polish kids jeered and spat at the Germans as they passed, eyes staring vacantly at the ground.

• • • • •

When Yurek first arrived in Stettin, it was still a city hastily evacuated by the fleeing Germans, empty of people but full of abandoned property and possessions. Only the main roads leading to Berlin were open; the side streets were still blocked by rubble from buildings toppled by bombs, destroyed by artillery fire. Many people stopped here on the way to conquered Berlin or on the way home from a German prison camp. Everybody was on the move, searching for a relative or a friend, for decent clothes, household goods. Some liked the place and stayed. Others, after finding their homes destroyed, settled in empty houses.

Stettin was to become part of the new Poland. A Polish authority was finally established. Transients became residents. A border city on the way to Berlin, Stettin soon became a center of the black-market trade with Germany—a smuggler's paradise.

With the smattering of Russian he had picked up, Yurek was seldom refused a ride in a Red Army truck. He journeyed back and forth across the border, exchanging Polish sausage for German textiles, and occasionally managing to pick up a gold piece. Dressed in the outgrown, boyish clothes that he kept for border crossings, he looked younger than his years—a destitute lad in search of his parents. But in Stettin and Berlin, he sported an array of fashions that gave him the look of a child dressed up in his father's clothes. He learned to dance, wore a gold wristwatch, a signet ring. He had grown a few inches taller and was shaving every third day. Still, no one called him sir, as befitted a grown man. Would people ever stop thinking of him as a child?

He frequented the nightclubs that were springing up all over the place. What else was there to do? Lonely evenings, a strange town . . . Crossing borders was a cinch, but there was no one waiting for him on his return. If he were to be caught and locked up, who would miss him?

Yuzka, the waitress in the hotel restaurant, made a point of confiding in him that she was half-Jewish. How did she know he was Jewish? Well, didn't he always hang around with Jews? She was too quick to agree to come to his room after work; she probably wouldn't show up, anyway . . .

·   ·   ·   ·   ·

He was awakened by a light tap at his door. It was Yuzka. She put a cautioning finger to her lips as he opened the door. She tiptoed into the room, shoes in hand. "I'd get fired if the boss knew," she whispered into his ear. Her hair tickled his face, her pungent perfume stirred his senses. He longed to put his arms around her, but didn't dare. "I'm so glad you came," he said, and tried to add an endearing word. "I'll bring you something nice from Berlin."

"I don't want presents," she pouted. "You think I came up here for that?"

"I mean something special."

"I like you, that's why I came."

"Kiss me, then."

"You first," she teased, and laughed when he put his lips against hers. "You call that kissing?" She took his face between her hands. He felt the tip of her darting tongue on his lips and almost fainted. His arms went around her and he pushed her down on the bed, lips clinging to lips. Somehow he got her blouse unbuttoned. Her body writhed beneath him.

"You're gorgeous, Yuzka, you're wonderful, you're—wait and see what I get you from Berlin."

"A diamond?" she laughed.

"You'll see."

"You guys with your big talk! You're not that rich."

"Just be nice and you'll see."

"Oh, how you all brag, all of you! If you've got so much money, where do you stash it?"

"In the PKO," he answered, his fingers fumbling with her underwear.

She was young, but not so young she didn't know the PKO was a prewar savings bank no longer in existence. "Aw, c'mon, Yurek, where do you keep all your money? Are you afraid to tell me?"

"Afraid? Why should I be afraid?"

"Hey, you've got me practically naked and you haven't undone one button of your own." She ran her hands down his trousers. "Aha! So that's where it is!"

He rolled off the bed and jumped to his feet.

"Where are you going?"

"To Berlin, to get you a diamond."

"I don't need any diamonds, I don't want any presents, I told you."

"Sure, you don't want any presents, you just want to know where pockface keeps his money."

"Come back here, my little pockface," she giggled as she slipped out of her panties. "Look at the present I have for *you.*"

No need to peep through a window. Here, in his own room not two feet away, was everything he had dreamed of for so long. A young, pretty girl with soft, maddening curves waiting for him in his own bed.

"Come, Yurek," her voice was lush with promise, her arms outstretched, her breasts beckoning.

With one sweep of his arm he gathered up her clothes and threw them at her.

"What are you doing?"

"Get out!"

"What's wrong?"

"I don't want any more."

"But I want you . . ."

"I want you out!"

"I risked my neck coming here, and you treat me like a—"

"I've got plenty of money and I know how to hang on to it! You want to know something else? I have a gun too. Want to see it?"

Not another word passed between them as she threw her clothes on and fled.

•   •   •   •   •

Yurek sipped his tea, grateful for the warmth the hot liquid spread through him. The café lights and murmuring voices cheered him; he could feel his tension ease away. Crossing the border tonight had been touchy; it was a miracle he hadn't lost his merchandise. His glance fell on Saltcha, sitting alone a few tables away. He caught her eye and nodded. Lazar had vanished weeks ago, and she was still waiting for him. Lucky guy! He must have been at least forty. How had he attracted such a young beauty? The one time Yurek had asked her to dance, she had accepted politely enough, but she could hardly wait to get back to her table.

Fighting on the Russian front, Lazar had lost a leg. A decorated war hero in the battle for Berlin, he had no problem crossing borders. But involving Russian officers in shipping his smuggled goods in military trucks, that was downright crazy.

Saltcha and Lazar had been in their room when Polish police and Russian soldiers surrounded the hotel. They were both led away under heavy guard. To everyone's relief, Saltcha returned a few weeks later. Now she was at her usual table at the café, looking frail and vulnerable. Yurek longed to comfort her, to let her know he cared. Could he ask to join her at her table? No, better to wait for the music and invite her to dance.

He watched her from the corner of his eye, her finely shaped head held high, her hair perfectly bleached straw-blond as in the old days. He walked over to her table. "May I join you?" He bowed. She gestured toward the empty chair.

They exchanged few words during the evening. The good food and lively music could not dispel the gloom that was a palpable presence at the table. His attempts at humor brought a wan smile to her lips.

Escorting her to the elevator, he had a sudden idea. "Would you have time to help me? I'm always on the move, you see. If I could count on someone to sell my goods for me, it would be a big help."

Saltcha studied his face. "Help for whom?"

"For me, I really need the help."

"I have the time, and frankly, I need the money. They took everything from us."

"Then we have a deal?" Yurek put out his hand. "Let's shake on it."

She shook his hand. "Until Lazar returns." Her voice dropped as she added, "If he ever does."

• • • • •

"Hey, Yurek!"

Olek, his one-time partner, caught up with him in the street. "Are congratulations in order?"

"What the hell are you talking about?"

"You know damn well what I'm talking about—you and Saltcha—you're always together. If it's not the restaurant, it's on the dance floor. Just yesterday I saw you two down by the harbor."

"You wouldn't be jealous, huh?"

"Jealous? Are you out of your skull? You can bet she's being watched. Don't say I didn't warn you," Olek added as he rushed off to catch a tram.

Yurek kicked at an empty matchbox. All the time he was showing off with Saltcha, he was sure the other guys envied him. What a laugh! She probably wouldn't have given him the time of day if she'd had a choice.

To hell with Olek and his poisonous tongue! He didn't have a better friend in the world than Saltcha. With the prices she was getting for his goods he hadn't lost one grosz sharing his profits with her. And she was truly loyal to Lazar, though maybe it was a good excuse to keep him at arm's length. Leaving all his savings with her may not have been such a great idea after all. What if she really was being watched? The gold pieces might be safer with him, even if he did have to carry them across borders.

The hell with it! He wouldn't give her up even if half the Security Police were watching her. Why was he dawdling? She was waiting for him. He rushed by the elevator and bounded up the stairs. He found her in her room, ironing one of his shirts.

"You shouldn't bother with that," he said, moved.

"We're going dancing tonight, aren't we? I thought I'd get a shirt ready . . ."

"Our partnership doesn't include doing my laundry."

Saltcha put the shirt on a hanger. "Why not? You're like a brother to me."

He swallowed hard. At last! Finally she had dropped the formal mister. "You're more than a sister to me . . ."

She came around the table and patted his cheek. "Don't make such a fuss. I like doing it. Besides, it may be that I need your company more than you need mine."

Suddenly, he found himself clasping her hand in his own, heard his voice sputter, "Saltcha, I love you—"

She was startled. "Don't be silly!" she said, and gently withdrew her hand.

He lowered his gaze. How the hell had an ironed shirt led him to such a confession? And what about Lazar? Hadn't he himself admired her loyalty to him?

"Don't look so downhearted, Yurek. There will be many loves in your life—real ones."

"This is real, Saltcha. Don't you understand? It didn't just happen on the spur of the moment. I've tried to resist it. Don't you feel something toward me?"

"I told you, I couldn't love my own brother more."

"Oh please, don't talk down to me. I'm not looking for a sister."

"I'm so much older than you—"

"A bigger difference in age didn't seem to bother you . . ."

"You mean Lazar? Maybe I was looking for more than a husband—he was like a father to me."

"But now all we have is each other. Let's get married, let's go to a rabbi."

She put her arms around him. "Poor Yurek, you lost your mother too early . . ." She put her lips to his cheek. "How old are you? Tell me the truth."

He didn't answer. It felt so good to have the warmth of her body against his.

• • • • •

Was it the endless rain, the dreariness of autumn that kept Yurek in his room? The change that had come over him was alarming. Only a little while ago it had been almost impossible for him to contain his ardor, and now it had become just as difficult to make him smile.

Saltcha reproached herself. He had come like a savior in her time of need; she was still a willing recipient of all he had to give, and to show her thanks—a peck on the cheek? It would be more merciful if she let him go his own way . . .

•   •   •   •   •

Saltcha wrung the cold water out of a towel and carefully placed it on Yurek's swollen face.

"You didn't have to start a fight. What do you care what Olek says?"

"I'm not through with that bastard. I'll bash his head in one of these days."

"Hush, don't get all riled up again. And he wasn't so wrong—"

"Stop that or—I'll let you have it too."

Saltcha smiled, but wished she hadn't insisted they go to the nightclub. On their way back from the dance floor Olek had stopped Yurek: "Why deal in secondhand merchandise? I can get you something straight from the mill."

Yurek had leapt at him with both fists. Before she could drag them apart, he had two black eyes and a bloody nose.

"Let's get away from here," he begged, throwing away the towel. "The border is getting worse, anyway. They say that in Lower Silesia, on the Czech border, the smuggling is much better."

He stretched out on her bed. She sat beside him and stroked his hair. "Go ahead, Yurek. You should. You're right. Here each day is worse than the one before."

"How fast can you get ready?"

"I'm staying here."

He jumped up. "You can't mean that! You'll never be free of Lazar's ghost if you stay here."

"I don't want to be free."

Yurek squirmed. If she were a prisoner of her past, he had to shake her out of it. "What about me?" he demanded. "What am I anyway, a mechanical toy—all you have to do is wind me up?"

Saltcha looked at him sadly. He was right, that was exactly what she was doing. She could see very well what was happening to him. How neatly she had justified her behavior. If she sent him away, she would break his heart; if she was too yielding, he would become even more attached to her. She was holding on to him because he provided for her. And she didn't exactly dislike him either. She was holding on to him as a stand-in—"Don't go, Yurek, please!"

He was stopped at the door by her cry. He could hear the anxiety in it but wanted to jump for joy. She did love him, even if she refused to admit it to herself! He rushed back and gathered her into his arms.

"I didn't want you to leave like this," she said, as they lay back on her bed.

His arms went limp. "Like what? What the hell do you want!" he shouted. "Are you playing games with me, or with yourself?"

The flicker of a smile and the shadow of remorse commingled around her pale lips. "Don't be angry with me, Yurek—I can't stand it," she pleaded.

The shadow blotted out the smile, her lips quivered at the edge of tears, and his heart contracted. Once more his arms wound around her and his lips reached for hers. Resting on the bed, her vivid features became even more expressive: her face younger, her complexion brighter, radiating freshness, innocence . . . The graceful line of her throat flowed temptingly into the open neck of her blouse.

He rested his head beside her. She turned, and the curve of her breast heaved toward him. His hands, with a will of their own, leaped into feverish struggle with her clothing. She closed her eyes and murmured his name.

Flesh met flesh, and a tempest erupted. His arms locked around her. His lips moved from her eyes to her earlobes, to her neck, to her stiffening nipples and down to her velvety belly, as his fingers lingered over every undulating line of her body. She moved closer, her body aglow. All of a sudden, she sat up: "Wait!" She rummaged in the night table, lay down again, and put something into his hand. "You know how to use this?"

He looked at her, incredulous.

"We've got to be careful, Yurek, I'm sorry—"

He just lay there, panting for breath.

She took the condom out of his hand, tried to help him. A strange chill went through his body the instant she touched him.

"You're still a virgin, aren't you?"

He shook his head.

She nestled against him, kissed him tenderly. His shuddering turned into sobs that he could barely restrain. In a little while he got up, put on his clothes, and left without a word.

• • • • •

When Yurek did not appear in the restaurant the next morning, Saltcha went up to his room. She found him packing his things.

"You're leaving?"

"Yes, for Walbrzych."

She turned away and took off her girdle. There was a muffled clinking of coins as she dropped it on the table.

He went on with his packing. "How much are you giving me?"

"All of it."

"We were partners; half of the profit is yours."

"Give me whatever you think is fair."

He ripped open the stitches of the girdle and stacked a pile of gold pieces in front of her.

"That's more than my share. I don't deserve it all, but I'll take it. Things will be difficult here without you. Thank you, Yurek."

"Don't thank me; you earned it."

"I hope we're parting as friends?"

"Why not?"

"Why did you turn away from me last night?"

"I don't know."

"Tell me, Yurek."

"There's nothing to tell."

"It was your first time and you were scared. It's nothing to be ashamed of."

He said nothing.

"Then why are you giving me all this money—charity?"

"That's just the point," he blurted out. "I don't want your charity, either. My first time was with an old peasant woman. I didn't know what the hell was happening. Then there was this girl who wanted my money. You wanted to do it out of pity . . ."

"That's not so. At first, you know, I tried to be faithful to Lazar. Then, frankly, I was afraid you might get more attached to me. But I'm human too. You're young and inexperienced, but you're a real man. I envy the girl who will get you . . ."

"Be that girl, Saltcha!"

"Do you want me now—a parting gift to each other?"

"That isn't all I want. I want to marry you the way my father married my mother."

Resignation and the sadness of parting were evident in his flagging voice. She put her arms around his neck, tears welling up in her eyes. "Will I ever see you again?"

His face remained expressionless. She withdrew her arms, wiped her eyes with a quick movement of her hand, and sank into a chair. "The world of your mother and father went up in flames," she said bitterly. "I got involved with Lazar because I sold myself for a bit of warmth. Maybe even for the bread he could give me. Evidently I haven't mastered that trade yet. I still feel I belong to him. So you see, I'm not a very good businesswoman."

"Cut it out, Saltcha."

"Why? Are you afraid to face the truth? These are whoring times and you have to keep up with them. The trouble is . . ." She stopped for a moment, then continued forlornly, "You see, you're too good, and I'm not bad enough yet."

She rose from her chair and turned toward the door. Yurek blocked her way. "Don't go, Saltcha. Not yet. We can't part this way. You forgot your money—"

"I didn't do enough to deserve all that gold, and I won't be useful to you anymore."

"You don't have to be."

"I guess you really mean it. You're a lousy businessman yourself, Yurek. You could have bought me for much less."

He took her hand from the doorknob and brought it up to his lips. "Don't do this to yourself," he pleaded. She let him lead her back to the chair. He knelt down beside her and laid his head in her lap.

• • • • •

"That peasant woman doesn't count. You were half-asleep, so that makes me your first."

"Does it really matter?"

Saltcha smiled. "You're dying to know how I feel about you, right? You are beautiful, Yurek. You always give more than you take, even in bed. Your passion was contagious yesterday—"

"And today?" He didn't wait for her answer. He grabbed both her hands and squeezed them beseechingly. "Marry me, Saltcha! You'll be happy with me, you'll see."

"You've got to get away from Stettin."

"We'll both go."

"I heard what Olek told you. He was right, you know. Don't get mad, Yurek. I know you don't care now, but I really am too old for you. Go away now, before I change my mind and marry you after all."

· · · · ·

They didn't leave her room all day, not even for meals. In the evening, Yurek went down to buy food, and they ate it in bed. There was no longer any need for Saltcha to reassure him or make commitments. The excitement was intense, mutual, and inexhaustible.

The next morning Saltcha insisted on going out to collect from a customer. Yurek left a note for her and went to his room. He threw himself on the bed and was asleep as his head hit the pillow.

· · · · ·

A beam of light fell on his face. He opened his eyes and raised himself on his elbow just as the door was closing. He stared into the darkness. Who had that been? He switched on the lamp and glanced at his watch. Eight o'clock. Must have been the chambermaid to turn down his bed. He had slept the whole day away.

He went upstairs to Saltcha's floor and met her in the corridor.

"Are you just coming in?" He leaned over to kiss her, but she brushed past him and put her key in the lock.

What was the matter? "I was sure you'd still be in bed. Didn't you get any sleep? Did you have trouble collecting today? Don't worry—money's not everything."

"There was no trouble with the money, but I met someone there . . . Come in, I'll tell you about it." She threw her coat over a chair. "Do you know Mr. Romanowski?" Yurek shook his head. "Well, he's supposed to have good connections with the Russians. Time and again I've begged him to do something for Lazar, but he didn't want to get involved. Today when he saw me collecting all that money, he got very interested and took some as an advance. Maybe he can do something and maybe he can't, but I have to take that chance. It's your money I gave him, Yurek. I hope you don't mind."

He lowered himself into an armchair. Saltcha was still standing near the mirror of her dressing table, but her eyes were fixed questioningly on him. He said nothing. "I hope you understand," she said, lowering her eyes. "I had to do it. No one else even remembers him anymore."

They went down to the café to eat. The place was jammed with people, many of them dancing. It was too noisy to talk. Saltcha was tired and hardly touched her food. They left early.

"I'm dead tired," she said as the elevator approached his floor. "Do you mind not coming with me?"

"I'll just see you to your door."

Yurek flopped on his bed fully clothed, and kicked his shoes off. In a couple of days they could have been in Walbrzych, and now this Romanowski had to turn up. He couldn't really blame her for trying to save Lazar, but he couldn't help it; it tore his guts out. Just like her handing him the condom. She was only trying to be careful, but it had ripped him apart just the same.

He was getting to be as nasty as Olek. Loyalty was something to admire. It wasn't just her delicate features that made her so beautiful, or the way she carried herself. She was truly a fine, devoted woman. If he had kept on insisting, she might have given in and married him.

Was that what he really wanted at age seventeen?

He slid off the bed and finished packing his rucksack.

2

When Yurek saw Berlin for the first time, it was one vast ruin. Signs were still stuck in the gaping holes of bombed-out buildings: HITLER PROMISED US LEBENSRAUM. HITLER GAVE US AIRY APARTMENTS. Did the Germans know yet who was to blame?

The signs soon disappeared, as did much of the rubble. Here and there, streetcars began operating. Before long, life resumed a more or less normal pace. New Allied currency appeared in all the sectors, but the German mark also came back into circulation, no less acceptable.

Strange: in Stettin he could have got a whole mountain of German marks for a smoked ham. A Russian soldier had once offered him a sackful of marks for a mouth organ. He had given in to the

Russian as a gift, rather than bother with the worthless paper of the devastated Reich. Who could have foretold that today's defunct German economy would be resuscitated by yesterday's enemies?

He wandered through the streets, peering into people's faces: which one of them had been with SS, which one with the vicious Rheinehard's Einsatz? Everywhere he looked for the murderers: on the sidewalks, in streetcars, in beer cellars, in the nightclubs springing up like weeds. Such easygoing people, so peaceful and polite—he could not even picture any of them in black-booted Nazi uniforms with instant death slung at their hips. Again and again he looked into a face: had that man ever fired into a baby's crib, split open a head with his rifle butt?

Most of the hotels had been wrecked. A black-market operator shouldn't be registered in a hotel anyway, he told himself, and took a room in a private home on the prestigious Kurfuhrstendam. They were decent, friendly people who supplied him with everything he needed at a reasonable rate.

When it came to business, he dealt only with Jews. He had his own customers and suppliers among the refugees who were stuck in Berlin. Most of them now lived in the displaced persons camps in Schlachtensee, and none of them had a good word for their German business associates.

•   •   •   •   •

At the Gedächtnis Kirche station, a young girl boarded the streetcar and took the seat next to Yurek. She arranged her schoolbooks neatly on her lap. He stole a glance at her. This was as good a time as any to find out if it was true that even schoolgirls . . . He leaned over. "Does the Fräulein like chocolate?" he asked in German.

She smiled.

"American chocolate," he emphasized, then added, "and Polish sausage."

"Cigarettes too?" she asked, still smiling.

He was surprised. She seemed awfully young. "You smoke?"

"My papa does."

The tram was approaching his stop. He stood up, walked to the exit. The girl followed him off.

He tried to sneak her into his room; his landlady might not take kindly to his bringing in a young girl. Later, coming out of the room, he found an extra towel hanging on the doorknob.

Gerda was young, good-looking, tactful, and thoroughly experienced. He, younger than she, was certainly not good-looking, but by the next morning he too was experienced. He helped her carry his gifts home; her mother, who let them in, did not ask her where she had been all night.

·   ·   ·   ·   ·

How Gerda occupied herself while he was away from Berlin was something Yurek refused to think about. He rejected the notion that the schoolbooks under her arm were mere decoration, but his trips to Berlin became more and more frequent.

From Stettin, the closest smuggling point was Berlin, but from Lower Silesia, where he now lived, he had to go through Prague, and from there it was easier to smuggle into West Germany. If it weren't for Gerda, he would have kept away from Berlin and the East German border. Smugglers had disappeared there without a trace . . .

"I could rent a room for you in Munich," he suggested to Gerda.

"All my friends are here."

"I don't have any friends but you."

"My parents won't let me stay by myself in a strange city."

"But you won't be alone. I'd be living with you in Munich. I'd only be away when I'm out buying."

She didn't reply.

"You don't want to go?"

"Please, Yurek, it's so unexpected. Give me time to think about it."

Before he left, he presented her with a wristwatch. Her parting kiss was long and ardent, as if she would never let him out of her arms.

·   ·   ·   ·   ·

Would she be the one, then?

Better not to think about it.

Was she the one to bind his life to forever?

He was too young to think about "forever."

He gave her more than enough goods and cigarettes for her favors. An Omega gold watch was no trivial thing.

Plenty of Jews were living with German girls. He had met an American officer, a Jew, who had taken a German girl with him to the States.

German, yes, but had she sold herself for ham?

It had been such a long war . . . so much hunger, starvation, what else could she have done?

Had the Jewish girls in the ghetto been any less hungry? They had fallen to the ground swollen from hunger. Graves multiplied, not whorehouses!

What whorehouses? If Gerda were selling herself to everybody, how did she find time for him the moment he set foot in Berlin? Maybe she did—

To hell with it! He used to prowl the streets like a stray dog— like the cow when she was in heat. All night long she had bellowed, had almost torn down the barn door. Gerda relieved him of this maddening restlessness, kissed his face until he almost forgot how bad it looked . . . A smuggler had to keep his wits about him, know exactly what he was doing every minute, or he was doomed. Gerda made him feel good, he could relax with her. To hell with the rest of it! He had suffered enough. It wouldn't make a damn bit of difference to the world if his bones were rotting in a ditch somewhere. But they weren't. He had survived. Didn't he have a right to enjoy life? Maybe this was his revenge on Hitler. He, Yurek the pockfaced, was sleeping with a pretty young Fräulein of the master race, and paying her mother and father in ham.

That wristwatch he had given her made it plain to her she could get a lot more. What if she really took a fancy to him and decided to tie him down for life? She could get pregnant without his knowing it. What would he do then? Would he be a father to her child, or would he go away and let it grow up to be a Nazi?

When he finally fell asleep, he dreamt there was a raid. Germans were in the courtyard and Mama was still looking for a place to hide him—the attic wide open—how had he allowed himself to take shelter in a place like that? Any German could get in. He tried to get out, but there was no door, not even a hole to crawl through. A trap! Running, running, and in the end—lured into a trap.

3

Yurek eagerly crossed the border between Lower Silesia and Czechoslovakia. It was unbelievably easy—some border! He climbed a mountain, spent the day with a shepherd; then at night he descended by way of a footpath, and there he was—on the other side. He boarded a train and by dawn he was registered at the Hotel Centrale in Prague. He had to get to bed early so he could be awake and alert through the following night. There were two more borders to cross before he reached West Berlin.

He slept, woke, slept again. By the time he got out of bed, it was too late for the train to the border. It was too late even for the restaurant in the lobby, which would be closed by now. He followed the sounds of music into a nightclub. They served no food, the waiter informed him. No tragedy—he had plenty in his room. Just one drink . . .

He drained his second glass and watched the dancing couple on stage go through their contortions. The alcohol made his head spin. From a nearby table came the accents of a familiar language. He strained his ears; yes, it was Hebrew, with all the Sephardic vowels as the Zionists pronounced them. He had studied the Bible with Papa, even some Hebrew grammar. If they wouldn't talk so damn fast, he might understand what they—he ought to go over to their table and say *shalom.* Hell, if those dolls on the stage wanted to dance in the nude, why did they paint their bodies green, like old copper statues? Yeah, really like statues, every curve molded, every line—Gerda wasn't bad either, but . . .

The dancers left the stage. The applause died down, and he could hear the sounds of Hebrew again. Should really say *shalom,* it was no more than right . . . if only the room would stop going in circles . . . It was so damn quiet in here now. Probably getting the stage ready for a new number . . . What did he need the stage for? He had a picture of Gerda up in his room that was a knockout. Gerda didn't paint herself green—pity you couldn't undress a photograph . . . Gerda with her baby face was much prettier . . . He would tell them about her in Hebrew, Zionist accent or no Zionist accent . . .

• • • • •

The next morning he awoke late, groggy and hung over. He stared at himself in the dresser mirror and ran his fingers over his sparse stubble. Probably too late for breakfast in the hotel again. Just as well; his mouth tasted like old shoe leather. A long walk would clear his head and make him feel human again.

He meandered through the streets of Prague, looking absently at shop windows that gleamed in the morning sunlight. Jewelry with crimson stones seemed to be on display everywhere. It would certainly be popular in Poland. Germany, too. He couldn't tell whether the stones were glass or genuine, but a lot of work had gone into those bracelets. Labor here was cheap.

He had his lunch in town and resumed his walk. Abruptly, he stopped in his tracks. A bridge in Catholic Prague with a Hebrew inscription? A quotation from the Jewish Bible! Such a sight would be impossible in Poland. He must find a camera when he got to Berlin and take a picture of this the next time . . . He glanced at his watch. Time to get back to the hotel if he didn't want to miss his train again.

He stepped into a line of passengers waiting to board the Number 7 tram to his hotel. He had traveled some distance before he realized he was on the right tram, but going in the wrong direction. He jumped off, crossed the street, and hopped on a crowded tram that turned out to be a Number 11. God knew where that would take him! He got off at the next stop in an unfamiliar area. No one had even heard of his hotel. He blundered from one street to another, forgetting that he had a map in his pocket.

When he finally made it back to the lobby of his hotel, he was exhausted. A fine state to be in when you made your living smuggling across borders . . .

He shook his head at his own ineptness. Each time he started walking a little faster, Lazar would come to his mind, or some other guy who had disappeared on a border crossing. Was it a premonition?

It was quite late, but he might catch the train if he hurried.

"YUREK!"

Before he could turn around, someone was hugging him.

"WICEK!"

"I hardly recognized you! A real fashion plate!" Wicek marveled.

They hugged each other, stepped back to get a better look, hugged each other again.

"So, you're alive, thank God! I searched for you all over. I was beginning to think the worst."

Yurek's lips trembled, smiling at the same time. "Look at me, bawling like a baby and I haven't even asked about Yuzek, little Milush, Stefcha—"

They were sitting in the lobby of the Centrale Hotel. Yurek kept breaking into Wicek's story each time he remembered someone else. The clock struck nine. Missed the train again. Oh well.

"And you, Yurek, whatever happened to you? How did you get out in one piece? Listen I've got to catch a train. How about coming with me?"

"Still smuggling?"

Wicek nodded, grinning.

"From Poland?"

"Sure. Where else?"

"What kind of stuff?"

"The most valuable."

"The most valuable? What's that?"

"Children."

"WHAT?"

"You heard me. Children."

"I don't understand."

"What's so hard to understand? Our children."

"What do you mean?"

"You don't know? Where have you—it's a long story, Yurek. The Central Committee in Warsaw? The Communists are running it. They say they want to rebuild Jewish life in Poland. How can you build anything on a cemetery? And will the anti-Semites let us? Fat chance! They're still killing Jews. Did you hear about the boys of a kibbutz who were murdered outside of Kraców? Where the hell have you been? You don't know what's going on right under your nose! A pogrom in Kielce—forty-two victims, some of them infants. The police joined the murderers."

"I did hear something about that. Listen, I can tell you some things you don't know, either. But what does this have to do with smuggling kids?"

"The Central Committee set up a few children's homes. Anti-Semites have already shot up one of them. We steal the kids out of those homes, take Jewish children back from Polish families, and smuggle them all out of Poland."

"We? Who's we?"

"I can see you don't know a damned thing. We have an organization called Brichah, to get survivors to Palestine. People from the ghetto underground. Some emissaries have come from Eretz, too."

"Palestine?"

"Yes. It's a well-run outfit. Today a train arrives with more than three hundred kids. I think the government couldn't be happier, our taking Jews out of Poland, I mean. Otherwise, we'd never be able to organize a whole trainload. They all hate us, you see. Sooner or later the government will have to defend Jews against the violence of the anti-Semites—and it won't make them very popular. Let's go, Yurek, it's late."

● ● ● ● ●

His name was no longer Wicek. "Shalom, Zev! Shalom, Zev!" he was greeted at every step as they entered the railway station.

"Has the train come in yet?" he asked.

Apparently it had arrived but was standing on a siding somewhere. Zev went to find it; Yurek tagged along. They hopped over rails and circled around long strings of cars. It wasn't difficult to pick out the transport among the other trains—the voices of children, like chirping birds, reached them from a distance. Here were the freight cars with Polish eagles and the initials of the Polish State Railway Line.

Zev shone his flashlight into the dark and was met by the screech of young voices: "Zev! Zev!" Little hands reached out to him, arms twined around his neck. They almost knocked him down in their excitement. One little girl held on to him for dear life. "She's mine," Zev explained to Yurek. "I stole her away from a Pole who wouldn't give her up for any amount of money. At first she cried, tried to run away; we had a devil of a time with her. Now, well you can see . . ."

The little girl finally allowed herself to be set down and they turned to leave. "Are you coming to Eretz with me?" she called after Zev.

"Certainly, but later. I still have a lot of work to do here."

Zev stopped to ask one of his comrades something.

"Galil, third car," the other replied, after a long search through his lists.

Zev pulled Yurek by the arm. "Come on! I've got a surprise for you!"

The word *Galil* was chalked on the side of the third car. Yurek's eyes followed Zev's flashlight as it played over the berths.

"Rinah, you have a visitor!"

A small girl threw her arms around Zev's neck.

"Stefcha?" Yurek asked uncertainly. "How she's grown! I never would have recognized her!"

"We call her by her Hebrew name now. Rinah, don't you remember Yurek? He took you to Shwider."

After a momentary hesitation, they kissed each other. Zev was disappointed. No joy, no tears—hardly a reunion. Rinah had forgotten Yurek.

"I'm hungry, Zev. Do you have a piece of bread for me?"

"They'll be bringing the soup around very soon."

Yurek was surprised. "Soup, like in the charity kitchen? The war's over."

"We don't have much money. We get some from America, but it costs fortunes to ransom these kids from the Poles who were keeping them."

"I'll be right back," Yurek said abruptly and jumped off the train.

"What's wrong?" Zev called, running after him. "Where are you going?"

"Don't worry, I'm not running away. Come with me, if you like."

They hurried to Yurek's hotel. He hauled his rucksacks out of the wardrobe and dumped them out on the bed.

Zev whistled. "That's worth a fortune."

"The kids are hungry," Yurek said, and strapped a loaded rucksack onto Zev's back.

•   •   •   •   •

Yurek stared at the empty rucksacks at the foot of his bed. Without any goods, it hardly seemed worth the trip to Berlin. He could exchange his German marks for dollars here in Prague. The profit wouldn't be as high, but there would be enough for a better meal than those kids were getting on the trains.

He thought about Zev's invitation. "You must come to Swinari and meet my Leah." Zev had clapped him heartily on the back. "You must have a girl of your own by now! No? Well, plenty of time for that—you're much younger than me."

Yurek knew about Swinari, that town in Lower Silesia not far from Walbrzych. The Hachshara kibbutz was there, the orientation center organized by the Brichah for children and teenagers. He was sure there wasn't one girl there who didn't have a sweetheart already, just like the girls in the refugee camps. All the time he'd been knocking himself out looking for bargains in the black market, others were acquiring more precious treasures . . . All you could buy with money was a Gerda.

Things were slowly settling down; pretty soon the black market would be out of business. He'd better grab whatever came his way. Without money, even Gerda wouldn't stay with him. He wasn't deluding himself about her, though it was good to lie in her arms, satisfied, exhausted, lulled by her caressing fingers . . . He must catch the early train to the border.

•   •   •   •   •

The journey itself was the same as always, but at the other end of the line something had changed. Was Gerda less affectionate because he had arrived empty-handed? Or was he just getting bored with her charms? She lay beside him fast asleep, but he tossed open-eyed, restless. All her soft words and embraces tonight had seemed as planned and mechanical as those of a wind-up doll.

Hard to believe—Stefcha had survived and he hadn't even known about it. He must have asked about the children when he went to Shwider after the war. No, that was the time he brought the gifts. The master was drunk and the mistress was away somewhere. Had he gone back there a second time? Had he even bothered to look at the lists of survivors the Jewish Committee had posted?

Now, how could he have taken time from shoveling in the marks and dollars? He had to make lots of money. Smugglers' hangouts and girls were expensive. The girls made more money than he—a smuggler crossed only one border a night, but a girl . . . Gerda had a blister on her lip. That was understandable. When your lips had to work overtime . . .

If he knew what was good for him, he'd get out of goddamn Berlin, the sooner the better.

• • • • •

He stopped in Walbrzych just long enough to change his clothes and went on to Swinari. Zev was away on a mission, he was told, but they would gladly take him to Leah, Zev's friend. He was painfully aware of the stares that followed him in his embarrassingly fancy clothes.

"Zev's told me all about you," Leah greeted him, shaking his hand. "He was so happy to find you again. He'll be back in a day or two."

He walked beside her, snatching frequent glances at her face. Was she pretty? It certainly wasn't Saltcha's kind of beauty. Leah's oval face was delicate, her olive skin smooth, her lips a bit too thin— but what eyes! The almond-shaped whites were almost blue; out of the dark brown depths of the pupils shone a compelling light; not a physical allure like Saltcha's, but a spirituality that was a kind of glow around her.

She showed him around the kibbutz. The sorrows of the war still smoldered in everyone's eyes, but no one was defeated. On the contrary, they were full of purpose, of hope, full of the energy of preparing for something real.

"I've got to go," Leah said after the tour. "My children are waiting. Want to come along?"

Yurek smiled. Zev with "his" children, Leah with "hers," about thirty of them, he saw, as they approached the group. A beautiful little girl looked up at him.

"What's your name?"

"Yurek."

"That's a Polish name."

"Yossel, then."

"Yosef," Leah corrected. "That's the Hebrew. Come on, kids, let's get to work!"

She sat on the floor, with the children around her in a circle. Yurek was filled with admiration for the imaginative way she conducted the lesson. It was no easy task, with such a large group of assorted ages brought together by chance.

The day was hot. "Read the next page," she instructed the children as she noticed Yurek remove his tie. "I'll be right back."

She took him to the supply room. When they returned to the classroom, he was wearing khaki shorts and a white pioneer's shirt. Now he looked like he belonged.

Normally a graceful dancer, he kept falling all over himself during the hora. Two left feet, he chided himself. Or was it because he was tripping over his thoughts?

In the evening he changed back to his city clothes and said goodbye to Leah.

"Will you visit us next week for the holiday?"

"Holiday?"

"Rosh Hashonah. Zev will certainly be back."

"I'll come," he said, hurrying off. My God, how could I have forgotten Rosh Hashonah?

• • • • •

It was not the Rosh Hashonah he remembered from home. But there was a lot of singing and dancing. He found himself replying to questions in Hebrew. Slowly, it was coming back to him, although his pronunciation needed a great deal of correction.

"What are you so busy with?" he asked Zev. "I came to see you, and you're never around."

"I'm sorry. And tonight I've got to leave again. But you stay, at least over the holidays."

"Another transport of children?"

"Only one child this time. Actually two people—a mother and child."

"Is it worth crossing a border for only two people?"

"What border? First, we've got to get them away. I told you, it's not an easy business. The mother was hiding out on a farm. I suppose the peasant took her in for the money, and then his son fell in love with her or something. We don't know the whole story yet. All I know is that when we first contacted her, she said she preferred to stay there. Now she's begging us to get her away. Her husband and his family watch her day and night."

"How will you do it?"

"If we can't find a peaceful way, we'll have to play rough. Something unpleasant must have happened there if she's asking for our help."

"Maybe she just wants to be with Jews again. I'm sure I could help. Let me come with you, Zev."

"Sure, if you want to. We can use a lookout in the village—and you've got a great face. You'll have to watch the house and figure out a strategy. But I warn you, this sort of thing can be riskier than smuggling."

"Are you scared?"

"I can't afford to be."

"Me neither."

"Okay. It's not too far from Kielce. They say the village had a hand in the pogrom."

"Hey, are you trying to scare me?"

"Why should I do that?"

"Then let me know when you're ready."

4

When the time came to contact the woman, Yurek went to the house with a valise, offering small wares for sale. A young woman with a baby on her arm answered his knock. She didn't need anything, she insisted. He looked at the number on the door. It checked. Was it the right street? She was blonde, with brown eyes and a pretty face, just as Zev had described her. The child seemed to be about the right age.

Yurek winked at her. Something was wrong. She didn't respond at all. Had she changed her mind again? After much urging, she agreed to look at his merchandise. She bought a pair of shoelaces, and the old peasant sitting near the window gave him a bank note. As Yurek handed the change to the young woman, he scratched her palm, hoping she would understand it as a signal and not a vulgar gesture. She dropped the change into the old man's hand. Repacking his valise slowly, Yurek glanced at her, his eyes questioning. Had she nodded her head or was he imagining it?

"Tomorrow is Sunday, but if you need anything else, I'll be in the village," he said at the door. He touched his cap and left.

The next morning, an automobile drove up to the peasants' house. Two men got out of the car and went inside. They identified themselves as members of the secret police and began asking questions. Where had the young man and the old peasant been during the night of the Kielce pogrom? The secret police had information that they had been seen in the mob.

"How can you accuse us of such a thing? Just the opposite—during the war we hid Jews. Our daughter-in-law here is Jewish."

"You're lying. She doesn't look like a Jew."

"Ask her. Tell them, Kasha. Tell the comrades that you're—that you were—"

"Go ahead, Kasha, tell them," her husband pleaded.

"You're liars, all of you!" one of the policemen snapped, drawing his revolver. "When we get you down to headquarters, you'll tell the truth!"

The door opened, and Yurek came in with his valise. The man with the gun turned on him instantly. "And who are you? Caught you red-handed, eh? Where do you get your goods, you smuggler?"

"A few pairs of shoelaces—you call that smuggling? I'm a war orphan."

The policemen turned back to the peasants. "We've got our orders to take you in. If you're telling the truth, you'll be back here in a few hours. You, old lady, you're coming with us. Your daughter-in-law can stay here with the baby. And you, young speculator, get lost! Find yourself an honest job somewhere. There's no room for peddlers in our new Poland!"

Yurek waited until they were all in the car and he heard the motor start. Then he turned to the young woman with a big smile. "Well, they're on their way." She tightened her grip on the baby. "Don't be afraid," he reassured her. "Take your baby and come with me. Hurry, please."

Outside, Zev was waiting. They cut through fields to a railway station past Kielce and caught the next train to Warsaw.

Meanwhile the automobile taking the peasants to Kielce had broken down on a lonely road. The men tinkered with the engine for a long time but couldn't find the trouble. All the while the peasants kept protesting their innocence. They hadn't done anything, they knew nothing, absolutely nothing—and who would tend the farm?

It was late in the evening when they were finally released.

· · · · ·

In the train, Zev feigned sleep. The young woman nervously rocked the baby in her arms. Yurek, at a window, tried to look nonchalant while he kept one eye on the platform. Finally, the train pulled out and he turned toward Kasha. "You can relax now," he breathed.

Zev straightened up and stretched his legs. Kasha transferred the baby to her other arm. "How did you know about Kielce?" she asked.

"Are you serious? The whole world knows about that pogrom."

"I mean about the old man and Maczek taking part in it."

"Don't let it worry you. It was only an excuse to get them out of the way."

"Only an excuse? You mean you really *didn't* know about them? The rumor spread like wildfire—the Jews in Kielce had killed a Christian. The whole village was in a turmoil. They grabbed axes, knives, clubs—I tried to stop Maczek, but he shoved me halfway across the room. They didn't return till late that night. The first word my husband said to me as they came back was Zhidova. And I was supposed to spend the rest of my life with him . . ." Tears streamed down her face.

"Shh," Yurek cautioned, "people are staring."

•　•　•　•　•

Yurek went to Swinari as often as his travels permitted. Kasha's adjustment to life on a kibbutz was instant, as if she had lived there all her life. People gravitated toward her, he noticed. Was it the dimples in her cheeks, or her rippling, infectious laugh? Whatever it was, he enjoyed seeing her and always brought a toy for the baby, sometimes American chocolate, occasionally a personal luxury for her.

But the smuggling business still demanded most of his time. By now the Germans had enough food of their own, and it was a relief not to carry sacks of smoked meat around. The big profit these days was in foreign currency and jewelry. Berlin was no longer on his itinerary. He confined his trade to the refugee camps of Munich, Feldafing, or Bergen-Belsen. In Poland, he was still Yurek; on the kibbutz he was Yosef; in the refugee camps in Germany they called him Yossel.

Why not? It was his Jewish name, after all, and the camp at Bergen-Belsen was a Jewish world. The first time he had set foot in the camp, they had given him a Yiddish newspaper published there. That same evening he'd been invited to a Yiddish play. They had started Hebrew classes, lectures. Things weren't ideal: there were hecklers at the political meetings; once even a fistfight. Yet they had a goal to fight for. Liberation had found these starved people on the verge of death. Before they had even put flesh on their bones, they began to transform their camp into a living Jewish community.

He half expected Zev to reproach him for his wayward life, and he had his defense ready: remember what happened to Milush? We wanted to support him, to keep him off the streets, but he wouldn't have any part of it, would he? In the end you had to set him up making cigarettes, didn't you? He was attached to his things too—after all he'd been through, how could he stand in line for the handout of a shirt and a pair of khaki shorts, so everyone would see that even his legs were pockmarked . . .

But Zev never uttered a reproachful word, did not even give him a critical look. Only once, when he was describing how he had become a medic in the Warsaw rebellion, Leah had sighed wistfully, "How we could use a medic around here!" And Zev had added, "Every kibbutz needs one."

Yurek had said nothing, but Leah persisted: "Our children have been through so much. It would be wonderful if a doctor could accompany every transport across the border, but there aren't any. At least if we had medics . . . We would pay them well."

"With what? You don't have enough money as it is. Isn't that what you said, Zev?"

"We'd take it out of the clothing budget, or even the food," Zev replied. "You can go hungry one day and eat more the next. But if something happens, and there's not even a medic . . ."

The conversation took place on an evening when Yurek's rucksack was already packed for the border crossing. He made the trip in pouring rain over perilous twisting mountain trails. One of the group, Heniek, lost his footing. Miraculously, he rolled only a few feet and escaped with a broken arm. A little farther and he'd have gone over the edge. Yurek watched as the other smugglers continued on their way without even a backward glance. Heniek's groans might give them away; they wanted to be as far away from the spot as possible . . .

Yurek found two straight twigs and bound the broken arm. He took a shirt out of his rucksack, tied the two sleeves around Heniek's neck, and made a sling. The fellow held on to his legs and begged him not to leave him alone to die in the night. It took some doing to get him to his feet and onto the path for the long hike back.

Heniek was a deadweight, hanging on as if his legs were broken too. They kept stumbling downhill while Yurek tried in vain to recognize a familiar landmark. All around them stood tall, pillared rocks, like gravestones.

"It's okay, we're on the Polish side," Heniek reassured him. He knew these parts well. Kudowa, the health resort, was not too far away. They were sure to have a doctor there.

Yurek stood at the window, staring at the park. The season was over, but people were still coming here for the mineral waters. What a beautiful view! How lovely it must be in full foliage. The door creaked and he turned around.

"Yurek! You're alive! Thank God!"

In the doorway stood Dr. Jendrichowski.

"Doctor!"

"It's good to see you! What brings you here?"

"This is my friend, Heniek. We—we were hiking in the mountains, and Heniek slipped. I think his arm is broken."

"You live in Kudowa?"

"Nearby, Doctor."

While the doctor examined Heniek's arm, Yurek's brain worked feverishly. The doctor would ask questions; he'd better have some convincing answers. Hiking in the mountains in a rainstorm? What a stupid excuse!"

"Well, my dear medic, your diagnosis was correct. Take your friend over to X-ray. Give them this slip. When you're through there, stop in to see me."

"I wish I *were* a medic. I mean a real one—"

"You'd make a fine medic, Yurek, but there's a question of your general education . . . Anyway, come to my office later. We'll talk about it."

•   •   •   •   •

Before leaving Germany, Yurek had bought some toys for Kasha's little boy and a cake of American perfumed soap, but when he went to Swinari, she was no longer there.

"We had to get her across the border in a hurry," Zev explained. "Her husband forced his way into a kibbutz in Lodz. Seems like he figured out who the guys really were who stormed into his house that day."

"But where is she? Where did they take her?"

"I have no idea. Maybe to a kibbutz in France or Italy. These things are decided in Prague."

Yurek had visions of Kasha climbing over mountain slopes with the baby in her arms. He wished she at least had a medic with her . . . He had helped rescue Kasha out of that godforsaken village. How sweetly she had smiled when he brought her something from his trips. But she had not thought to scribble shalom on a scrap of paper, or leave word for him with Zev.

Why should he care, anyhow? Let her go wherever she wanted, and God bless her. Even to her peasant, for all he cared. He couldn't worry about the whole lousy world. Did the world worry about him?

5

Yurek sat on the one chair in his hotel room in Prague, trying to decide whether to go down to the nightclub or get undressed and get into bed. He was in the doldrums these days. The Hotel Centrale could be a pretty lively place. Still, he wasn't much in the mood for . . .

A sudden thought cheered him up. Earlier he had again overheard some Hebrew conversation in the lobby. The fellows had been so deeply engrossed in their talk that they were oblivious to what was going on around them. Must be Brichah people—shouldn't be too hard to find out what rooms they were in, if they were staying here. He called down to the desk clerk and in a few minutes was put through to one of them. In a mixture of Hebrew and Yiddish he invited them to join him for a drink.

Two young men appeared in the arched entryway of the club and peered into the dimly lit room. Yurek stood up and waved.

"Shalom. Please sit down," he greeted them, holding out his hand.

They remained standing. "What do you want?" one of them asked.

"Have a seat. I only wanted to spend a little time with my own people." Not until they had a drink did he dare ask: could they tell him where Kasha and her child might have been taken?

They stared at him silently. He looked from one to the other and added quickly, "I helped get her away, so I feel close to her somehow."

"What are you doing in Prague?"

"I'm on my way to Feldafing."

"An emissary? What organization?"

"No, no, I'm not with any organization. I smuggle goods between Walbrzych and Feldafing."

"What do you smuggle?"

"You know, whatever comes to hand. If the German economy is hurt by my dealings in the black market, I don't exactly lose any sleep over it."

Yurek ordered another round of drinks and returned to his original question: Did they have any idea where he might find Kasha? Could he trace her through their Prague center? His guests mouthed compliments about the singer on stage, but his questions remained unanswered.

He awoke early the next morning. His train was not due to leave until evening and he was too restless to sit around the hotel. He walked along the street and wondered how to fill the hours before his departure. He could go to the Marahal's Synagogue, or to the Jewish Museum that Zev had told him about. Better not risk getting lost again . . . He turned to go back for a map of the city and almost bumped into one of the Brichah people. It was not either of the men who had been with him last night, but there was no mistaking him.

With the map in his pocket, Yurek was soon on his way again. He stopped to look into a display window. The glass reflected the face of the man he had bumped into near the hotel. In the Marahal's Synagogue he saw him again. Were they tailing him? Brichah was a secret organization, after all. Someone who neither looks nor acts like a Jew, comes from nowhere to ask about a person they had whisked out of Poland. If they suspected him of spying, they could finish him off in a Prague alley. That's how underground organizations deal with such things.

•   •   •   •   •

If he was alarmed by the Brichah, he should have run off to Germany. There, at least, he could do business. What the hell was he doing back in Walbrzych with all his stuff? He would even have sold it in Prague instead of carting it all the way back to Poland.

Yurek punched the pillow under his head. Hunger pangs grumbled in his stomach. Another mealtime had come and gone, but he could not work up the energy to get out of bed.

A knock on the door. He didn't answer. No one ever came to see him anyway. He certainly didn't want company now. The knocking continued. Someone called his name. Zev? He jumped up and opened the door.

"What are you doing here?"

"Are you sick? How come you haven't been around?"

"I've been on the road."

"A bad border? You look terrible."

"I'm okay."

"A bad business deal?"

"No, nothing like that."

"What's wrong, then?"

"I don't know. I don't feel well."

"Come back to the kibbutz with me."

"I can't, not yet."

"I only meant you should come for a rest. Hey, you said 'not yet'—does that mean—"

"Look, I can't think straight. Don't worry, I'm not sick. And I'm glad you came to see me."

Zev turned and walked to the window. "The truth is, I didn't exactly come to visit. I came to ask for something, it's no small thing."

"For you, half my kingdom."

"It's no joke—"

"What's up?"

"We've gathered almost three hundred kids, but the money for fixing up the train hasn't come yet. Things are getting too hot for us here. The Jewish Communists are dead set against our work and are putting up all sorts of obstacles. Now we hear that the matter is being discussed by the Polish Communist party. We also hear they've sent a delegation to the president about it. There's a danger they'll seal the borders altogether."

"Are you considering sending them in small groups? I'm ready to go with them anytime—I know the border like the back of my hand."

"We can't do that. It's snowing in the mountains already. It's only a matter of money, and that's bound to come soon."

"Can't you hurry them up?"

"The way things are going, we're even afraid of the JOINT—I mean the Warsaw Bureau of the American Jewish Distribution Committee. We suspect the Polish secret police have an agent there . . ."

"And you think I can help you?"

"Let me finish, Yurek. There are rich Jews among the smugglers, and you know them. If you could persuade them to lend us the money . . . We could pay them back in dollars right here, or instruct our people abroad to give it to them there, whichever way they want."

No sooner were the words out of Zev's mouth than Yurek ran to the bed, lifted a corner of the mattress, and pulled out a woman's corset. He handed it to Zev. "Eight hundred dollars in gold. It's all yours."

"In this thing?"

"Is it enough?" He took a gold watch off his wrist and ripped a diamond out of his trouser cuff. "Here, take this too."

"It's wonderful of you to do this, Yosef." Zev put his hand affectionately on Yurek's shoulder, and his voice fell. "But I'm afraid it's not nearly enough."

"Then let's go get some more! Come on!"

"Remember, what we're doing with the kids is illegal—"

"Don't worry, leave it to me!"

6

When Yurek had crawled across borders in any wretched weather he had felt as strong as an ox. Now that he hadn't crossed one in more than two weeks, his head ached, his back was sore, he was dead tired, and he couldn't fall asleep. Should he run over to Kudowa for the mineral baths? His father had weak lungs; Hannele too. And mud baths were supposed to be dangerous for people with weak lungs. Perhaps he should ask a doctor. Dr. Jendrichowski had invited him to come there.

•　•　•　•　•

Kudowa was one of the finest spas in Europe for heart disease and nervous ailments. Was it really the baths and the mineral waters that helped, or was it just the serenity of the natural surroundings? The mountains in this area were not as steep or imposing as farther south in the area of Zakopane. Here the hills seemed to have climbed up slowly, with steady, regular steps, leaning on a cane, just like the patients. Tall, pointed rocks stood along the slopes in perfect harmony with the pines and oaks. In this spa, which catered to the weak heart and the frayed nerve, quarreling was forbidden, so tree made peace with cliff and coexisted amicably. Tranquility reigned supreme at the spa, guarded jealously by nature—and by the patients.

•　　•　　•　　•　　•

Sitting in the doctor's waiting room, Yurek wondered what the devil he was doing there. Was he inventing imaginary ailments? Was it the pain of loss? Kasha, whom he hardly knew, or Gerda, whom he knew only too well? Could a mud cure wash the mud out of his soul? He bemoaned his pockmarked face. The trouble was that his scars went much deeper than his skin. One day he was in love with Saltcha, the next he was ready to marry Gerda, the third he felt romantic about Kasha. One day he was filled with saintliness and wanted to devote himself to the poor orphans in the children's commune; the next day he was smuggling across borders, hanging around nightclubs, smoking, drinking, and all the while the stuff was choking him. Was there a cure for this kind of head at the Kudowa spa?

The doctor greeted him as he walked into the room.

"Good to see you again, Yurek. How's your friend doing—the one with the broken arm? And how is Stakh? Is he continuing his medical studies?" The doctor noticed the change in Yurek's face. "He survived, didn't he?"

Yurek shook his head.

"What happened? A stray bullet?"

"Not a stray one." The words almost scorched his lips: "A Polish Nazi of the Naro gangs."

"Scum of the earth!" the doctor exploded.

"It's good to see that the doctor is among those who are not indifferent."

"And you are *not* indifferent?"

"How could I be? It was only my looks that saved me."

"I suspected all along that you were *amkho* . . ."

Yurek's mouth dropped open. *Amkho?* It couldn't be. If he prac-

ticed under the name of Jendrichowski, then his diploma must have
been under that name, a Polish name.

"What is your real name?"

"You want to know if I'm—here, they don't know. But yes, I am
amkho."

"And your uncle the priest?"

"He's not my uncle and he's not a priest. He survived disguised
as a priest . . ."

•   •   •   •   •

The doctor found Yurek healthy enough, but nervous, and exhausted.
He prescribed mineral baths. "They certainly can't do any harm," he
smiled.

When Yurek arrived for his regular bath a few days later, they
informed him that the doctor wished to see him. Dr. Jendrichowski
had arranged for him to work as a medical aide in his clinic, where
he would have an opportunity to further his studies. The doctor himself was giving a course on anatomy to the nurses.

Who wanted to study anatomy? The only reason he wasn't crossing borders was that he had loaned all his capital out, but when he
got it back, well—didn't like to lie around idle.

On the other hand, what could he lose by taking a few lessons in
anatomy? He had little formal education. Lucky his father had forced
a bit of Torah into him. In the kibbutz they didn't eat as much meat,
eggs, and butter in a week as he polished off in a day, but with the
little bit of money they did have, they bought books. If only he'd
been lucky enough to find a kibbutz before he had become such a
hardened smuggler.

•   •   •   •   •

Yurek went to Swinari for a visit. Zev caught sight of him and drew
him aside. "Come into the office and get your bundle."

"What bundle?"

"Your money."

"It doesn't belong to me anymore."

Zev stared. "You don't want your money back?"

"No."

"Don't make any rash decisions. The money was sent here to pay debts. Come and get it. If you have second thoughts after the money's been spent, you'll yell for it till you're blue in the face and it won't do you any good."

"What makes you so sure I'll have second thoughts? If I move in here, I'll get my share of it along with everyone else."

"Are you really ready to join us?"

"Isn't that the whole idea of a kibbutz? How can you become a member of a collective and still hold on to your own little bundle?"

Zev grabbed Yurek's hand and dragged him into Leah's classroom. "What did I tell you about Yosef?" he shouted.

"Zev, I'm in class now," Leah gasped, shocked by the interruption.

"Leah," Zev continued excitedly, "didn't I tell you he would come?"

"You interrupted a class to tell me this?"

"Answer me, it's important. What did I say?"

"Zev believes in you"—she turned to Yurek—"but I . . . to tell you the truth I'm not exactly crazy about smugglers or smuggling."

"But what did I say?" Zev persisted.

"Zev feels that you're one of ours."

"He *is* one of ours. He's joining the kibbutz."

Leah studied him silently, then smiled. "Yosef, will you be able to give up your silk ties and—"

"He's already given everything he owns to the commune," Zev interjected.

Leah hugged Yosef and kissed him on both cheeks.

7

Night blanketed the white snow on the peaks of the Alps, the green fields in the valleys, the brown slopes of the mountains, and the blue Rhone at their feet. Dense, misty darkness hovered close, as if a heavy curtain had been suspended over the earth. No breeze, not even the faintest stirring, as if even the river itself had stopped flowing. On the tracks running parallel to the river, a flash of a locomotive cut a tunnel of light in the darkness.

• • • • •

"Grab some sleep, Yosef," said Leibl, who was in charge of this trans-port. "Tomorrow will be a tough day: checking lists of arrivals, as-signing quarters, distributing food. Try to catch a few winks."

"*You* get some sleep, Leibl. Last night while you were jumping the border, I slept on the train."

"Forgot that this time you were traveling with a passport and a visa? Nice to travel legal for a change?"

"Nice? All those immigration officers, so many checkpoints. When you travel 'black,' you know that everything will go smoothly because it's greased. Here all those searches, questions. I'm not used to crossing a border 'white.'"

"You've got a point. Under the Nazis, the only lawful thing for a Jew was to die. Now you have the right to rot in a displaced persons camp and stand in line with your soup cup. I only hope that when we finally do win our rights, we'll still be able to respect the law. Grab a snooze. Stretching out on a bench may be illegal, but sitting upright and dozing is still okay."

Yosef sat in a corner near a window. He leaned his head against the cold pane and tried to close his eyes. Leibl noticed that he was twisting and turning restlessly. "It's hard to rest the second night on the road with so many little kids. Well, take the first-aid kit and make the rounds of the coaches, since you're not sleeping anyway."

• • • • •

"Everything okay?" Yosef asked the monitor of the coach.

"Fine," the boy answered. But in the corner near a window, a little girl was still crying. Her mother scolded her, and the child wailed even louder. Yosef crawled over parcels and outstretched legs to reach the kid. The coach was dark, but he could see that the woman holding the child was in an advanced state of pregnancy.

"Everything all right?" he asked and knew it was a foolish ques-tion. "The child is tired. Half an aspirin, perhaps?"

"I've tried that. She spat it out. She's grinding me down."

"You're exhausted too."

"I just hope she doesn't get sick. Such a tiny thing, and already sneaking across borders," the mother murmured.

"I have some candies. Shall I give her one? What's her name?"

"Hannele."

"Come here, Hannele, your mommy's tired. I have a lollipop for you."

Yosef settled himself on a rucksack. The child struggled when he lifted her out of her mother's arms, but settled on his lap when she tasted the sweet. She soon started crying again. The candy fell out of her mouth and was lost in the dark. Yosef took a bottle of water out of his kit, held it to the little girl's lips. She grew quiet. The mother started to say something, but her head sank down on her breast. Yosef tried to soothe the child.

"Sleep, Hannele, close your eyes and sleep. Shall I sing you a lullaby? Shall I tell you a story? You're tired, Hannele, and scared. I understand. But there's nothing to be afraid of. If you were a little bit older and knew where we were going, you'd jump for joy. We're going home, Hannele, home!

"Ah, how would you know what a home is? You must have been born in an attic, a cellar, maybe in a camp. In the DP camp everyone lives together in one big barrack, one cubicle separated from the other by a curtain. Did you live in a camp like that? Just when you wanted to laugh, a child on the other side of the curtain would be sleeping, and then when that child cried, it woke you up. A home is different, Hannele. In a home, all four walls are yours, the floor, the ceiling, everything, just for you. You'll be able to laugh whenever you feel like it. You'll be able to sleep whenever you want to. A whole big home, just for you. And Sorele will have her home, and Yankele his home . . .

"I know what you want to ask: Where will they give out the soup? No, Hannele, in a home you don't have to stand in a line with a bowl to get soup. Each home has its own kitchen, all to itself. Your mommy will buy white dishes and silver spoons, and she'll cook food for you whenever you feel like it. If you want chicken soup with noodles, she'll cook that; if it's rice and milk you want, she'll cook that. And—I know, Hannele, you don't understand a word of what I'm saying. You're a good little girl to let me keep talking . . . Are you asleep? Ssh . . ."

Yosef's own eyes grew heavy, but he was afraid he might move and wake the child. "When I get to Eretz Israel, the first thing I'll do is catch up on my sleep. I'll do nothing else for three days and three nights. People will laugh and call me the sleepy pioneer."

Dull gray light was showing through the coach window when a

man on the bench awoke and took the child from him. "Thank you very much. I'm Hertzke Kempinski, and this is my child."

"I'm one of the medics with the transport. If you need something for her—my name is Yosef."

• • • • •

The sun was shining brightly when the train chugged into Marseilles. Passengers, with all their belongings on the train, began to pour out into the station, looking for porters, but the transportation workers were on strike.

"By the time we get all our people unloaded, the British agents will know all there is to know about us," Leibl complained bitterly to Yosef.

"Weren't our men here aware of the strike? They should have delayed the transport."

Suddenly, the platform filled with porters, and before anyone realized what was happening, children, invalids, baggage disappeared from the coaches. Yosef soon found himself on the back of a large truck. "I'm a medic with a special transport," he protested, but the French didn't understand a word he said. The truck bumped through narrow streets. A transport of two hundred immigrants, and here he was on a truck with no more than twenty people. Where were they all? The vehicle turned into a narrow road between fields. Had they lost the way, or was he on the wrong truck? A gate opened for them. They came to a halt in a spacious yard filled with wooden barracks.

A group of tanned youngsters ran from one of the wooden structures. Yosef watched them, looking for a Jewish face, when one youth asked, "*Ha-kol beseder?* Everything okay?" Before he could reply, the gate swung open again. Another truck drove into the clearing. One truck after another pulled up with screeching brakes. They had followed different routes, because a convoy of trucks would have aroused suspicion. What kind of connection did his people have with the transportation workers of Marseilles that in the middle of a strike they could mobilize porters and drivers? Was it possible that they were not altogether alone in the world?

Clamor and confusion. One person looking for a relative, another for his baggage. Yosef was searching for the pregnant woman and her child. Was it always like this—that when you helped someone, that person became dear to you? Apparently there were a number of pregnant women in the transport, but none with children. Ah, here they came, a hefty man with a child in his arms, behind him a woman with a large belly. They came closer. Could this be the child from the railway coach? Well, a pretty face wasn't everything, he would be the first to admit that. The woman walked awkwardly as if on stilts.

Why did he turn away from the woman as soon as he got a closer look at her? Was it her swollen face? What was he standing around for? He was a medic, he had to look after the whole transport. He'd better go see what was happening in the barracks with the red Star of David, the infirmary.

The pregnant one, perhaps because her face was swollen, resembled his Aunt Beila. He hadn't been overly fond of Aunt Beila. Why? Never mind, didn't he have a right not to like her for no reason at all? Well, he also had a right to dislike the pregnant woman for no reason at all.

The following day he had a good reason for disliking her. They were involved in confidential work in the office, and someone kept pounding on the door. Yosef opened it, and the pregnant woman tried to push her way in. He went out, shutting the door behind him.

"What are you pushing me for? I've been pushed around enough. I need to see Leibl! Do you think I have the strength—"

Suddenly she fell silent. The shadows under her eyes grew darker. Her eyes became slits that cut into him like knives. Now he remembered why he hadn't liked Aunt Beila: when her slitlike eyes used to stare at him out of her fat face, he felt as if she were scrutinizing his pocks. He shouldn't hate this woman, but—"How's Hannele?" he asked abruptly.

The slits widened, revealing eyes filled with blue and dark with fear. The eyes again vanished behind the shadows. Only the fear remained, hanging between them like an impenetrable curtain. A vague premonition tightened Yosef's chest. Or was it fear? Alas, these poor pregnant Jewish women . . . He remembered the sow when her time came, how she had prepared a bed for herself. These days, where could a Jewish mother find a secure corner when her time came? A Jewish mother nowadays didn't even have . . .

"You really can't go in there now. I'll come for you when he's free. Just tell me your name and barracks number."

"Kempinski, Golda Kempinski," she spoke hurriedly, as if to get it all out at once. "A difficult pregnancy, and we also have a small child. I heard about Immigration Dalet, where you're certain to reach Palestine. My husband—" her eyes were now shut completely. She sucked in a deep breath. "Kempinski is the name of my second husband. My first husband—I lost my first husband and children." She stood only a step away from him, but her answer reached him as if her hoarse whisper had, on its way, become entangled with the echo of another voice. It was a hot day, but an icy frost hung between them.

Yosef coiled up as if to confront an adversary. His glance traveled to her feet—she limped, she was a strange lame woman. He wanted to flee, but his feet stuck rooted to the ground. he heard a voice—his voice? "Your children—how many did you have?"

"With my first husband, three."

Yosef kept his eyes lowered, but he no longer saw anything at all. He wanted to speak, but his tongue cleaved to his palate; only single words slipped out against his will: "Nenna? Yossel? Hannele?"

•   •   •   •   •

Golda lay on a stretcher as two pairs of strong arms carried her to the infirmary. All the old pains awoke and burned in her body, from the tips of her fingers to the toes that were no longer there. Her brain pressed against her skull as if it wanted to fly loose; questions bombarded it like icy arrows: Who did she belong to and who belonged to her? Kempinski? Heshl? A Hannele from Shiya, a Hannele from Hertzke. Where was Shiya's Hannele? What would she say to Shiya's Hannele about Hertzke's Hannele?

Her thoughts began to come through more clearly. Yossel was walking beside her. He was holding her hand. She didn't open her eyes. If she opened them, she would have to talk to him, and she didn't know yet what to say. She must tell him everything, she must make him understand. Yossel, her own flesh and blood. Yossele—the apple of her eye—now beside her. Where had he come from? What did he think of her? He had been twelve years old when the burden of feeding the family was thrown on his childish shoulders. He had climbed over the wall to smuggle because she had shouted at Shiya. Surely he remembered that. Did he also remember that she herself had gone to the Umschlagplatz to be with Hannele? Did he remember—dear Father in heaven, you kept me alive so I should live to see my child saved. Grant me, then, that he should understand me and judge me mercifully. Otherwise your blessing is a curse.

•   •   •   •   •

How did she get trapped in a blockade? She had to get out of here. Her lean-to must still be in the forest. The storm had ripped chunks out of it, but it was better than nothing. The war couldn't last much longer.

But the war was finished, wasn't it?

The war was over, and again a blockade. They must hide the children in the attic. Hannele, where have you disappeared to? Shiya, where in the world . . .? No, Shiya, I'm not looking for anyone. She called Hannele, and the little girl with the blonde curls came running, the Hannele with the—wait, Shiya, I'll let you in in just a moment.

Where could she hide her? Shiya was coming.

The door opened a crack, and she could see a head of black hair. The door opened wider. It was Hannele, her black hair bathed in cold sweat, her dark eyes red. The blonde Hannele clenched her fists, wouldn't let the older Hannele get close to her mother. Out of the dark Hannele's mouth came dark screams. Don't scream, no spoiled-baby tantrums, you can't stay the youngest forever. She must get her to shut her mouth because . . .

It was too late, she heard the soft patter of Shiya's slippers moving across the floor. The roots of her hair were on fire, her eyeballs strained to get out of their sockets, a scream tore against her mouth and couldn't come out. H-E-L-P!

Hertzke shook her.

"It's nothing, Hertzke, just a bad dream, a nightmare."

A dream in which Shiya was alive was bad? Woe to her if Shiya's presence was evil and Hannele's a nightmare.

Why Hannele? To whom did she owe a Hannele? Now she would have a boy and call him Yossel, or a girl and call her Nenna, and then one fine day the door would open and in would walk the real Nenna and Yossel, and Hannele and Shiya would also enter. Would that really be a fine day, or—?

Why had she been in such a hurry to name the child after Hannele before she knew what had really happened? "Hannele is no more—no one is alive any longer to come back and find me with a bastard." Was that it?

Yes, that was it. A mother waiting, hoping for her child to come, doesn't forget the child's face. She hadn't recognized Yossel in the train, perhaps because it was dark, perhaps because his voice had changed. But afterward she had stood before him in broad daylight. She had seen the pockmarks on his face and hadn't even given it a thought. Had she refused to think?

She was used to nightmares while asleep, but nightmares with wide open eyes? No, she refused to be driven into madness. As long as there was a breath of life in her, she would be happy with her newly discovered son as well as with the new children. She would be happy, SHE WOULD BE HAPPY! If there were no Shiyas, then let there be Herzkes—let there be Hanneles, even if their eyes were gray, their hair sandy, and their potato noses like Hertzke's . . . She would be happy!

8

He was keenly aware that he was among the lucky few who still had someone alive, so why did he feel so all alone? The same restlessness that had churned in him during his smuggling days still pricked him. He scurried around and worked harder than any of the others. Yosef is an idealist, they praised him. Was it idealism or . . . Was he punishing himself because *his* Hannele was gone, or was he taking revenge on this live Hannele? Did he really have to volunteer for double duty and extra tasks, especially when his mother begged him for more time?

Of course, whenever he had to go into town, he first ran to his mother to ask if she needed anything. But why did he lose his tongue when he was with her? Getting a word out of him was like pulling teeth, she complained.

His mother believed he had become a big shot here so he could keep his hand in the till and get extra privileges. Her wants were modest enough, perhaps some additional straw for her bed, some fresh milk for her little one. And she was ready to pay. Hertzke had money, but where could he buy anything when no one was allowed out of the camp?

He'd been on his feet now almost twenty hours. He ought to go straight to his cot. But then it would be after midnight when he awoke, and he wouldn't be able to see his mother. He'd wash his face and run over to her for a few moments.

• • • • •

He shouldn't have come when he was so tired. He sat there uncomfortably, not knowing what to say. His mother too was silent. Was she annoyed that he sat so glumly? Maybe she didn't know what to say either.

Golda's gaze moved from Yossel to Hannele and back again. In the train on the way to Marseilles, when he still had no idea who she was, he had cradled Hannele in his arms and tried to make her forget her tears. Now that he knew she was his little sister, he didn't speak to her, didn't even touch her.

"What do you think of your sister?" she asked abruptly, and regretted the words even before they were out of her mouth.

Yosef looked at the child: a broad nose, a red face. "A big girl," he muttered.

"Just over a year old," Golda responded, barely able to conceal her irritation.

A year and a half. Yosef recalled what Golda had told him on the train. She'd said that if she made the child younger, she would have a better chance of getting in on the legal immigration. "God bless her," he replied, "she looks more like two."

Golda turned her head away to hide the flush that suffused her face. If Yossel knew Hannele's real age, he would be able to figure out that it had all started when nothing had been known for certain. Yossel would think the same kind of thoughts that had tormented her then.

"I don't know what I struggled and suffered for," Golda sighed after a long silence.

"Don't talk that way, Mother!"

"I had no one, I didn't even know about you. The truth is that I thought you—God forbid. What was I thinking? Those who thought too much didn't survive."

"Why are you torturing yourself? It's a miracle, a thousand miracles. Why can't you just enjoy being alive?"

"I swallowed garbage, was eaten by lice—is that a miracle? A pig, too, eats out of garbage cans. Is a pig's life a miracle?"

Why was she torturing Yossel? What did she want of him? Every time she opened her mouth, she twisted the dagger in his heart.

"To overcome such miseries, Mother, is more than a miracle, it's heroism. I know, from my own experiences, it would have been easier to surrender to the Angel of Death than to stand up to him."

She strained to control her tears. Her swollen red eyes yearned for them as a parched lawn craved rain, but tears would only frighten Yossel into silence. When she was a little girl and was crying, her father seldom gave her a pat, but he always had calming, soothing words. Yossel was like her father; let him speak. But, before he could say anything else, her mouth opened and the words poured forth of their own volition.

"Those days pass before my eyes like a movie on a screen. What do you say to this: I lay asleep in my shelter in the forest. I don't remember dreaming. I woke up, restless, climbed out of the shelter, and paced back and forth. A peaceful summer night. I listened to the sounds of the forest, the whispering of trees, the chirping of crickets, the distant hoot of an owl. I sniffed the air like a hunting dog. Only the odors of moss and sap. I tried to lie down again, but something kept pulling me out. My heart fluttered and my feet carried me; where to, I had no idea. My eyes pierced the darkness, my ears pricked up like a rabbit's. Dawn broke and I went on, into a thicket where one could hardly take a step.

"I don't remember whether I found any food. I don't even know if I lay down to sleep. It grew light and dark and light again, I don't know how many times, before I made my way back to the shelter. Don't ask me how. I haven't the faintest idea. When I got back I discovered eggshells, empty tins, pages from a German newspaper. Germans had camped there, no doubt about it. Heroism or madness, I don't deserve any praise for it. I wasn't even aware of what I was doing."

"Maybe you dreamed the whole thing?"

"The dream is called survival. The word became part of me, like a *dybbuk,* a ghost, when the roundups in the ghetto became more frequent and we started running from place to place. It was like a fever, an illness. The fever subsided when things grew quieter and rose when danger approached. The *dybbuk* guided me across a narrow board laid over a chasm when I fled the Umschlagsplatz. Even in the hell of Treblinka it lifted me out of a group of naked women and carried me over fences and mines, through ditches and under search-light beams. The mother that you knew remained in Treblinka. Golda Heshl was stripped away from me with my clothes. Only the *dybbuk* remained. It beat inside me like a pulse: survive, overcome. It crowed like a rooster and barked like a dog to survive. When I couldn't bear it anymore, the *dybbuk* wrapped me in a dream of No-volipki 51. Your father, Nenna, everyone came back by some kind of sorcery. Your father was a father until his last moment. Me—I was only a *dybbuk*."

She had begun to explain herself but ended by accusing herself. What new kind of *dybbuk* was it that forced her to demean herself in the eyes of her child?

"It was you, not Papa, who carried the whole burden of the household," Yosef murmured.

"Your father ran to the left willingly to be with Nenna. I ran . . ."

"But you *had* to run to the right. Hannele and I were hidden up in that attic! What kind of mother would you have been if you hadn't? And now you're poisoning your life with self-recrimination. That's worse than any *dybbuk*. You're being your own anti-Semite."

"Maybe I want you to console me."

"Enough! Stop! What you're accusing yourself of is exactly what our enemies always threw up to us. Even before the war, when we were told to get out of Europe, vicious tongues began spreading the slander that the Zionists were exploiting Jewish suffering for their own propaganda. Certain Jews argued that Jewish blood is the oil that drives the wheels of Zionism. And today? 'The Zionists are using Jewish victims to beg: a groshen for an injury, a permit to enter Palestine for one who was gassed, a visa for one who was cre-mated, immigration for a piece of human soap.' That's the charge I read in a newspaper printed in the Jewish alphabet. Don't do it, Mother! Survival is still the order of the day; survival as individuals, survival as a people."

"Yossel, my son, when I parted from you, you were a child, and now—"

"If Father knew there was no chance to save Nenna, and he went over to the left only to die with her, then he did wrong."

Golda could no longer keep back her tears, nor did she wish to. They streamed down her face as if they would never stop.

"You're exactly like your grandfather," she gasped when he fell silent. "Only he could understand things like that, speak like that."

Hertzke, who had been sitting silently in a corner, nervously · scraped the floor with the heels of his shoes. Golda hastily wiped her tears. "Yossel, now that you know what I've been through, maybe you'll be able to get us visas under the legal quota?"

Wearily Yosef dragged himself to the door. Hannele, the new Hannele, had a flat nose, as if the tip had been broken off. *His* Hannele had no nose at all because he'd let her freeze in an icy attic. He resembled his grandfather, Mother had said. If she only knew . . .

• • • • •

Day followed day, week followed week, and no ship was in sight. The crowd in the Marseilles Brichah camp was beginning to fret. How long could they continue like this, a hundred souls to a barrack? At least the meals had been regular in the refugee camps in Germany. It had been possible to carry on a bit of trade too. Why couldn't they have waited in Germany? "Who knows when a ship will come, *if* a ship will ever come?" A few Zionists had decided to wage war on the British Empire, so they had to lie around here under inhuman conditions.

The leaders tried to assuage them with the promise that a ship was expected any day, but they had heard that refrain too many times.

One day, Golda noticed that the leaders had stopped making promises. Something must have happened, something must have changed, maybe for the better. She could hardly wait for Yosef's return. "Is there news of a ship, Yossel? A ship is on the way, right?"

"How do you know?"

"I'm right, then!"

"Don't tell anyone. There's been trouble enough all along the way. If Uncle Hertzke doesn't know yet, don't tell him."

"What do you mean? I can't keep secrets from my husband."

"It's not *your* secret, you're not even supposed to know. Don't you see, one person tells another, and in no time the British will know. They might have spies in the camp. Whoever told you—"

"No one told me, Yossel. I figured it out for myself. But don't worry, I can keep a secret."

• • • • •

"Yossel, you remember you have a mother, don't you? You might as well be on another planet."

"He was here day before yesterday," Hertzke reminded her.

"Yes, for all of five minutes. We've been in this camp now for—how long? Over three months and—"

"Good news, Mother!"

"Good news? That you can stay for ten minutes? Sorry, Yossele. What is it?"

"In a week, ten days, we'll be aboard ship."

"What did I tell you, Hertzke? Legal immigration, right?"

"No, Mother, illegal—an illegal ship"

"Which will go straight to Eretz Israel?"

"Of course."

"I mean, have they made sure the ship will arrive?"

"How can anyone be sure? The British are stronger than we are."

"So I could end up in Cyprus or God knows where?"

"Mother, everybody here has gone through the same hell. You think there are entry certificates just lying around to be snatched?"

"People do go legally; it's an open secret."

"People with tuberculosis or other such illnesses. There are only a few places. They weigh and measure a thousand times before they give someone a legal certificate."

"I'm not exactly in perfect health. My feet—and what if I have a miscarriage?"

"Mother!"

"I may be lame, but I'm not blind. You can't stand your new sister. And you're ashamed of my belly, as if I were carrying a bastard!"

"Mother!"

"God punished me—I stayed alive. You want me to go and bury myself? I *was* buried already, but Hertzke saved me. The war is over, but—"

"The war is over, Mother . . ." Yosef felt short of breath. He dragged himself over to the bench and sat down. Elbows on knees, head propped in both hands, he inhaled deeply, raised his head, and continued. "The war was over, there was plenty of food, but the kids in the orphanages still hid bread in their cupboards. The war was

over, but I still ran like a hunted animal. I jumped borders, smuggled—I could have been shot. Why did I need the dollars that I
sewed into my pants? I didn't even know that I had anyone left in
the whole world."

"Now you know."

"Now I know that I have you, your child."

"Your sister."

"My sister, and a lot more brothers and sisters. We're all in this
together, we've got to trust each other, help each other, otherwise
we'll all go down. You remember the 'snatchers' in the ghetto who
used to grab the bread right out of your mouth? Now we must learn
to share every bite."

"Are you making a speech to me, Yossel?"

"Mother, I'm still a pretty smart smuggler. The first months after
the liberation I ate and drank as if the world were ending. But the
war was not over for me until I became a member of the kibbutz. In
the kibbutz we ate dry crusts of bread, but we were one big family. I
don't want to be a thief anymore. I can't steal certificates, not even
for you, when there is someone else who may need it even more."

"I'm in the last months, Yossel, it's almost my time."

"There will be a few others aboard ship in the same condition.
That's our fate."

"If only you'd speak to Leibl . . ."

"He is aware of the situation. He goes through hell himself every
time he has to distribute the few legal places."

"I'm so weak, so broken, Yossel. It's so hard for me."

"I did get you one concession. I'll be going along with you."

"I don't want to be separated from you, Yossel, not even for a
day. I just want you to show some love for your sister—and for me
too . . ."

9

During the war, the old tub had ferried American soldiers across the
Atlantic. After the war she had been put up for sale as scrap. Brichah
emissaries had bought her and taken her to Baltimore to repair and
refit.

Junkyard ships had become more expensive than their scrap value when the dealers realized that a new, mysterious market for them had opened up. The British too soon knew who the buyers were and made representation to the maritime nations to refuse registration flags. In Europe, people without homes were rotting in camps; in American shipyards, ships without homes and registration were available. The ships had to find fictitious addresses before they could set out with cargoes of homeless people. The name of this ship was supposed to be *Moledet*, or *Homeland*, but first an "innocent" name was needed that would allow her to dock at any port for water and supplies.

There was a possibility of registering the ship under the Honduran flag. Someone got hold of a Spanish-English dictionary and searched for a fitting name for a Honduran vessel: *bajona* was a sea lion, *agila* an eagle.

"An eagle flies, it doesn't float."

"*Agila del Mer*, or *Leon del Mer*—the *Sea Eagle* or the *Sea Lion*. Or maybe *La Regina del Mer*, the *Sea Queen?*"

"Let's not get carried away! Eagle? Queen? She's a patched-up old tub. Where's the map of Honduras?"

"Maybe name her after the capital, Tegucigalpa? There's a bay called Carotasca, a Puerto Cortez, a town Santa Rosa—"

"A Christian saint for a Jewish ship? It doesn't make sense."

"Doesn't make sense? Perfect! It might fool the British."

* * * * *

Yosef's head rocked back and forth against the headrest on the bench of a rushing train. He was used to night journeys and usually slept like a rock, except when he was on medic duty. Now he was on his way to Paris, alone, to meet a group of refugees and take them to Marseilles. He could have slept for as long as he wished, but memories of Saltcha suddenly surfaced in his mind. He wondered why. Opposite him sat a young couple, the girl sleeping against her boyfriend's shoulder. Was that the reason? He had never gone anywhere with Saltcha on a train. She had never slept on his shoulder like that. Why Saltcha all of a sudden?

On the other hand, how had he avoided thinking about her for so long? He lived like a monk these days, but there had been times when he had lived almost like a married man. He had been happy with Gerda.

Happy?

He had had some happy moments in his life . . . dewy-eyed, his head in the clouds, his heart sprouting wings . . . he tried to hold on to every one of those precious moments. Yes, he had experienced happiness . . . but never with Gerda. His moments of real happiness lay elsewhere: when he had suddenly met up with Wicek in Prague, when he had given all his money to outfit the train for the children, when . . . yes, of course he had felt like that when he found his mother. He had been confused, of course. His mother, yet not altogether his any longer. His father's Goldele, and yet Hertzke's wife . . . Of course it was marvelous that Hertzke had rescued her and that there were new children. But it would take time to get used to it, to realize that it was all to the good, to get it straight in his head, in his heart.

The truth was that somewhere deep inside him was a nagging doubt about having given away all his money. But he was proud of what he had done. There, that was it! Happiness was being both pleased and proud of oneself. He certainly had not felt that with Gerda. Indulging oneself like a pig didn't mean happiness. Did it at least indicate pleasure?

Gerda certainly knew her trade. She knew how to make him never want to leave her. He used to run back to Berlin like someone possessed, and now . . . He remembered a good many of her features, the way he remembered the credit balance of a successful smuggling operation. He no longer took pleasure in it.

But Saltcha? He had loved her, yearned for her, lain awake nights thinking about her. For a long time she had been a dream beyond his reach. He had spent sleepless nights undressing her in his fantasies, the lines of her beautiful body emerging like the blazing sun from behind a cloud. Then came the night when it was all more than a dream, when she stopped resisting him and lay before him with all her sensuous magic. He had become terror stricken and impotent, but her gentle caresses had restored everything.

Saltcha had wanted to be careful, however. Why had this shocked him so? Saltcha had been loyal and good to him, and he had gone off and forgotten about her, just as he had forgotten Gerda. If Saltcha remained in Stettin, she would end up in jail. She too was an innocent child, lost among strangers, who needed to be rescued.

Odd. He remembered Saltcha only as he had pictured her in his imagination. Twice she had undressed before him, and yet he couldn't remember her body as he had beheld it with wide-open, fascinated eyes.

Dear Saltcha:

I don't know if you're wondering where I disappeared to. I'm surprised myself that I haven't written to you before this. I came out of the war with my brain in a fog. Maybe the fog hasn't altogether lifted yet, but I'm beginning to see things a little more clearly. I'm no longer a smuggler. I'm active in Zionist work and preparing to settle in Palestine. If this letter reaches you and you want to answer, write to me at the Jewish Agency in Paris. I don't stay in any one place for very long, but I'm in Paris pretty often.

It occurs to me that I know very little about your life. And I understand you even less. But I do know enough to be able to say with all my heart that you are truly beautiful. It would be a great waste if you were to spend your life in Stettin waiting for the past to return . . .

No doubt you're amused that the boy Yurek would take it on himself to show you the way to a worthwhile life. But really, it's time for you to stop living "for the day." No good can come to you in Poland. If you should decide to move to Palestine, get in touch with a Zionist organization in Stettin, Lodz, or Warsaw. Write to me. I can help you get out of Poland.

It would be good to hear from you, no matter what your decision. Perhaps you've already found a "friend"? Even a husband? If a miracle happened and Lazar did return, give him my love. Come to Palestine, both of you . . .

I wish you all the best. Your,

Yurek

P.S. My mother is alive and here with me.

10

The only way to break the British blockade was to flood the shores of Eretz Israel with so many illegal immigrants that the mandate authorities would be swamped. Even in the dilapidated Brichah boats, it took only a week to cross the Mediterranean. The overcrowding and the unsanitary conditions would have to be ignored and as many passengers as possible loaded on the ships. That was the decision, finally, of the Mossad Aliyah Bet, the underground responsible for bringing refugees from Europe.

The refugee camps around Marseilles were buzzing like so many beehives. Every day brought new transports of people. With three- and four-tier bunks hastily thrown together in every available centimeter of space, the barracks looked like chicken coops. The kitchen staff worked around the clock.

•   •   •   •   •

It was Yosef's turn at kitchen duty. He had already peeled a mountain of potatoes. Earth and potato bits stuck to his hands. He wiped the sweat from his face, leaving a muddy track across his forehead. His work finally done, he was standing in line at the water faucet to wash when he heard his name called on the loudspeaker. He left his pitcher with a boy standing behind him and ran to the office.

"Yurek! Is that you behind the mud?"

"Saltcha!"

He threw his arms around her, kissed her, smudging her face too. "I didn't believe you'd really come. I was peeling potatoes," he explained.

"In Paris they told me you were a big shot, and you're peeling potatoes?"

"It's like in the kibbutzim in Eretz Israel—the higher you rise the harder you work."

"*Zu Tora v'zeh skhara?*—This is Torah and this is her reward?" she quoted an old talmudic saying.

"Saltcha, you know Hebrew?"

"You think I'm a *shiksa,* a Gentile? I studied in a Hebrew school. I thought you might help me get a better bunk, but I see you've become an idealist: the more you suffer, the bigger your portion of heaven. Look, here I am fighting with you already! Tell me what you—is there a place to wash up?"

"I was in line for the faucet when you called me out. Where are your quarters? I'll wash up and come right over."

"My quarters? In the Grand Hotel. Barrack 12, row 3, bunk 5, level 3. How do you like that for an address?"

"Better than the Grand Hotel."

"I'm not complaining. Wash up, I'll wait for you at the entrance to my barracks."

•   •   •   •   •

"Are you getting married, or what? You're dressed fit to kill," a friend called out to Yosef.

His shirt and jacket were creased from having lain so long in the rucksack. Yosef patted his clothes, trying to smooth the wrinkles, but it didn't help. His blue tie had disappeared into thin air.

"I'd almost given you up. I thought you were angry with me," Saltcha said.

"Why should I be?"

"I made fun of your life here."

"We live like soldiers on the front lines here, not like smugglers in hotels."

"Soldiers are forced to go to the front. Who's forcing you?"

"The whole world is forcing me—and you—and all the rest of us. The lousy, indifferent world."

"It was a miracle we didn't know."

"Know what?"

"I'm a graduate of Auschwitz and Matthausen, as you know. Does anyone who hasn't been there know what it means to watch the smoke curl out of chimneys until one becomes that smoke oneself? What kind of joy does life have hidden away for me to make it worth hanging onto with rotting teeth and crumbling fingernails?"

"The joy of victory."

"Victory? Yes, I used to dream about that. I used to comfort myself that the world didn't know what was going on. I don't have to tell you about the death marches in the last days before the liberation. Tens of thousands perished on those marches, or because of them. No one did anything to stop them. Obviously no one knew what was happening there, that's how we consoled ourselves. But when the world learned the truth—"

"What's happened to you, Saltcha? You've changed."

"I used to believe that when the world beheld the destruction, when the nations learned of the terrible slaughter, they would fall on their knees and hide their faces in shame. The pitiful remnant of Jews would be enveloped in a spontaneous outpouring of warmth and benevolence, we would recognize the profound regret of the world, and that would be balm to our wounds."

"You had a beautiful dream."

Disregarding his interruption, she continued as if she had been waiting all her life to express these words. "We would all be surrounded with loving-kindness to make up for the days and nights of Auschwitz and Matthausen. Above all, to atone for the crime of locked gates and closed borders to those who had been looking for refuge, they would restore us to our land, and restore the land to us; they would drain the swamps, water the deserts, and build palaces for us—"

"Palaces, no less!"

"The most marvelous beauty, the greatest comfort imaginable, would be a compensation for the filthy, cold barracks, lice-infested straw sacks, rotting rags, and moldy bread of the camps. They would mobilize the most luxurious ships in the world to lead us out of exile."

"Were you waiting for a ship like that?"

"Why not? The leaders of the world would come to greet me as I stepped onto native soil. Roosevelt, Churchill, and Stalin would carry me in their arms to my new, secure home—"

"Those old fogies? Are their arms better than mine?"

"Don't laugh at me, Yurek. Did you ever imagine that today we would be faced with blockaded ports, camps with four-tier bunks, and lines waiting to use the toilets? Would you have wanted to survive if you could have foreseen that two years after the war, we would still be living like hunted animals?"

Yosef stroked her forehead. "You wanted to escape reality by hiding under Lazar's wings. I'm beginning to understand you."

"I wish I could . . ."

He combed his fingers through her bleached hair.

"Don't, Yurek, you're making a mess of my hairdo, the entire facade of a carefree lady."

"I must admit, Saltcha, that I took your mask to be the real thing."

"Maybe it is—by now—"

"I too assumed that my mask was my real self, and you see what happened—the daring smuggler was no more than a scared kid. It's good that you came, good that we found each other again. We're beginning to know each other as we really are, and that's wonderful."

• • • • •

All night Yosef had helped in the superhuman task of preparing one large Sabbath-eve dinner to which everyone would sit down together. Weary as he was, he managed to sit beside Saltcha for the singing. She had a pleasant voice. Her Hebrew was better than his and she knew a world of songs. Between songs, Yosef stole kisses.

In France it was acceptable to kiss a girl in public. Others behaved more freely, but he was among the few fortunate ones who still had a mother to answer to. Bad enough that he was going around with a girl who was older than he was and who bleached her hair.

Soon Yosef was able to calm his mother by assuring her that Saltcha had stopped bleaching her hair. He wanted to bring her to visit Golda, but Saltcha was reluctant to go half blonde, half brunette. Her hair grew fast, however. Soon, very soon . . .

• • • • •

It was a while since they had announced in the refugee camp that a ship was on the way. A storm on the Atlantic, difficulties getting fuel in Portugal, slipping through the Strait of Gibraltar on a moonless night so the British wouldn't see . . . At the camp meanwhile, more people were arriving. The crowding was unbearable. Nor did the weather help much—one heatwave after another.

"A ship is on the way," the refugees kept comforting each other, and made sure never to miss a Hebrew class. A journalist from a Yiddish newspaper in Poland began putting out a mimeographed news bulletin. Amateurs from the DP camps in Belsen and Munich prepared a theater revue. The children's classes were the pride and joy of the refugees. Even English, the administrative language of Palestine, was being taught.

To solve the problem of her hair, Saltcha had the camp barber give her a boyish bob. When she looked into the mirror, she wept. The camp barber was an amateur too. "By the time you're a bride, it will have grown out," Yosef joked, but she was inconsolable.

"I hope that's the worst thing that ever happens to us! And honestly, you look younger and prettier than ever."

"What about you, Yurek? You used to dress so well. Now you

walk around looking like a mess, and it doesn't bother you that my head is a mess too?"

"Come on, stop wailing. I know what! I'll dress up in all my finery and take you into town to a real French coiffeur."

"You're teasing me."

"In such a serious crisis? God forbid! Seriously, we'll go into town very soon."

"On what excuse?"

"Only Yurek the smuggler needed excuses. Yosef tells the truth."

"Stop being a fanatic. When you're prepared to lie for me I'll know you love me."

"Will you accept a forgery instead? I'll give you a forged permit to enter Palestine. We need a photo for the document, so I'll take you to town to a hairdresser and then to a photographer. We'll stay in town all day, and there you'll have to prove to me that you love me too. Here I hardly ever get a chance to kiss you."

"On the streets of a French town we can kiss as much as we like. Every step a kiss."

"That night, our last night together in Stettin, it was more than a kiss, a great deal more . . ."

"I wasn't sure you remembered it with pleasure."

"We'll go tomorrow. I've reserved a room in a hotel. Are you angry?"

"No."

"Do you have any money? I've given all mine away."

"How could you give away your last groshen?"

"Had I known you were coming . . ."

"I had no idea you wanted me to come. You left angry."

"You refused to marry me then. Now you've joined me . . . you came here because of me, didn't you?"

"Will it make you happier if I say yes? Yurek, dearest boy, you think you've finally reached shore? The truth is you're grasping at straws. I'm not nearly as clever as I seem, nor as good. I'm not as determined as you think, either. I'm tired! I'm looking for security, for rest, but fate throws me from one stormy sea to the next. You are really very dear to me. Maybe I really do love you. You see, I need someone who will take me into his strong arms and carry me. Do you have strong arms, Yosef?"

She had called him Yosef for the first time. It gave his arms added strength.

• • • • •

The day that Yosef and Saltcha were supposed to go into town, an entire refugee camp arrived from Lille, and Yosef was kept busy. They tried to go the following day, but the *Santa Rosa* docked at Marseilles. Security was tightened, and no one was allowed to leave camp.

11

Yossi boy
Don't groan oy
Relax, enjoy.
Get a little tipsy
And taste the Gypsy.

Thus quipped the American volunteer sailors on the *Santa Rosa* when the Mossad people refused to join them for a drink at the Sans Souci Café. The Americans thought they had the mentality of old men, and funny names too: Avi, Uzi, Yossi, Dossi. To be sure, there was plenty of trouble: the ship rocked at anchor in the port; they couldn't outfit her; they were having a hard time getting fuel for the long journey. But what could the volunteer sailors do? Recite psalms? One of them in fact did just that, the Methodist minister, Nobel. The Mossad boys sat on the hot deck, furrowing their brows and wringing their hands. The Americans were a cheerful bunch. They wanted to help but they didn't believe in agonizing.

They thought at least one of the Yossis, Yuval, was a regular fellow. He allowed himself to be taken along with the Yankees on their bar-crawling expeditions. He was a skinny lad with flaxen hair and a grayish-white skin, like half-baked bread. One day someone saw him enter a hotel with the Gypsy from the Sans Souci. When he returned to the ship, the Mikes (as the Yossis called the Americans) applauded him.

"Want to go halves with me on your Gypsy, Yuval?"

"You're already going halves with a Britisher. What she learns from you she sells to him as well as to me."

"You're spying on us?"

"I'm spying on the British. I have to know everything they know."

"Why didn't you tell us she's a spy? Okay, fellows! From now on we'll tell the kinds of stories that will make the British dizzy."

"She's not the only one. All the dancers, all the waiters, even the whores sell information. You get drunk but they stay sober; they're experts at loosening their clients' tongues. It's part of their trade."

"So what do you want us to do—behave like choirboys? We volunteered for a ship, not a monastery," Ike muttered.

"You've boarded the ship here," Nobel, the Methodist minister, joined in. "I know the Americans better than you do. Do you have any idea what they've been through on the *Santa Rosa* up to now? Some of them left us. Those aboard now are ready to go through thick and thin with the ship. They drink? So what? Did you ever know sailors who didn't?"

"What about you?" one of the sailors joked.

"He gets drunk on psalms," Willy answered for the minister. "I admit we're not professional seamen. But once you've been through a storm at sea, at the mercy of the waves, and you survive to sleep with a hot-blooded Gypsy instead of on the ocean bed, and you can pour whiskey down your gullet instead of saltwater—who can resist? Drinking comes with the job."

"And the Mossad boys?"

"They're drunk with power. Bossing us around is their whiskey."

"That's true," Ike commented. "We helped prepare the ship in America, we brought it all the way over here. The Reverend Nobel can testify that we kept our noses to the grindstone. Now you come along and tell us where to go, how to speak, who to talk to and who not to, even whose bed to stay out of . . ."

•   •   •   •   •

Some of the Americans returned from a night of drinking and set about picking on the Yossis. They were spoiling for a fight, singing, yelling, and finally throwing up all over the deck. The following day they slept till noon. The Yossis got busy with a Hebrew-English dictionary and dragged Nobel into their conspiracy. When the Mikes came back on deck, the Yossis greeted them in English:

We like you,
Ike and Mike,
And Hy and Sy,
But why oh why
Do you turn our ship
Into a sty?

Instead of responding angrily, the Americans were delighted. "Bravo! Hurrah! If the Yossis have a sense of humor, there's hope for us all. We'll soon teach them how to enjoy life."

The Americans took up the jingle and started kidding Sy, the cook, one of the few who had made friends with the Yossis. Sy was a first-class cook, but the kitchen always looked as if it had just been hit by a hurricane. He obviously enjoyed his own meals. He had a goiter that hung in folds on his chest and a belly that hung over his none-too-clean pants. "My name is Simon, Sy for short," he had introduced himself. The Yossis called him by his full name, Simon, and he never failed to add, under his breath, "Sy for short." When the Yanks started chasing around Marseilles and Sy remained aboard in his kitchen, the Yossis took to calling him "Shimon." He would mutter, "Shim for short."

Willy was a jovial type. His last name was Blau, but his hair was red as fire and his white skin was covered with freckles. Once, when he was in town, he bumped into Sy. This would be a great chance to introduce him to a girl, Willy thought. But Sy vanished into thin air. When Willy mentioned it later aboard ship, Sy denied he had been in town at all.

"Don't be embarrassed, Sy. I've suspected for some time that your passion isn't just in your belly."

"Quite an operator," Ike laughed.

"I never left the ship!"

"Willy, you only thought you saw Sy. It was really a pregnant French woman," Ike bantered.

"It was Sy, I saw him with my own eyes. What's he so upset about? We're all human."

"On my word of honor, I never left the ship!"

"Between your word and my eyes, I'll bet on my eyes," Willy insisted.

The usually good-natured Sy turned on Willy, both fists ready. "You red pig, shut up!"

"Hey, Sy, where's your sense of humor?" Ike tried to separate them.

Sy now turned on Ike. Willy tried to calm him.

"You red sonofabitch," Sy screamed at him, "you're the one who started all the trouble."

Though shocked by Sy's outburst, everybody soon forgot the incident—everybody but Yuval. Two days later the Gypsy informed him that Sy was selling ship's provisions on the black market. The Gypsy said her information came from a Brit. Willy was convinced it was a provocation by the British. They too were aware she was a double agent.

• • • • •

At last Yosef was able to take Saltcha into town to get her photograph taken. He would have liked to show her the town, but the truck that picked them up from camp was going straight to the ship, which they both wanted to see. They sat on the packages in the back of the truck, holding hands and looking at each other with a new shyness. No sooner had they arrived at the ship, however, than Yuval dragged Yosef off. "Come with me."

"I'm not alone," Yosef protested.

"Let her wait aboard ship. This is urgent."

"But—"

"There's no time to lose!" Yuval drew Yosef after him to a taxi. From a distance, Yosef signaled to Saltcha to wait for him.

"Anybody who sells food can sell secrets too," Yuval told Yosef as they got into the taxi. Sy had sneaked off the ship looking fatter than ever. He had to be followed. Yosef, whom Sy didn't know, would have no trouble keeping an eye on him. Not too many guys Sy's size were seen wandering the streets of Marseilles.

They followed Sy's cab while Yuval, assuming that Yosef was innocent about the workings of the black market, tried to fill him in. "The British either control or have an interest in all the major oil companies in the world, so it's easy for them to block the sale of fuel to us. But no matter how tough it is to get oil on the black market, it's even tougher to get coffee and tea. Any black-market dealer would jump at the chance for a trade. You see?"

Of course he saw. They should just leave the whole thing to him, he would . . .

They had managed to buy the fuel for hard cash, but the stores of coffee and tea had disappeared.

"If you know what he's been doing, why do we have to follow him?"

"To catch him red-handed, otherwise the Americans in the crew will take his side. They might even accuse us of framing him."

"Are there problems with the Yankees?"

"They're first-rate guys. Without them the whole operation would be impossible, but—and maybe it's as much our fault as theirs—so far we haven't become—I don't know quite how to explain it—we're still in two separate worlds. An American makes friends quickly, opens up with people. They meet a stranger and— hey, driver! Don't lose him! He might turn at the corner!" He continued his explanation. "An American meets a stranger, and inside of two minutes they're on a first-name basis. We've had it too hard, been betrayed too often by friends. Maybe it's just shyness. Or maybe life has been too easy for Americans generally."

"What do we need them for? We can find plenty of volunteers in the refugee camps."

"Now you're talking like a child. You just agreed to leave your girl at a moment's notice and go with me. I am sure that very few of our American volunteers would do that. It's easier for them to take a ship out into dangerous waters than leave a girl that way. But somebody has to know how to handle a ship. We've had no experience with oceans since Moses divided the Red Sea. True, the Americans are not really professionals, but they know much more than us."

The taxi in front of them stopped. Sy got out and started walking. Yuval stayed in their cab while Yosef got out to tackle the cook. Sy went into a barbershop. Half an hour later he came out—without a haircut—and began pacing to and fro on the sidewalk. Yuval sat quietly in the taxi.

Suddenly, a small truck pulled up to the curb, so close to Yosef that Sy bumped into him as he climbed into it. The pickup screeched off at top speed and Yosef ran toward the taxi, but Yuval wasn't waiting. The truck and the taxi both disappeared from view, leaving Yosef in the wake of grinding gears and squealing tires. What should he do now? Sy would surely return, and even if he didn't, Yuval would return to take him back to the ship or give him new instructions. He had no choice but to wait where he was.

The sun crawled lazily over the Marseilles rooftops. Yosef didn't take his eyes off the entrance to the barbershop. Nearby was a café with little sidewalk tables. People came by, sat down at tables under the awning, left, and others took their places. How he longed to sit down in the shade for a few minutes to rest his hot, weary feet and wet his parched throat. Right now he'd give his ring and his gold Omega for a bottle of ice-cold Perrier, even for a single gulp of tepid Marseilles tap water, but he had no money. At the tables the customers changed and so did the choice of food. First it was long sticks of French bread with coffee, then all kinds of shellfish on and off their shells. The late afternoon aperitifs were finished and there was still no sign of Sy or Yuval. He had to stay where he was, eyes glued to the barbershop. In the Clemenceau Hotel a cool room with closed shutters and a clean bed was waiting for him. And here he stood surrounded by the thick, stifling walls of a commercial district, while Saltcha waited on the sweltering deck of the ship, with no idea of his whereabouts.

Not until the barbershop had been locked up for the night did Yosef decide to leave his post. He felt guilty, nonetheless; leaving an observation post before the designated time was the same as desertion, but he simply had no strength left. He had to get back to the ship. "*Le port?* The harbor?" he asked passersby. He didn't understand their answers; perhaps they didn't understand his question. He tried again. "*Au port?* The way to the harbor?" This time a Frenchman pointed to a bus that was just pulling away. He chased after it but abruptly stopped. He didn't even have the few centimes for a ticket.

Again he asked questions, and again a man pointed to a bus. This time he pulled his empty pockets inside out. The man took out a coin and paid for him. He thanked his rescuer profusely. Hot as he'd been before, now he was shivering and could barely drag his feet.

His benefactor tried various languages until they discovered they could communicate in German. Yosef did not know many English words, but he was sure the man had tried that language. Moreover, he asked too many questions. Were all Britishers that curious, or was he a spy?

Just as the bus began to move, Yosef jumped off and ducked into a courtyard. Before he emerged cautiously, he scanned the street. Too many people; impossible to tell if he were being followed. He ran across the street, dodging cars. He heard a policeman reprimand him and was grateful he hadn't stopped him. Further on was a boulevard with benches. He must sit down, his left ankle was killing him. Maybe he had pulled a ligament jumping from the bus. Would he ever manage to get back to the ship by evening? Saltcha must be worried sick.

• • • • •

Yuval had made a spot decision that he couldn't risk losing the truck with Sy in it. He was sure Yosef would simply hop into a taxi and return to the ship. He followed, watched, chased, and finally caught the cook red-handed. It took hours.

When Yosef at last dragged himself back to the ship, it was past midnight. They woke Yuval, whose eyes opened wide in astonishment. "I was sure you'd be back in the camp ages ago."

"Where's Saltcha?"

"Oh, your girl? Where's the girl that was here with Yosef this morning?"

Someone recalled that Willy had taken her out to show her the town. She would certainly be back at the refugee camp by now. They went to wake Willy, but his bunk was empty.

They applied ice to Yosef's ankle, which eased the pain somewhat. No, he didn't want to lie down, he'd wait.

• • • • •

Yosef woke Yuval again. "What time is it?"

"Two-thirty."

"How do I get into town? I have a room at the Clemenceau."

At the hotel, they told him that Saltcha had not checked in. He returned to the ship, but Willy's bunk aboard ship was still empty.

Some of the crew members were beginning to get up. The ice on his ankle had melted again. It wasn't the ankle that bothered him now. He was a lump of pain abandoned on the deck, a heap of smoldering embers turning slowly into ashes. Saltcha's and Willy's voices and giggles broke into his pain.

"What're you doing out here?" Saltcha asked. He could smell the alcohol on her breath.

When he did not reply, she motioned to Willy to leave them alone.

"You're mad at me—"

From between clenched teeth, only one word tore loose: "Whore!"

Saltcha stood absolutely still for a long moment, then turned and began to walk away. Yosef tried to get to his feet to follow her, but the pain in his ankle flared up, and he fell back on the bench.

Gray ash . . . the last living embers of thought dissolved into gray ash. Only the eyes remained open and watched the slender figure disappear into the pale light of dawn . . .

•   •   •   •   •

"You said a terrible, terrible thing to me, Yosef, but I'm not angry. You can believe it or not, but Willy only took me from one night spot to another. Nothing happened between us."

"I'd had a miserable day, Saltcha. I came back ready to fall into your arms and you—can you forgive me? I felt so lousy that I—no, it's no excuse. You're an angel to come back to me. I can't even ask you to forgive me—"

"I have to forgive you, because I want you to forgive me. Nothing physical happened between me and Willy, but something else did. Maybe something would have—I mean—it's not easy for me to tell you this—"

Yosef's eyes were wide, questioning.

"I'm a piece of flotsam. How does it go in Hebrew—*ud mutsal me'esh*—a cinder out of the flames. I'm no good for you, and you're no good for me, and that's the truth. You're too serious, too sad, too . . . Willy's lightheartedness, his silly antics, are good for me. A clown, a happy-go-lucky . . ."

"An American."

"That too. I hate camps. My belly's full, yet I'm still terrified of going hungry. They branded a number on my arm—you can't see what they burned into my soul. Believe me, I wanted to love you, Yurek, I truly did. But apparently, fear is stronger than love. I'm afraid . . ."

She no longer called him Yosef, her hair was again bleached . . . She wanted to go to America, not Palestine.

Saltcha started to say something, then suddenly turned and walked away.

Later his mother gave him a little parcel that Saltcha had left for him. Inside was a note: "I took too much from you because at that time I needed it. Now you need it more, and after all, it belongs to you." The gold coins clinked inside the envelope.

• • • • •

The American consul in Marseilles had his doubts about the legality of a Jewish wedding performed by a Methodist minister on French soil, so Willy found a rabbi who performed another ceremony in the American consulate. If the British captured the *Santa Rosa,* they could hardly send the wife of the American Willy Blau to Cyprus. Mr. and Mrs. William Blau had a country, and its consul would protect their interests. It was crucial to make sure that someone from the *Santa Rosa* would arrive in Eretz Israel directly to make a full report to the Central Command of the Hagannah, the Jewish underground in Palestine. The British spy network was familiar with those who left the ship regularly on business or pleasure in Marseilles. Nobel rarely did this. If he shaved the beard he had grown since he boarded the ship in Baltimore and donned his minister's garb, he had a good chance of getting a visa.

The streets surrounding the British consulate in Paris were watched by both the French Sureté and the British undercover agents. The offices of the Jewish Agency and the Hagannah were also watched by spies, Nobel had been warned. Better to transact his business by telephone than try to set foot in these offices.

He entered the American Embassy still bearded, dressed like an ordinary citizen. When he left, he was clean-shaven, wearing the cloth. In his pocket was a letter from the American cultural attaché, requesting the British consul to do everything possible to enable the reverend to visit the shrines in the Holy Land.

The guards at the British consulate saluted him and the consul promised to do whatever he could, but the matter had to be transmitted to London for approval. Mr. Nobel was surely aware of the difficulties caused by Zionist extremists.

It took only a few days for Nobel to get his visa, but when he returned to Marseilles he learned that the *Santa Rosa* had already set sail for Portevenire, in Italy.

By the time Nobel arrived in Portevenire, a "customs brokers agency" staffed with people from Scotland Yard was already ensconced in a house on a cliff overlooking the harbor where the *Santa Rosa* lay at anchor. Yuval had one of his girls working as a secretary in the agency office. Nobel suddenly felt the urge to paint. He clapped a beret on his head and set up an easel right next to the house occupied by the British. He borrowed a stool from the agency's office and set about making sketches of the scene. As his eyes measured the landscape, they also noted carefully who went in and out of those offices.

Unexpectedly a small gunboat sailed into the port and dropped anchor in the isthmus close to where the *Santa Rosa* was docked. Days passed. Apparently the gunboat was there to prevent the *Santa Rosa* from sailing. What could be done? They began to prepare the ship for her long voyage. Labor was plentiful and cheap. In Baltimore only the most necessary repairs had been made for the Atlantic crossing. In Marseilles they had removed fittings that were no longer needed. Here they finally tackled the enormous task of preparing her to receive thousands of passengers. A new "Yossi" joined them, by the name of Amnon: a communications expert who could handle the ship's radio as well as the Hagannah code.

Hammers pounded, metal clanged in the innards of the ship, typewriter keys tapped in the Scotland Yard's office on the cliff. Companionways from an abandoned passenger ship were fitted into the *Santa Rosa* in broad daylight—what did they have to lose? It was no longer a secret that the ship was preparing to sail with a full load of passengers. If they couldn't get away from the British on land, they would try to give them the slip on the high seas.

In Marseilles, Leibl's office was again out of bounds: they were busy forging passports. The Colombian consul promised to stamp visas. It would thus be easier to obtain Italian visas. "If the passports are phony, why do we need legal visas?" a baffled Yosef asked.

"Checking whether the Polish government issued a passport in such-and-such a name is a complicated business," Leibl explained, "but it's easy enough to phone the local Colombian consulate to find out if they issued a few thousand visas. When do you go to Paris again? The daughter of a Warsaw Yiddish poet is married to a minister in the Italian government. Find out her name and address, ask the Yiddish writers in Paris. Maybe she'll turn out to be a new Queen Esther for us."

• • • • •

Horace Caldwell, from the house on the cliff, invited Yuval into his office for a Scotch and opened his files to him. "I want to spare you futile labor and unnecessary heartache. You have absolutely no chance of getting through. They have already suffered so much—why expose them to more?"

Yuval sipped his drink. "A good question. I ask it and the whole civilized world asks it. Britain will not be able to rationalize her actions."

"Yuval, I didn't invite you here to preach at you or to be preached at. We're both logical, practical men. That's why I put my cards on the table, hoping you would draw the logical, practical conclusions.

"My people have learned in the course of their long history that it isn't always logical to be practical, nor is it always practical to be logical. Their very existence defies logic; their determination to remain Jews is far from practical."

"Britain is a great power. The shores of Palestine are guarded by sea and air fleets. How can you possibly hope to overcome them? I suspect you don't believe in miracles."

"You, Horace, have your home, and your government to protect your home. You can afford to live without miracles. My people have nothing concrete to hold onto. The world abandoned us, everything is in ruins, only the dream of a home remains. They must hang on to that dream or go under."

"Stop preaching and speak to the point."

"You want to know if I believe in miracles? Does one need a miracle to make people act like human beings again? I believe in people. I believe that you, Horace, will one day be ashamed of your present work. I detect a human being under that uniform."

"You know perfectly well that Italy will not risk a confrontation with Britain over a few hundred Jews."

"No, no one will risk a confrontation with anyone. No one raised a murmur over a few million Jews."

"Your ship is blockaded. Your interventions with the Italian government are useless. Unless, of course, Moses appears with his magic rod to divide the port's breakwaters."

"Moses didn't always use his rod. Sometimes he used his head."

"You mean he'll beat his head against the barriers?"

"Sometimes our miracles come by way of the heart. Occasionally, God softens the heart of Pharaoh . . . Even you, Horace, are not immune. Someday, after a sleepless night, you might offer to help us. Chaim Weitzman, the president of the Zionist organization, says that a Jew who doesn't believe in miracles is not a realist."

•   •   •   •   •

Aboard ship, the day started like any other. Workers came from town and the crew worked with them, outfitting the ship. When a special messenger came on the afternoon train from Rome, work stopped. The workers from town left the ship, and they and the crew went to the ship's captain. He hurried to the office of the port commander.

The captain had brought a sealed letter from Rome to the commander. The commander opened the letter, read it through, and proceeded to examine it carefully on all sides. No doubt about it; the paper, the seal, were from the Italian admiralty. It was an order to remove the gunboat that was blocking the *Santa Rosa*'s departure.

The commander scratched his head, drummed his fingers on the table, and once more examined the paper and the seal he had broken. If it were forged, it was a damn good forgery. Should he show it to Signor Caldwell? There was nothing in the order to say it was a secret document, but Italy was, after all, a free nation. She didn't have to account to the British for all her actions. Everything looked authentic, but why take a chance? He would call Rome.

The captain agreed. "If you have any doubts, call Rome, by all means."

Easier said than done. The telephone system in Italy had never been efficient, and the war had destroyed a good deal of equipment.

"Say it's an emergency," the captain suggested.

"It's an emergency," the commander shouted into the mouthpiece.

"We have orders to sail before dark," the captain said. "The telephone operators are lazy. You have to pressure them."

The commander continued to call the central operator but could not get through to Rome. No matter what he did, he was taking a chance. If he let the *Santa Rosa* sail and it turned out the admiralty hadn't issued the order, he'd be in hot water. If the order were authentic and he detained a foreign ship illegally, he'd still be in trouble. Once more he lifted the receiver and shouted a few curses into the telephone, but the line to Rome was still clogged.

"You're sure this is authentic?" he asked the captain.

Up to this point the captain had waited patiently, but now he was insulted. Would he, an officer, a ship's captain, risk his entire career if he had the slightest doubt about those papers? The ship had better be released immediately. It was almost dusk, and he had no intention of staying here one extra minute.

The commander finally decided that he was commander of a port, not a detective. He had received orders and had to carry them out. He hadn't called Rome when Caldwell had brought him orders to place the gunboat in the isthmus to block the *Santa Rosa*.

When the port commander finally got through to Rome, the workday at the admiralty was over and the officer to whom the commander wished to speak had left the office. The officer whom he finally reached handed his call over to another, who in turn handed it to still another. They started hunting for the *Santa Rosa* file, and meanwhile the connection was broken.

The *Santa Rosa* had already slipped her moorings. Horace Caldwell raced to the port commander and established a connection with the British Embassy in Rome by radio. By the time the commander got an order to pursue the *Santa Rosa* and bring her back to port, it was well into the night. Maybe the pursuing gunboats couldn't catch up with the larger ship, or maybe they didn't want to. In any case, at dawn, when the *Santa Rosa* reached French territorial waters and the captain sighted a gunboat through his binoculars, it seemed to him that someone aboard the small boat was waving a blessing.

* * * * *

What they had not managed to accomplish in Portevenire they completed in De Bok, a small port near Lyon. When Horace ran into Yuval on the street he greeted him like an old friend. "Chalk up one for your side," he said graciously.

"It's not a sports contest, it's Russian roulette," Yuval responded. "There are lives at stake."

"You're the ones who are putting them on the line."

"Horace, you're a better spy than preacher. Don't lecture me."

"You're the one that's threatening me with lives at stake."

"I see you can't swallow this mess with complete indifference. A point in your favor. Listen, what about coming to work for us? You can follow your profession during the day and still be able to sleep at night. I'm sure you know that the first Hagannah instructor was a British officer."

"There's a limit to everything, Yuval. Before she left, you brought a huge number of lifeboats aboard the *Santa Rosa*. According to my calculations, enough for five thousand people. We both know you won't be able to get through."

"Many have."

"Not this time. We've got you in our sights all the way. Did you notice the planes circling your ship? Outside the territorial waters there are warships waiting for you. If you're out to demonstrate against the Palestine immigration restrictions, you don't have to endanger the physical and psychological well-being of thousands of refugees. A few hundred would be enough."

"When I suggested that you come to work for us, I was only kidding. But from the way you worry about us, it seems to me you *are* drawing closer. Will you consider it?"

"No more jokes, Yuval."

"Seriously, then. I work on a Honduran vessel that belongs to an American company and is preparing to sail for Venezuela, or Panama, or some other South American port. We haven't got our exact instructions yet."

"I'm ready to help you get the ship out of the Mediterranean."

12

Information came to the central office of the Mossad in Paris that Ernest Bevin, the British foreign minister, was exerting pressure on Foreign Minister Bidault to curb the Aliyah Bet operations from France. The *Santa Rosa* received urgent orders and vanished from the port of De Bok.

British agents searched for her in every small, out-of-the-way port and found her in Sette, a busy place where ships of all sizes were being towed by tugs in and out of the numerous slips and barriers. A steady stream of trucks was bringing more and more passengers to the ship. The order to load had arrived unexpectedly, and the mobilization of transportation to the vessel was a superhuman task. Those on duty were exhausted, but the people in line at the gangplank moved in a quiet and orderly fashion. Once aboard, everyone received a hall and bunk number, as well as the number of the group to which they were assigned. The passengers were surprised when they were asked to surrender their passports, but gave them up without a murmur. When the order to load the ship had arrived, fewer than two thousand passports had been prepared, and the passenger list numbered almost five thousand. The passports of those who had already boarded the ship were collected to give them to those still waiting in line.

Yosef ran down with a batch of passports, which he hurriedly distributed to those standing nearest the ship. He noticed a face that seemed familiar, but he had no time to stop. No one must get to the immigration control officer without a document.

He was already standing before the immigration official when he realized he had a girl's passport. "*Allez, allez. Bougez!* Go, go. Move on!" The official winked and hurried him on.

Even before the loading was completed, they knew all about it at the Quai d'Orsay. The Mossad had received reliable information: Bevin was demanding that the ship be detained, and Bidault was on the verge of yielding. The ship must sail immediately.

It proved impossible to line up a tug and a pilot to guide the ship out of her berth. All the pilots were occupied, all the tugs were busy, and it was plain who had arranged matters so.

"How much do you want? Give me a price, any price, and you'll get it," Uri, the ship's captain, pleaded with one of the pilots. "Tell me where I can buy a tug and I'll give it to you as a gift afterward, if you'll lead us out of here."

"Ten thousand dollars in gold."

"Fine."

"At midnight."

"Midnight is fine. It's a deal."

The ship's captain invited the port officials to a farewell banquet. The cook, with the help of a French chef, prepared hors d'oeuvres. Drinks were served in glasses and bottles, the latter as souvenirs. After a few rounds, Uri announced that the ship's stores were overstocked with coffee, tea, and canned meats. The guests would be doing him a favor by taking some of the extra supplies off his hands. The crew prepared parcels.

The port commander poured himself another glass of cognac, led

Uri off to a corner, and began to speak with a thickened tongue. "A port is a port. Even under Marshal Pétain it was a port. I mean that when the marshal was cooperating with that traitor LaValle in Vichy, I became commander of the port. And a port is a port, not politics, *n'est-ce pas?* A man is but a man," he beat his breast. "My brother-in-law from Paris was also sent to a concentration camp. I'm talking about your cargo. Don't give away your provisions. You'll be here a long time. I'm telling you and I know what I'm talking about. Now it's dark, but as soon as it gets light I'll lead your ship to the other side of a drawbridge. When the bridge is lowered—*fini.* A port is a port, and an order is an order, *comprenez?*"

"Don't worry, *mon ami,* our people in Paris know how to open doors. The order will be canceled, I assure you."

They were still drinking aboard ship when Mike slipped over the railing and into the water. He swam silently to the post where the ship was moored against the cement wall of the basin. He raised his head. A lantern was directly over the post, and a policeman was standing under the lantern.

What now? Should he pretend that he had decided to take a swim in the filthy waters of the port? A wild idea struck him. "Monsieur, monsieur!" he called. Knowing no French, he explained in English what he wanted and then resorted to sign language.

The policeman understood his frantic signs and released the rope from the post. Only a thin wire now remained to hold the ship until the pilot arrived with his tug. They would cut the wire with an ax, otherwise suspicion would fall on the policeman.

All the people on board were in their bunks. The last guests had departed on unsteady legs. A church clock tolled twelve. The package of gold was ready, but there was no sign of the pilot or his tug. Anxious hearts beat impatiently. Long minutes passed, and the clocks tolled one. But what could they do without a pilot? Even an experienced captain couldn't sail out of the post at night with no pilot to guide him, so how would Uri manage?

The pilot didn't appear, and the clock ticked off the seconds relentlessly. The greatest risk was to do nothing at all, to wait around until the ship was isolated behind a drawbridge. If the pilot didn't show up by two, they would have to try it on their own.

The second toll of the second hour was accompanied by the sharp whish of severed wire. "Start up the engines," Uri's voice came over the loudspeaker.

The back-and-forth maneuvers to turn the ship around threw the passengers out of their bunks. Under the impression that this was normal procedure, they picked themselves up and went back to sleep. Though the *Santa Rosa* took a battering, it was worth it. With her bow now facing out to sea, she glided away from the port area. When they had arrived here, no one aboard had calculated how many canals, basins, and breakers they had passed. They could hardly believe the number of ships, boats, and barges moored in every berth, every inlet—. It was a labyrinth through which the vessel had to maneuver like an elephant in an ant colony.

"I've got more luck than brains," Uri commented. During the constant shuttling back and forth, he bumped against walls with the ship's bow, with her stern, with her sides, but had managed to avoid a collision.

The port guards were asleep, or pretended to be. The *Santa Rosa*'s engines groaned as she churned up a white foam that pounded the port's cement walls. All of a sudden, the engines died. What new disaster now?

Uri came close to panicking. Had the ship run aground? The darkness was beginning to fade, there was no time to lose. Once he got the engines started again, he gave them maximum power, the throttle open all the way. The ship rolled convulsively, the propellers flailed the mud as she plowed ahead bit by bit, until she lurched, slid forward, and was sailing free, her bow straight toward the open sea.

● ● ● ● ●

The loudspeakers roused the passengers. Weary from traveling all night to reach the ship, then standing in line for hours to board her, they hadn't unpacked but had gone straight to their bunks. Now a mild, rosy-blue dawn greeted them on deck.

Leibl was at the loudspeaker. The name *Santa Rosa* was fictitious, he announced. They were aboard the Hagannah ship *Moledet*. The ship had an "escort"—that black spot on the horizon was a British vessel. A good many difficulties had already been overcome; if everyone was disciplined and followed instructions, there was good reason to hope that they would arrive safely. He would speak to them again later. Meanwhile good morning and a hearty appetite. "Enjoy your breakfast," he signed off.

13

The heat was suffocating, the crowding inhuman. The ship was a modern Tower of Babel. Children born in Siberia spoke only Russian; those from North Africa only Arabic. Sounds of Yiddish, Polish, Hungarian, Rumanian, French, Italian came from all sides. The passengers were studying Hebrew, but few could communicate in it.

At first Yosef felt there were too many monitors, that it was only adding to the chaos. He soon realized, however, that Leibl knew his job. Everyone on board had been given some kind of task, which provided a sense of responsibility and kept each person at his station. It would have been disastrous to have people wandering around the overcrowded deck.

Yosef was summoned. A woman had just given birth, but the ship's doctor sent Yosef to the crew's quarters. "Give him something," Nobel said, pointing to Willy, whose eyes were now redder than his hair. He was pounding his fists on the sides of his bunk. "It should have happened to my child, it should have happened to *mine!*" he shouted and refused to allow anyone to call Saltcha.

"Calm down, Willy—what happened?"

"The newborn, it's dead! If it was mine, the American consul would have intervened. The *New York Times* would have protested! Who will speak for an infant who hasn't even been named yet but is already being chased by battleships?" He refused to take the pill that Yosef offered him, but rocked back and forth as if he would never stop. "Yosef," he asked suddenly, "what's my Hebrew name?"

"I don't know—and you'd better take this—"

"I'm named after a grandfather, Gedaliah-Wolfe."

"Gedaliah Zev."

"I want a shorter name, like all the Yossis have."

"Zev is short, and the first letters of Gedaliah make a short name—Gad. But it's not the same—"

"Let it be Gad. 'Willy' died with that infant. Yosef, you hate me. I don't blame you. Forgive me."

"Just be good to her, that's all I ask."

"Can you forgive me too? Don't hate me, Yosef."

"I don't hate you, Willy."

"Gad."

"We have enough enemies. Why should we hate each other?"

"I came here to rescue children—look what I've accomplished."

"We mustn't despair. Despair is a luxury—and our worst enemy."

Willy embraced him. "You want me to be good to Saltcha? You're really as generous as she says. She talks about you so much it makes me mad sometimes. She thinks about your happiness too. We all deserve it, we should love one another, we've had enough misery."

"Have you been drinking, Willy? I can smell it—"

"I'm not drunk and I'm not Willy, I'm Gad. No, the bottle is no cure-all. You refugees—and the Yossis—you know better. How do you say it—*afalperken,* despite everything? I must learn Hebrew. Come with me to see Saltcha, Yosef. What's her Hebrew name?"

"Sarah."

"Sarah? That's also English. Come with me—"

"Not now."

Yosef extricated himself and ran to his mother.

"What's happened, Yossel? You look terrible."

"How do you feel?"

"Not bad."

"Honestly?"

"I'm fine, Yossel."

"Four more days, Mother. Don't lift Hannele. Maybe it would be better if you stayed in bed altogether. In four days we'll be in Eretz Israel."

"You've heard about the baby?"

"You know? Be careful, take care, Mother."

"You too, Yossel." She placed her hands on her enormous belly. "I need this like a hole in the head—"

"Don't say that! You do need it. We need it. Our enemies want to wipe us out. We must multiply in spite of them."

"I thought I was all alone in the world. If I'd known that you still—"

"Don't, Mother. You know what 'Yosef' means?"

"It's a name—the first Yosef was mother Rachel's son."

"Yes, and Rachel longed for children, the Scripture tells us. So she called her firstborn Yosef, which means, 'May the Lord grant me more.' May the Lord grant you more sons, Mother. We need them desperately."

14

Leibl had first noticed him back in Sette. The sparse blond hairs on his chin and cheeks were curled like question marks: boy or man? He stood patiently in the long line at the ship. The heavy black hat over his black skullcap gave him the look of a little boy in his father's headgear. Despite the heat, he did not take off the hat or his long black cloak. Someone started to tease him but grew silent once he met those deep brown eyes under the long golden lashes. They seemed unfathomable, but their glance was soft and warm. The scholar Hillel, who never lost his patience and was never provoked to anger, must have had eyes like them.

Most of the passengers came from concentration camps in Germany or from Siberian exile. They had arrived without visas, been smuggled across borders, and still had to cross the sea illegally. But everyone had some baggage: a rucksack, a child in arms or in a sling on the back, a valise in hand. Anyone without a child could carry an extra pack. They had lost so much—yet the sense of possession was still strong.

Their treasures consisted of a few torn pieces of clothing, a pair of patched shoes; one or two even carried a quilted tunic shiny with age. In the wilds of Siberia they had begrudged themselves bread to save for the tunic, so how could they now discard it? They had heard that the nights in Eretz Israel were cold. Anything rescued from their destroyed homes was particularly precious—a chipped enamel pot, a broken stool, anything that offered mute testimony there had once been a home. There were only a fortunate few whose wealth included a photo album. It was as if the ashes scattered by the wind had been gathered together here and given human images.

The one exception was the black-garbed, blond lad who carried only one small parcel under his arm. His pockets, however, were full—phylacteries in one, a Bible in the other.

"That's all you've got?" Leibl had asked him.

"My belongings are already in Eretz Israel."

"Then do me a favor, take this aboard with you. And don't let it out of your hands—it's the ship's flag."

• • • • •

By the time the ship was loaded the sky had grown dark. It had taken a long time to get all the passengers settled. The orders were to turn in at once. The following morning a call came over the loudspeaker: Whoever had the flag should bring it immediately to the topmast on the upper deck.

It was Leibl who kept the ship's log. The *Moledet* was not simply another ship, and the log could not be simply the record of another sea voyage. The log of this ship and its passengers would become a page in Jewish history. Although he himself had given the flag to the blond lad with the black hat, Leibl began to question him closely, as if he had never seen him before.

"How do you come to have a Zionist flag?"

"Every Jew has a share in Zion."

"But you Hassidim don't believe that Zion and Zionism are one and the same thing, do you?"

"The flag is precious to me. It is going with Jews to the Land of Israel."

"My father, of blessed memory, was a Hassid like you, but he would have said it was nothing but a rag."

"Where is your father now?"

"You would say in Paradise. He ascended via the chimney of the crematorium in Treblinka."

"Your father has gone to the true world, so he knows the truth. A piece of cloth, whether it's silk or crude cotton, is no more than a piece of cloth. But if one hangs it over an ark of the Torah, it becomes a *parochet,* a holy curtain. Our prophets spoke of the flag of the 'ingathering of the exiles,' and we pray three times a day: 'And raise thy banners to gather us from exile.' If this flag has the power to give Jews a little bit of faith and confidence, a renewed will to set out on the long, hard road again, then it's in the same tradition as the redeeming banners of the Lord. It was a rare privilege for me to bring this flag aboard ship."

"How come you're not waiting for the Master of the Universe to raise the flag?"

"The author of *Or ha Chaim* was a cabalist and a great sage. He said that only a hurried salvation will come by way of a miracle, but salvation in its time will come as it is written: *'v'kam shevet m'Ys-rael*—and a tribe will arise in Israel'—that is, it will arise out of the natural world. Jews will go toward salvation in a natural way, as in the days of Cyrus. I envy you, Leibl, you and your friends are fulfilling this prophecy."

"I still don't quite understand what you're doing aboard our ship. You have a Palestinian passport, you could travel legally."

"I want to be here with them." He pointed to the people on the deck.

"The truth is, you're risking nothing. If the British capture us, they'll put the Hagannah people in jail, they'll send the refugees to Cyprus, but they'll have to let you go."

"Can you use my passport?"

"You're a strange one! No, we can't. It has your picture on it. And none of the refugees looks like you."

"I can exchange clothes with somebody. My beard is quite short. In a week someone could grow one almost as long—some fellow in danger of imprisonment."

"We might be able to pull that kind of trick on a legal ship. Here they'll check everyone much too closely."

"Think about it, anyway. Maybe there's a way I can be of some use," the young man urged.

·　·　·　·　·

Life aboard the ship fell into a pattern. Each person belonged to a group, and each group had its regular tasks. The little rabbi, as they nicknamed the young Hassid, was not assigned to any group. He attached himself now to one, now to another, and read to them passages from his Bible.

"The prophet Jeremiah witnessed the first destruction. He then brought God's Word to the Jews: 'Thus saith the Lord of Hosts, the God of Israel, unto all captivity . . . Build ye houses and dwell in them and plant gardens, and eat the fruit of them; take ye wives, and beget ye sons and daughters . . . Multiply ye there, and be not diminished . . .'"

·　·　·　·　·

The sea was no longer as calm as it had been during the first two days out. The waves rolled higher, the force of the current rocked the ship; the wooden structures that held the bunks, the hastily constructed companionways, groaned and creaked as if they were about to fall apart. Many aboard were stricken with diarrhea, most were seasick. Even those who turned up at the discussion groups complained of headaches, stomach pains, or nausea.

The little rabbi joined a group that was supposed to hear a lecture on Palestinography. Everyone was talking about the rough seas.

"The roar of the wind is the voice of the Lord. The Lord cries when his people suffer, and His voice is heard from one end of the universe to the other. The Lord of the Universe weeps when His children are tormented, and two enormous tears fall into the sea. That's what the Midrash on Scriptures says. Perhaps that's why the sea is so stormy today."

"So the Lord is weeping for our fate? Tell Him, Rabbi, not to weep so hard. Two tears rock this ship and make us sick; a few more tears will sink us altogether."

"The Lord is with us, daughter."

"Where was He when we were in Auschwitz?"

"With us, daughter."

"Don't daughter me! You're too young to have daughters. I was in Auschwitz, Rabbi. I looked for Him. I couldn't find Him."

The girl jumped up and ran away. The little rabbi's eyes followed her sorrowfully. "Believe me," he pleaded with the others, "it's a privilege to come to Eretz Israel through great suffering. Indeed, the Gemarrah says so: The Lord gave the Jews three gifts—the Torah, Eretz Israel, and the world to come—and all of them can be reached only through suffering."

"If the Lord wanted to bestow gifts, why did it have to be through suffering?" someone asked.

"It is written that God punished the serpent by causing it to crawl on its belly and eat earth. One might think that wasn't much of a curse. After all, if the serpent crawls on the earth, it will find its sustenance everywhere. The rabbi of Kotsk, of blessed memory, explained that the very fact that the serpent had everything he needed without even having to stoop over was the real curse. Man, on the other hand, was blessed by God in that he could sweeten his bread by labor, he could enjoy the result of his own creation. The Jews in the desert complained, they preferred slavery to suffering in the wilderness. Therefore Moses told them angrily: 'God will do battle for you.' We here have earned the privilege of doing battle for ourselves and gaining our freedom through suffering."

•   •   •   •   •

Dawn. The sea had grown calmer. It was now possible to lie quietly in the bunks and sleep. The girl from Auschwitz stood at the rail on the upper deck, her eyes on the horizon, where a soft, rosy hue was beginning to climb the sky. She felt someone approach.

"Good morning," the little rabbi greeted her.

"Good morning, good year."

"That's God's world for you—yesterday a storm, today a marvelous calm."

"What did He need the storm for? To tease us?"

"If a father always carried his child in his arms, it would never learn to walk. When a child falls, it cries, but the father knows that the fall is the first stage of learning to walk."

The girl pointed to the silhouette of a warship. "Did the good Father send us that too?"

"The child takes a few steps and the father moves backward. The foolish child might think that the father was abandoning him, but a father doesn't abandon his children."

"And if he does, he isn't really a father."

"You have an Auschwitz number on your arm. God couldn't bring himself to see your complaints in a negative light. If you do murmur against Him, however, it means that you believe in Him despite Auschwitz. What's your name, daughter?"

"I no longer have a name, only a number."

"You're right, daughter, they tattooed it on your arm because you're a Jewish child, so it has been transformed into a mark of honor rather than shame."

"Don't call me daughter; my name is Masha. Everything that was done to me because I'm Jewish—does that mean it's good and honorable? You weren't there. You don't know anything about Auschwitz."

"It's true I wasn't in Auschwitz, and I can't forgive myself for it. My flesh hurts because it never became bloated with hunger, nor was it torn by flogging. My bones ache because they were never broken by savage blows. My eyes throb in pain because they never looked at the chimneys of the crematoria. Forgive me, Masha, you were tormented there also for me."

"Rabbi, I see your tears. They fall into the sea and don't create a storm. You weep because you were not in Auschwitz, and He—"

"He was there, He was in Auschwitz. The Gemarrah says:

'No matter whether Jews may be driven, the Divine Presence accompanies them into exile, and returns with them when they are redeemed.'"

"There too?" Masha stretched out her tattooed arm.

"Yes, there too. And if one can imagine the Divine Presence in human form, It too has an Auschwitz number tattooed on the arm."

Masha let her arm drop and lowered her gaze to the sea. "You weren't there! If you had any idea what Auschwitz was, you would realize that you are profaning the name of God with such talk."

"It is not written He had returned *them,* but *He* had returned. From this we learn that the Holy One himself returned along with them from the place of exile. I believe with perfect faith that the Divine Presence was with you in Auschwitz and is now coming back with you on this ship."

"You don't know what you're saying! You don't know!" Masha almost screamed. "And what did you say—the Divine Presence has a number tattooed on Its arm? What does It have tattooed across Its breast?"

The little rabbi seemed to be struck dumb. Masha turned to him with a sudden movement, opened a button of her blouse, and exposed the top of her chest. "Here! A rabbi should know how the Divine Presence looks. What do you see, Rabbi?"

To her surprise, the rabbi did not lower his eyes. "I see a scar, the mark of a wound. I hope it has healed properly."

"It will never heal," she said emphatically as she buttoned her blouse and turned again toward the sea.

"Don't say that, Masha."

Her eyes bored into his face with almost intolerable intensity. "There was a tattoo here too once." She lowered her eyes, her voice so soft he could hardly hear her. "Does the Divine Presence also have the letters F.H. tattooed across Its breasts—Field Whore?"

The silence that followed was long and painful. Finally, the little rabbi stepped closer to her and in a trembling voice said: "What the Germans did to you, the Romans did to the daughter of Rabbi Yohanan and also to the daughter of the martyred Rabbi Hanina. This girl was the sister of Bruria, who was the wife of Rabbi Meir. Bruria was famous for her piety and wisdom."

"Is this supposed to console me?" Masha asked and turned her back to him.

He grasped her arm and turned her around toward him. Looking steadily into her eyes, he said: "You asked me a question before. The answer is yes."

"Yes what?"

"You asked me about a tattoo and the Divine Presence."

"You can't bring yourself to utter the words."

"The answer is yes, you were driven into Auschwitz because you are a Jewish daughter and 'in all the places of their exile the Divine Presence is with them.' So the Divine Presence was in Auschwitz along with you. When they tattooed the words . . ."

"Say it, say it!"

"When they tattooed the word WHORE across your breasts, the same word appeared on the breasts of the Divine Presence, if one can imagine the Divine Presence with breasts . . ." his words trailed off.

"You profane God."

"No. Quite the contrary. I am confirming my belief in the Lord our God and everything our sages have said about Him."

"Did the Divine Presence also allow itself to have plastic surgery performed?"

"The Divine Presence experienced the torment of it along with you."

"Forgive me for forcing you to say things that are alien to your tongue."

"It is difficult for me to say many things, many words are alien to my tongue, particularly in the presence of a woman. But anything that might ease your pain is a service to the Lord, a healing also for the wounds of the Divine Presence. Man has a private organ that is considered shameful to mention in public. Yet the Lord chose to symbolize His covenant with us by a cut on that very organ. The scar on your body is a sign of the covenant with God. Your Jewishness has been carved into your flesh."

"You live in the clouds, Rabbi, but what about an ordinary man? What will he say when he sees the mark each time he comes close to embrace me? He will see the carved word, even though the letters have been removed."

"Do you have anyone, Masha—a boyfriend, I mean?"

"Me? Are you kidding?"

"You have no bridegroom, I have no bride."

"I haven't, nor will I ever have, nor do I want one. Never!"

"Don't talk like that. I want you to be my bride."

Masha was stunned.

"Will you be able to run a kosher home?" he continued. "I'm not setting conditions, but—"

"Rabbi—"

"My name is Shlomo. My father, of blessed memory, was a rabbi, but I'm not."

"What would your father say to this match?"

"All I know, I learned from him. I am only trying to follow in his footsteps. Yes, Masha, I believe he would have approved. Did I tell you I've lived in Eretz Israel? I've been there for years, but I wanted the privilege of arriving in the Holy Land along with my brothers and sisters, through suffering. I'm beginning in believe that destiny guided me to this ship. Don't you see, Masha?"

"Your compassion is comforting. Even heavenly. But is it enough to cement a union between two earthly creatures? Marriage is for a lifetime."

"God has chosen you to suffer for me too. His mysterious ways have brought you to me. Please think about it . . ."

* * * * *

Willy—redheaded and snubnosed—looked out of place among the oval-faced, long-nosed, dark-haired youths from Morocco. During the long weeks in France, Willy had picked up very little French. The girls in the bars spoke to him in English. He learned Yiddish from Saltcha, which the Moroccans didn't understand. How he managed to communicate with them, nobody could fathom. They had been stiff and reserved when Willy had tried some of his pranks on them, but once he had won the hearts of their children, the adults began to include him in their group. They remained a clique apart even with Willy's friendship, but he assigned them a special task. Eighteen young men were now organized into a unit called "The Moroccan Brigade" and were given detailed instruction on how to defend their positions in the event of a British attack. Day after day they practiced defense measures and refined their strategy.

Saltcha and Willy had been seen hugging and kissing in public just like the youngsters on the streets of Paris. It irritated some of the passengers, but Yosef regarded them kindly. Only a short time ago he had dreamt that one day Saltcha would come to him weeping that the Yankee had deceived her, that it was really him, Yurek, whom she loved—fantasies of a defeated child. Let her go on believing that Willy was the most handsome, the finest, the best of all possible men . . .

•   •   •   •   •

The little rabbi noticed Masha on deck, walked over, and greeted her.

"Oh, it's you again," she responded impatiently.

"You want me to go away? What do you have against me?"

"I don't know, Rabbi Shlomo. I'm not in a very good mood today. When I'm like this—"

"Let's drop the title and the formality. Call me Shlomo, just Shlomo."

A bitter and mischievous grin appeared on her face. "Are you serious about your proposal? Then how come you keep your distance from me? Come closer, take my arm, I'm used to a great deal more . . ."

Shlomo seized her arm. "Why do you torment yourself like this?"

"Does what I said hurt you?"

"Only because it hurts you."

"And if it didn't hurt me? Kiss me," she challenged him.

Shlomo hesitated momentarily, then bent over and touched his lips to hers. There was a murmur of voices all around them. Masha took his hand firmly in hers and pulled him after her to the railing. Both were silent for a long time.

"If I hadn't asked you, would you have kissed me?"

"I would have waited until after we were married. That's the way it's done among us."

"Then why did you do it?"

"Because you wanted me to."

"Are you ready to do anything I want? And if I should ask you to eat something that isn't kosher?"

"God forbid!"

"Then why did you listen to me just now?"

"You could have thought—you might have gotten this idea that—that I didn't want to kiss you for other reasons."

"What other reasons?"

"Masha, you are torturing me and you are tormenting yourself even more. Don't do it, Mashele!"

"Had I been a kosher girl, you wouldn't have kissed me. You would have waited for the wedding night. That's how it's done among you. But because I am what I am, it's permissible to kiss me in public. Otherwise, I might think it disgusts you to kiss a whore."

"I forbid you to talk like that! I never want to hear that word again!"

"A dreadful word, isn't it? You can't stand it, can you? You kissed me just because you can't forget it. You were disgusted, weren't you? But you overcame your repulsion, you're ready to sacrifice yourself to atone for His sins." She pointed heavenward.

Shlomo's large innocent eyes seemed even larger as his trembling lips spoke. "How can you talk like that, Mashele? Marriage is not a game for me. I come from a long line of saintly Jews. I am the only one of my family who has survived. I was just bar mitzvah when my father, of blessed memory, sent me away. That was before the war, but he had a premonition. He constantly spoke to me, a thirteen-year-old boy, about my responsibility to carry on the family line, to forge the next link in the chain. I want you to be the mother of my children, the children of my father and my grandfathers, all the way back to the holy preacher of Kozenic. They should be born through you and be a part of you, just as they will be a part of me and my forefathers. How can you think even for a moment that I do this lightly, thoughtlessly? Suffering purifies. You have emerged as pure as the biblical Hanania, Michael, and Azariah from the fiery furnace."

Masha's eyes seemed to sink deeper into her head. The heavy, swollen lids drooped toward the dark lines under them, but she couldn't close them, just as one cannot bend a swollen knee. "Do you really mean what you're saying?" Her voice came as from far away.

"A man cannot live at peace with himself if he feels one thing and says another."

"I doubt if I'll ever be able to be at peace with myself."

"Do you know what the Gemarrah says about that? The rabbis taught that he who loves his wife as himself and who honors her more than himself, about him it is written: 'And thou shalt know peace in thy dwelling.'"

"What does that mean in simple language?"

"When husband and wife love each other, peace and contentment reign in their home."

"Do the Hassidim talk about love?"

"Maybe they talk less than others, but they don't love less. I've only known you for a couple of days, yet I feel our souls have been close for a very long time. We were destined for each other even before we were born. When you were chosen to be my destined one, you were also chosen to suffer for me. When you become part of me and I part of you, then I will feel that I too was in Auschwitz. You were there for me too, you suffered there for me too. Our Torah was given in two tablets, like bride and groom. But it is one Torah, just as bride and groom are two souls that become one. Open your heart to me, Mashele . . . When your heart is no longer full of pain, there will be room for God and happiness. When you have God in your heart, then there will be room for me too, because God is love, God is life."

Masha's eyes filled. Shlomo's words kept flowing. The film of tears trembled and broke, like a dam burst by the waters of a flood. She wept for a long time, her head over the railing, her arm against his. He put his hand over hers and whispered, "Don't be ashamed of our tears. This ship of the hunted is an island of tears. Cry, it will do you good."

"Teardrops in a vast ocean, that's what Jewish tears are these days. Who will see them, who will take any notice?"

"He who sees everything, who hears everything," replied Shlomo, his own tears flowing.

"You really believe that?"

"With perfect faith."

"Good for you."

"I believe with perfect faith that it will be good for you too. Tell me that our souls have flowed together and become one, just as our tears have mingled. Say it, Mashele."

"I don't know what to say. I'm in a fog. All my limbs ache, yet the aching feels good. I imagine that's the way a person who has been paralyzed feels when he begins to experience pain again. I have to sit down, or I'll collapse."

The ship's loudspeaker announced that dinner was ready for Group G. She felt a hollowness under her heart; perhaps some warm food would help.

•　•　•　•　•

"Maybe I shouldn't have told you. What you don't know can't hurt—"

"Mashele, does that mean you accept? Mazel tov—congratulations—to us both!"

"Did I say I accepted?"

"From what you said—"

"Is that how it sounded? I don't know yet. I don't know anything. If God were as good as you, it would be easier to believe in Him."

"God's benevolence manifests itself through people who do His will. If I am good, then it is His goodness."

"I'm all confused, mixed up. I don't know anything yet."

"Do you find me repulsive? Do you object to my appearance? To my behavior? Is that it?"

"God forbid. You have pierced a blister. Now the pain is stronger, but—what do you know about me? You're not doing it for me. You're doing it for God. That's why it doesn't matter to you."

"I know a great deal about you. You're honest. You can't tell a lie. Your straightforwardness is almost saintly. The only thing God demands of us is an upright heart."

"And suppose I can't become the mother of your children?"

Shlomo's knees buckled; he gripped the rail. "Did they operate on you?"

Masha didn't answer.

After a moment he looked directly into her eyes and said firmly, "If that is so, then it's a sure sign that I am not destined to bring children into the world."

"And your family line?"

Shlomo shrugged.

"But your father—"

"My father and I, both of us, can only do what the Lord has willed. If the Lord wants to snap the thread of our family line—well, it has happened to many holy lines . . ."

"They didn't operate on me."

A cloud cleared from his eyes, a sunny radiance shone from them. "I rely on my intuitive perception, on my faith; but you are cautious, you try me with all manner of tests. Praise be to God that I have passed them all."

"I'm not testing you. I often speak against my will, as if to spite myself. I speak nonsense and you make a big thing of it. My father was the same way. If one of the children so much as burped, he was enchanted with its brilliance."

"Praise the Lord you were spared that terrible operation. I felt instinctively that we were destined to raise generations of children."

"I haven't felt it yet. Don't think I'm giving myself airs. Just the opposite. I've never known anyone like you. If you're trying to sacrifice yourself to heal my wounds, it can't last. You can have a moment of altruism, but if you have to sacrifice every minute of every day—an entire lifetime—even you will become restive and overburdened."

"Why don't you believe me, Mashele?"

"Except for what has happened to me, you're a learned man and I'm just an ordinary girl. I was thirteen when the war broke out. How much could I have learned by the age of thirteen?"

"Your common sense and inborn intelligence are nothing to scoff at. Your maturity is admirable. Your attempts to degrade yourself come from the same source as your tendency to torment yourself, to cause yourself pain. You spoke about your father's behavior with children. Did it ever happen that he spanked you and then you were so angry that you refused to touch the food he later gave you? You are now acting in the same manner with God. You refused to accept His goodness. But perhaps it's true that I am hurrying you too much. You are, God bless you, intelligent and astute. I'll wait for your answer, Masha."

15

Black silhouettes loomed on the horizon—four towering escorts. One of the warships drew closer and closer to the *Santa Rosa.* The others hung back. The escort cruised alongside the refugee ship as if showing off its superiority. Red stains showed where only an undercoating had been used to paint the *Santa Rosa,* patches of various hues where even the topcoat was wearing thin. And the motley collection of people on its shabby decks—hunched, bent figures in shapeless garments of every color and description.

The British ship had a fresh coat of green-gray paint. Between the gun emplacements stood orderly rows of sailors in spanking white uniforms, staring across at the refugees. The silence on the battleship contrasted with the noisy confusion of the *Santa Rosa.* At the head of these neat rows of sailors stood an officer. Someone handed him a megaphone and sudden silence fell on the ship of refugees.

The British officer was aware that most of the refugees had been in German camps. Perhaps someone had told him that their language, Yiddish, was like German. In any case, he spoke to them in German.

"We know who you are, and where you are heading. It is forbidden by law to enter Palestine without visas. Return to Germany where UNRWA will look after you until you get legal visas to countries that encourage immigration."

Uri replied in English. "We have no idea who you are. You're flying the Union Jack, but you're speaking the language of Hitler, and you want to send us back to Hitler's camps."

The British officer ignored this reply but continued in English. "My name is Stuart Bentley, captain of the cruiser *Ajax* of His Majesty's royal fleet. It is our duty to see that the law is adhered to."

Uri replied. "How do you do, Captain? Nice to meet you. The League of Nations gave Britain a mandate over Palestine to establish a Jewish homeland there. If it's the royal fleet's duty to carry out Great Britain's international obligations, then sail to Germany, pick up shiploads of Jewish refugees, and bring them to Palestine. We, aboard this ship, will manage without your help or advice."

The British ship veered away before Uri had finished. "Villains! For shame!" The megaphone of the *Santa Rosa* shouted after them. Then Uri turned to the refugees. "Friends, we are not without plans or without means. Our ship has escaped a number of traps and avoided all sorts of dangers. It is still possible that we can land you safely on the shores of our homeland. It is also possible that the British will win. If it should come to a showdown, we have to put up a token struggle. But remember: they are well armed. Our struggle should arouse the conscience of the world, but no one must sacrifice himself in combat. We've had enough sacrifices."

Amnon was in constant communication with Tel Aviv and a plan was worked out. The *Santa Rosa* had shallower water draft than the heavy warships. She also could move at a higher speed. The British had no sanction to attack outside the territorial waters of Palestine, so the *Santa Rosa* would sail alongside the shoreline just outside the territorial limit. Opposite the appointed landing place, the *Santa Rosa* would suddenly steam at full speed toward the shore and perhaps succeed in reaching shallow water before the British ships could overtake them. If the British didn't know where the *Santa Rosa* was landing, a good many refugees could manage to disembark and vanish in the towns and villages along the coast before the mandate forces could get ashore.

• • • • •

Uri received instructions from Tel Aviv to head south and lead the British to believe they were planning to land in Raffah. Only later would they veer north. Meanwhile, they were to stay outside the three-mile limit. When they were parallel to Bat-Yam, they were to change course sharply toward the coast and ground the ship on the sandbars. All those who could swim were instructed to swim ashore. All lifeboats and belts were to be used. The people on shore were prepared to surround the refugees and whisk them away without a trace.

"Won't the British open fire when they realize that we're slipping out of their hands?" Uri asked.

"The British are not Nazis," Tel Aviv replied.

• • • • •

Uri sat hunched over his maps. "Are we near Tobruk?" Amnon asked.

"We're alongside the coast of Egypt. We'll soon be approaching Rosetta."

"Where the devil is Rosetta?"

"Don't you remember? They learned how to decipher hieroglyphics from a stone that one of Napoleon's soldiers found in Rosetta. I found something in Rosetta too."

"When were you ever in Rosetta?"

"My index finger is there right now, here on the map. You know what I found?"

"What?"

"Sand."

"Beyond the Rosetta inlet, the water gets shallower and shallower until it turns into the Dalmatian sand dunes. Shall we play a game with the British? A draft of three meters is enough for us. They're sticking so close to us that maybe we can get one of their destroyers grounded in the sand."

The *Santa Rosa* did sail across the shallows into Egyptian territorial waters. The British now had the legal right to halt the ship. However, they were familiar with the terrain and kept their distance. A sudden thought made Uri break into a cold sweat. The British had four ships and a good many more along the coast. They could line up at the edge of the shallows and capture the *Santa Rosa* before she got out again past the three-mile limit.

The *Santa Rosa* made a sudden run for the open sea. For a short while the lights of the pursuers were invisible, but soon enough their beams were again trained on the refugee ship through the black night.

•   •   •   •   •

A new day began to lighten the sky behind the coast of Eretz Israel. The commanders of the ship huddled together to read the Hagannah orders, which had been held waiting in sealed envelopes. The Hagannah people with whom the British were unfamiliar were instructed that if the ship were captured, they were to mingle with the refugees and allow themselves to be sent to Cyprus. Those whom the British knew were instructed to go into hiding. The prearranged hiding places were equipped with food, water, and work clothes. The first work crews sent to clear out the ship would be Hagannah people. The code would be a song from the Sabbath prayers, "*Kumi Tze-ee M'toch haHafecha*—Come ye out from the midst of destruction." Those who were hidden would then emerge dressed in work clothes and mingle with the work crew.

The Hagannah people were still discussing their plans when the alarm was raised from the helm:

"Man overboard!"

Most of the passengers were still asleep. Shlomo was on deck reciting the morning prayers and was just winding the phylactery around his left arm. He was standing at the rail on the starboard side facing east when he realized that there was a commotion on the port side. When he got there, he saw Mike being pulled up with the drowning person in his arms.

It was Masha.

Shlomo could only stand there murmuring prayers as the doctor and some of the sailors applied artificial respiration. Her expressionless face was as green as the seawater she had swallowed. Her eyes, which had always seemed to him to be pools of suffering, were covered by her swollen lids. It seemed as if all the pain and torment had been drained from her in the water. She lay there inert and peaceful, as if the doctor's efforts were only disturbing her.

A scream tore from Shlomo's lips: "God forbid!" It seemed to him that she responded to his cry as a faint tremor went through her body. He noticed suddenly that he still held the headpiece of his phylacteries in his hand, and attached it high on his forehead. With the strand of leather, he formed the letter *shin* over the back of his hand. The prayer over the phylacteries now took on another meaning.

"And I will betroth thee unto me forever, yea I will betroth thee unto me in righteousness and in justice, and in loving-kindness, and in compassion. And I will betroth thee unto me with faithfulness, and thou shalt know the Lord."

● ● ● ● ●

Fervently praying it would be unnecessary, they began preparations to defend the ship. They strung barbed wire around the promenade deck and over every opening that the British could use as entry. Uri felt uneasy. They would have a serious problem if a fire broke out anywhere. The refugees worked like demons and paid no attention to his concern. The trained hoses from the oil tanks across the deck to make the boarding areas slippery. They piled sandbags around the helm and the lookout. Willy inspected his Moroccan Brigade to make sure they weren't hiding any weapons. Leibl warned everybody again and again: "We must not provoke the British into firing."

● ● ● ● ●

Shlomo stood on deck, his eyes trying to pierce the darkness. The ship was now sailing along the coast of Sinai. Somewhere on the far side of the coast stood the mountain on which the Torah had been received. All the Jews had been there, and with them the souls of all Jews to be born to the end of days, Masha's and his among them. She had been fully purified by her sufferings. What had happened this morning could either be a punishment or a test for him. If it were a punishment, he would accept it with love. If it were a test, let the merits of his ancestors be in his favor. "The dead don't praise God, nor do those who descend into silence." Masha was saved to demonstrate that the Lord had turned His face away only for a short while. Those whom the Nazis had wanted to defile would yet, with God's help, bring into the world generations of pious and holy Jews. He completed his evening prayers with a feeling of relief and went below to the infirmary.

He sat beside Masha's bunk. In the dark he could not distinguish her features, but her hand lay in his unresistingly. For the first time he felt that his words were reaching her soul.

"Why must it be today, Shlomo? I'm so weak."

"The marriage canopy wipes out all sins. Tomorrow, with God's help, we shall be in Eretz Israel. I want us to set foot on the Holy Land cleansed of all sins."

"They'll laugh at us."

"Making people laugh is also an achievement, especially in these days and in our situation. There's a tale in the Gemarrah about two clowns who made the people in the marketplace laugh. Elijah the Prophet said that they had thereby earned for themselves a place in the world to come."

"Do as you think best. I only hope I may be worthy of you, Shlomo."

•   •   •   •   •

Shlomo was convinced that Masha's "falling" overboard was a sign from heaven. "Out of bitterness came sweetness." Now she had the ritual purification without which they could not perform the marriage ceremony. The only problem that remained was the *ketuba*. Any Jew could perform the ceremony, but where could they find a marriage contract? He did not know the long text by heart.

A request was made over the loudspeaker. One woman who had her *ketuba* with her responded, and Shlomo copied the text.

A prayer shawl was spread out as the marriage canopy, and candles were lit. A British ship sailed close by and threw a beam of light. The activity on deck was making them suspicious.

"What are they looking for, secret weapons?" someone joked.

"This is our secret weapon," Shlomo pointed to the prayer shawl.

The weakened bride had to be supported on either side, but the ceremonial prayers rang out through the night. The British ship moved away, extinguishing its searchlight. The stars were not shining brightly, but like the people gathered around the canopy, quivered and twinkled. "*Od yishama,* there will yet be heard in the cities of Judea and in the streets of Jerusalem the sounds of rejoicing, the sounds of jubilation; the voice of the groom, the voice of the bride . . ."

Hearts fluttered. A momentous silence descended on the ship. Tomorrow they would be swarming toward the shore of Eretz Israel.

Serene darkness. Even the faint lights from the British vessel seemed to recede. Why had they fallen behind? Were they, too, moved by the solemnity of that night?

16

Willy took over a lookout in the wheelhouse. The ship cruised slowly, almost serenely, over calm waters. With her lights out she blended into the mysterious darkness of the night. The stars faded one by one; sky and sea—one dense blackness. Then suddenly a blaze of light! The *Moledet* was trapped in the blinding light of reflectors. The British had surrounded them.

• • • • •

The orders from London had been to halt the refugee ship at all costs. The captain of the destroyer *Checkers* had come up with an idea: attack now even though the ship was still about thirty-seven kilometers from shore. The Jews had blundered into the Dalmatian shallows, which showed how little they knew about navigation. Why not surprise them now in the dead of night, when everyone was asleep, and convince them that they were already in the territorial waters of Palestine?

The wail of the ship's siren made the skin crawl and the nerve ends tingle. No, not again! All the dulled fears, all the half-scarred wounds burst open and screamed in unison with the wail of the siren. Do or die!

Each commander pushed his way through to his group; the key personnel took up their positions. From the bridge they lowered the insignia with the fictitious name *Santa Rosa* and raised it again, reversed. The British reflectors lit up the luminous paint: HAGANNAH SHIP MOLEDET.

From the storm deck the young people lowered a large sheet with the drawing of a mother nursing her infant and an inscription: "Is this your enemy?"

A destroyer cruised closer. A voice reached them over the waves: "You are now in the territorial waters of Palestine. Turn off your engines; our ship will tow you to Haifa."

"Liars! Pirates!" they shouted back from the refugee ship.

Was it the shock of the sudden attack or the inspiration of the new name of the ship? The instructions about a limited counterattack were forgotten. Each man stood with clenched fists: "Over my dead body! They won't take me alive!"

A short, sharp whistle. The *Moledet* replied: "You know perfectly well we are in international waters. You have no right to attack us. We shall lodge a complaint with the proper authorities." They waited for an answer.

A mighty impact shook the whole ship. Two destroyers slid in on either side. Many on board were knocked off their feet. As they scrambled up again, they could see the British sailors running across rope bridges, which the destroyer had thrown over to the upper deck of the *Moledet.* The upper deck was defended by children, who pelted the attackers with potatoes, tin cans, bottles.

The first British to board the ship made straight for the wheel-house. By the time Uri came racing up with a group of crew members, the British sailors had barricaded themselves inside. All attempts to mount an attack on the wheelhouse were repulsed. A bullet grazed Ike's arm. But the wheelhouse had to be retaken. They climbed into the lifeboats and from there jumped onto the roof. In the lifeboats they found some smoke-signal containers. They broke a hole in the roof of the wheelhouse and tossed down the containers. The British sailors, thinking it was tear gas, surrendered and were locked up. Uri took over the wheel and began to maneuver the ship.

The landing bridges were wrenched from the attacking destroyer. Another ship tried to slip into position, but the backing and forthing of the *Moledet* became progressively more methodical, more precise. The attackers were left without a landing bridge; those aboard the *Moledet* were cut off from their ships and in danger of being surrounded. One of their small groups was overpowered. Leibl collected the prisoners' weapons and threw them into the sea. It was safer to be without live ammunition.

As Yosef was dressing the prisoners' wounds, he gathered the weapons he had found and rushed up to throw them overboard. "We may need the weapons," someone objected, grabbing his arm.

"This is our weapon," he replied, raising his finger to the tip of the mast, but he was disappointed to see that the flag was not there. "How come the flag wasn't hoisted?" he asked in dismay.

"The rope got tangled."

Yosef made straight for the mast.

British sailors were now trying to swing across to the *Moledet* on ropes. The defenders were able to catch them while they were still in the air and throw them into the water. The attackers were now searching the waters for the light signals on the life jackets of their sailors. One succeeded in swinging across into one of the *Moledet*'s lifeboats. The boys of the Moroccan Brigade stood guard over him. If he tried to get out, he would fall right into their hands. The British sailor would no doubt have preferred to return to his ship now, but the movements of the *Moledet* forced his ship to change course. He drew his revolver. The boys didn't budge. The destroyer again headed for the *Moledet* and bumped her. The sailor in the lifeboat wavered, lost his balance, and fell. A boy with a knife leapt forward to cut the rope, and the lifeboat with the sailor inside fell on the heads of those on the destroyer.

The warship abruptly shut off its beams. In the distance the heavy curtain of darkness was hedged by a pink streak where night was ready to give birth to a new day. It was still difficult to guess what the enemy was preparing to do, shrouded as they were in blackness.

Then an explosion of brilliant light blinded the defenders of the *Moledet*. Even before they realized that the British had put on gas masks, the *Moledet* was pelted with tear-gas bombs. The entire ship was wrapped in a cloud of gas. A medic carried gassed children to Nobel, who tried to wash their eyes, but found the water pipes had been broken. He grabbed a pot of cold coffee and washed their eyes with that to ease their agony. Portholes were shattered by bullets. "Flat on the deck!" Nobel shouted to the children and ran to the steps. At the top he was met by the British with drawn revolvers. Nobel pointed to his arm band with its American flag. "American. Correspondent for a Christian magazine."

"Maybe you can do something to bring this suicidal madness to an end?" the British officer asked him.

Before Nobel could reply, Ike ran up behind him with an ax in his upraised arm: "Murderers! You're slaughtering our children!"

Nobel grabbed the ax out of Ike's hands before the British could shoot. "I'll see what I can do," he replied to the officer, and dragged Ike off with him.

Some of the British soldiers who had managed to get aboard were still surrounded and isolated, but they could not be overpowered.

Mike examined a crack through which water was seeping and declared, "It's not serious, we've got a good pump."

Uri's report was less optimistic. "The entire structure of the ship has been loosened; we can't take chances with five thousand lives."

"We're not fighting for those five thousand alone," Ike protested.

"How long will we allow ourselves to be slaughtered and not do something?" a volunteer from among the refugees shouted.

•   •   •   •   •

Yosef had climbed the banner mast to raise the flag. It wasn't easy to unravel the tangled rope. Beneath him the battle continued. His comrades were throwing cans from the food stores, pulling out stair railings to beat off the attackers.

Each one to his task, Yosef told himself. The flag would give the defenders new morale. He must unravel the rope and raise the flag.

Hertzke had promised Yosef that he would make sure Golda got enough rest. She lay on her bunk as she had promised. The collisions, the shouting, had awakened her, but she had dozed off again. Was it weariness from her pregnancy, or had Yossel put something into the hot milk he had brought her, Hertzke wondered. Suddenly they heard the shooting. Golda jumped up and started for the deck. Hertzke caught up with her. She pulled her arm away and ran on. "Where?" she demanded when she reached the top deck. "There," someone pointed to the banner mast.

•   •   •   •   •

The face was a mass of pulpy flesh and blood with unidentifiable features. "Who is it?" they asked one another. A heap of broken bones in short khaki pants, a shred of blue-and-white cloth clenched in his fist. "Who is it?" Golda repeated the question only to delay the knowledge that pressed on her consciousness. Then it broke on her with horror, and she went down like a sinking ship.

•   •   •   •   •

Golda opened her eyes. Was it she who was uttering those hideous cries? But her mouth was locked by her clenched teeth. Were the screams splitting her face? Were they getting stuck in her ears . . .

ringing, ringing, ringing? A piercing scream was again splitting her head. Everything was splitting . . . the boards of her bunk, the sky outside . . . Or was it only her body that was splitting and tearing into shreds?

Were the pains too early? She didn't care now whether the child was a girl or a boy. No, it had to be a boy, born to take Yossel's place, as her little girl had taken Hannele's. She couldn't see Hertzke, she couldn't see the child. She was utterly indifferent to those replacements. No one could take Yossel's place, nor Hannele's, not Nenna's, least of all Shiya's. She had seen them all, seen them standing around Yossel's body, as if they were alive. Now they were floating outside above the waters, keeping her company. She had only to call and they would enter. But how could she call them now when she was being split and torn to pieces? No, Shiya and the children were not there, outside, they were all inside her. She wouldn't scream anymore. Let them nestle inside her—all of them: Shiya, Nenna, Yossel, Hannele—Hannele the first, the little dark beauty! Let them nestle inside her and burn her insides, like salt on an open wound . . .

Epilogue

Yes, thou shalt be as that lieth
down in the midst of the sea,
Or as he that lieth upon the tip of a mast.
Prov. 23:34

The battle was over. The *Moledet* had fought valiantly before her surrender. All the passengers were now prisoners on the British ships. Leibl, his head still swollen and raw, his eyes as red as the bloodstained bandage over his forehead, remained on board to keep watch over the woman in labor.

He was sitting across from her berth in the tiny dark cabin, adding another page to the ship's log. His tears blotted the words as he wrote them; the tears were as much a part of the ship's story as the words. He was fortunate he could still shed tears; she at the height of her agony had none left. He was with her because Yosef, her son, the medic, was no longer there to take care of her. Leibl was adding to the log because the story of the *Moledet* had not ended and the struggle was not finished with the surrender of the ship.

She lay there with wide open eyes, eyes like gaping, suppurating wounds. The birth of a child, though accompanied by pain, should bring joy. For her, the pains of birth were accompanied by those of loss. She didn't cry, she didn't moan, her silence frightened him, and the fear grew from hour to hour. At last he heard a low, harsh groan. "Hannele in some godforsaken forest. Nenna in the furnaces of Treblinka, Yossel in the depths of the sea. Lord of the universe, have you more grisly ways to destroy my offspring? What have you in store for the newborn?"

Leibl recorded her words and chewed his pen in frustration. On paper, the words were bereft of the sore hoarseness of her voice, shorn of her mounting rage and bleak despair. Was it because he could not share that despair that the words fell lifeless from his pen? He sat there beside her and did not see the *Moledet* as only a rusty old freighter at the mercy of the waves. The ship was like the nation—without a home, without a haven. *Moledet*—homeland—without a homeland. He was angry that his sorrow was not as bitter as hers. On the contrary, he could not help but see something symbolic in the infant born on the *Moledet* at dawn. A new Jew born in the wake of a new dawn . . .

Foolish hyperbole?

So many rifles aimed at the flag, but it still hung at the top, at the very tip of the mast. When one says that a person is "on the tip of a mast," it means that he doesn't have an inch of ground under his feet. But when a flag flutters at the tip of a mast . . . No, he was too superstitious, but if it were without meaning, why were so many sailors determined to shoot to ribbons that fluttering scrap of blue-and-white cloth? Their bullets had ripped and shredded it, but a remnant still floated at the top of the mast. The remnant, burned and ragged, like the nation, stubborn like the nation, still floated in the wind and signaled to shore: We shall be back.

•   •   •   •   •

Leibl added a footnote: All the above happened after the flood. The pandemonium of war had died down, the horror of destruction had ceased. The righteous had been victorious and could afford to be generous. Tranquility reigned. Spacious new homes arose in the devastated cities of the enemy. Along the Rhine and the Oder, hammers and trowels were in use. The wounded were healing their wounds, the exiled returning to their homes.

All of them?

And it came to pass in those days that the Jew Hertzke knew his wife Golda, and she was with child. Both, embers rescued from the fire. Golda longed to bring her child into the world in a new home, a home where that child would not be surrounded by the ugliness of hate, a home where his neighbor would not shame or betray him, where death would not hover over every rooftop nor lurk in every dark corner. But the gates of the longed-for homeland were locked. Golda's hearth was a half-demolished ship that lurched from wave to wave. Only one of her children had come out of the Holocaust. Now his bullet-riddled, broken body lay at the foot of a destroyed mast while in a corner of the hold of the ravaged ship she gave birth to a new son.

•   •   •   •   •

The full moon over her bed was not the moon at all but a porthole. The doctor handed her a small bundle. The bundle chirped like a little bird. She took it and pressed it to her breast. Lips, soft warm little lips, searched for the nipple. A warm tremor passed through her body. She was suckling her own flesh and blood and . . . and the new day was beginning to light the porthole. A chirp from the infant came to her like the echo of words that she considered her son's last will and testament. She would call him Yosef as if to say: May our sons increase and multiply.

Under international law a ship has the extraterritorial rights of the nation under whose flag she sails, and a child born aboard ship is given the citizenship of that nation. All this took place aboard the ship *Moledet,* and the shredded, bloodstained flag was the flag of the Jewish *Moledet*—homeland-to-be. Was the infant Yosef, born even before his homeland, the first citizen of that homeland?

Postscript

Leibl fell near Latrun in the War of Independence, in the battle to reopen the road to beleaguered Jerusalem. A generation later, an author doing research for a novel happened upon the log of the ship

Moledet and saw it fitting to finish this chronicle in the style of the ancient biblical book:

Now more on the newborn Yosef, the battles he had to fight, the struggles he had to endure, behold, it is written in the books of Chronicles of his homeland, Israel.